# Love at Second Sight

RETHINK WHAT IT MEANS TO LOVE.

# Love at Second Sight

Ayoka B.

AYOKA
Joyinhome Publishing

Love At Second Sight

Ayoka B.



Published by Joyinhome Publishing

ISBN: 979-8-9897325-0-0

Cover art by Keiona Clark, keionaclarkart.com

Cover design by Akesha Scott

Editing by Gina Foshee

A specially-curated playlist is available for download on Spotify and YouTube Music (Love At Second Sight: A Novel).

*To JJ:*
*Cherished wife, mother, sister, daughter and friend. I know you would have loved reading this book.*

# Table of Contents

# Intro

# A Beautiful Surprise

She met him in Walmart of all places.

After being laid off, Shane and Tonya went there regularly to peruse the CD section. There was a great selection and the prices were decent. It had become their shared ritual.

Shane didn't know what she was looking for, but would know it when she found it. Tonya was in the next aisle. New releases, classics, soundtracks, greatest hits, what would she pick today? Shane was lost in the endless choices.

She heard someone coming up the aisle. Shane assumed it was Tonya coming to find her. When she raised her eyes, she saw him and everything seemed to slow down. His lean, muscular body took long strides in her direction.

He was about 6'1" and the color of brown sugar. His deep set eyes were framed with heavy brows and they locked with hers; the two stood in silence for a moment. Tattoos adorned his forearms and his lips were so....

She shook her head quickly to clear it.

"How you doin'?" He smiled. Why'd he do that?

I'm fine now, she thought. But she only smiled. Just then Tonya walked over and stood beside her. She followed Shane's line of sight and looked from him to her friend then back at him.

"Hey, how are you?" Tonya beamed.

He laughed, nodding his head in acknowledgment. Shane pushed

her cart around the corner to the next aisle. Tonya followed close behind.

"Did you see his lips?" Tonya asked between clenched teeth.

"Yes," Shane whispered, hoping Tonya would take the cue and
lower her voice.

"I saw him looking at you." Tonya nudged Shane. "Go talk to him."

"I will not!"

"Whyyyyy?" her friend whined.

Tonya wished Shane would get out of her own way. It was time for
her to end this "man sabbatical." And she needed some fun. Shane
was a great Single Mom, but she was also a loner who spent too
much time in the house. She knew Shane didn't trip about having a
man, but Tonya was in love so she wanted her friend to find love too.

"If you don't go talk to him, then I'll do it for you."

Tonya ran down to the end of the aisle in search of the mystery
man. Shane grabbed the cart and hurriedly pushed it, trying to catch
her; the right front wheel was slowing her down, dragging across the
linoleum.

"Tonya!"

And there she was, smiling up at him two aisles over.

"Oh, so you're a tattoo artist," she nodded her head. "Me and my
girl have been talking about getting tattoos."

Tonya spotted Shane in her periphery.

"Shane, you hear that? He can do our tattoos!"

He looked in Shane's direction as Tonya called to her.

"So can we have your number so we can call you when we're
ready?"

He smiled revealing even, pearly teeth. "Sure."

Shane reflexively swallowed and watched as he wrote his number
down. Tonya read the slip of paper as she took it.

"Mike. Well it was nice meeting you, Mike! My girl Shane will call
when we're ready." Tonya jerked her head toward Shane.

"Aight ladies. Until then." He smiled that smile and began walking
to the front of the store.

Shane held her hand up to stop Tonya from saying anything more while he was within earshot. She waited about a minute.

"Dayum! He was delicious."

Shane laughed. She didn't disagree.

Shane pulled into her driveway. Tonya was laughing through the blue tooth.

"Girl are you serious?"

"Yes! I finally called his ass and got some chic's answering machine. I thought I had the wrong number. I was like I know this muthafucka didn't give me his woman's number! Gurrrrl!!!!! This is exactly why I don't want to be bothered with anybody… this ignorant type of shit right here!"

Shane put the car in park and turned off the ignition. Damn it! She accidentally disconnected the call. I'll call her when I get in the house, she thought. Shane pressed the button to open the trunk. She opened the door and walked around to the back of the car. After looking at all of the grocery bags, she knew she'd have to make several trips. She sighed and put her hands through several of the bag handles, heaving them up out of the trunk.

After she had the last of the bags, she used her palm to close the trunk. She sighed. Now she had to put everything away. It was still early so she had plenty of time before she had to pick-up Sean. She was so glad that DC had all-day kindergarten programs. She had friends in Maryland whose kids went only half-day. What was the point? Were they learning anything in four hours?

Shane looked across the dining room table. She'd start with the frozen items. Then, separate the fish and freeze it in individual packages, same with the chicken. Shane loved doing this when she was alone. She could take her time, put everything where it belonged and it gave her time to gather her thoughts.

As she methodically put away the groceries, her mind began to drift to the tall stranger from Walmart. Maybe he had a woman and that was their home number. Tonya had asked for his number to get a tattoo. Perhaps she'd misread his energy. It was probably for the best.

After she'd transferred the chicken and fish to the kitchen counter beside the sink, she got the plastic wrap and freezer bags. She wanted the area set up before she began separating.

Shane washed her hands and began loading the packages into the freezer. Once she put in the last package, she sprayed down the counter and sink with bleach. After it sat for a minute or two she would rinse thoroughly, then scrub. There would be no food borne illness on her watch.

The bags containing toiletry items were waiting in the foyer so she'd remember to take them upstairs when she went. As she bent to grab the handles, the phone started to ring. Tonya was calling back.

Shane walked across the living room, into the dining room where the phone sat on a cherry wood side table.

"I was going to call you when I got situated," she said as she walked back to the foyer to take the bags upstairs.

"Okay," answered a male voice. "Call me back when you're situated."

Shane stopped at the foot of the stairs.

"Hello, who is this?" But she already knew.

"I thought you were going to call me back?" he quipped.

"Who is this?" she repeated.

"This is Mike… the tattoo artist. Is this Shane?"

"It is.…"

"Hey. I saw that you called the other day... You didn't leave a message."

Damned caller ID.

"Oh, yeah... I wasn't sure that it was the right number. A woman's voice was on the message."

"Yeah. That's my kids' mom, Sherri. I spend a lot of time there so I figured that was the best place to catch me."

There was an awkward silence.

"Okay, well... Do you work at a shop or something? I haven't come up with a design yet, but maybe there are some I can choose from?"

"Yes, I work at a shop. I also do parties. But before you come in, you should think about what you want, what type of design. This will adorn your body forever. Be sure about it. Your body is a temple."

"So you thought through all of your tattoos?"

"Not all, but most of them. But we're talking about you, especially for a virgin, a tattoo virgin," he added.

"Oh I'm not a virgin… for tattoos I mean…. I have a small one."

"Oh. Your girl made it seem like this was a first."

"For her, not me. But it's been a while." She sat on the bottom step.

"What do you have, if you don't mind me asking?"

"It's a heart with my fiancé's name. He was killed when we were in college."

"Shane, I'm so sorry to hear that! I apologize. I didn't mean to bring up some painful shit."

"It's alright. You didn't, I did." She paused. "I'm not sure that I want another tattoo. I may want this to be the only one."

"I get it. It can and should be very personal."

Silence, again.

"I have one of my younger brother on my left bicep. He was also killed."

Shane's stomach clenched. "Oh Mike, I'm sorry. How old was he?" Shane stopped. She shouldn't have asked him. He didn't know her!

"Never mind. You don't have to answer that," she said quickly.

"He was 18. He got into some shit that he didn't have no business. …"

Wow. They shared an awful bond that she'd give anything not to have.

# First Verse

# Hey Gorgeous

Shane used the fluffy, beach towel to dry Sean's stomach. They were leaving the neighborhood water park after two hours. She had no idea this existed in her SE neighborhood until recently; her cousin told her about it. It was quiet and they'd had it to themselves. He chortled as she tickled him.

"I've got your tickles!" she exclaimed.

Shane scanned the deck area to make sure she had everything. No pool toy left behind. She heaved the tote bag onto her shoulder, grabbing her son's hand.

They sang as they walked to the parking lot, their arms swinging with the rhythm. It was some catchy Backyardigans tune. Sean loved the Backyardigans!

When they reached the car, she threw the bag in the back seat and helped Sean into his booster. She made sure he was securely strapped in then kissed his nose. He giggled as she closed the car door.

Shane climbed in, closed the door and started the car. She slid in a CD and began the short ride home. She looked in the rear view mirror; Sean was asleep before she made the first turn.

When they got home, she had to carry him from the car up to his bedroom. Man was he getting heavy, she thought. She'd have to get him out of his damp trunks before she put him in the bed. She sighed.

Finally, he was down. After she changed her clothes, she tossed their wet clothes and towels into the wash. Shane thought about taking a nap herself. But Sean would be hungry when he woke up, they'd only had snacks at the pool.

She headed downstairs to find something to fix for lunch. As she reached the bottom step, the house phone rang. Shane glanced at the caller ID. Mike. She smiled.

"Hey! What's going on?"

"Hey Gorgeous! How are you?"

"Good, good. Me and Sean just got in from the water park. I'm trying to see what's for lunch while he's taking his nap. I feel like I need a nap! Whatchu got going on?"

"Ain't nothing! Just wanted to check in on you."

Shane and Mike talked sporadically for months. She enjoyed their conversations and was excited whenever he called, but he wasn't interested in her. Besides, she wasn't clear on the relationship with his kids' mother. They had three children together!  But this was cool. They had a funny and friendly banter. She could always use a friend; it's what she could handle.

"You still haven't seen his ass again? What's up wit this dude?!??" Tonya was far more upset than she was.

"I don't know Tonya. We just talk. It's cool, we're friends."

"Nope! I saw how he was lookin' at you. He was checkin' for you. What's his game?"

"I don't know, but if it's a game he's playing, I'm out. I told you the number that he gave me was a woman's number… And, I don't ever call him. He calls me."

There was so much she still didn't know about Mike. She knew his full name was Evan Michael Jeffries. He was a tattoo artist and aspiring rapper. Yup. He actually spent a lot of time in the studio. It was a dream of his. She hadn't heard any of his stuff to know if it was a dream worth pursuing, but maybe she'd find out.

———— ა ————

Mike didn't know what to do. He really wanted to spend some time

with Shane and see what she was about. It was something about her
that he couldn't shake, he didn't want to shake. But, from their conversations he knew she had been through a lot of bullshit with her son's
father and he wanted to come correct.

He had messed up giving her Sherri's number; he didn't know why
he'd done that. There was nothing going on with Sherri besides co-parenting. They'd tried over the years. He had great love for her and they'd
been through a lot. She'd helped get him through the murder of his
brother, but that was gratitude. Sherri wanted more than that but gratitude was all he felt. He just didn't want any static when it came to the
kids.

He and Sherri had an infant son and that was a mistake. To be clear,
he loved his son but he let alcohol and grief cloud his judgment one
night and found solace with Sherri. They hadn't been together sexually
in years and now they shared three children. He hadn't had a drink
since.

Mike thought about his hand — he knew a lil' something about cards
— and knew his wasn't strong. He had three children, he was focusing
on his music and was a tattoo artist. He didn't own a home like Shane
and he wasn't sure of what he had to offer. Shane needed a helpmate,
someone to love and take care of her. At least that's what he wanted to
give her, but everything in his life was a work in progress.

Mike could tell that Shane was curious about him and his intentions,
but she never asked. He wanted her in his life, but he didn't want to be
selfish. Maybe he needed to back away from her to leave room for
someone more worthy of her time.

He decided to talk to his Mom. She would give him good advice. He
knew she would be happy that he met someone whom he wanted to
get to know better.

"What's up Ma?"

"Hey baby, what's going on? I haven't seen you much lately, coming
in all hours from that studio. You better be careful being in the street
so late. Don't nothin' good happen at night in these streets." His
mother looked at him squarely in the face to make sure he was hearing
her.

"Ma, I know. I got it."

He knew he couldn't keep staying so late in the studio. His mother worried and why wouldn't she? She'd already lost a son to nonsense. Now, she only had him and her grandchildren.

"I hear you. I'll try to plan my time better so I'm not out so late." Mike paused. "Come sit down. I want to talk to you."

His mother stopped going through the mail and turned to look at her son. His voice was serious, not playful. It made her nervous. Mike saw the shift in her body language.

"Everything's okay," he assured her. "I just want to talk to you. We haven't had a good talk in a while."

He walked toward the kitchen with his mother following behind. He pulled out a chair for her and pulled one out for himself, sitting next to her.

"You're making me nervous!"

"Ma, chill. It's all good, I promise." He smiled.

She couldn't help but smile back at her handsome son.

He sighed. "A few months ago, I met someone. I wasn't trying to meet anyone, but I guess I was supposed to meet her… Her name is Shane. She has a young son. She's different from most women that I meet. She's smart, confident and beautiful. She's really funny and real chill. You'd like her."

This was not what she expected. Mike was smiling, waiting for her to say something. He looked expectant, like he wanted permission.

"So what's the problem?" his mother asked, sensing a but.

"I don't know how to approach her. We talk off and on but I haven't seen her since we met."

"Well, why not?" His mother was surprised. Mike was a confident man and he never lacked attention from women.

Mike's head was down and his eyes were on the table.

"Mike. Look at me. What's going on?" She put her hand under his chin and gently raised his face to look at her. His eyes were watery.

Mike was silent. She knew not to rush him, so she waited.

"I don't know what I have to give her. You know what my time is like and after I spend time with the kids, I don't really have any left. I'm trying to build my life… Right now, I don't know what I have to offer."

She chose her words carefully. She did not care for Sherri and that hadn't made things easy in the past.

"Well have you asked her what she wants? What's her name again?"

"Shane."

"Have you asked Shane what she wants?"

"Well, no…."

"I think if you want to get to know this woman, that's the first step. You need to know what she's looking for."

His mother stood up from the table and went to the fridge, opening it. She took out the roast that had been thawing since last night and sat it on the counter. She opened the fridge again taking out carrots and celery.

"Hand me some onions and potatoes," she called over her shoulder.

Mike sat a pile of potatoes and a few onions on the counter beside the oven. He walked to his mother, bent down and kissed her smooth cheek. She smiled.

"Thank you." He smiled at her.

"Boy you're worrying before you have to! Take the woman out and have a real conversation."

He frowned. "We've had real conversations!"

"Well not real enough if you don't even know if she wants a man! You come in here moping and you haven't even asked the question." She sucked her teeth and shook her head.

Mike walked into the other room and sat on the couch. He thought for a few moments then reached for the phone on the coffee table.

"Hey, Gorgeous! "How you doin'?"

He would see Shane that weekend. She'd agreed to go out with him and he could not wait. It had been four months since he'd met her and that was on him. They were going to a late movie. He wasn't sure how they'd have a conversation but that was the plan.

## What a Woman Wants

Mike rang Shane's doorbell and was a bunch of nerves. Cool out, he told himself. He couldn't understand why this woman had him in knots. He shook his head trying to clear it when she opened the door.

Her skin was smooth and beautiful. And her hair was a wild, curly crown. She had almond eyes that greeted him warmly, but looked directly into him.

"Hey," she said softly.

"Hey Gorgeous!" He had the overwhelming urge to kiss her, but he knew that wasn't the play. But her lips were full, the kind he liked, and they curved just so when she smiled. He needed to pull his shit together if he was going to make it through this date. He wanted to focus and listen, to make sure Shane Mathews was the woman he thought she was.

Shane moved back from the doorway, allowing him to walk in. Her home was a beautiful, historic DC row house with oak floors and a wide staircase. He stood in the foyer and panned the place quickly not wanting to seem nosy.

"I just need to grab something. You can wait in the living room or take a look around if you want." She laughed. "I'll be right back."

Mike watched as she walked up the stairs, trying not to stare. She was wearing platform heels and a dress. Her legs looked shapely and thick, like they would wrap nicely around his waist.

He walked into the living room and sat down on the sofa. Focus. He could feel that there was something special about this woman and he didn't want to get caught up thinking about sex.

He looked around the room. It was a warm, burnt orange with nice art pieces adorning the walls. He stood to get a better look at some of the art. Shane came into the room when he was studying a painting; he hadn't heard her come down the stairs.

"Ready?"

"Yes. Let's go."

About 30 minutes into the movie, Mike was ready to leave. All he wanted to do was talk to Shane, to look at her. Shane caught him looking in the dark of the theater.

"What's wrong?"

"Nothin'... are you enjoying this?"

"You don't like the movie?" she whispered.

He didn't answer.

"Do you want to leave?"

He nodded. She took his hand, stood and they inched down the row. People were not happy at the timing of their exit. They walked down the aisle and out into the movie lobby.

"My bad."

"It's okay," answered Shane. "I'm not a big movie fan."

"Why didn't you say something when I said we were going to the movies?!"

"I thought you wanted to go and it didn't matter to me... I just wanted to spend some time with you."

Mike smiled. Right answer. As they walked through the lobby, Mike took her hand. Shane stopped abruptly, so he let it go. Shane looked at him and rejoined their hands.

"I just want to get some Raisinets before we go."

They walked to the concession stand and ordered the $5 Raisinets. Shane grabbed the box and tore into the cellophane.

"If you're hungry, we can get some dinner," chided Mike.

Shane rolled her eyes, popping a few into her mouth. She closed her eyes. "I looooove these!"

Instead of finding the car, they took a long walk. The narrow streets were uneven, the sprawling tree roots upending the bricked patterns. He held her hand steadying her. "Be careful Gorgeous!"

"You'd think the residents of Georgetown would demand that the sidewalks be repaired," she huffed, trying not to twist an ankle.

They strolled past stores peeking into the large windows, looking at the wares on display. After some time, they walked to Canal park, found a bench and sat down. The street lights cast shadows from the manicured shrubs and trees. They talked about their upbringing, their children, their art.

"I write poetry. Did I tell you that?"

"No, you didn't. What kind do you write?"

"No kind in particular, whatever comes out. Sometimes they rhyme, sometimes they ramble, some are really short… Just whatever I'm feeling at the time."

"Nice." Mike wanted to read some but thought it too soon to ask. He wrote lyrics, but he wouldn't characterize them as poetry, per se. He wasn't sure if he would share any of them with Shane.

"I saw you looking at the painting earlier at the house. Do you paint?"

"Naw, I sketch and draw. I haven't ever tried painting but the strokes fascinate me. I always wonder about the order that the artist made the strokes. Did they sketch it out first? Did they have a plan or just a blank canvas and painted what they were feeling at that moment?"

"Wow! You're an artist."

Mike laughed nervously. "No. I do tattoos."

"So that means you're not an artist? Is that what your clients would say?"

Mike didn't answer.

"Didn't you once tell me what I put on my body should be special? I'm sure your clients come to you with a particular design… that's art. Besides, only an artist would give so much thought to brush strokes."

Mike silently agreed.

"So when can I see some of these sketches?" Shane had an eyebrow raised.

"Oh, um I guess whenever you want."

"You're just gonna let me bully you? If you don't want me to see your art, you can say that. I know it's personal."

Mike smiled. "I'll show you. One day...."

Shane laughed. Her laugh was like music. Mike dragged his thumb across her cheek. Her eyes fluttered open and her laughing subsided. He looked at her, wondering what she was thinking at that moment. He leaned in and kissed her lightly on the lips. They were soft and luscious just as he'd imagined.

He kissed her again, this time urgently and then slowly licked her lips. They still had a hint of chocolate on them. He leaned slightly away from her.

"You taste good!"

Shane looked as if she was startled. Then she smiled a small smile and that was the permission that he needed.

Mike moved closer, closing the space between them. He wrapped an arm around her back and placed his other hand against the nape of her neck, in her soft, curly hair. He paused and studied her face. She had small freckles on her nose and cheeks. He wanted to kiss those too. Mike kissed her deeply, her mouth opening to allow his tongue to search hers. His kiss was slow and deep; he wanted to explore more of her.

Slow down, he told himself. This was their first date. He didn't want her to think that he was trying to sleep with her. Not that he didn't want to. Mike finished the kiss and opened his eyes. Shane was looking intently at him. He still had his arms around her. He'd forgotten that they were outside, sitting on a bench.

"Well... that was... unexpected."

"I know... Shane, what do you want? No wait. Before you answer, I have some things to tell you."

Mike released his embrace and took her hands, wrapping his long fingers around them.

"I know that we had a strange start. That was my fault. I gave you Sherri's number because I wanted to keep some distance and have our exchange be about business. I didn't want to get into anything. I've got a lot going on and I don't have a lot of spare time. But I need you to know, there is nothing going on with me and Sherri besides our kids."

He stopped. This wasn't coming out right.

"I think about you a lot. And that hasn't happened to me before. I have all of these things that I'm trying to do, for my kids and for my life. But I want to get to know you. I feel like you are supposed to be in my life and not just to talk to on the phone sometimes. We've discussed so many things, but we've never talked about us. I know why I didn't; I was afraid. But I talked to my Mom and she said-"

"You talked to your mom about me?" Shane smiled, her eyes twinkling.

"I didn't mean to say that, but yes, I did."

"And what did she say?"

"She said that I need to ask what you want." Mike looked at Shane, watching her eyes trying to gauge what she was thinking, feeling.

"What I mean to say is, I want to spend time with you. I want to know if that's what you want."

Shane was quiet for a long time. Mike didn't know if she wanted him to sweat or if he was mistaken about their connection.

"I would love to spend time together."

This time, Shane leaned in and kissed him slowly and softly. Then she rested her forehead on his. Mike smiled. His heart was beating wildly in his chest.

"Okay! It's late. Let's get you home."

When they walked into the house, Shane put her purse on the dining room table and asked Mike if he wanted anything. "A drink?"

He declined. "I don't drink."

Shane raised her right eyebrow. That was a new piece of information. It was for the best because she didn't need a drink.

"Okay. I'll be right back."

Shane walked upstairs and into her room. She shut the door and took a deep breath. She needed to get her mind right! That man downstairs was foine! And more than that, he was sexy. Sex appeal was always more important to Shane and Mike had it in spades. She was glad he didn't recognize his power because her panties might drop.

Damn! She shook her head trying to clear it. She was super attracted to him. How was she going to make it through the evening and be good?

They sat in the living room and talked into the wee hours. When Mike stood to leave, he didn't want to go. He just wanted to be in her space. He reached out to Shane and pulled her up to stand beside him. They walked to the door hand in hand. He raised their intertwined hands and kissed hers.

"Let's talk soon," said Shane.

"Soon? Don't play with me woman, you better call me tomorrow!"

Shane laughed. "I would need your number to do that."

Mike stopped. She was right. He technically never gave her his number and he always called. Damn. He was lucky that she was giving him this chance because he almost fucked it up. Shane went to get a pen and a pad from the kitchen drawer. He wrote down two numbers.

"The first is my pager number. The second is the house number."

Mike tore off the page and pressed it into her hand. He bent down and kissed her lips, then forehead.

"Do you believe in love at second sight?" he asked her.

Shane didn't answer.

"Don't break my heart, okay?" he said then smiled.

"Okay," whispered Shane.

Shane closed the door behind him. She walked up a few steps to watch him walk to his car. After turning on the alarm, she walked upstairs.

At the landing, Shane closed her eyes and thanked God for sending Mike.

Mike opened the car door and sat in the driver's seat, pulling the door behind him. "Love at second sight", what the fuck was that?!?? He put his head on the steering wheel. This woman had him twisted. He was gone.

It was late. He'd better get home. He started up the car and blasted the radio. He needed some music to clear his mind; it was clouded with Shane. At least there's no traffic, he thought as he turned onto Naylor Road. I'll be home in 20 minutes.

The streets were mostly empty. Now and then, he would come across a knot of cars, most likely coming from a club or breakfast after the club. He heard snatches of music as they whizzed by.

Although he worked and was frequently in DC, he missed it: his old neighborhood, the energy, the people. But after his brother was killed, his Mother was desperate to leave the city.

Shane was from the 'Southside' like him. Now, she lived in Anacostia but grew up closer to Randall Highlands. He grew up off of Martin Luther King Avenue and went to Ballou. And even though she went to some private school uptown, she was still an around the way girl. He liked that. She was smart but from the hood. Shane was different and didn't care what people thought about that. He didn't care either.

⸙

"It's about time y'all went out! I thought something was wrong with the brother…How was it?" Tonya wanted details.

"We went to a movie, but we left in the middle. Then we walked and talked for hours."

"Yeah, he's an artist. He likes all that romantic, share-your-dreams type shit just like you! So when are you gonna see him again?"

"Soon."

Over the next few weeks, Shane saw Mike at least three or four times per week. She knew that he was making time for her.

One afternoon they had been riding for a while. She recognized that they were heading towards southern Maryland.

"Where do you live, Waldorf?"

"Let me find out you know about the country!" Mike laughed. "But, no, I live in Brandywine."

"My family is from southern Maryland so I know this drive well," explained Shane.

They turned into a cute community across from a park that she'd been to once or twice. They rode to the back of the development and parked. When they walked into the small town house, Shane was overwhelmed by the smell of chicken. It smelled delicious. Mike called out.

"Mom, we're here."

Mom! As her thoughts raced, a woman stepped into the room. She was a shorter, darker version of Mike. As Mike reached out to hug her, she pushed him out of the way headed toward Shane.

"I've been waiting to meet you, Shane!" She put her arms around her. "I'm Jessica."

Shane laughed as Mike looked mock hurt. She was surprised to meet the woman. He hadn't mentioned that they were going to see his mother. Mike was watching Shane.

"It's nice to meet you."

"Mike, take her jacket. Sit down honey, make yourself at home." Mike's mother sat down next to her and looked at her. "He didn't tell you, did he?"

Mike walked back into the living room and his mother looked at him. "Mike, you can't just be springing yo momma on people! You're gonna run her away."

Mike looked at Shane and shrugged his shoulders.

"I wasn't trying to be secretive, I just wanted you two to meet."

Dinner was wonderful and the company was even better. Shane could see where Mike got his big personality and easy smile. The three of them laughed and talked, then laughed some more.

"Ooooh Mike, I like her! I see why you were all tied in knots. This one here is special."

Mike and Shane looked at each other. Jessica looked at them.

"Y'all are in love already," she said, shaking her head. "I knew it when he said he was bringing you."

After the three of them cleaned the kitchen, his mother packed a container for Shane.

"Next time, I want you to bring Sean."

"Yes ma'am, I mean Jessica."

Sean hadn't met Mike yet. Shane spent time with Mike when Sean was with his dad. Mike would ask after him and had spoken to him on the phone, but that was the extent of it. She wanted to wait, to be sure it was right.

# Dirty Street Clothes

When they got to Shane's, she hung her jacket in the hall. After washing her hands, she put the container in the fridge.

"Why do you do that?"

"What?" asked Shane, closing the fridge door.

"Wash your hands as soon as you get in the house?"

Shane thought about it. She always did; it was second nature. She was very particular about germs and her son was the same.

"Because it's dirty out there and I don't want to spread germs into my home. That's why we take our shoes off and that's why we take our street clothes off when we go upstairs."

"Oh, okay," said Mike walking to the kitchen sink. He washed his hands slowly, watching her. As he dried his hands, he walked toward her.

"I want my hands to be extra clean, especially when I touch you."

He grabbed Shane and bent down to kiss the base of her neck, trailing kisses up to her chin and cheekbones. He laid kisses on her eyelids, the tip of her nose and then landed on her soft lips.

Shane savored the feel of his lips. She put her arms around his waist, raising one hand to caress the back of his head. She kissed him fiercely until she lost her breath. Shane broke away and walked out of the kitchen.

"Remember," she called as she began to walk up the steps. "You have to take off your street clothes when you come upstairs."

Mike stood there for a moment listening to her feet on the steps. "Awww shit.

He jogged over to the steps, then took them three at a time. He caught Shane in a bear hug in the hallway, making her shriek.

"Now let's get these dirty street clothes off you!"

Mike released her and put his hands on her shoulders, running his hands lightly from her neck to her arms and back. He looked into her eyes; the brown of her eyes was lighter than he remembered. He saw fire in them and they danced with mischief. But he saw something else: a vulnerability, almost shyness. She took his hand and brought it to her lips, kissing his open palm.

With the same hand, he pulled the tie of her wrap dress and watched it fall open. Mike involuntarily sucked in his breath. He stared at her light brown skin against the lacy, yellow bra and panties that she wore. Her breasts were beautiful, small mounds that he wanted to savor. Her thighs were thick and taut below her small waist and wide hips.

Shane let the dress fall to the floor and reached for Mike. She stood on her tiptoes and pulled off his sweatshirt, then t-shirt. As she looked into his eyes, she unbuckled his belt. He bit his lip as she slowly lowered his zipper. Not taking her eyes from his, she tugged at the belt loops, forcing the jeans down to the floor. He slowly stepped out of his pants, one foot at a time.

She wanted to feel his skin. She reached up and touched his chest. It was smooth and hard. Her other hand rubbed across his abs and down to his navel. She rubbed her fingertips into the fine hair that was below his navel, then dropped her hand into his boxers. He closed his eyes as she began to stroke him.

After a moment, he opened his eyes. Shane loved the way he looked at her, like no other woman existed. That look made her flush.

She involuntarily licked her lips and Mike's dark eyes blazed. He picked her up and she wrapped her legs around his waist. Cupping her butt, he carried her into the bedroom and laid her back onto the bed. He slowly peeled her panties down and threw them over his shoulder. Shane giggled.

She watched as he stood above her, sliding his boxers down his legs. His broad shoulders narrowed into his torso and divine pelvis. He was long and lean and she wanted to ravage him.

Mike grabbed her leg at the back of her knee, extending it. He put her big toe in his mouth. He rubbed the arch of her foot and gently sucked as he locked eyes with her. His other hand began to softly caress her. Then, he slid a finger inside which made her moan. Mike took his time, caressing until she was soft and wet.

Just when Shane thought that she would explode, Mike put her leg down and flipped her onto her stomach. He gently pushed her up onto her knees, spread her legs and buried his face.

"Mmmmmmmm," she moaned.

Mike's tongue was gentle, tasting and savoring her. Then it became ferocious, darting in and out and flicking. She was losing control.

"MIKE!!!" she screamed.

"Not yet Gorgeous. Wait for me."

He flipped her back over and slid inside her. It felt exquisite. Shane no longer had control of her legs and her eyes were fluttering. There was a slow burn running through her body. She felt like she was floating but she was very present. Shane opened her eyes to see Mike watching her as he stroked steadily.

She grabbed his hips and began to rock with him. That seemed to take him to the edge.

"Awww Shane, I wasn't ready!"

She wrapped her legs tightly around his waist and clenched her walls.

"Arghhh!"

Her legs shuddered and she moaned loudly. He stilled and she grabbed him raining kisses on his chest, arms and neck. He collapsed beside her.

Mike reached for her and wrapped his long body around her short one. Soon, they were asleep. Sometime later, she awoke and looked at him in the twilight. They were tangled in the sheets.

Dark was falling as she watched him sleep. He was absolutely beautiful. His body was adorned with tattoos. She'd only seen those on his arms but now she could see his back and legs. The black ink against his brown skin told a story, Mike's story.

Shane reached over the side of her bed for a journal. She kept a stack of them there. As she scribbled a few words and phrases, she could feel Mike stirring. She was re-reading what she'd written and she felt his lips on her shoulder blade. He gently kissed her tattoo and slid closer to her. He put his arms around her and nestled his face in her hair.

She put her pen inside the journal as a bookmark and turned to face him. Mike put his hand in her hair and twisted the curls between his long fingers. Shane traced his lips with her thumb. He kissed her thumb, then he bit it.

"Owww!"

"It didn't hurt."

"How do you know? Lemme bite you and you tell me how it feels!"

"Please do." A smile crept over Mike's face.

Yes! Round two. She pulled back the sheet and climbed over Mike, straddling him. She leaned down and bit him hard on his chest.

"Aaaaghhh!"

"Are you okay?" Shane said in an overly sweet voice.

She bent down and kissed the spot. Then, she slowly kissed his shoulders, his neck, his face and ears. She paused to look at his face. He was watching her intently.

She leaned back down and kissed his stomach. She ran her tongue over his abdominal muscles, tracing them slowly. Then, she dipped her tongue into his navel. Mike ran his fingers up and down her spine.

Shane took each of his wrists in her hands and pinned them at his sides. Then she slid down his body, still holding his wrists. She raised her eyes to look into his, then slid her mouth down over his stiffness. His eyes grew big, then he slowly closed them.

Shane worked her tongue and lips. She began slowly, then picked up the pace. Just when Mike began to clench his toes, she released him, crawled up and eased down onto him.

"Damn Shane," he growled.

She raised his wrists and pinned them beside his ears. He let her have control. He loved how aggressive she was. Shane was working her hips and ass, raising up just enough to glide back down so he filled her. It felt soooo good.

Mike tried to lift his hands and she loosened her grip. He gripped her butt cheek with one, the other began to rub her clit. She kept her pace savoring the sensations running through her body. She looked down at him and watched the faces that he made, loving that she could make him experience such pleasure. Slowly Shane began to speed up. He wrapped his arms around her back and pulled her to him. He kissed her deeply. Then, he reached his peak and let out a yell.

Shane lay on top of him, sweating and smiling. He looked down and wiped the perspiration from her forehead.

"Yessssssss! That's what I'm talking about!"

Mike laughed a big laugh. "You good?"

"Oh, I'm great!" exclaimed Shane rolling over to lay beside him. She stretched her entire body like a cat. "I'ma sleep good!"

"Glad I could help."

"Yeah, you helped a lil' bit…"

Mike laughed again.

"I love you Shane."

"I love you more."

———— ❧ ————

Shane lounged on Tonya's couch suffering from the itis. She'd dropped by her friend's apartment with fried fish dinners from Levi's. She hadn't seen her friend in a minute. Sean was with her sister at the zoo today and Mike was at the studio. After they finished eating, they listened to music and caught up. Tonya was sprawled on the carpeted floor with a stack of CDs beside her.

"So where's Joe?"

"Girl he has a big assignment due so I haven't seen him much in the past two weeks." Tonya sighed. "I'll be glad when he graduates. I'm starting to get lonely!"

"You just make sure that you behave yourself," warned Shane. "You know how you can get!" She frowned.

Tonya waved her off. "That was the old Tonya. I'm chillin'."

"Okay…." Shane said slowly, giving her side eye.

"I'm serious!" said Tonya, throwing a decorative pillow at Shane's head.

"Now what's up with you and Mike…" Tonya did a little shimmy, her ample breasts undulated.

Shane snickered. "We're good!"

"Oh bitch don't gimme dat! I want details." Tonya rubbed her manicured hands together.

She and Shane had the type of relationship that knew no bounds. They typically shared intimate details of their lives, including sexual encounters. But only when it was just a fun fling. They didn't talk that way about Joe, at least not in a long time.

"Tonya, mind your business! I'm not telling you about my man!"

"Okay, okay," yielded Tonya.

She knew that meant it was getting serious.

"What I will say is that he can handle me. And he always makes sure that I'm satisfied." Shane winked.

"Okay Mike!" Tonya snapped her fingers. Over the years, there had been a few that seemed promising, but didn't make the cut when it came to laying the pipe. Both Shane and Tonya were comfortable and bold in their sensuality and absolutely unapologetic. The difference being Tonya was more overt with her sexuality; men never saw it coming with Shane.

"But it's so much more than that, Tonya," Shane explained. "He has such a kind heart. I don't think many people know that about him. They assume that he isn't as beautiful on the inside… I'm happy that he lets me see that side of him."

Tonya smiled at her friend. "He trusts you."

Shane nodded her head.

"And you loooove him!" teased Tonya. "You're welcome! If I left your ass to your own devices, you wouldn't be getting that premium shit!" They laughed out loud in unison.

Tonya stood up and opened a wooden box that was on her mantle. She took out a jay, inserted it between her full lips and cupped her hand to protect the flame of the lighter. She took a few quick puffs and slowly blew the smoke out in rings. She took another puff, inhaling deeply and walked it over to Shane.

Shane took the jay and closed her eyes as she puffed. She didn't smoke often, mostly when she and her girls went out, but she enjoyed that light and peaceful feeling that it gave. She never smoked at home because she didn't want to when Sean was at home. Besides, she didn't even know how to roll.

Tonya took a sip of her over-sized half and half that was on the coffee table. Her long legs stretched before her. She was so glad that her girl was getting that "D" on the regular. Shane deserved it. She deserved to be happy after the sorry asses that she'd dealt with, including Sean's father.

## Quality Time

Shane stood in the threshold of her son's room. She watched as Mike and Sean built Lego structures while sprawled across the floor. They each had a creation in their hands and were crashing them into the other complete with sound effects. She leaned her head against the wooden, door frame.

It had taken some time for her to let Mike meet Sean. This was the first man that she'd let him meet, not that there had been many in between. She wanted it to feel right, not forced or awkward. Mike was so good with him as she knew he would be. He was a great father to his children. They'd all spent time together at Mike and his Mom's house and even been on a few outings together: the circus, the park. It gave her such joy to see them like this.

"Hey Mommy!" Mike turned slightly and winked at her.

"Me and Mike are playing Power Rangers!" Sean held up two Lego people in his small hands.

"Oh, that's what I walked in on."

"Yeah! GO, GO Power Rangerrrs!" he sang.

"Okay, well I'll be down the hall." Shane laughed and walked to her "office".

She sat down at her desk and turned on her desktop. She'd decided to show Mike some of her poetry. She hadn't shared her poetry with anyone except two of her close girlfriends from college, Gail and Chanté.

Only once, she showed a poem to Sean's father. By then, their relationship was in real trouble. She'd written a poem about how she was feeling and shared it with him, hopeful that it would get through when nothing else seemed to. She remembered that he shrugged. "What does that have to do with me?" Her new family was falling apart and there was nothing more to do.

Shane cringed at the memory. Poetry was very personal, it was her art. But she knew that she could trust Mike with it. He was also an artist. But she'd wait until later to show him; she didn't want to disturb playtime. Maybe after lunch when Sean was taking a nap. Right now, she'd just type up some of her more recent stuff that was handwritten in her journals.

After she finished, she went to the kitchen and fixed Sean a turkey and spinach wrap with provolone cheese drizzled with balsamic vinegar. He was a particular eater and he hated mayonnaise. She put a bunch of green grapes on the plate and a small pile of plain chips.

Now what were she and Mike going to eat? She didn't know about Mike, but she wasn't going to eat a wrap. Shane wasn't fond of sandwiches, except PB&J of course. She opened the fridge and spotted some leftover vodka sauce that she'd made. Yes! I'll just fix more pasta, she thought. She grabbed the step stool and climbed up to the upper cabinet to get a box of linguine. They could have that with a spinach salad.

After they'd cleaned the kitchen and Sean was napping, Shane called Mike upstairs.

"C'mere. I want to show you something."

Shane sat quietly at the computer screen as he read over her shoulder. She realized she'd been holding her breath.

"Love, that is beautiful!" He bent and kissed her shoulder.

"Thank you."

"Explain the title to me. I feel like it's a reference that I don't know."

"Sure. Zora Neale Hurston is one of my favorite authors. Well she was way before her time! Audacious, unafraid, fearless. In one of her books, *Their Eyes Were Watching God-*"

"Okay, I've heard of that book...!" Shane waited. My bad love. Go 'head."

"Well in that book, she says that *'the Black woman is the mule of the world.'* You know, a tireless worker who is at the bottom, the one who gets kicked often... that always stuck with me... When I wrote this poem, I had just gotten back to college after taking time off. When Bernard died, I took a semester off. I was trying to get my life back on track, but I was having a really hard time. That's when I started writing poetry. They were just spilling out of me. This is one of the first ones." She paused. "I'm going to publish a series of poetry books. The title of the first book is *Mule of the World.*"

"Do you have the rest of the poems for this book?"

"Yes."

"Can I read them?"

Shane clicked the mouse and sent the pages to print.

"There aren't many. My vision is of small, illustrated books."

When the printer stopped, she pulled the pages from the tray and handed them to him. He took the pages, went downstairs and sat on the couch.

After Shane turned off the computer, she went downstairs. Mike looked up briefly and waved for her to sit beside him. Once she did, he put his arm around her. Shane laid against him.

When he finished reading, Mike looked down at her.

"Babe, you have a gift! When are you gonna put this into the world?"

"I don't know. I need an illustrator."

After a moment, Shane sat up and turned to him.

"Why don't you do it?"

"Do what?"

"Illustrate my poetry books! I've been looking for an artist to do it, that's why they've been sitting. I hadn't found the right person… but you, you could do it!"

"Oh Shane, I don't know…"

"What's to know?"

"I just sketch here and there… I don't want to disappoint you."

Shane frowned. "Okay, well, just think about it."

Mike took her hand. "I will. I promise. Thank you for sharing these with me." He kissed her softly on the lips. Just then, Sean came bounding down the steps full of energy from his nap.

"What's for dinner?"

"I was just wondering the same thing, lil' man… I don't know. Mommy?" They looked at her.

"Why are y'all looking at me?"

Sean ran into the living room and jumped on Mike. Mike grabbed him and laughed. "I can't stay, man. I've gotta go and do some work."

"You mean lay some tracks down?"

"Listen to you with the lingo!"

"What's lingo?"

"It means you know some words that have to do with Mike's work in the studio," explained Shane.

"Oh. Well Mom, what are we going to eat?"

"Didn't you just eat lunch?"

"He's a growing boy Shane, right?" Mike looked at Sean. On cue, he raised his bicep to show Mike his muscles.

Mike squeezed it. "Oh shiiiiyoot!" Mike corrected himself as Shane shot him a look.

He grabbed Sean as he stood up, hoisting him into the air. Sean squealed as Mike threw him up near the ceiling and caught him.

"You be good, okay? Hold it down for me!" He kissed Sean on the forehead and threw him on the couch.

He looked at Shane. "You be good too Mommy!" He kissed her on the forehead, then quickly on the lips.

"Hey!" yelled Sean.

"What? I can't kiss your Mommy?!??"

Sean frowned.

"Don't you worry. I have more than enough kisses for you!" Shane tickled him as Mike walked to the hallway to put on his jacket.

At the doorway, he turned and waved. "I love y'all!"

Mike was spending less time with Shane. He still logged plenty of studio time and he'd taken on a full-time job, but cut his hours at the tattoo shop. She knew that he was trying to put things in place, but she barely saw him. And it was starting to take a toll on their relationship.

Shane opened her eyes to see Mike watching her in the dark.

"Gorgeous, I'm about to head out. You all have a good day." He bent down and kissed her nose.

She glanced at the clock. 3:57am. These early hours were for the birds. She raised up and swung her legs over the side of the bed. Damn, it was cold. She grabbed her terry robe from the back of the door and slipped it on.

Shane walked down the steps as Mike was coming back into the house. He'd started his car and was letting it warm up while he went to the kitchen to grab his lunch from the fridge.

She grabbed his hand and led him to the living room.

"Gorgeous, I gotta go."

She stopped in front of the over sized chair and pushed him back on it. Shane straddled him and kissed his lips. She lifted up onto her knees creating the space she needed to unbuckle his belt. Shane needed Mike. Right now. He bit his bottom lip as she eased herself onto him. They rocked quietly as the sky began to lighten.

He called her at lunchtime. "Just called to tell you I love you."

"Were you late?"

"Whatchu think? I told my supervisor that I was on the toilet." He laughed.

Shane shook her head.

"Gotta go. Love you, bye."

Mike would have many other mornings that he was "stuck on the toilet."

~

"Hey Gorgeous. I'm just leaving the studio. I know it's late, but can I come see you?"

She'd been to the studio only one time. Mike wanted her to sing the hook on a new song he was working on. When Shane was in high-school, she sang in a group. Shane hadn't sung in years, but finally agreed to do it. She met him at the studio one Sunday afternoon. Her throat had been scratchy so she'd been drinking tea all morning, trying to soothe her voice; she didn't want to disappoint him.

Once in the studio, after introductions, the owner asked her if she thought about recording any of her poetry. Mike's big mouth. She wondered if he'd put him up to it.

"No. I'm a writer, not a performer. Big respect to those who are, but I only write."

She never made it into the booth to record the hook. Shane got upset with Mike for something, she couldn't even remember what it was, and she'd left without saying goodbye.

Shane eased down the creaky steps. She padded into the living room and curled up on the sofa under a throw blanket. If she fell back to sleep, at least here she would hear him tapping on the door.

She awoke to a light tapping and opened the noisy security door. Shane paused, giving him a look.

"I know, I know. I just wanted to see you. I miss you."

She turned and walked back into the living room, wrapped in the blanket.

"Well whose fault is that?"

She sat back on the couch and watched him as he locked the door. He took off his boots and jacket, hanging it on the banister.

He walked over to the couch and stood her up peeling away the blanket. Once it fell away, he picked her up and kissed her lightly.

"Put me down," she protested, wanting to stay mad at him.

He put her down softly. Shane walked over to the stereo system.

"Can I play you something?" she asked, stealing a line from one of her favorite movies.

He waited, curious.

"I want you to listen to the words."

A soft melody flooded the room.

*It's like yesterday I didn't even know your name...*

Shane put her arms around his waist and sank into his warmth. They danced slowly in the darkness. The lyrics of this song expressed exactly how she felt about Mike and the impact that he'd made in her life.

As they swayed, she felt safe and happy. She wanted to live in that moment. That night, they fell asleep whispering and laughing.

⁂

Tonya was planning something for Shane's birthday, she just didn't know what. On the night of her birthday, a small group of her friends came over. The dining room table was set up with salsa, spinach dip and Shane's favorite lime flavored tortilla chips. On the other side were shot glasses, a platter of sliced limes, tequila salt and gold Jose Cuervo.

"We're going to a club in Adams Morgan for salsa lessons," Tonya announced.

"Oooh, this is going to be fun," Shane exclaimed as Tonya pinned a pink satin birthday girl pin on her.

The doorbell rang.

Shane skipped to the door. It was Mike. He was carrying several shopping bags. Shane hurriedly opened the door and planted a long, wet kiss on his lips. She loved those lips.

"Alright you two, break it up," called Tonya.

"Hey Gorgeous!" Mike ignored Tonya kissing Shane again. He held the bags out to her. "Happy birthday!"

Shane jumped up and down, the stiletto heels of her suede boots loudly tapping the hardwood floor. There were the new Alicia Keys and India Arie CDs that she wanted. Isse Myake perfume that she loved. A beautiful bound journal. When she got to the last bag, Mike took it from her. It was a pink, Victoria Secret bag.

"Nooo, not here."

"Looks like that one's for you anyway." Shane snickered.

Mike smiled, wiggling his thick eyebrows. "For us."

He kissed her slowly and deeply. Shane wanted to take him upstairs right now, but she had a house full of guests. If she'd already had some tequila, she wouldn't have cared. They walked arm in arm into the dining room where the others had started taking shots. Her friend Gus poured one for each of them.

"Time to catch up!"

Shane raised her shot glass and clinked it with Gus's.

"He doesn't drink, so both of these are mine."

"Such a square!" yelled Tonya.

"You all over here!" Mike yelled back, picking up the camcorder that was sitting in a nearby chair.

"How's everyone feeling tonight?" Mike spoke to the room.

"Wassup Mike," her friends echoed one another, smiling, and some nodding in acknowledgment.

He aimed just as Shane and Gus knocked back a shot, then Shane chased it with the second.

"Gus, watch her ass while y'all are out!" Mike said from behind the camera. He was walking around getting footage.

"OR, you can watch me!"

Mike paused the camera and looked at her guiltily.

"I gotta go to the studio."

Tonya anxiously glanced at Shane, then quickly poured a round for everyone. "Y'all let's toast Shane," she said, handing out shots and lime wedges.

Her friends all took a shot of tequila, except Mike.

"But before we go, we have to hit the piñata!" Tonya dug into a large bag in the corner to produce a Dora the Explorer piñata.

"What's in it?" asked Shane.

"You'll have to break into it and find out."

Gus secured the piñata in the ceiling of the large entryway between the dining and living rooms. Tonya blindfolded Shane and gave her Sean's plastic toy bat.

"Everybody stand back!"

Tonya stood Shane in front of the piñata to speed things along. After four good whacks, Shane heard objects raining onto the floor. She pulled off the blindfold to find a variety of liquor miniatures, liquor filled chocolates, flavored condoms and colorful tubes of lube littering the floor.

"What the...?"

Tonya did a little shimmy. "I put some fun stuff in it!" She winked at Shane who laughed.

"Okay, who am I riding with?"

⸎

Shane was excited. She was hosting Thanksgiving at her house for the first time. Her family rotated locations for Thanksgiving and went to her Grandmother's for Christmas. She was now part of the rotation. As host, she'd make the turkey and everyone else would bring the fixings. Her cousin served as coordinator, coming up with the menu and assigning items to the rest of the family.

She'd gotten up early in the morning and put the turkey in the oven. Mike was helping set up additional tables and chairs. Jessica usually traveled south to spend time with extended family, but instead she was coming to Shane's.

"Babe, why are you so nervous? These are your people."

"I don't know. I guess because this is my first time hosting. And I don't want no mess... There's always mess with my family during the holidays."

He leaned over and kissed her as they put the long table into place.

"There will be no mess today. Now where did you say I could find the tablecloths?"

Sean was in charge of setting the tables. Shane bought table decor from the store which Sean had selected. He also made some construction paper turkeys from his hand print. He was excited to get started.

"Not yet man! I've gotta put the tablecloth first. Come help me find them."

As Mike predicted, for the first time in years, there was no mess. The turkey was juicy, her aunt's mac and cheese was on point as always and her Mom's potato rolls melted in your mouth. The men in her family plus her aunt, cousin and Mike were watching football, of course. Shane was putting cream cheese icing on a carrot cake which is her favorite. And since they were engrossed in the game, she could have first dibs and maybe even put a slice away for later.

"Mommy. Can I have some pie?"

"Yes, give me a minute honey. I'll get it for you."

"I've got it Shane," said her mother, Dorothy, coming into the kitchen for a plate and knife.

She and Jessica had been in the dining room chatting.

"Shane, do you need any help?" called Jessica.

"No thanks. Do you need anything?"

"No honey, I'm full as a tick!"

Her mother leaned over to her.

"So Mike... I like him. Why have you kept him a secret?"

"He's not a secret." But she hadn't introduced him to her Mom until now. There was no real reason... Shane was just kinda greedy when it came to Mike. She couldn't explain it. It was like he was so yummy that she didn't want to share. Shane looked at her Mom and shrugged her shoulders.

"Well, I like him. And his Mom."

Shane only smiled. Her house was brimming with the people whom she loved. She had never been this happy.

That night when she lay down in her bed, her body thanked her, especially her feet. Shane hadn't realized how exhausted she was; she'd been going nonstop for the last few days. Although she felt tired, her mind was filled with overlapping thoughts. It was always this way when there was quiet.

Shane reflected on the day and smiled. She mused on what life had in store for her. What was coming and would she be ready to tackle it? She wondered who Sean was going to be and what he would contribute to the world. For that matter, what would she contribute? These inner conversations frequently kept her up at night, but they were productive. They helped her formulate and tweak personal goals. There was so much she wanted to do but she hadn't committed to a path. Besides writing and Motherhood, she hadn't committed to anything… except Mike.

An old coworker and friend, Lisa, was expecting her first child and due any day. She'd checked into the hospital that evening. Everyone was excited. The next morning, Shane received a call from another former co-worker.

"Shane, Lisa lost the baby."

"What!!!"

"I don't know the details… They had the baby on monitors once she checked in and everything seemed to be going fine. I don't know what happened from there. Lisa's still in the hospital."

Shane hung up the phone in shock. She cried aloud for her friend, praying that God would help her through this somehow.

A few weeks later, she went to Lisa's house to attend a memorial service for Baby Chloe. She'd been cremated and there was a beautiful silver urn inscribed with her name. Shane stood in the front doorway because the house was overflowing with people. There were others standing outside with her. They silently listened to the service. Shane wiped away tears as her body shivered in a winter cold that she could barely feel.

When the service ended, she entered Lisa's house wading through people until she found her. She hugged her tightly and kissed her forehead and cheek.

"Thank you for coming, Shane."

She left before Lisa could see the tears beginning to well up. She didn't know what to say, but she knew that her tears wouldn't help her friend.

Mike came over later that night. He massaged Shane's body with oil, quietly listening as she cried.

"How is she going to ever move past this?"

"Baby I don't know that she will. All of you just need to hold her up and let her know you're there for her. And pray for her."

Shane's tears eventually slowed as Mike continued to massage her. She reached a place of calm that was because of him. He broke the silence.

"What should I get lil' man for Christmas? Has he asked for anything in particular?"

"No, he hasn't asked for anything. Sean is excited for the lights and tree and seeing his family." Shane thought for a second. "He'll love whatever you give him."

Shane was relaxed, enjoying the feel of Mike's hands. She languidly turned her head to gaze up at him.

"And what do you want for Christmas?" Shane asked, smiling at him.

Mike was quiet for a moment.

"To marry you."

Did she hear him right? Was he serious? There were a million thoughts careening in her mind. She was terrified. Since Bernard died, Shane didn't think that she would ever consider marriage.

Shane laughed. She hadn't meant to, but that's what came out. Mike didn't mean it, she thought, he was just talking. And so she let it hang in the air. She never said anything and neither did he. She couldn't know that years later, this would haunt her.

Mike came over early one afternoon, straight from work. When she opened the door, she could tell that something was off.

"I got an award today."

"That's great!" She went to put her arms around him. He walked past her embrace and began to pace in the foyer.

"We were at a company-wide program when I got the award. When I was leaving, a man approached me, asking if my name was Evan Jeffries. Then, he asked if my mom's name was Jessica."

Shane tensed as she sat on the bottom step.

"He tells me that he knew me when I was little. Then, he asks about my brother. Turns out, he's his dad."

Mike silently kept pacing.

"I say, 'I'm sorry to have to tell you this, but my brother is dead'… He looks at me and tears start coming down his face." Mike stops to look at her.

"That white man slid down the wall to the floor. He was hysterical!" He paused.

Shane didn't react when he said white man, but this was new information.

"The thing is, I can remember us spending time with a white guy when I was young. He would come get me, Steve and my Mom and we would do stuff, go places."

"So what happened?"

"What do you mean what happened? I just told you."

"What happened after the guy started crying?"

"I left."

"You left?... Just like that?" He didn't respond.

"Well do you know his name?"

"Yes, he introduced himself. Something McDoogle."

"Can you find him?"

"Find him for what?!" Mike was yelling.

"To connect with him. You all obviously spent time together at some point. You should talk to Jessica. You could spend some time with him."

"For what?!"

"I don't know… Maybe you two could build a relationship. You don't have one with your father, maybe…."

"Shane. I'm a grown fucking man. I don't need a father now!"

"I just thought it may help you. Maybe you could help each other. You have all this rage. I keep telling you, you can't keep all of that inside."

He looked at her briefly.

"I have to go."

Five months slipped by and she barely saw Mike. Shane tried talking to him, to reconnect.

"Gorgeous, I'm doing my best. You know I have a lot going on! Just bear with me."

"Mike, we barely see you. I call, I can hardly get you on the phone. I haven't seen the kids in forever… I'm always waiting. When is it going to be time for us?"

She didn't know if he didn't care or just couldn't see it. Shane was tired. She spent too much time missing him and felt like she would always be waiting on him.

Shane asked Mike to come over. She couldn't deny that she was drawn to him like a magnet. Actually they were drawn to each other.

But they weren't on the same page. It was time for them to go their separate ways.

Mike was sucking on Shane's big toe. God, she loved this man and she was going to miss him. But her heart couldn't bear it any longer. She just needed a final taste.

"I just can't do this anymore. I feel like I'm in a relationship by myself and it's draining. I need to think about what's best for me and for Sean."

Mike didn't seem surprised. In fact, it didn't seem like what she said was registering.

"Ok Gorgeous." His face was expressionless. "I totally understand. Thank you for being patient with me."

They embraced for a long time in the foyer, neither of them wanting to move. Shane wiped her eyes.

"Okay then. Take care of yourself." She attempted a smile.

"Okay." He looked at her for a long moment then walked out the door.

Shane was doing okay for the first month or so. Then, the sadness began and it came in waves. Most times she could move through it, focus on a task. But sometimes, it was too heavy. It sat on Shane's chest, squeezing the breath from her body. At times like this, she stayed very still and let the wave overtake her. That's when the tears wouldn't stop and her body rattled with her heaving. Only when it passed could she catch her breath.

Mike was EVERYTHING. He wasn't perfect, not by anyone's standard. But Shane felt that he was perfect for her. So what was the problem? It seemed like timing was the only issue. Surely they could work through that! They fit like a hand in a glove and yet they were apart. His smile haunted her. She made herself not call him, but could not resist answering his calls.

"Hey Gorgeous."

"Hey."

# Chorus

# Always Been Your Girl

She sat in a Thai restaurant in Foggy Bottom with Tonya. Between forkfuls of pad thai, Shane relayed the breakup to her.

"It was like he was unphased. Like I said I'd lost his Outkast CD or something."

Tonya listened, shaking her head occasionally.

Shane suddenly felt sick. She put down her fork and breathed deeply through her nose.

"What's up Shane?" Tonya's concerned eyes searched hers. "You okay?"

Shane's voice cracked. "No! Far from it!" She lowered her voice and leaned across the table.

"I'm pregnant!" She hadn't told anyone else.

"Oh sweetie… When you told me how passionate that last time was… I had a feeling… Are you gonna tell him?"

"I have to tell him… but Tonya, I can't have this baby! I still don't have a job. We're not together.…" Shane stopped abruptly and began to cry. She felt overwhelmed. Just when she'd found the strength to try to move on without Mike.

"Can we just go?"

"Yeah, sure. Let me find our server and get some boxes."

Shane was waiting for Mike to come over. Her stomach was flip flopping from a combination of nausea and nerves. She was dreading this conversation and even more, his reaction.

Mike's face lit up and he grabbed Shane lifting her off the ground. His excitement waned as he realized that Shane didn't feel the same.

"I can't have this baby Mike."

She would never forget the look on his face. But he didn't fight her.

Shane scheduled the appointment and Mike took her. They headed to a facility downtown. He dropped her near the front door and then he searched for a parking lot or space. While she waited, a white guy approached her and got into her personal space.

"Why are you here? Don't you know that abortion is murder? You are killing your child!"

Shane ran down the street until she reached the end of the block. She was crying uncontrollably and trying to catch her breath. She was thankful that he didn't follow her. Once her breathing was almost normal, she wiped her face. Mike tapped her on her shoulder.

"What are you doing down here?" He could tell she'd been crying. "Shane, what happened?" he demanded.

She wanted to tell him, but she was afraid of what he might do. Besides, the guy was nowhere to be seen. He'd disappeared into the concrete and asphalt of downtown.

"Let's just go in before we're late."

For such a life-changing decision, Shane wouldn't remember much when she reflected back on having the abortion. She could only recall the clinical smell and the artificially lit rooms. There was a heavy feeling of sadness and tension in the Planned Parenthood clinic. What she remembers with clarity was regretting the decision before she and Mike even left the facility, but some things can never be undone. And she didn't dare tell him.

They drove to her house in silence. She was in physical pain but was emotionally numb. When they got there, Mike carefully helped her undress and tucked her in. Then he gave her some of the prescribed pain medication. Mike helped her sit up so she could drink some water to get it down. Once she was comfortable, he announced that he couldn't stay.

"Shane, I have to go."

WTF?!?? Shane didn't ask why, she just nodded her head. She was glad that Tonya had Sean for the night. Once she heard the door lock, the tears flowed freely. At some point, the medication kicked in and she finally drifted off. She awoke during the night to go to the bathroom. Good thing. She needed to change the over sized pad that she was wearing. Then, she took more pain meds and laid back down.

Shane stared into the darkness feeling empty, wondering how her life had taken this turn. Everything was so wrong. It would probably never be right again. She was so angry that Mike hadn't tried to talk her out of it. She knew that wasn't fair; she knew what she was like once she'd made up her mind about something. But she wanted, needed to be angry and he was the perfect target. Deep down she knew that they would never be the same. And it was her fault.

⸺ ✺ ⸺

Mike's birthday. She texted him. No response, not that she expected one. Shane lay on her back, on the carpeted floor of her bedroom. As she stared at the ceiling, *I Am Ready for Love* echoed through her room. Arie's plaintive ballad bounced from the ceiling to the wall and back again. Shane laid still as the tears crept and pooled inside her ears. What she couldn't understand was how he could bear to be apart from her. Because she felt like she was slowly dying.

They hadn't experienced many of the milestones that you have as a couple: celebrations and vacations, but also the small moments in between that strengthen a bond. So why was she so connected to him? A wave was coming to overtake her.

Later, her son came into her room. She was sitting on the floor in her terry bathrobe, silently crying. Though she tried, she couldn't stop the tears. He put his small arms around her neck.

"It's going to be okay, Mommy."

That's when Shane knew she had to pull herself together. She couldn't bear for Sean to see her like this. Usually she was able to hold it in until he was asleep. But lately the tears came unannounced, falling as she did the laundry and cooked dinner.

Another year had come and gone. Shane had a good job that she enjoyed. It wasn't a career, but she was putting money in the bank and it kept her busy. Mike would call or text once in a while to check on them, but she couldn't bring herself to answer.

She missed him. Sometimes, there was a pain in her chest from his absence. It was at these times that she would break down and call him, but he would never answer.

One morning at work, she was conducting research on an account. Lately, she had a feeling in the pit of her stomach. She learned over time not to ignore her intuition. Let's see, Shane thought as she typed "Evan Jeffries". She got a few results that led her to some sort of lightweight background check. She had to know what this feeling was. She opened the lower desk drawer and retrieved her wallet.

After inputting her credit card info, she waited. Data started populating the screen including past addresses. She scrolled down; she knew all of that. She kept scrolling, then she stopped. Shane stared at the screen. Spouse: Sherri Jeffries. It was dated a few months ago.

Shane's heartbeat quickened and her body began to shake. She turned off the computer and yanked her purse from the drawer. She stood up, sending her chair rolling across the office. She strapped her purse across her body and ran to the office door snatching her coat from its hook. Then, she hurried down the hall and across the reception area.

"Shane," the receptionist called after her. "Are you alright?"

"No, I'm leaving for the day."

Shane ran past the elevator bay and into the stairwell. She ran down four flights of stairs, then sat down on a landing. Her chest heaved and her blouse was wet with tears. Her cell phone had been vibrating since she left. She peeked at it recognizing a co-worker's number. She couldn't talk.

I'm not feeling well, she texted. Heading home.

She probably shouldn't have been on the road but she had to get out of there. Somehow, she made it home. Shane was lying in the tub, in water that was now cold. She thought about Mike's Christmas wish. Why hadn't she said something, anything? She wasn't ready to be married, but she should've talked to him and explained how she was feeling.

Bernard's sudden death had sent her spiraling and it had taken years to regain her footing. Grief was an elusive companion. Just when she believed it had released her from its steely grasp, it would reach out to claim her once more. Even when she was in the relationship with Sean's father, she held back part of herself. She didn't realize it at the time, but she was trying to shield herself. Mike was the first relationship when she'd finally let go and fully committed, emotionally. She wasn't aware then, but she was truly happy to move forward.

I have to get out of this tub, she thought a bunch of times. Finally, she did, trailing water everywhere. She walked to her room and put on her white, terry robe. Shane climbed into bed, her wet legs soaking the sheets. She reached over the side of the bed and picked up her phone. She dialed Mike's Mom's number.

"Hey baby! How you doing?"

Shane began to cry.

"Shane, what's wrong?"

Shane kept crying, not able to find the words.

"Hello?!?? Baby say something, you're scaring me!"

"I can't believe he got married," Shane uttered, not believing the words as she said them.

"Who baby? Who got married?"

"Your son!" she spat.

"What are you talking about Shane? Mike's not married. Besides, he loves you. He's not gonna marry anyone but you."

"Why are you lying for him? Don't lie to me Jessica, please."

"Shane, I don't know what's going on, but I wouldn't lie to you honey."

"I saw it. I saw it with my own eyes. He's married... I can't believe he did that. After everything!"

Shane gulped for air and began to cry harder. "I'm so sorry!"

"Sorry for what baby?"

"I was pregnant," wailed Shane. "I had an abortion. I should've had our baby. I'm so sorry. I was afraid… I shouldn't have done that!" Shane cried uncontrollably. Her eyes burned and snot ran from her nose. She reached for the box of tissues on her nightstand.

Jessica was silent for a long while. "Oh Shane, why didn't you come to me? We coulda worked it out. I would've helped you!"

"God, I'm sorry! I wish I could change it but I can't!"

"Ok Shane, calm down honey."

Shane cried until she wore herself out. "He's gone from me. He married Sherri."

"To Sherri?" Jessica paused. "Baby, he is not married. I don't know what you saw- "

"Ask him Jessica. The next time you see him, ask him. I can't believe he would do it and not tell you, but Mike is married."

———— ⚭ ————

Shane was going to meet Tonya to get a pedicure.

"My treat," she said on the phone, finally coaxing her friend out of the house. She was truly worried about Shane.

Shane sat in the car. She opened the console between the front seats; she always kept a few CDs inside that she was feeling at the moment.

Right now, it was Heather Headley. She thought back to the concert that Tonya attended with her because Mike couldn't make it. Heather Headley opened for India Arie.

Mike was her "beautiful surprise." She was so excited to hear the band play the opening melody of that song. She quickly dialed Mike's number so India could serenade him. He didn't pick up.

Mike saw Shane calling and stepped out to answer the phone. Then, he hesitated. He'd disappointed her again by not going to the concert. Shane had been so excited when she surprised him with the tickets. He remembered dancing in her living room to an Arie ballad, then making slow love to her. Mike bowed his head and put the phone back into his pocket.

"Okay, I'm ready," he yelled. "Can you run that back for me?" he asked the sound engineer.

Shane loved India and Heather, but right now Heather sang the soundtrack to her life. She must be going through some shit, just like me, Shane thought. Or she has a friend who is serving as her songwriting muse.

*Can you tell me that I'm not her,*
*That I'm not the one who completes your world?*

*Always Been Your Girl.* That song took Shane to a place that she kept locked away. Although the song broke her down, it somehow temporarily eased the pain, just a hair, enough for her to breathe and not cry.

Shane pulled into the parking lot of her and Tonya's favorite spot for mani pedis. She dreaded going in and being "okay". Tonya was only trying to help but it was all so exhausting!

She sat in the pedicure throne next to her friend with a glass of wine in her hand. Tonya held hers up for a toast. She waited until Shane reluctantly lifted hers.

"This is to you Shane. I know you've been struggling… but I know that great things are coming your way. So this is to the future. May it be so bright that you forget the darkness."

Shane clinked her glass with Tonya's and placed it on the side table next to her. She exhaled and looked down at the nail color that she selected. At least her feet would be cute, that was something. She would count the small wins for now.

⸺ ❧ ⸺

Mike called and asked to see her. She'd agreed, wanting to get it over with. He stood in her living room and told her what she already knew. She sat on the couch listening as silent tears followed their regular tracks.

"I didn't think we had a future... And Sherri was telling me that some dude she was seeing was moving to North Carolina. He wanted her to come with him. She was going to take the kids with her! So I did what I had to do."

"And just like that, she married you?"

"Yeah."

"So what happened to the guy?"

"I don't know... I guess he left!"

"And that didn't strike you as odd, how easily she agreed?" Shane paused. "And you didn't even tell your Mom!?!!" Her voice raised a pitch.

Mike was uncharacteristically quiet. "Shane, I'm sorry... I still love you. That hasn't changed. It will never change."

"Please, just go."

Shane walked to the living room and opened the bar. She seldom drank and especially alone, but she needed something to smooth out the edges of her mind. "This should do it," she said to her quiet house.

Shane sat at her dining room table and sipped a dry martini. I'm so stupid, she thought. She'd always thought that he would come back for her, that they would work things out. We should be building a life together.

She went back to the bar and fixed a second martini. After draining it, she put her glass in the sink. She cut off the lights and went upstairs. As usual, she cried herself to sleep.

# SECOND VERSE

# Onward and Upward

Shane was an advertising major in college. She wanted to be a copywriter and dreamed of power meetings in power suits with her hair in a severe bun, but she didn't have the stomach for the cutthroat nature of the business. And she didn't want to move to New York, the center of the ad world. She only wanted to write.

One day, when she was about to leave work to pick up Sean from school, her phone dinged with a text notification. She grabbed her jacket, shoving her phone into her purse. She'd check it later.

Once she and Sean were home after playing at the park, she stretched across the couch as he played in his room. She remembered the notification and checked her phone. It was her friend Gail from college. She was in town for a meeting and wanted to connect. Shane missed her friend; she hadn't seen her in a long time. She texted back a time and place to meet.

It was a bright Saturday. They met at Old Ebbitt Grill and caught up over a long lunch and cocktails.

"When was the last time you talked to Chanté?"

"Oh, it's been a minute… probably a few months now. You know she's killing the Miami real estate game! She could sell snow to an Eskimo!" exclaimed Shane.

"Remember how she used to get us into all the campus events when we didn't have one ticket between us, even when it was sold out!"

"And she would get us into clubs with no ID? Chanté would flip into the hard sell and we were in!"

They laughed hard, wiping their eyes. It grew quiet.

"So what are you doing with yourself Shane?" Gail listened as she pushed up her expensive, olive-colored frames.

"Still writing, mostly poetry and working a 9 to 5 to pay the bills! Looking for that big break...." she laughed and her voice trailed off.

"Well...." Gail took a sip of her cocktail. "I have this client who I'm working with on a major rebrand. We need some fresh eyes and talent on the project. Why don't you come to the City for a meeting?"

Shane put down her glass. "Are you offering me a job?"

"Maybe... I remember your writing... I also remember how you chickened out of New York. I know how talented you are!"

"I didn't chicken- "

"Yes you did," said Gail matter-of-factly, cutting her off. "Not a judgment, just a fact." She locked eyes with Shane. "So take the train up for a meeting."

She took the final swig of her drink.

"I'll think about it."

Gail exhaled. "Shane, you're always in your head... Don't think, just do! I'll send tickets. Tell your Mom you have a business trip. You know she'll keep Sean."

Gail stood up, her tall frame dwarfing Shane. "I have to run. I have a few more stops to make before I head back tonight."

Gail grabbed Shane's hand pulling her up. She embraced her old friend then kissed her cheek. Gail looked at her for a moment; she knew Shane was struggling. Gail swiped at a tear that was threatening to fall.

"This was so great! I'll see you in a few weeks then."

Shane watched as her old friend strode across the restaurant, her stilettos impatiently tapping the historic tile.

In New York, Shane met with Gail's team and her client. She listened to the vision for the corporate rebrand, taking copious notes. She was excited, but still unsure about how she fit on the team. She watched Gail, admiring her confidence and control. She owned the room, her full figure was slaying in a tailored, cream pantsuit and magenta stilettos.

After the meeting, she and Gail went to a late lunch. Italian, Shane's favorite. Gail was trying to close the deal. They sat in Gail's regular booth.

"So Shane, I need you to come up with a tagline and write a jingle for the commercial. It will launch the campaign."

Shane gasped. "I've never written a commercial let alone a jingle!"

"C'mon Shane! You are one of the most creative people I know. I know you can do this. Besides, this is a marquee client and I need something spectacular!"

"So no pressure."

"Look Shane. You need something…." Gail waved her hand as if to summon something. "A challenge." Shane was grateful that Gail didn't name the unspoken something that was hanging in the air. "See this for the opportunity that it is."

That evening Shane sat in her plush hotel room, courtesy of Gail, reading through her notes. She could do this. She would. That night, Shane awoke from a dream. She sat down at the desk and began scribbling on the hotel notepad. She wrote for hours, climbing back into bed as the sun came up.

She wrote the jingle. And many more for many clients. She was great at it. Shane was Gail's secret weapon. After a couple of years they branched out, opening their own shop, SAG Advertising. Gail handpicked a few from her old team and slowly brought them over.

Their company was responsible for the success of products and companies up and down the eastern seaboard and into the mid-west. Shane would travel up to the City for client meetings and presentations, but maintained DC as home base. Her Mom helped with Sean when Shane traveled and couldn't bring him.

⁓

Tonya and Joe got engaged! Shane was happy for her friend. Joe was good for her; he grounded her. Recently, Joe was offered a great IT job and they were moving to Colorado.

"When are you gonna come visit? It's beautiful, but you know it ain't nothing there except white folks and a bunch of trees!"

"Me and Sean will come out as soon as he's out of school." Shane paused. "I can't believe I won't be able to just stop by…." Her voice trailed off.

"Now don't start that shit! You know this is hard enough. I'm trying to support my man."

"I know," Shane said quietly. "I'm trying not to be selfish."

"You know I'm only a phone call away! Well, not really. I hate when people say that!" Tonya laughed, then was serious. "I've always got your back Shane."

Mike called periodically. Shane refused to answer. On occasion, he would leave her notes at her back door, flowers sometimes.

One evening after Sean had gone to bed, she scanned the channels looking for something to watch because she knew she wouldn't be able to sleep. She landed on a Will Smith movie, Hancock. Shane fell asleep on the couch that night dreaming of the god-like characters in the movie. That was her and Mike; they were stronger apart. When they were together, they grew weaker and lost their power.

Shane had a business meeting in New York the next week. She would catch the train up; she loved riding the train. Shane seldom flew to NYC.

It was a quiet night and one of her besties was checking on her. They laughed easily, but she wasn't able to hide the sadness that laced her voice.

"So have you heard from him?" asked Chanté.

"Not in a while. It's better this way. When he reaches out, it puts me in a tailspin… I need something different for my life."

"Girl, I know. It takes time, but it'll be alright."

Chanté had met Mike once when they drove to Pennsylvania for her baby shower. Her and Gail knew the details of her and Mike's saga and had lent a supportive ear on many late nights. They'd both thought the couple would find their way back to each other.

"So what else is up? Have you done anything fun in New York? I need to take a trip so we can have a girl's weekend!"

"Yes. Let's make it happen!" said Shane with an enthusiasm that she didn't really feel.

She heard a light tapping. Her heart lurched. She got up from the couch and walked over to the front door. Shane peeked out of the inset window and into Mike's eyes.

"Chanté, I gotta go. Mike's here."

"Oh shit. Girl, be strong!"

That night, Mike and Shane cried and kissed each others' tears. They made love and Shane knew it was the last time. He left and Shane dreamt about the wedding and babies that they'd never have. She once told him that he would always love her. Perhaps she had cursed them both.

~

The train ride was peaceful and gave Shane time to think and write. She watched as the landscape transitioned from verdant country to urban concrete.

One of her many journals was open on the seat beside her. She stared down at her words on the page:

*Sometimes like a spring rain*
*We need tears to wash away dirt, debris and*
*Pain…*
*And to renew and strengthen.*
*But they never come when I beckon.*

A dam was built so long ago
I cannot recall gathering the sticks and mud and leaves
That created the mortar.

A lump formed in her throat. She thought of him, in these times of quiet. He would fill up the space, leaving room for little else. Shane sighed and swallowed. Just then, she felt eyes on her. She turned to meet the stare of a Black man about her age. He was a deep, rich brown with a tight fade and an immaculate beard. He wore a tailored, navy suit with a plum-colored, patterned tie. She glanced down at his shoes. Very nice.

"You look deep in thought."

"What's that?" Shane asked.

"I said, you were deep in thought. I didn't mean to disturb you."

"You didn't. But I felt you watching me."

He looked a bit embarrassed. "My apologies." He stood. "I'm headed to the dining car, can I get you anything?"

"Um no, thanks… On second thought, I'll join you, if you don't mind."

"I do not."

Shane stuffed her journal into her backpack and followed him through the train. When they reached the dining car, she sat down and extended her hand. "I'm Shane."

"Robert."

"It's good to meet you Robert."

Shane ordered a coffee and a cinnamon raisin bagel, toasted with butter. Robert had a cheese and tomato omelet with a glass of fresh-squeezed orange juice. After an hour, they were chatting and laughing like old friends. Robert was a music publisher and was headed to the City for a meeting with a record label. Shane shared that she worked in advertising and branding.

"Mostly I create brand stories, but also copy for jingles and commercials," she explained.

"Have you ever written a song?"

Shane shook her head. "Lots of poetry, but never a song," she explained between sips. This was her second cup.

"Is that what you were writing when you caught me staring?" Robert laughed.

Shane smiled. "You got me."

Robert looked at his watch. "We should be in the City soon. What time is your meeting?"

"Oh, not 'til this afternoon. I like to come up early. I don't like to be rushed."

"A true artist," he remarked. "Well, I need to go gather my things so I can get to my meeting on time."

Robert stood. He extended his hands and she gave him one of hers. He closed both hands around it.

"It was so good to meet you Shane." He paused and looked at her.

He released her hand and reached into his pocket, bringing out his wallet. Before Shane could object, he put bills on the table. Then he took a card from his wallet and pressed it into her hand.

"When you get bored and want a new adventure, give me a call. You could be a songwriter."

Shane followed Robert back to their car and grabbed the rest of her belongings. He picked up a briefcase and a wool coat, wrapping a scarf around his neck. He was a good looking brother and could wear a suit, okay?

He winked at her and she waved. They stepped off the train, headed in opposite directions.

Later that afternoon, she told Gail about her new acquaintance.

"Oh girl, it's about time! I was starting to worry about you."

She slapped at her friend. "Not like that!" She hesitated. "But I have been thinking about what he said."

Gail turned to look at her friend. "Are you serious?"

Shane looked at the ground, then up at her friend. Things were going well. She'd made and saved quite a nest egg, even made some investments guided by one of Gail's Wall Street buddies. But she felt a pull inside her. Her creativity was ready to grow and expand. And she was intrigued by the idea of songwriting.

"Gail, it's been eight years… Yes, they've been great but…."

"Oh, I knew I wouldn't have you forever! I knew the artist inside you would grow tired of the ad game." Gail looked at her friend. "I created a monster," she laughed, but it was hollow.

"Oh I'm not gone. I haven't even called him!" she huffed.

"Yeah, but you've got that look…."

"What look?" Shane raised an eyebrow.

"That faraway Shane look, like you're looking to the horizon."

# New Musings

Music had always been a huge part of her life. Every celebration and milestone was framed by music. Each time she had to pull herself from a valley, music had been an integral part of the journey. And every celebration and high-point was punctuated with music. Shane knew she could be a fantastic songwriter. But she wouldn't leave her partner in a lurch; she'd still be involved. Together, they eventually found someone to take on Shane's role. She would remain part-owner and agreed to serve as a consultant for another 18 months.

Life was good, but BUSY! She and Sean moved to Chicago. Why Chicago? Shane hated the cold, but she loved Chicago in the spring and summer. And she needed a change… besides, she found a great piece of property, a historic Greystone.

She rented the DC house to a young, Black family and began packing their life headed for the Windy City. Before they moved, she wrote Mike a letter. She didn't know where he was in life so she sent it to his Mom.

Dear Mike,

I pray that you are well. I'm starting a new career as a songwriter. All of the poetry and journals have finally paid off! We shared a love of music and now I'll be immersed in it. Can you believe it! I hardly can.

I've made another big decision. Sean and I are moving to Chicago. It's time for a new beginning and I can't have that in DC… too many memories....

You're probably wondering why I'm writing. We haven't spoken for some time, but it didn't feel right to leave without telling you. That may strike you as strange, but you are still with me. You're in my thoughts and my heart.

I want to thank you for loving me so fiercely that I was able to get over the fear and give you my heart completely. I thought our story would be a long, rich one but it didn't turn out that way. Still, I am truly glad that you came into my life. I learned a lot about myself and understand that our relationship was not a failure, it was simply an ending.

Kiss the kids and give Jessica my love.

Shane


The Greystone was beautiful and inexpensive but it needed a lot of work! It was a multi-family property with three apartments, one per floor. She would take her time restoring it and convert it back into a family home for her and Sean. They'd live in the top apartment during the renovations. Their new space had two spacious, sun-filled bedrooms, two and one half bathrooms, a fireplace, a small, utilitarian kitchen, living room and a den which Shane made her home office. Best of all, it had a window seat in the front bay window.

Early mornings, she would sit and gaze out the bay window onto the street with a journal and a cup of coffee, scribbling intermittently, while Sean was at school. It had to be early because the contractors would start banging away downstairs and frequently the general contractor needed her opinion on some detail or another.

Shane had an architect friend from college, Bryan, with a local firm who found the general contractor for her. He'd come and walked the property with her taking notes and video along the way. Bryan was talented with years of experience under his proverbial belt. He knew Shane wanted to preserve the history and charm of the place; she was looking for more restoration than renovation with a few modern upgrades, mostly to the kitchen and bathrooms.

"When it's done, I'll have you and Imani over for dinner! I expect to host plenty of dinner parties!"

"Oh, well you and Imani will get along great because she loves going to dinner parties," he laughed. Imani had done well to snag this one. He was a handsome, intelligent and genuinely nice guy. She and Bryan had been two peas in a pod in college, but had lost touch over the years. She'd attended their wedding and they swapped pictures of their kids, but that became the totality of the relationship, until now. She was so glad to have her good friend back in her life!

"Tell Imani she can come see me before then if she doesn't mind a little dust… She may need to bring her hard hat!" Shane laughed. "On second thought, maybe we'll just hang out or grab some dinner."

"That might be best," agreed Bryan. "She's not the construction site type."

"No? Given the work you do I thought she may be used to it."

"She'll come once a project is done and pat my back for bringing a vision to life, but nah. It's cool though; she supports me and recognizes my talent, she just likes to come once it's clean and pretty." He snickered. "She has a great design eye though… You may want to talk to her when you get to that phase. She knows all of the spots for decor, antiques, art, you name it."

"Note to self: Imani is decorating the house!" she proclaimed.

There were a total of seven bedrooms, three kitchens, three fireplaces, one dining room, two dining nooks, five full baths, three half baths, a laundry room and two dens across the floors. She had a lot of decisions to make. Bryan was very helpful with his recommendations and was able to draft new plans for the project. In the end, there would be four bedrooms, four full baths, two half baths, a kitchen, butler's pantry, formal dining room, parlor, laundry room and an office. Someday Shane hoped to convert the basement into a recording studio.

One afternoon, as Shane finished going over plan changes with the general contractor, her phone rang. It was a Maryland area code. Shane still hadn't changed her number. She couldn't bear to give up her 202 area code.

"Shane Mathews."

"Well hello Shane!" She knew the voice right away.

"Jessica! How are you?" Her heart started beating faster.

"I'm fine honey. How are you doing? How's Sean? Mike told me that you all moved to Chicago. Now what are y'all doing up there in all of that cold?"

Shane laughed. How she missed Jessica. At one time, she believed this woman would be her mother-in-law.

"What's all that racket? Did I catch you at a bad time?"

Shane went upstairs to get away from the construction noise and dust.

"No, not at all. I'm having some work done in our new house and I was downstairs in the midst of it. It should be quieter now."

"How's Sean?"

They talked for hours catching each other up with the details of their lives. Mike had relocated to California. He had finally left the music behind and was starting to take his visual art seriously. Shane couldn't believe that he moved that far away without his family.

"Oh, I'm sure he'll be back this way at some point. But I'm proud of him. He's finally using the talent that God gave him."

Shane was proud of him too. She hoped that he was happy.

After getting off the phone with Jessica, Shane walked into her office. She went online to check in for her and Sean's flight. Tonya and Joe's wedding was the following week in Maryland: the couple's families and most of their friends lived there.

Shane was the maid of honor and Sean would serve as an usher. They were arriving ahead of time so Shane could help with any last minute tasks and host the bachelorette party. She and Tonya were also hoping to find some time for just the two of them. They hadn't seen each other since she and Sean visited Colorado the previous summer. That was over a year ago.

It was a large wedding with more than 100 guests. Tonya was beautiful in her designer wedding gown. She wore a slip silhouette to accentuate her slim, curvy figure and long legs. The gown was antique white and puddled at her feet. It was perfect against her chocolate brown skin. She'd cut her hair in a pixie style and wore a simple cap veil pinned to her hair. She was radiant and glowing, smiling the entire day and night.

And it was a party. Both Tonya and Joe love a good time and the wedding reception didn't disappoint. They had a live band playing covers of all the current hits and some classics. Tonya changed into another slip gown that stopped mid thigh so she could move. The guests partied into the night and brunched the next day. That next night they left for the Maldives for two weeks, sponsored by her parents. Before a car picked them up, Shane was able to steal a few moments with her.

Shane held her friend for a long time. She was so happy for her, but she missed her. Their lives were drifting farther apart.

"I love you and I am so happy for both of you!" A tear slid down Shane's face. "I know that y'all are gonna take care of each other and be good to one another because you've been doing that."

When they broke apart, Tonya wiped the tears from her eyes and Shane's.

"This is a happy day, no more tears!" Tonya laughed. "It's been so good to see you. I wish we had more time."

"Girl please. You better go on with your husband on your fantasy honeymoon."

"I know, right! I need to make sure I'm popping those pills cuz we gonna be fuckin' on the beach!" Tonya grinded the air.

"You so nasty," Shane said, shaking her head.

"I know, but he loves it," she said, grinding again.

"Hey, where's my wife!" Joe bellowed.

They turned in unison to see Joe headed in their direction, strutting like George Jefferson. Tonya and Shane cackled.

He smiled a huge smile. Shane hugged him. "Congratulations!"

"Thank you, thank you." He released her and took a dramatic step back. "You're looking beautiful this evening!"

"Why thank you sir." Shane did a mini curtsy.

"My boy is asking about you."

"Who?" Tonya asked, her lip curled in a half snarl. Shane held up her hand.

"It doesn't matter... not interested."

"Aww Shane. You don't even know who it is!" he protested.

"Doesn't matter. I'm not about to hook up with somebody at y'all's wedding. Direct him toward someone else."

"It's like that?... Well, me and my lady need to bounce." He looked at Tonya. "You ready to go?" He re-started his strut.

"Are you serious with that walk?" Tonya had a pained look on her face.

"Dead ass! C'mon now wife, let's do this! We have a plane to catch." She turned to Shane. They hugged once more and kissed.

"Until next time," Shane whispered.

<hr>

More than a year into her songwriting career and she and Robert were connected at the hip. Although he was based in Jersey, he knew everybody, everywhere. They would meet in New York or LA sometimes, others, he would come to Chicago. He introduced her to entertainment attorneys, producers, up-and-coming artists, sound engineers and other songwriters.

She enjoyed Robert's company and more than that, she was learning so much from him! Although Shane was a creative, she had a head for business and an MBA to match. After much negotiation on her part, they entered into a co-publishing agreement. This meant she did not assign all of her song copyrights to him like many traditional agreements, but instead retained a percentage of the copyright. In other words, Shane kept a greater share of royalties because she also earned a portion of the publisher's share.

Besides, one day she may want to start her own publishing company. And although they had a great relationship, this was business. Just to be sure, she had an acquaintance from B-School who went on to become a contract lawyer, giving the agreement a once-over. She was not about to be a struggling artist!

"I know we need them all, but what's the difference between the ISWC code and the other identifiers?" she asked Robert.

"The ISWC is for each song, so you'll be assigned many of them. The others are tied to you so you'll only have one from each entity."

"Ohhhh," Shane said, the light bulb coming on.

So as a creator, she also had identifiers. All of the codes track how songs are used on streaming services to make sure they would be paid accurately.

Additionally, she was registered with ASCAP, a performing rights organization, and the Mechanical Licensing Collective (MLC) to ensure that she received any royalties that were due to her; Robert made sure that the paperwork was complete and submitted.

In time, they also registered for a synchronization license. She knew about synch licenses from her jingle work. This was necessary if your work was incorporated into any audiovisual work such as a film, video game, TV show or commercial. Master use licenses were new to her but she'd done her research. Robert would handle those if and when any of her work became a sound recording.

Whew! It was a lot at first, but once the paperwork was done, she only needed to concentrate on writing the next great song. And she did… many times over. In the first few years, Shane wrote over 50 songs; 32 of them had been sold or otherwise licensed. Shane Mathews was in demand!

Shane didn't have a process or particular songwriting ritual. Songs just came to her, the way poetry always had. She kept journals beside the bed and in her car. She drew inspiration from the many art museums, architecture, parks, people and of course her life and that of those around her. She'd always been a keen observer, preferring to listen rather than talk. Once Shane tweaked and perfected lyrics, she let them marinate for a few weeks, if time allowed.

Once she'd shared something with Mike that her grandmother told her back when she was a college student.

"She said that in relationships, one person always loves the other more. This time, I guess it's me."

Mike disagreed.

*Grandma Told Me* was Shane's latest song.

 *Love is sweet but it's never even*
 *I've learned that lesson through a lot of livin'*
 *Someone always loves stronger*
 *Someone always holds on a little longer*
 *Baby, let him love you more she said, let him love you more.*

---

"I knew it," Robert reflected one night. "When I saw you on the train with that journal, you had this dreamy look in your eyes. I knew you were a songwriter!"

They toasted. Shane sipping her crisp white wine, Robert sipping his bourbon. They were in her parlor, in front of a low fire.

"Ugh, I don't know how you drink that!" Shane made a face at Robert.

Robert ignored her. "Shane, you did the damn thing with this renovation, pardon me, restoration."

Shane smiled and looked wistfully at the grand wooden doors at the entrance of the room. She'd found them while out for the day sourcing the finishing details for the house with Imani. They were in an antique store that stocked many 20th century, locally-made pieces. She'd gotten to know the owner, Ahmed, while frequenting the store during the restoration of the Greystone.

"Shane, so good to see you!" he purred his native language, enriching his words. He leaned toward her in a light embrace, kissing both of her cheeks. "I want to show you some new things that I think you'll like!" his voice trembled with excitement.

"Lead the way!"

When she saw the dusty doors leaning on each other, her eyes lit up. They were at least 10 feet tall with raised, intricate carvings. Imani jumped up and down beside her, clapping her hands excitedly.

"The contractor is gonna kill me! How are we gonna make these work? The doorways are finished…"

"What about the parlor?" said Imani slowly. "That entrance might be wide enough…," she continued as she began to pace. "They may have to open it up a bit, but I'm sure Bryan can advise them. Lemme call him!"

And, of course, Bryan made it work. Those doors paired with the coffered ceiling made this room her favorite.

"The credit goes to Bryan and my general contractor. Yes, I had a vision, but they made it a reality! And I can't forget my girl Imani with the designer's eye, but thank you!"

She sipped her wine. "I am very pleased with it. Next up will be the studio."

"This is a big ole house for just you! Sean is going to go off to school soon. You betta get a dog or something!"

"I know," whined Shane.

She stared into the fire, watching it pop and crackle. She'd always thought that she'd get married one day and maybe have another kid, but time was marching on. Shane was kicking ass as a songwriter but her personal life was non-existent. Her social life was nonstop: she had many friends and went to plenty of parties and events. But she didn't have a plus one. And she had been on too many dates and had a few short-term relationships over the years.

There was one love, Chad, that had been promising. Chad was an accountant with a big ego and a wide, gap-toothed smile. She'd loved Chad with his dry humor and thick brows. They were together for four years. He was the first to meet Sean since Mike; he loved Sean and the three of them had good times together. He'd wanted to get married but whenever he brought it up, she'd get skittish. He finally called her on it and she admitted that she wasn't ready to get married or to slow down in her career.

"Then what are we doing Shane? You know that I want to get married and have a family."

"What do you want me to say?"

"I guess there is nothing more to be said." And he was gone.

If she was being fair and honest, she would've just told him that he wasn't the one.

"We need to introduce you to somebody!" Robert stood up and headed to the kitchen to refill her wine glass. She followed behind him pouting.

"Now you sound like Imani! I told her, 'Everyone doesn't get what you and Bryan have.'"

Shane sat at the island, swinging her feet. She tapped her empty wine glass. Robert laughed as he opened the wine fridge to get the bottle. He poured the wine, then looked at her.

After a few moments, he said, "you know, I admire you Shane. You go after what you want. You've accomplished so much but I feel like you're just getting started! People better look out!"

Shane nodded her head. The loneliness was creeping back in.

"Robert, this wasn't the plan for my life… Don't get me wrong, I am thankful. My son is happy and healthy, I love my work and I have a lot of people who love and support me."

"But not that special one," finished Robert. Shane tilted her head in his direction.

"You never talk about Sean's dad, what happened? Is he the reason you stay single?"

Shane sipped her wine. She was quiet for a while.

"Shane, I'm sorry, you don't have to answer."

"No, it's okay. I'm just not used to talking about the past… only rehashing it in my head…." Shane had a distant look. "Sean's dad is an asshole, but nobody else could have given me Sean, so I feel that was his purpose in my life." She paused.

"He turned out to be a very selfish person, not who I thought he was… And as you know, he doesn't have a relationship with his son. That part is the hardest. But no, he's not what keeps me unavailable."

"Then what is it Shane? You are so talented, you're a great Mom, you're beautiful… And the songs that you write, whew, you write the hell out of a love song. So I know you have passion and that longing."

Shane smiled a small, sad smile.

"I think I've had my quota of true loves Robert. Not sure it's gonna happen a third time."

Is this about your former fiancé?" He looked at her and said softly, "Do you think he'd want you to spend your life alone? It's been a long time."

Shane grabbed her wineglass and got up from the island. "Now you need a refill."

After Robert freshened his drink, Shane gave him the short version of her love affair with Mike. "We are the greatest love story never told." She closed her eyes. "A lot of my songs and poetry are about him. He's still my muse."

Her eyes began to tear up. "Guess I'm not quite over him."

"Damn Shane." It was all he had to offer.

"So what about you Robert? You're not going to meet anybody hanging out wit me!"

Robert sighed. "I had my version of a Mike once, Erika. Not as tragic but I was shut down for a while! She couldn't handle my schedule; she wanted me to spend more time with her. But I was grinding and building — for us — she just didn't see it like that."

"C'mon home to me Charlene!" sang Shane.

"What's with men spending all their time "building" instead of living and being present with the woman who loves you? We don't want a bunch of shit, we just want y'all to be there!"

Robert pensively sipped his drink.

"It's a man thing, I guess. We want to take care of our woman in a way we believe you deserve. Sometimes, I guess we can't see the forest for the trees and we get in our own way… Shit, I dunno."

"We are pitiful!" exclaimed Shane.

Robert sat his drink on a coaster. "Speak for yourself. I ain't pitiful." He smoothed his shirt. "Shiiiit, I'm an eligible bachelor!"

"Ok!" Shane held up her hands. "My bad."

She and Robert had become really great friends and business partners. Robert encouraged her to apply for membership to the Recording Academy. Now, Shane was a voting member. People respected her songwriting power, so she had a voice. She set out to quietly recruit other voting members and shift the paradigm of who and how the best in the music industry were chosen.

They'd also changed the nature of their business relationship. He still served as her publisher but they were now in an administration agreement, which meant that Robert was no longer assigned a portion of Shane's copyrights. But he still performed administrative duties for a fee: registration, licensing, royalty collection and income distribution. Shane had earned it; to date, she'd written songs for over 20 new and established artists. Besides, they were both making a lot of money between the licensing deals and royalties.

Most of Shane's songs were available for streaming and a few appeared on movie soundtracks. Now, the pair considered a sub-publisher agreement. As a result of the international tours of some of the bigger artists Shane had written for, some songs were hits in other countries. The sub-publisher agreement uses a foreign publisher to represent and promote a songwriter's musical works in different countries. They handle all of the services that Robert typically did, in that respective country.

Of all the songs Shane had written, she kept a few for herself - about Mike, inspired by him. Writing them helped when she was lonely and wondering about his life. There was *Invisible Me*, *And Then He Came*, but one of her favorites was *Naysayers*:

*It may not be perfect,*
*But he's perfect for me.*
*He ain't got degrees,*
*But, his tongue is a master of lyric and rhyme*
*And these curves of mine.*
*I have all that I need*
*As long as I'm loving him*
*And he's loving me.*

# CHORUS

# Mule

Shane loved coming to the galleries in New York. She grabbed a coffee, then headed to Chelsea to see some art. There were always new, up and coming artists to check out whose work inspired her and stoked her creativity. She also liked discovering established artists whom she didn't know so she could watch their careers. Afterward, she would stop by the Market and have a fabulous lunch.

It had been a minute since she was in the City. She thought about reaching out to Gail or one of her other friends there, but decided against it. She wanted a "me" day in Chelsea. And art was a personal experience for her. She liked to take her time and admire the pieces, quietly. Today, maybe she'd stroll through the High Line too.

Shane was glad that she'd gotten an early start. Chelsea would be bustling soon. Shane was wrapped in her thoughts, when something caught her eye. She looked up to see that she was standing in front of the Cavin-Morris Gallery. Through the floor to ceiling glass, she could see a huge, colorful painting.

She pulled the heavy door and stepped inside. Shane headed down a short flight of open stairs that were in the center of the gallery. Then, she saw it. Shane stopped and stared at the over-sized painting.

"Breathtaking, isn't it?" The British accent broke through her thoughts.

"It is," she answered, not taking her eyes from the piece.

It was awash with deep, rich and vibrant colors and texture. The orange, turquoise, rose and crimson danced with energy and excitement. There was movement in metallic golds and azure. Every inch of the canvas crackled before her, except the center. There were a pair of eyes, light brown but not too light, clear and penetrating staring at her beneath dark lashes. There was a soulfulness to them but also sadness. She knew those eyes.

"Do you know the artist?"

"What?" Shane finally looked to her right to find a spindly, blond woman wearing a tailored suit, stilettos and perfect make up looking back at her.

"Are you familiar with the work of Evan Jeffries?"

Shane turned back to the painting.

"Yes. I've seen his work."

The woman had been watching, evaluating her. Probably to see if she belonged in a gallery such as this. If she could afford to be in a place like this. Shane could feel the blue eyes appraising her worn jeans and leather jacket. She removed her scarf and unzipped her jacket, revealing a Lenny Kravitz concert tee.

The woman dragged her eyes back to the artwork.

"It's a stunning piece. One of a kind, entitled *Mule*."

A small smile crept to Shane's lips. Mule of the world, she mouthed.

"What was that?" the blond asked.

"Nothing. I'll take it."

"What, you want to buy it? It's not for sale," she stuttered. "It's simply on loan from the artist. I can show you another Jeffries piece that…."

"No… I'll take this one."

"As I said," huffed the woman. "This piece is not for sale."

Shane reached inside her jacket to produce a linen business card. She held it between her index and middle fingers, extending it to the woman. Her name was embossed on the card in crisp font. The woman hesitantly took the card, her fingers caressing the heavy paper stock.

"Call Mr. Jeffries and tell him that someone is interested in this piece. Tell him who the buyer is. My contact is on the card."

Shane turned to admire the painting one last time before she left the gallery.

———~———

Glad to be back at home, Shane sat in her office staring out of the window. Snowflakes were silently blanketing the street, the crooked branches, everything. The fire crackled and danced in the fireplace on the far wall of the room. Her gaze crept up the plaster wall to the intricate ceiling. She loved the original architecture of her Greystone.

The restoration had been exciting but kinda brutal to live through. But she and Sean pitched in and got their hands dirty and learned a lot! Shane had loved it: it fed her creativity and love for all things HGTV-related. There was a time that she never dreamed that she would own such a home.

The doorbell interrupted her reverie. It was early and she didn't have anything on her calendar. Maybe it was her assistant, Stephanie. She jogged down the stairs and looked out of the enormous bay window. It was some sort of delivery truck.

A gentleman was bundled on her doorstep with a clipboard in his hand. She walked through the foyer into the vestibule to let him in. He wiped his feet vigorously before stepping inside. His gaze swept the foyer approvingly.

"Nice," he said, shaking his head.

"Thank you."

"I'm looking for Shane Mathews."

"That would be me," she said brightly.

"Ok. I have two items for you. I just need you to sign, but first I'll need some form of identification."

Shane walked to a carved, wooden console table that abutted the opposite wall and slid open the drawer. Removing her wallet, she fished out her driver's license. After glancing at the ID, the gentleman handed her the clipboard to sign. Then, he handed her an envelope.

"This is the first item. The second is coming off of the truck."

Two gentlemen walked up the wide front steps carrying a huge flat box. Her eyes began to sting a little. She put the envelope on the table and walked to the doors, opening both this time. The men stopped at the top of the steps, resting on the porch under the overhang. The box was about seven feet high and wider still.

"Where do you want it?" one of them asked.

"Could you take it to the parlor?" She motioned them in, past the foyer to the hallway. "It's the first door on the left."

"Thank you!" Shane closed and locked the double doors and looked toward the parlor. Her eyes followed the path across the floor noticing a trail of water with scattered mini puddles. I'll get that up later, she thought. Shane walked to the console table and gingerly opened the envelope. Inside there was another envelope with a handwritten note clipped to it: "Hey Gorgeous. This is for you."

She opened the envelope to find a cashier's check for the amount she'd wired to the gallery. She tucked it back into the envelope and put it inside the console drawer. Shane looked at the note again, slid it into her back pocket, then she headed for the butler's pantry. After rummaging through a drawer, she found a utility knife. This will work, she thought.

She walked into the parlor and carefully began to cut the top seams of the box, then down the right side and down the left. The cardboard fell toward her and onto the wool rug covering the floor. Shane took a deep breath then poked a hole into the brown paper. She wiggled her index finger making the hole grow, then pulled through the paper making a widening gash. Colors began to appear; she stopped tearing and slowly put her right hand into the gash.

Her fingers touched the canvas. She closed her eyes and slowly ran her fingertips over the expanse of the canvas. There was a topography to the painting and her fingers lingered over the texture. She imagined him as he painted: stepping back to admire after he completed bold strokes. She opened her eyes and used both hands to pull back the paper. She knew exactly where to hang it.

The next week, her assistant sat on the chaise in Shane's office. Shane watched as Stephanie gazed at the painting hanging above the fireplace.

"Niiice," the young woman remarked. "This is the one you saw in New York?"

"Yes."

Stephanie studied the eyes in the center of the piece. "You said that you know the artist?"

Shane nodded. "From DC, a long time ago… So what's on the schedule?"

"Well, your producer friend from the Recording Academy wants to know if you're going to teach the master class. They need to know this week."

Right. The songwriting class in LA. She would have to be on the west coast for at least two months. At least the weather would be better and she wouldn't be so lonely with Sean away at school.

"Tell them I'll agree, but I need them to secure some options for accommodations. You're coming, right?" She looked at the young woman.

"I'll come out with you, but I have to come back in a few weeks. Remember that I have to defend my dissertation."

"Of course, that's right," said Shane. It wouldn't be long before her talented assistant left her for bigger and better things.

"Also you have the ASCAP Experience coming up after you get back from LA. You'll need to start working on your presentation and content for that."

Shane nodded her head.

Stephanie looked at Shane as if a light bulb turned on. "I should rsvp for a few events for you to attend while you're there. Let's keep the buzz going ahead of the bio...." She started texting furiously on her phone. "How's it coming anyway?" She waited.

Shane exhaled. "It's coming, but I owe the publisher some chapters."

Stephanie abruptly put down the phone and looked up. "Shane! I thought you said you turned those in last week?!!?"

"No. What I said was they were *expected* last week."

Stephanie threw a crumpled paper at Shane, hitting her shoulder. Shane laughed.

"I'm going to get it done!"

"I know and preferably before we leave for Los Angeles," Stephanie retorted.

"So bossy! C'mon. I'll make us some coffee."

Shane stood up from behind her desk and walked across the room. She glanced at the painting. Stephanie raised up from the chaise.

"It is stunning."

"Yup."

She and Stephanie sat at the kitchen counter enjoying their coffee. Stephanie went through a few more items with her to keep things progressing while they were in LA. She pushed her locks back from her face.

"What about the house? Do you want to hire a service to watch it while you're away?"

"Do you think that's necessary? I'll reach out to Imani to see if she can come by once or twice a week. Or maybe I'll see if my Mom will come out here."

"Okay. Also, when I'm back, I'll still come a few times per week to work... if that's okay."

"That's fine. I know you need quiet!" Stephanie had a roommate and it wasn't always easy for her to work in her condo.

Stephanie wrote a few notes, then closed her planner.

"So what's up with the book?"

"What do you mean?"

"Shane, c'mon. You attack everything head on and writing is like breathing for you."

"Well look at you, Ms. Persistent!"

"That's why you hired me." Stephanie took a bite of a flaky croissant.

"'Tis true, 'tis true…."

"So what gives?" she asked between bites.

Shane was indeed struggling with the book. How was she going to write about her life without including Mike? He wasn't some footnote. Mike was a constant. He was always there, in her songs, in her breath, in her heart.

"I don't know. I don't want to write a boring biography. That's not me… I've been doing some research and I was thinking of shifting to a memoir. I'd focus on my career starting with writing jingles and give some backstory that shaped me as an artist and writer. I'd use poetry or lyrics as the constant, to tie the pieces together."

"Sounds great. Have you mentioned it to your publisher? That's who you've gotta sell, not me."

Shane refilled her coffee mug.

"I was still working it out in my head and on paper. I'll give her a call this week. Before you say it, I know that the timeline has slipped a bit, but I think now that I have this new concept I can make up the time. And I can use the chapters that I've already submitted. Besides, I will write while I'm in LA. So don't go overboard with scheduling events for me!"

"Okay, okay. Just doing my job."

"And I have a favor. Could you help me plan a little soiree before we leave for the west coast? I haven't hosted a dinner party in a while. I'll ask Imani if she can help too."

Shane tapped her wine glass with a fork.

"Can I get everyone's attention?" Most of the guests were in the formal dining room. "Steph, can you try to corral people from the parlor and the kitchen?"

As people crowded into the room, Shane took a moment to gather her thoughts. "I want to thank everyone for coming tonight." She could see Imani, Bryan, Stephanie, some recording artists she'd worked with, a few producers she knew and friends that she'd made since moving to Chi-town.

"Girl you know we wouldn't miss one of your dinner parties!" responded Imani to laughter. Bryan had his arm around her waist. She was dwarfed by her husband's broad frame.

"Well I know you wouldn't!" laughed Shane.

"No, but seriously. Thank you for coming." She paused. "Most of you have become my second family. I moved to Chicago on a whim. I was changing careers so I wanted a big change. Sean and I knew no one, except Bryan, and I hadn't seen him really since college. I am so lucky that Sean didn't hold it against me, dragging him here for our big adventure!" Shane looked around the room.

"You all have loved and supported me and I want to say thank you. I'm about to embark on some new projects and things that may take me outside of my comfort zone, but I know my people will be here for me. Bryan and Imani, thank you for helping me build my home, for being my friends, well really, my family." Imani nodded and blew her a kiss.

"Stephanie — this is my right hand y'all — thank you for keeping me on point and organized. Because of you, I get to focus on what I love to do." Stephanie smiled and nodded. "And Robert, where's Robert?"

Robert held up his highball glass.

"Robert, you have held me down, shown me the ropes and pushed me when I needed it! Thank you for being my business partner and much more for being my friend. And for those of you still holding on to hope, this man is like my brother. There is no match to be made!"

There were a few protests from the group.

Shane rolled her eyes and chuckled. "Anyway, I wanted to have one last get together before I head to LA to teach this class."

"MASTERclass," Stephanie corrected.

"Yes, masterclass. I love you all." Shane wiped at her eyes and took a sip of her white wine.

"And we love you!"

# THIRD VERSE

# Masterclass

Shane and Stephanie flew into the Los Angeles International Airport two weeks later. Shane was feeling good. The prior week, she'd met with her publisher who loved the idea of a memoir. Shane sold her with original poetry running through the chapters. Her poetry led to her stumble into songwriting so it was quite apropos. There were great stories and memories from her work at SAG, her early days as a songwriter but most importantly the origin of her poetry as a young college student. It was relatable, compelling and it would sell.

They deplaned and were met by a driver holding a sign with her name on it.

"Nice touch," Shane remarked to Stephanie with a raised eyebrow.

"Don't look at me. I didn't arrange this. It must be the Recording Academy."

"Okay!" Her pitch raised as she smiled.

They climbed into the back of the town car while the driver hurriedly put their luggage into the trunk. Shane's class would be held at the University of Santa Monica on Wilshire Boulevard. The house they'd occupy was close by, as were plenty of shops, stores, the beach and Bergamot Station, a complex of art galleries and creative businesses. She couldn't wait for some down time so she could explore.

Right now, they were headed to the house to drop their luggage. Then, straight to the university to get a temporary ID and a quick tour so she'd know where to go on Monday. At least later, she could take a walk on the beach.

Stephanie would be spared the mini campus tour. She headed to the Whole Foods to stock the house, then she would set up their office. The owner had graciously removed furniture from one of the bedrooms, but left a desk and chair, a lamp and a chaise. Anything else they could grab at a Target that she spied in the area.

Once she left the University, she took a walk. She'd insisted that the driver stay with her assistant to run errands. If she needed to, she'd grab an Uber. Shane headed straight for the beach. She could smell the salt in the air and the crashing waves grew louder as she headed west. She'd also have to make time for the Santa Monica Pier, having never been. I'll be here for almost three months, she thought. I have time.

Shane saw stairs that led down to the sand. Yes! She took off her Chucks and socks so she could feel the sand between her manicured toes. Shane shoved the socks into her tote bag, then bent down to roll up her jeans. She wanted to get her feet wet.

As she started to run towards the surf, her phone began to vibrate. She dug around her bag feeling for it. Sean's handsome face and wild hair flashed across the screen.

"Hey!"

"Hey Ma. I guess you made it there safely."

"I did. I'm sorry honey. I meant to call when I landed but we've been moving since we touched down. I just got some time to myself and- "

"You're at the beach." Sean laughed.

"Yup. I was running to dip my toes in when you called. What's up with you?"

"Nuthin'. I did some studying earlier, now I'm lookin' for something to get into tonight. I was about to fix me something to eat when I noticed what time it was. So I called to check on you."

"Uh huh. Whatchu getting into tonight?"

"I said I don't know."

"Yeah, okay. Well be safe."

"Always. You too. LA isn't that safe. Don't be out by yourself once it gets dark."

"Okayyy Sean. I don't need a lecture. Now I'm going to run into this ocean before my phone starts ringing again!"

"Aight, Ma. Talk to you soon."

"Love you SonSon." Shane made a kissing noise and disconnected the call.

That evening, Shane cooked her and Stephanie dinner: pan seared salmon with honey glaze, garlic spinach and lemon and herb roasted potatoes. She enjoyed having someone to cook for, for a change. Besides, they'd had a long day and neither wanted to go out for dinner.

"Shane, that was fantastic! I'm going to miss your meals."

Shane took a sip of wine and nodded her head approvingly at Stephanie's choice.

"Oh, now that you're going to be a PhD., you're not gonna come around?"

"Of course I will! I just mean, it won't be like this…."

Shane could sense her apprehension. She put down her glass. "Steph, what's up?"

The young woman didn't answer.

"What's going on? You've been working toward this for as long as I've known you. Now you're almost there, honey…."

Stephanie stood up, walked to the couch and collapsed on it. Shane followed her.

"Steph, look. You are young, talented, intelligent and beautiful. The world is your oyster right now! Whatever you want to do next is up to you."

"That's just it! I don't know what I want to do and, at this point, I feel like I should."

"Well… you can slow walk it. I know being my assistant isn't as cerebral as you may want, but I'm in no rush to replace you. I don't want to be selfish, but I will be."

Shane looked at Stephanie.

"You don't have to have it all figured out," she said in a soothing voice. "And be thankful that you don't have pesky student loans to worry about. Just focus on kicking ass when you defend in a few weeks."

Stephanie smiled and finished her last sips of wine. "I'm going to bed," she declared. "See you in the morning!"

<hr>

Thank goodness she was able to sleep in! Sunday morning and Shane sat looking out of the bedroom window. She couldn't quite see the ocean but she could faintly hear the surf and smell the salt in the air. It was sunny and people were out: jogging, walking dogs and some were leisurely strolling.

Shane had one of her journals spread across her lap. She was working on her memoir, recalling the turns and choices in her path that led her to today. On one hand, her journey seemed to have started long ago, but on the other it seemed to have happened so quickly. How could it be both?

> For as long as I can remember, I've loved words. This love affair with words pulled me from some dark, frightening places throughout my life and buoyed me so that I could enjoy the sweet simple joys that were coming my way. I love that many of us know the same words, but some people have a gift to put them together in such a perfect way that it can bring us to tears, evoke long forgotten memories and even provoke gut-busting laughter. That power simply enthralls me and quite frankly got me hooked to writing. What sequence of words could I create that could move someone?

Shane made notations in the margin next to memories that she wanted to expound upon and jotted details. What was the weather that day, at that time? Were there smells that she could remember? What was she wearing and who was there? Most importantly, what music was playing?

She smelled coffee. God bless Steph. She put her pen in the journal and threw it on the bed as she got up from the chair. She put on a light robe and opened the door.

"I thought you were gonna sleep forever!"

Shane rolled her eyes. "Chile, I've been up for a while. I was people-watching, listening to the sounds of the neighborhood."

Steph was already pouring Shane a cup of coffee. It smelled divine. The sugar and creamer were waiting on the counter.

Shane sat at the counter, lifting the cup to her lips.

"What kind is this?"

"I'm not sure. Something fancy that they recommended at Whole Foods. I told them that I wanted a medium to dark roast but nothing bitter or too strong… They grind the beans right there. I've already had a cup. You'll thank me."

"Mmmmmm! You don't know the brand or anything? We're gonna have to find out!"

Shane took another long, slow sip and rolled it around on her tongue.

"This is fancy! I'm gonna have a hard time sticking to my two cup maximum."

Shane looked at Steph who was leaning on the counter on her elbows. "So will you be practicing your presentation while you're out here?"

"Yeah, a bit but I don't want to overdo it. I'll think about it too much and be all up in my head."

"Well we don't need to talk about it. Do I really get to chill today?"

"Yes. Nothing until your first day of class tomorrow. There are twenty-two people in the class. I have their applications if you want to look them over."

"Nah, I like to be surprised. I like to spend the first day feeling everyone out and having them introduce themselves, share what they want folks to know about them."

"Okay well I'm going for a walk if you don't need anything."

"I'm good. Go enjoy yourself. But be careful," she called after Stephanie.

Stephanie waved, heading out of the front door. She was ready for the day and had obviously been up for a while. So what, thought Shane. I've earned this lazy Sunday. And she savored the rest of her coffee, then poured herself another cup and headed back to the bedroom and her journal.

After writing for a few hours, she took a shower and headed out. She would not let this sunshine go to waste. Shane decided to walk the neighborhood to see what was around before she headed to the beach. She'd actually walked for a while, listening to a new artist that she agreed to write for when she saw a spa. Yes! Self Love Spa.

Let me just check out the lobby area and see what type of services they offer, she thought. Shane pulled the glass door open and was greeted by a heavenly scent. What is that?, she wondered. There was faint, new age music playing from the sound system.

"Welcome to Self Love Spa! How may I assist you today?"

"Oh, hi. I was just walking around the neighborhood and noticed the spa. Can I see your menu of services?"

"Sure. Are you new to the area?"

"Yes and no. I will be here for a few months to teach a class so I'm a temporary transplant."

"Ok, well welcome. My name is Shani. Here is the menu of services. We also offer packages and a few specials from time to time. Is there any service in particular that you were looking for?"

"Not really Shani. I think I'm in need of a spa day!"

"Well we can definitely help you with that!" Shani beamed. "We are pretty booked for today. Is there another day that we can schedule for you?"

"Yes, sure. I wasn't prepared for today so that's fine. Do you have anything for Saturday?"

Shani checked the system. After a few mouse clicks, she nodded her head.

"Do you mind early morning?"

"No, actually I would prefer it. What time?

"8:30am. Would you like a half day or full day service?"

Shani itemized the options and helped Shane customize her day of pampering. Shane opted for an hour massage, full body scrub, facial and a mani pedi; it included hot, herbal tea, lunch and light snacks throughout the day. She smiled as she thought back to the mani pedi dates that she and Tonya used to have so long ago. She missed her friend. She'd have to check in on her and Joe soon.

"Okay so we'll see you this Saturday. We'll send you a reminder text 24 hours in advance. Please respond to confirm."

Shane left the cute spa, excited for her upcoming pampering. Now, off to the beach. As she walked, she breathed deeply and enjoyed the bustle around her. Not as busy as Chicago but that was good. She could use a slower pace for a while.

Her phone began vibrating and Shane hesitated before she checked the screen. She wanted a "me" day before she had to be back on the clock tomorrow. It was Gail. They hadn't talked in a while. A video call, now this was special.

"Hey girl!"

"Hey. I heard you're out in Cali for a few!"

"Yeah. What's going on?"

"Look at all that sunshine. I'm jealous. How are you Shane?"

"I'm really good, Gail. How are things?

"You know, busy busy. How's my nephew doing in school? I know he's killing it."

"And you know this! The apple don't fall far...." Shane laughed. "So what's up? You never do the video thing."

"I know. I wanted to see your face when I tell you who I ran into last night at this little soiree in the City."

"I don't know, who?" She didn't feel like guessing.

"Mike Jeffries."

Shane's heart picked up its pace.

"Oh?"

"Oh! That's all you got? Don't give me, oh."

"Go on…"

"He was there with a small group. He's in New York for a new exhibition of his work. He invited me and Sam to go check it out."

"Are you going to go? He has great work."

"Yeah, I'll see what Sam wants to do. Anyway, he's still living on the West Coast. And, he asked about you."

Shane wasn't expecting that last part. "What did you tell him?"

"I told him that you were doing quite well and that he's probably heard a bunch of your songs." Gail paused.

"He was alone Shane."

Shane was quiet. She'd stopped walking.

"His wife wasn't with him?"

"No. He was with a couple of guys and one woman. They were fellow artists; he introduced us. And Shane, he still looks damn good."

Shane didn't know what to do with this information.

"Shane. You heard me, right?"

"Yes, Gail I heard you."

"I thought that you'd be more excited."

"Gail, what do you want me to say?"

"Well think of something because I gave him your number."

"Damn it Gail! Why did you do that?"

"Shane, you know why! How long has it been? Fifteen years, more? You're not married or even dating right now. All you do is work… You need to get over this hump one way or another."

"But that's not your decision to make!"

"Well, I made it! You don't have to answer, but he's going to call." Gail looked at her. "I guess you're not going to thank me."

"No, I am not."

"That's okay. Seeing you turn a page in your life will be thanks enough. Enjoy the beach. I'll talk to you later."

Shane was truly annoyed. Why would Gail do that without talking to her first? And why was he asking about her? Shane took a deep breath and exhaled. You know what, she thought. I am not going to get caught up with this. I'm going to walk on the beach, stroll on the pier and enjoy the rest of my day. And she did.

The next morning Shane was off! She walked down Wilshire Boulevard to the University. It was a beautiful sunny morning, not too cool, not too hot. Shane wore a pair of cargo pants, a pullover, white linen shirt and a pair of Doc Marten boots. She had a denim jacket tied around her waist just in case it got a little cool. And her hair was doing what it does, all over her head. They were getting the artist, honey! She was not about to spend the next couple of months getting dressed up.

When she walked into the classroom, there were already a few students inside chatting and drinking their morning beverages.

"Hello beautiful people!"

"Ms. Mathews, hello!" blurted one young woman excitedly.

"Okay, hold it! There will be none of that! Please call me Shane."

Shane shook the young woman's hand and welcomed her to the class. She scanned the room glad to see a diverse mix of people trickling in: Black, white, Latinx, old, young, artsy, not-so-artsy… Yes, she squealed internally. They will all bring a unique perspective. She went to the board and had a giddy moment, writing her name in large letters. She turned to the class.

"Welcome. I'm Shane Mathews, please call me Shane. This is *A Songwriting Masterclass*. First, I am very excited! And a wee bit nervous if I'm honest. But that's why we're here. To be honest, and vulnerable and to talk about feelings and experiences. Please don't think that you will be in this class and not share. To get the most from this experience, you need to be unafraid and bold! You need to pretend that nobody is going to see the lyrics or hear the song. You need to let loose!"

Shane did a little shimmy which earned her a few laughs.

"We're going to learn, we're going to connect and we're going to HAVE FUN! Let's start by getting to know each other. Stand up — bear with me — stand up where you are just to get the blood flowing. Move your body a little bit: rotate your shoulders, roll your head, jump up and down. Now, each of you tell us your name, where you're from, why you're here and something most people don't know about you!"

To finish out the exercise, Shane took her turn.

"Shane, originally from DC. I'm here to teach the class and I hated writing poetry when I was young! I really did! But when I needed it, it began to literally pour out of me. Some of you may know that I started writing in high school, short stories here and there. In college, I began to dabble with poetry. What you don't know is that when I was in college, my fiancé was murdered." She paused. "Writing got me through it. It's about the only thing I could do... I wrote and wrote. And I kept writing. Whenever I needed a release, I wrote. I have journals of my writing. That's why I opened this class by saying that you have to be comfortable with being uncomfortable, being vulnerable and expressing yourself."

"The best songs are those that make us feel something, right? Whether it's sadness, joy, excitement, loss, passion or anger. Music also has a strong connection to memory; you may not remember what you wore to that dance but I bet you remember the songs that played!"

Heads were nodding. There were a few smiles. She pointed to a middle-aged gentleman sitting further back.

"Sir, tell me your name again."

"Oscar."

"Oscar. What is your favorite song?"

"Right now or ever?"

"Whichever you want to share."

*"Sara Smile."*

"Ahhhh, a man after my heart! Hall & Oates. We may have to school some of these young folks in here... Why is that your favorite song? Well, first tell me how it makes you feel."

"It makes me feel happy and young!"

"Can you tell me what about the song makes you feel happy and young?"

He thought for a moment. "The music and the words. It makes me think about falling in love."

"Interesting. Thank you. Somebody else. Your favorite song, shout it out."

*"My Life* by MJB!"

"Yesssss! Why?"

"Because it makes me feel powerful and uplifted. And the lyrics are dope!"

"Anybody else?"

*"The Bones* by Maren Morris."

"Anything by Dua Lipa!"

"Lizzo is my favorite songwriter cause she's real!"

"I love Adele. She uses her pain to write the most phenomenal songs!"

"Whoa! A lot of women. All great artists, more importantly great lyricists! But where are my men? I feel like we need some balance."

There was a brief silence.

"Oh, so there are no great male songwriters? C'mon! What about Prince, Adam Levine... Lionel Richie, you've heard of them right? Let's see... J. Cole, Bruce Springsteen, Bob Marley, Eminem, Stevie Wonder, Elton John, Raheem DeVaughn and the list goes on! Those are just some of my favorites...."

Shane paused and stood up. She had been sitting on the edge of a desk in the front of the room. She walked to the board and grabbed a piece of chalk from the tray.

"Now, who has ever written a poem? Don't be shy. Let me see a show of hands?"

A few hands slowly raised.

"Okay, okay. Well song lyrics are basically a poem. So for those of you who have written one, you're halfway there… Although I suspect we have some closet poets in the house today.…" She raised her right eyebrow.

Shane wrote a list of words on the board. They were random words: paint, teeth, bored, grass, adore, clouds, arid. After she finished writing, she turned back to her students.

"Let's take a break and meet back in 15 minutes."

As her students streamed back into the classroom, Shane jumped right back in.

She walked around the desk.

"So this is an assignment that a creative writing professor gave my class when I was in college. My words were milk, tire, spring, heavy, broke, lost."

She read a poem aloud:

*Your letter came late that Spring afternoon,*
*As I lounged on the back porch.*
*Warm rays filtered through the screen and bounced off the letter,*
*As I read.*
*Words…careful words,*
*Heavy with sweet memories and bitter regret.*
*Of missing my lips brush against your eyelids*
*And the love that nurtured you like a mother's precious milk.*
*Now, you are envious*
*That a new love found the smile you stole.*
*I can empathize,*
*Because whoever said, "it's better to have loved and lost…"*
*Never lost anyone.*
*But,*

Shane paused for a beat. "That is entitled, *Hindsight*. Any thoughts?"

A young Asian man named Luk raised his hand.

"How long did you have to write the poem?"

"Lemme see… I think I had the class every other day, so about two days."

"Wow. How did you approach it?"

"I remember thinking about which word was the most difficult… for me it was milk, so I started there. How could I use milk that wouldn't be awkward? I started thinking of what I associated with milk. I thought of a mother and baby. I can't recall how the poem took this direction but I do remember it sort of falling into place… It just started coming to me as I looked at those words."

"Any other thoughts?"

"Was that poem from a personal experience?" the young woman asked who had called her Ms. Mathews before class began.

"No it wasn't. I mean I'd had my heart broken by then but it wasn't something that happened to me."

"But it seemed so real."

"Good. I tapped into real feelings that I've felt and sentiments that I thought would resonate with people. Universal topics like love and heartache are always relatable. I also tried to paint a picture: warm rays bouncing, Spring afternoon, tangerine sun, a bald tire… Actually this is a great segue into the five senses."

She returned to the desk's edge.

"Now, music already gives you one of the senses, but what about the other four? She paused. Our senses provide the strongest tie to memory. When you write, you want to paint a picture. I don't care what you're writing, you will draw someone in if you can excite their senses."

Shane pointed behind her.

"Check out the words on the board. Write them down… I want you to write a poem using all of the words listed. Don't worry about structure or rhyme, I only care about the content! Evoke as many of your senses as you can without it sounding forced. That's all for today. Thank you! I look forward to seeing you all on Wednesday and reading your poems. Impress me!"

Shane strolled down Wilshire then cut right to explore other blocks in the neighborhood. She was of course headed to the pier to walk on the beach. Her hair blew in the breeze as she approached the pier. It was crowded with people walking, jogging, skating and laughing; she was enjoying the vibe. She shoved her jacket into her tote bag and fished out her shades and a box of Raisinets. The sun was bright and felt good on her skin.

Now what is for lunch, she wondered as she popped a handful of the candies into her mouth. Her phone began buzzing. Shane sighed. She dug around for her phone; it was Stephanie.

"Hey Steph. What's up?"

"Shane, I just got us into a MusiCares fundraiser for Wednesday night!" she squealed.

"Okayyy… what else?"

"Nothing else! It's a great organization and there will be plenty of artists and industry execs there as well as celebrities. You can chat people up about your bio, I mean, memoir."

"Do I have to?" Shane whined.

"No, you don't have to but this would be a good opportunity for you to do so."

Shane sighed.

That night, she slept fitfully. She awoke with lyrics to a song, or a hook at least.

*Do you know what it's like,*
*To have love and your life slip through your fingertips?*
*Do you know what it's like,*
*To have memories and time just slip through your fingertips?*

# A Night Out

She and Stephanie scurried around the house putting the finishing touches on their evening looks. Shane had contacted the Self Love Spa to see if they knew or could recommend any makeup artists in the area. Luckily, they had a great one and she'd just finished their faces. Thank goodness because makeup was not Shane's ministry. She only wore it at times like these.

After seeing the finished product, she was digging the smoky eye that the young woman had given her. It complemented her almond eyes. The shadow and blush were gold-toned and gave her a sun-kissed look. Her freckles still peeked through which she liked. Not too made up. She'd finish her face with a nude lip using lipstick from her personal yet limited collection.

Shane had packed two formal dresses and one cocktail since she knew that Stephanie would be scheduling a few events. Tonight, she was wearing a leaf green one-shoulder dress that just brushed the floor with a side train that was a tad bit longer. It had layering and ruching across her breast and abdomen, with a high split on the right.

Her hair was pinned on top of her head with gold pins with a few tendrils spilling down the sides of her face. She wore an understated, diamond choker that was a splurge gift to herself and a pair of diamond stud earrings. In her hand was a gold, studded clutch. Her stilettos were rose gold colored and beaded.

When she walked out of her room, she gasped. Stephanie was stunning! Her slim, tall frame was rocking a sleeveless, low-cut, white goddess dress. There were gold seams that accented the gown beautifully. She wore gold, stiletto slingbacks to complete the look. Stephanie's makeup was a muted coral palette which accentuated her cinnamon skin. Her honey colored locks were pinned in a crown encircling her head. She looked regal. Shane had given her a gold lariat necklace to wear that dangled low, between her breasts.

"Don't hurt 'em Steph! Be careful tonight." she teased.

Stephanie blushed. "I think our car is here."

It was 6pm sharp. The fundraiser was being held at the LA County Museum of Art. It would be an hour ride to the event. The windows were up to preserve their hair and makeup. The air was on and it was a little chilly.

"Sir, could you turn the air down a little?"

Stephanie turned to her, opening her silver clutch.

"So I have a few bullets for you to use when you're chatting with people."

Shane smiled at her and took the folded paper that she extended.

"You are off duty tonight. Enjoy yourself. There will be a lot of young, beautiful people there. Meet them. Have some drinks, dance, laugh."

Stephanie smiled.

"Alright. As long as you do the same."

Shane would try. She would probably know most of the folks at this event but Stephanie wouldn't; it would be a fun night for her. It wasn't that Shane didn't enjoy getting dressed up and going to swanky events from time to time, it was simply draining. But it was a great organization and she believed in the work that it did.

In the car, they munched on apple and pear slices, manchego cheese and sparkling water that Shane packed so they wouldn't be starving when they arrived at the event. She'd carefully chosen snacks that would not make a mess or stain their dresses. They reapplied their lipstick as they pulled up to the venue. They looked at one another and collectively inhaled and exhaled. Shane winked at Stephanie.

Later as Shane floated through the crowd, she would catch a glimpse of Stephanie smiling and laughing. Good. She'd checked and they were seated at a table near the stage with people whose names Shane didn't recognize. This might be fun, she thought. Shane crossed the room and someone caught her arm.

"Shane! I'm surprised to see you here." His large, penetrating ebony eyes danced.

It was Grover, a composer who had worked on a few sound recordings that she'd written for. It had been about a year since she'd seen him. She leaned in to hug him and he kissed her cheek. She'd have to remember to tell Robert that she'd seen him.

"Grover Fanon…how are you? What are you working on, cuz I know you're into something!" she laughed.

"You know me… always busy like someone else I know. I heard you're working on a book?"

Here we go, she thought. She gave him a brief one minute spiel.

"Oh, so we get to peek behind the Shane curtain a little bit." He smiled, his full lips framed his white, large teeth.

Shane shrugged. "I guess." Shane noticed a tall gentleman approaching them.

Grover, good to see you!" He gave Grover a healthy handshake and pulled him in close, touching his shoulder to his, careful not to spill his drink.

Grover nodded in Shane's direction. "Shane, do you know Anthony?"

"I do not. It's good to meet you." She extended her hand to the handsome stranger.

"What?!?? I'm introducing you to someone whom you've never met? Mark the calendar!"

Shane punched Grover in the arm.

"Shane Mathews, this is Anthony Dekra. Anthony is an entertainment lawyer. Shane is a songwriter extraordinaire! You're just in time to hear about Shane's upcoming book."

Just then, the lights flickered and began to dim.

"Saved by lighting," Shane smiled.

"It was nice to meet you Anthony. Grover, good to see you. I'm here for a couple of months so let's connect."

Shane found her way to her table, pulling out the chair next to a waiting Stephanie.

"Ooh my feet are killing me," she murmured to Stephanie.

"Unh unh, no you don't!"

What?" Shane asked, confused.

"Who is tall, dark and fine that you just left standing there?"

"What, who?"

"That's what I'm asking you? He watched you walk over here."

"Oh, Anthony something. Grover, remember Grover the musician/composer? He just introduced me before they signaled for us to find our tables."

"That's it? That's all you got?"

"Shhhh! They're starting."

Stephanie gave her an eye roll and turned her attention to the stage.

"Thank you everyone for joining us for the MusiCares' Annual Fundraiser."

To her delight, the special guest performer was Ledisi.

———— ✺ ————

Shane was glad to finally make it back to the house. She walked barefoot, carrying her heels in one hand and holding her dress up in the other.

"Whew! What a night!"

She admittedly enjoyed herself. She actually met a few new people and had some great conversations. But she was tired. Shane dropped her purse on the counter and plopped onto the couch. She began to rub her feet as Stephanie laid on the other sofa across from her.

"So, did you have fun? More importantly, did you meet anyone?"

"Yes and yes," giggled Stephanie.

"Do tell!"

"I danced a few times and met a guy from New York. He is a musician and is in town working on a movie score."

"What's his name?"

"Why?"

"I may know him."

Stephanie paused. "Okay, I'll tell you… but if you don't know him, promise you won't go asking people about him."

"I can't promise that."

"Shane!"

"I will promise that I'll only ask about his character. As long as I don't hear anything bad, I won't dig any further, deal?"

Stephanie smiled. "His name is Tom Juarez."

Shane thought for a moment. "Doesn't ring a bell, but I'll do some light checking." She yawned. "Okay, I'm going to bed. I've got a class to teach!"

It was already Friday! Shane was enjoying the class and LA. She was also looking forward to her spa day tomorrow. She'd received the confirmation text earlier in the day. Damn, I should've made an appointment for Steph too, she thought. Turns out, Stephanie was having lunch with Tom. Shane would have to get to her recon on Mr. Juarez quickly.

As Shane was reaching out for information about Tom, Stephanie was doing her own research.

"Robert, hey this is Stephanie. Good, how are you? Things are going well here. From what I hear, Shane is enjoying the class… Give her a call and I'm sure she'll tell you all about it. Do you have a number for

Grover? I don't have a last name but Shane said he's a composer. We ran into him the other night at an event."

Stephanie waited for him to scroll through his contacts.

"Okay here it is. I just sent it."

Next, Stephanie called Grover and set up dinner for him and Shane the next week.

"Okay great! She needs to have some fun while she's here. By the way, what is the name of the gentleman to whom you introduced her at the fundraiser? Oh! He's an entertainment lawyer… Do you have his contact information?"

Anthony Dekra. He and Grover had known each other for over a decade.

Shane strolled back to the house after her spa day. It was amazing and long overdue. The staff at Self Love Spa knew how to treat you! She was full and satisfied but she felt light and rejuvenated. The sun was high and bright and the salt air tickled her bare shoulders. It was a perfect day. She wondered how Steph's lunch date went. She was sure to hear about it soon enough.

Shane listened to the sounds of her new neighborhood. People running errands, street cafés spilling over with hungry patrons, seagulls flying overhead. An occasional horn jerked her out of her thoughts, reminding her to be aware of her surroundings.

Her phone began to vibrate in her bag. She stopped on the corner and dug around her tote bag for it. It was a California number but she didn't recognize it.

"Shane Mathews."

She pressed the phone between her shoulder and ear, hoisting her bag up on the opposite shoulder. Shane combed her wayward strands behind her unoccupied ear.

"Grover! What's going on?"

That Stephanie had been busy! She and Grover had a dinner scheduled for Thursday at some fancy place that she was sure to hate, but Grover loved. He was a people watcher. No doubt the reason for the selected restaurant. It was all good. She loved Grover's eccentric manner and wanted to hear about his latest project. The way he talked about his compositions made the music leap from the page and dance around the room.

"So how was lunch?" Shane called as she put her keys on the kitchen counter. She could hear Stephanie moving around in the office.

She walked toward the room and leaned against the threshold. Stephanie was going through a stack of papers and looking at a laptop screen. She peered over the screen and smiled.

"It was great." She had a soft, dreamy sound to her voice.

"Uh oh! Looks like you've been bitten!" Shane laughed.

Stephanie groaned. "He is so great!"

Shane looked at her young assistant and was a bit envious.

"So when are you seeing him again?"

"Later in the week. He's got a few recording sessions and I've got to give some time to my dissertation notes."

"Is that what all this is?" Shane motioned toward the pile of papers in front of Stephanie.

She nodded.

"Well I'll leave you to it then. I've got a memoir to write." Shane turned and headed to her bedroom. But maybe I'll take a short nap first, she decided.

Shane was awakened by her buzzing phone. The room was dark. How long a nap did she take? She sat up trying to orient herself.

"Shane Mathews."

"Hey Gorgeous."

# BRIDGE

# Evan Michael Jeffries

Mike was in LA. They agreed to meet at Bergamot Station, the creative space that Shane was excited to visit.

It was a blue, cloudless sky. Shane decided to walk to the gallery. It was a long walk but she needed the time and fresh air to calm her, so she got out early.

Shane was nervous. She hadn't seen him in almost 10 years. A lot had changed, she had changed. And she'd gained weight. Chanté called it thick, but she looked different. Well, her body looked different. Her midsection and thighs had grown and both areas seemed to scoff at her yoga practice.

She realized that she was being silly. Why did she even care? She exhaled. Because it's Mike. He had this effect on her; he always had since the day they met. Which was interesting because she'd always felt truly herself with him.

Get it together Shane, she scolded herself. As she walked, she tuned in to her surroundings. The sun was high, but the rays were soft and dreamy. Although she couldn't hear the surf, the salt lightly tickled the air and pricked her nose.

She'd worn a loose fitting, off the shoulder dress today with a bold, flowered print. It was long-sleeved and she wore a wide belt just below the bodice with her maroon, pearlescent Doc Martens. Her heavy, curly strands fluttered in the air.

The walk wasn't as long as she'd anticipated. She could see the modern, behemoth structure in the distance and it was beautiful. It looked as if its galleries had dropped from the sky into the middle of a neighborhood. And as she got closer, she could see him. There was Mike.

He was bigger, more muscular than before. He had a beard as opposed to the trim goatee he had long ago. But he looked the same, handsome as ever. He hadn't aged at all.

Mike wore a navy, long-sleeved button down and black jeans with casual, black oxfords. The shirt accentuated his broad shoulders and chest. His arms hung at his sides while his long fingers fidgeted. She resisted the urge to run to him.

Shane recognized the moment that he saw her: his quick intake of air, as she approached. As she came closer, he drummed his fingers against his left thigh.

"Hey stranger!" She stopped short in front of him.

He smiled. "Hey Gorgeous."

Those words. She didn't know how much she missed his voice until that moment. Her eyes stung and she blinked back tears.

Mike closed the space between them and pulled her into an embrace. He smelled heavenly. She inhaled his scent and put her arms around him. She wasn't sure how long they stood, oblivious to passersby. She listened as his heart beat wildly in his chest just as hers did. Shane didn't want to move.

Finally, Shane let go and stepped away. Mike reluctantly let her go. She looked up at him. "Mike."

"Shane."

In all these years, she'd only heard him say her name a dozen times but she loved the way it sounded when he said it, like he meant it.

"I guess we can thank Gail for this meeting." Shane snickered.

"Yes. I will be sure to thank her. How are you, Gorgeous? More beautiful than I remember!" He smiled widely taking her in.

"I'm good." And she was. "How are you?"

"I'm blessed."

"So why'd you drag me here?" She smiled. "I'm kidding, this is on my list to visit while I'm in town!"

"Well then, let's go. There's a lot to see!"

As they walked, Mike explained the different galleries. They were unique and eccentric with different personalities. Some looked like you were in an expensive gallery with white, crisp walls and dramatic lighting. Others had a warehouse feel with a corrugated metal ceiling and cement walls which didn't take away from the aesthetic or the art.

The varied artwork was awesome. Every medium was represented from paintings to sculpture to ironwork and glassblowing. Mosaics and loom work. The colors and textures were mind-blowing and her greedy eyes devoured everything. She could feel Mike watching her as she admired the pieces.

"You really have a keen eye."

"I don't know about that," laughed Shane. "I just know what I like."

"Is that right?"

"It is." She looked squarely at him.

Mike cleared his throat.

"You may know that there are galleries here that are dedicated to up and coming artists and makers. They really give great opportunities for unknown artists to display their work. Artists can also teach classes here in their discipline based on their experience and portfolio rather than classic training or works sold. I teach a few myself."

"Really! What do you teach?"

"Well it's been a minute because I've been traveling to promote my new work, but I've taught *Beginner's Painting*, *Abstract Painting* and *Multimedia Art*. A requirement is that my classes are open to the public and free."

"How does that work?"

"I wrote that into my contract. I subsidize the classes and the gallery matches my commitment through its philanthropic arm. I also teach classes specifically for the youth when I can."

Shane beamed at him. She was so proud. "Woooow."

Mike had a multimedia exhibit on display there. That was also part of his negotiation of the free, public classes; he had to lend enough pieces for an exhibition. She followed him as they stepped into a brightly lit corridor. There were large, metallic letters on the left wall at eye level: *Evan Jeffries: Love's Testimony.*

The corridor led to a large room with moody, midnight blue walls and recessed lighting. Over-sized canvases adorned the walls. There was one, tall canvas in the center of the room on a white wall unit.

Shane was drawn in not only by the vivid colors but by the raw emotion that leapt from the art. She crossed the room over to a canvas that took up the better part of the wall on which it hung.

There was a tall window at the top right of the painting and an inky darkness that colored in the panes. The majority of the piece was made to look like bed sheets, cradling a shadowy figure. The sheets were crumpled and bunched and three-dimensional, coming out from the canvas. And they truly looked like sheets!

Shane wanted to touch them. They were made of some sort of papier mâché looking material. A lone moon beam shone through the window alighting upon the curvy figure under the sheets. Her back was to the viewer and the sheets bunched around her waist, accentuating her butt. There were wild tendrils of hair splayed on the pillow. Another figure stood at the far side of the bed hidden in the darkness, looking down at her. A placard hung beside the piece. It read: *Salty Sheets.* The entire piece was made up of shades of black, grays, whites and blues. Yet it had a brightness due to the moon beam.

She walked to the next piece which shared a wall with another. Both were abstract paintings. The first was bright with yellows and oranges with white swaths peeking through. The strokes were light and wispy and covered the entire canvas in that manner. There were blush colored sections layered with lime green and light splatters of shades that she couldn't quite name. It was a joyous work, in contrast to its neighbor.

The next painting had wide, deliberate and erratic strokes of black, gray and red. There were streaks of navy and white in sections of it. It was frantic and made her breathing quicken. Her eyes checked for the name of the piece, *Heartbreak*. Its wall mate was entitled, *Happiness*.

She was so caught up in the art, that she had lost track of Mike. He watched from a distance, observing her while she observed his work. She hadn't noticed that they were alone in the gallery.

Just then, she noticed a familiar figure in her periphery; it drew her to the center of the room. The tall canvas on the wall unit featured what was really a silhouette. But the hair, the body shape was hers. The figure was dancing or spinning and there was a colorful aura around her. Metallic sparks outlined the aura and, as she drew closer, she realized that there were words and phrases beyond the metallic sparks, over the expanse of the canvas. Mother, bright smile, independent, willful, creative, soulmate, poet, passionate, loner, brown-eyed girl, gorgeous, intellectual, word lover, bibliophile, heart-breaker and countless more. It was called *Poetry In Motion*.

Tears began to well in her eyes. She looked over at Mike. He had a goofy smile on his face. All of this time, she had been his muse. Just as he had always been hers. She walked over to a far corner determined to finish looking at the exhibit and keep her cool.

This one was calm and ethereal. Beautiful clear turquoise water under a vibrant baby blue sky with thin, wispy clouds. Cirrus clouds, the name popped into her mind. The shore had light, almost white sand and laying on it was a small, sleeping baby. Curled in the fetal position, the baby was the color of brown sugar with dark curly tendrils and a button nose. The infant was surrounded by light.

The painting began to blur. Fat, sloppy tears ran down her cheeks but before they could drop, Mike was there holding her up. He wrapped her in his embrace as she sobbed loudly, her cries shaking her body. They stayed that way for a long time, long after her tears stopped. Mike kissed the top of her head. Mike painted their baby.

"I should've said something," he said.

"What?" Shane raised her head from his chest and looked up at him confused.

"When you told me about the baby, I should've said something. When I saw you weren't excited, I should've asked you why. I wish I had fought you!"

Tears began to slide down his cheeks. "I'm so sorry that I didn't. My mom told me how you called her the day you found out that I'd married Sherri. She waited a long time, but she told me."

Mike wiped his eyes. He looked down at Shane and cupped her face in his large hands.

"Shane, I was hurt. I was hurt that you didn't want my baby. Then, I guess I figured it was best... but it wasn't. And we should've talked about it so many times... Please don't carry that weight Shane. That decision was on me as much as it was on you."

Shane's voice trembled. "I regretted it before we even left the clinic," she confessed. "But I couldn't tell you that! I was so ashamed and so angry at myself."

"We made a huge mistake Shane."

They embraced, silently looking at the painting for a long while. The placard read *Angel Baby.*

"I wasn't prepared for this," Shane said with a wry smile, breaking away from Mike.

"I know and I apologize," Mike said softly. "I guess I should've warned you about the exhibit."

Shane wasn't angry; she felt like she had been emotionally wrung out. She smiled a small smile and wiped at her eyes.

"It's okay... I'm alright." She looked at him. "Guess I better look at this last one."

To their right was another over sized canvas. There were two huge butterflies on invisible wire protruding from the painting: one butterfly was larger and they were slightly touching. The smaller one was predominantly orange with pink and yellow veining, the other was royal blue with kelly green and yellow veining. They were amid an oil painting of an enormous sun-dappled poppy field under a clear blue sky with cumulus clouds. *Next Lifetime* was the name of the piece. Shane looked up and he was standing beside her. She stood on her tiptoes and kissed him lightly on the lips. Mike closed his eyes.

"It's beautiful," she breathed.

After staring at this final painting for some time, Mike took her hand.

"Why don't we go somewhere to sit and talk."

"Yes, let's. You got me all emotional up in here and now I'm starving!"

"C'mon woman."

They sat down to order lunch at one of the many outdoor gallery eateries.

"How's Sean?"

"Sean is a freshman at NYU and he's doing very well."

"I'm not surprised. He's had a wonderful teacher."

"I've been blessed that my work has allowed us to travel and expose Sean to different experiences and cultures. He had many more stamps in his book before he left for college than most grown folk! We took trips to places around the globe that we chose. We've also been to Sundance and movie openings in different countries where my songs were part of the soundtrack."

"Look at you, Big Time!" exclaimed Mike.

Shane did a mock bow. "So how are your kids doing?"

"The oldest, Frank, was in school in North Carolina but now he's working. Kaya is working and in school for costume design. The baby, Steve, he's struggling a little bit… spoiled and hardheaded…."

"Well, he got it honest!"

Before Mike could protest, Shane held up her hand. "Whatever you're going to say, I know better."

Mike shook his head and laughed.

They caught each other up on their careers and respective lives. Jessica was doing well. He and Sherri divorced about five years prior. Mike had exhibits in several countries with more to come. And when he wasn't traveling, he was teaching or painting in his LA or NY studio.

As they ate, Mike told her about an exhibit that's currently in NY that features his series entitled, *The Kids*. He pulled out his phone to show her pictures of the pieces and a short video of the exhibit.

One painting, *Playtime*, was two pairs of hands, one of a man, one of a child stacking Legos. Another was the front view of a row of four pairs of tennis shoes, in different sizes and one pair was pink; the next three were oil paintings of each of his children, close-up their faces taking up the entire canvas. The last one, *Lil' Man*, was Sean's six-year old face staring from the canvas. He stopped swiping and sat the phone face down on the table.

Mike looked at her. "You and Sean have always been with me."

Shane was silent.

"Shane, I know that I hurt you." He paused. "I had a lot of growing up to do and I know myself now. I can't say that I did back then."

The waiter came by to check on them.

"How are we doing over here? Can I interest you all in dessert or coffee?"

Coffee. Coffee would be awesome right now.

"Shane, anything for you?"

"A coffee please. Two creams, one sugar."

"Could you make that coffee to go please?" Mike stood up and came around the table to Shane extending his hand.

"Sure Mr. Jeffries. Should I put this on your tab?"

"Yes, thank you."

Shane didn't realize they were going anywhere.

"Let's grab your coffee and take a walk. Is that okay with you?"

Shane nodded her head and stood.

They left the grounds of the gallery and ventured into the Santa Monica neighborhood. They walked silently for a while as Shane sipped her coffee.

"What's up Mike?"

He looked nervous. She thought they were past that by now. They were passing by a park and Mike grabbed her hand. They walked into the park and he led her to a bench. She sat down and he remained standing. She looked up at him.

"Shane. I know it's been a long time." He took a deep breath. "But when I look at you, I feel as strongly as I ever did… If you let me, I'd like to make things right between us. Please allow me the chance to give you everything that I wanted to, back then. I love you."

Shane reached for his hand. He opened his hand and held hers. She took a deep breath.

"For so long, I wanted to hear those words. And ten years ago, I probably would have followed you anywhere. It took me a long time to be okay and I was only okay… But now, I've grown and gotten stronger." She paused and her chin trembled. "Mike, I love you. I probably always will. But I have a great career and I'm ready to be settled, not jet set around the world."

"Shane. If that's what it takes, for me to slow down- "

"Let me stop you there. I would never want you to change your career for me. I wouldn't ask you to do that. Besides, you would only end up resenting me!"

"Shane, you don't know how I feel. You don't get to tell me how I will feel." He sat down beside her on the bench.

"I know I'm dropping a lot in your lap but this has been years in the making," he shook his head. "I didn't plan any of this but this is how I feel."

Shane looked down at her lap and studied her hands for a few minutes.

"Mike, I want you to be happy. We tried, but it just wasn't our time."

"Maybe not then, but now things could be different. I know I'm different and we still love each other… just tell me you'll think about it… Can you do that for me?"

Shane smiled and cried at the same time.

"Look at me, I'm a mess!" she laughed.

"You're perfect." He kissed her eyes and cheeks as her tears fell. Mike wrapped his arms around her.

Shane's head was spinning. Over the years, she'd convinced herself that Mike had been put in her life to show her how to love and trust again. Was it more than that?

"Okay," she conceded. "I'll think about it."

And he smiled that smile and kissed her deeply yet tenderly. Oh, how she'd missed him, his touch.

That night, she barely slept. She could smell Mike and taste his kisses. What was she going to do? Shane was tempted to call Tonya or Chanté to ask for advice but decided against it. She had to make this decision alone.

⸙

Shane looked at her watch as the driver pulled up to the french restaurant. She was running about ten minutes late, but she texted Grover to let him know. She was sure that they wouldn't lose their table; Grover knew everyone.

As she stepped out of her car, she smoothed her dress. Shane was wearing a sheath black dress with a sweetheart neckline and intricate lace cap sleeves. There was a modest split on the left. She wore a gold choker and gold kitten heels. Her hair was slicked back and pinned into a high bun. She'd opted for a bit of mascara and a nude lip.

"Shane!" Grover was waving her over to a table for two near a large window. Perfect for people watching, she thought.

She made her way through the busy restaurant as people watched. No doubt they wanted to see who Grover was signaling. He was a regular at A-list events and popular in most circles. He stood as she approached the table.

"Shane! You never disappoint." He appraised her then he kissed her cheek. Grover crossed to the other side of the table to pull out her chair. As he sat down, the waiter hurried over.

"Ah, give us a few minutes, will you please?"

"So Shane. What are you drinking? And before you tell me nothing, that's not gonna work tonight baby. We're gonna catch up, laugh and close this place down. I want to hear about this book, all these songs that I hear everywhere I turn and the latest in Chi-town."

"You finished?" Shane raised an eyebrow. "Damn! Can a sista sit down before you start?"

Grover laughed a hearty laugh. "You're right."

He waved over the waiter.

"Sir, can you direct the sommelier this way?"

"Oui monsieur!"

Shane laughed as the waiter hurried in search of the wine expert. "Why do you have that man running like that?"

"Did I tell him to run? He chose to run!"

"These people are in here tripping over themselves for you. I see you Black man, in command per usual!"

Grover smiled. He was an attractive man with wild hair and a clean shaven face. Tonight, he wore a tailored black suit with a black shirt and bowtie, but usually he could be mistaken for a rock musician. Grover was an old soul, an anachronism really. He should've been born in the 60s a midst the beatniks, hippies and jazz artists.

The sommelier came to the table and asked her a few questions about her wine preferences. He returned with a bottle of the most delicious white wine with a mineraly finish that Shane had ever had.

"I should take a picture of this bottle," exclaimed Shane. "I need this in my life!"

"See, you need to hang with me more often!" Grover raised and lowered his thick brows in quick succession. He looked so mischievous she almost spit out the wine she had just sipped.

"Okay, get me a menu before you have me tipsy up in here, showin' out!"

This was just what she needed. Grover was like the younger brother that she didn't have who was always up to something. He was silly and knew how to have a good time. And just because Shane thought of him as a brother, it did not stop his constant flirting. But she was used to it.

"So how long do we have you here on the West coast Shane?"

Shane was in mid chew of something delectable and buttery that Grover ordered for her in French. He was such a showoff! His family was originally from Haiti. She hoped it wasn't snails.

"At least another month," she said before taking another bite.

"Okay, so time for more dates before you go…." Shane laughed as Grover offered her a bite of his dinner. "Try it. You won't be sorry."

She hesitantly opened her mouth as Grover slid his fork into it gently. It was even better than whatever she was eating. He watched her lips as she closed her eyes, savoring the forkful. He was watching closely, admiring her. She opened her eyes.

"Do you ever quit?" Shane leaned over and hit his arm.

"Would you want me to?" He winked, then took a sip of wine. "Your assistant called… She was asking a lot of questions. She asked me about Ant."

"Who is Ant?" she asked as she raised her wine glass for another sip.

"Ant, the one that I introduced you to at the MusiCares event."

Shane wrinkled her brow and thought back. The one that Stephanie asked about when Shane made it to the table.

"Oh yeah? What did she ask?"

"For his contact information. I mean, it wasn't a problem. I gave it to her, but I was curious."

Steph, that little sneak.

"She didn't mention anything to me...."

"Oh. Well he's a good friend. I've known him a long time. He's a solid dude."

"Well, since we're talking about people's character, do you know a Tom Juarez? He was at the event as well. Stephanie is interested in him and I want to know that he's a solid dude."

"Way to change the subject!" He looked her in the eyes.

"Oh don't give me that look. I think Steph is trying to be a matchmaker, that's all." She sat back in her seat.

"Tom Juarez?" she waved her hand, spurring him on.

"Yeah, I know Tom. He's a cool cat. Plays the bass guitar. He's really good. We've worked together on a few pieces and scores. I like to think that I've given him some guidance, some wisdom."

"Oh so you're his mentor?"

"Something like that. Tom is super talented and young. I just hip him to the business and make sure he doesn't make too many missteps is all. But you have nothing to worry about Mama Bear, he's a good dude."

<hr>

Three weeks had blown by and Stephanie was heading back to Chicago. She'd decided to stay at Shane's so that she could focus and prepare. Lately, her mind had been on Mr. Juarez and she didn't get much done in terms of her dissertation defense.

"Call me when you land," Shane reminded her. "Oh and I arranged a car to pick you up from the airport."

Before Stephanie could protest, Shane waved her off. "It's already done."

Shane was glad to have her class to keep her busy. She channeled all of her feelings into the class, challenging her students to pour into their craft. The poem that everyone was assigned the first week of class would be the basis of each student's song. A handful of students wrote new poems, abandoning the initial one and some had journals of ideas that they were going to use. This week, they were delving into song composition.

"There are six parts to a song. Can anyone tell me what they are? Feel free to yell them out."

"Verse!"

"Okay, yeah we all know that one… what else?"

"A chorus which repeats. It's the climax of the song."

"Very good. The chorus is also where you find the hook of a song. Okay, what else?"

"The intro and bridge!"

"Great! That's four out of six. We're almost there!"

The class grew quiet, expectant.

"That's all you've got? Nothing else?"

Shane hopped off the front desk and walked around to the board. She wrote the numbers one through six. Beside the one, she wrote Intro. Next to the two, she wrote Verse. She skipped three, then wrote Chorus as number four. Bridge was number five and she left the sixth spot blank.

"These next two weeks are dedicated to song composition. First, we'll review the six parts and the function of each one: Intro, Verse, Pre-chorus, Chorus, Bridge and finally Outro or Coda." Shane filled in the blanks on the board. "Then, we'll get into song structure. Bars, the different forms and variations of those forms. Consider this the meat and potatoes! Ask a lot of questions and take a lot of notes."

Shane walked back to her perch on the desk.

"So we'll start at the beginning. The Intro eases us into a song. Its tempo is slower and catches the listener's attention but only teases them for what's to come. It establishes melody and rhythm and also introduces the singer's voice or voices."

"Any questions?" Shane looked around the room, then continued.

"The most known part of the song is the verse. This is where you as the songwriter begin to tell your story and emotionally connect with your listener. You also begin to build anticipation. The listener should be waiting and wanting to know what's coming next. Your story is divided into verses. So think of your poems. What story is at the heart of it? What do you want to say?" Shane jumped from the desk and stood at the front of the room.

"We will begin to flesh out your stories and you will write a song with correct composition and a popular structure. But first, we'll continue with the parts of a song."

"The chorus, haha, the chorus. This is the most important part of a song. It can make people love your song… it can carry a song up the charts! When people like a song, they don't know the lyrics, but they know what? The chorus!" Shane turned to the class. "THIS…" her arms opened wide for dramatic effect. "… is the culmination of all the big ideas in your song. Think about how often the title of a song is embedded in the chorus." She paused. "This is also where you'll find the hook which is the catchiest part of the song. It's the song's climax." She winked and a few students snickered. "It builds to this point, then there's that release of tension."

Shane ran down the final three parts as students frantically took notes.

"Next up, is song structure. Each major part of a song gets a letter starting with 'A', not including the Intro."

She went back to the board. Next to Verse, she wrote a capital A. Next to Chorus, she wrote a capital B. Next to Bridge, she wrote a capital C.

"The most common structure in contemporary songwriting is ABABCB. In the first part of the 20th century, what's called the 32-bar form was popular or AABA. Over time, songwriters have increased the intricacy and complexity of their works. In addition, the instrumentation has become more complicated to evoke emotion and feeling. Adele, who is one of my favorite songwriters, is masterful at this. Her songs are textbook when it comes to the function of the song parts and the accompanying instrumentation of each part."

She went to her bag and pulled out a stack of documents. She began to hand out a few worksheets around the room.

"Please pass these back. Everyone should have three different worksheets. These are popular and classic songs; you should recognize at least one of them." She smiled. She'd included one of her own.

"Your assignment is to label all the parts of each song. Then, I want you to label the structure. Next class, bring in the lyrics of your favorite song. We will dissect each one and you will tell me how well the songwriter did."

That afternoon, Shane headed to the grocery store. It was time to restock the fridge and buy more of that delicious coffee that Stephanie found. Besides, she needed some comfort food and Raisinets. After putting the groceries away, she decided to call Mike. She'd thought about his question and it was time to give her answer.

She would cook, he'd always enjoyed her cooking. Besides, they needed privacy when they talked. Unlike their last conversation: they had been so open to the public and vulnerable. And Shane was on her turf, kinda.

"Hey Gorgeous! How are you?" Mike answered the phone on the first ring.

"Busy, but good. How are you doing?"

"Better now that I hear your voice." She could hear his smile through the phone. "I told my Mom that I saw you. Of course she wanted a blow by blow reenactment," he laughed. "She always loved you."

Shane smiled a half smile. "Tell her hello and that I miss her."

"I most definitely will… so what's up Shane? Have you given any thought to what I asked you?"

"Yes, that's why I'm calling. Can you come over for dinner?"

"Sure, when?"

"Whenever works for you."

"Ok. I'm in the middle of a piece… How about tomorrow night?"

"That'll work. So tomorrow.…"

"Tomorrow. I love you Shane."

"I love you back."

It would be so easy to say yes to Mike… part of her wanted to, but she was afraid. Not the kind of fear that you have when you start a relationship, that mix of fear, excitement and anticipation, but fear of what would happen if she put her trust in him again. It was a sinking feeling that she couldn't shake.

Mike arrived right on time, looking and smelling delicious. He wore distressed blue jeans and a light sweater. And Timbs. She shook her head and laughed to herself when she saw he was wearing them. She had her Chucks and Doc Martens, why shouldn't he still rock Timbs?

"What's so funny?" he asked while wrapping his arms around her.

"Nothing," she insisted. She inhaled his scent, then reached up and kissed him lightly on the lips.

"It smells good in here! Whatchu cooking up woman?"

"Some shrimp pasta with white wine sauce. And a spinach salad. I have sparkling water and iced tea, which would you like?"

"No beer or wine?"

Shane stopped on her way into the kitchen to look at him.

"I'm kidding! Iced tea will work."

"I was about to say, some things do change!"

Shane opened the fridge and grabbed the pitcher of hibiscus iced tea. She sat it on the counter.

"This is a nice place! Is it yours?" Mike walked around the house. She noticed that he'd removed his boots at the door.

"For the next four weeks it is!" Shane reached into the cabinet to get two glasses.

Mike came to sit at the counter opposite her while Shane finished cooking. She sat two chilled bowls of salad on the counter and a jar of homemade vinaigrette. She looked at him and he locked eyes with her. Her stomach tightened then felt fluttery.

"So do you have an answer for me?"

He wasn't wasting any time.

"I do," she said, dishing pasta into two pasta bowls. She turned to place them on the counter. Then she opened the drawer and put flatware beside the bowls.

She walked over to the other side of the island and sat beside Mike. She looked at him and put her hand on his jaw. He was so handsome. She brushed his cheek.

"You're not going to like it," she said softly.

Mike leapt from the stool at the counter and walked across the room. He turned to look at her. He was sure when she'd called and invited him to dinner, it would be a new beginning for them.

"Why Shane? This should be our time!" Mike looked stricken.

"Mike, I love you… but I don't trust you, not with my heart." Tears began to well in her eyes. Slowly they crept down her cheeks.

"You don't love me Shane! If you did, you wouldn't do this."

"Don't you dare!" screamed Shane. She startled herself. "You got married and you have the nerve to say that I don't love you? I waited for you, emotionally I never left you, and you never came back!"

Shane was angry and trembling. She couldn't remember ever being this angry.

"Shane, I'm sorry. I was wrong to say that. I know you love me, I've never doubted that."

Shane inhaled. "You have no idea how hard it's been for me to let you go and get on with my life." she said angrily.

Mike crossed the room and knelt before her, taking her hands.

"I told you that I wanted to marry you… remember that Shane?" His voice was almost a whisper. "Do you remember?" Tears welled in his eyes.

Shane nodded slightly.

"You didn't say anything… you laughed!"

"I know," her voice was hoarse. "You don't know how many times I've replayed that moment." Tears rolled down her chin. "I was shocked and afraid… I'm ashamed, but that's what came out. I don't understand so I don't expect you to."

He stood up and sat beside her. "As much as I loved you, I told myself that I would never ask again."

He rubbed her back until her sobbing slowed down. He hated to see her cry and once again he was the reason.

She looked up at him. "I'm sorry Mike. I just can't. As much as part of me wants to, I can't."

Mike hung his head. Shane was the one thing in his life that he could not get right.

Shane spent the evening crying silently and sipping from a glass of wine. It hurt to see him leave. Mike was hurt and she was the cause. Oh God! Did she make the right choice?

# CHORUS

# A New Song

Grover called to invite Shane to a dinner party. There would be some folks there that Shane hadn't seen in a while and some new people in the business to whom Grover wanted to introduce her. Shane wasn't really up to it and with Stephanie gone, she'd have to go alone; however, Grover wasn't taking no for an answer.

"That assistant of yours told me that you needed some fun while you're here so that's what you're gonna get!"

Grover had an amazing industrial loft with two floors. There were concrete walls and exposed steel beams. The floor to ceiling windows gave a breathtaking view of the LA night with all of its twinkling lights.

"Fancy seeing you here."

Shane turned from the window to see Ant, Anthony standing there with a drink in his hand. "It's Shane, right?"

She snickered. He knew her name. Men were funny as hell.

"Yes, Shane." She stuck out her hand. "And you are?"

"Anthony Dekra," he said, taking her hand in his. "Grover introduced us at the MusiCares event."

"Oh right, right," she nodded.

Anthony stood over six feet tall and was slim like a basketball player. He was the color of chewy, sweet dates... Shane loved dates! His large, dark bedroom eyes took her in. He'd rocked the black tie attire when they met, but the man looked good dressed down as well.

"Your assistant contacted me about a consultation for an artist that you were working with."

"Did she now?"

"She said that you would follow up with me. Do you still need the consult?"

"Mr. Dekra, I think we both know that I don't need the consult."

He smiled and his right dimple popped. "Okay. So tell me something about yourself Shane. Better yet, tell me about this biography that you're writing."

Shane sighed. She might as well get some practice.

"It's a memoir really...."

They moved over to a sleek, sectional leather couch. After she gave him the spiel about the upcoming book, she moved to refill her glass.

"Oh no, I'll get that. What would you like?"

As he walked away, she caught a glimpse of Grover in the distance. He winked at her. Anthony returned with a glass of Pinot Gris and handed it to her carefully.

"Grover says you're the hottest songwriter in the country. Have I heard any of your stuff?"

She looked at him. "Cut the shit," she said good humoredly. "I know Grover gave you the 4-1-1 on me! Now if you want to have a real conversation, let's do that."

He put his hands up defensively and laughed. "Whoa, I was just making small talk."

"I don't do small talk." Shane looked at him squarely with her right eyebrow raised.

After they got through the initial hiccup, they had a great conversation. Anthony, originally from Ohio, lives in Burbank. An entertainment lawyer with an impressive client roster. He divorced about nine years ago and has three children. The divorce was amicable and they spend a lot of time as a family; his ex-wife has since remarried.

Anthony had an easy way about him and a suave coolness that was magnetic. His bald head and salt and pepper goatee upped his sex appeal. Before she left, he asked if he could call her.

"Yes. Grover has my number."

"I'm sure he does," he said, helping her into her jacket. "But I'm not asking Grover, I'm asking you." The dimple popped again.

Oooh. She liked his persistence. She gave him her number.

Two days later, she had a message from Anthony. She'd been in class when he called. She listened to the message during the class break. He had a sexy, baritone voice.

"It was nice spending some time with you the other night. I'd like to do it again soon. Let me know if you'd like that."

Shane would like that. She'd call him in the afternoon after class. Right now her students were trickling back in.

"Okay. Who's ready to share their song?" Resounding silence. "You will all have a turn so don't everyone speak at once!"

The next morning, she called Tonya.

"Tonya. I met someone!"

"Well shit who is he? Don't have me guessing." Her voice was gravelly.

Shane could tell she had awakened Tonya. It was early, but she was excited.

"His name is Anthony. He's divorced and he lives in Burbank. He's an entertainment lawyer... He has this smooth roughness that I'm digging!"

"Okay, okay. How did you meet?"

Shane runs it down for Tonya who listens patiently. She hadn't heard her friend excited about a man in a long time.

"So are you gonna see him again?"

"Yes. We've talked and plan to go out soon."

"What does your friend Grover say about him?"

"He says that he's a solid dude. He's known him for over a decade, so they met when he was still married. I think Grover is trying to set us up."

"So what do you like about him? I can't remember the last time you were this excited." Actually, she could but it didn't warrant a mention.

"I don't know… there's just something about him… a confidence and swagger that I like! And he's interesting. I've never known a Black man who surfs!" She laughed.

"He surfs?" repeated Tonya. "Oh wow." She paused. "Are you ready?"

"Am I ready? What do you mean?"

"Honey, all I'm saying is the last guy that you were in a serious relationship with, you let go. You said he wasn't the one… I'm just asking that before you start down a road, make sure you're ready to give him an honest chance."

Shane knew Tonya was right. But she was ready. She never told her about reconnecting with Mike, so Tonya couldn't know that she'd turned a corner. She'd tell her one day, but it was still too fresh.

"I hear you. But I can say that I'm finally ready. I mean, I don't know if this will turn into anything, but I'm open to the possibility."

"That's my girl."

"Who is that?" She heard Joe's groggy voice in the background. "Is that my Shay Shay?" he yelled loudly.

"Yeah, it's her. Who else could call this early and not get cussed out?"

"Shanie poo! What's going on girl?"

"Nothing Joe. You treating my girl right?"

"And you know this!"

Shane laughed. Joe was so silly. She loved how much he loved Tonya. They were good together. She definitely had to get back to Colorado. It had been a while.

"Shane met somebody!"

"Whaaaat? You want me to do a background check? I need this dude's name, birth date and social!"

Shane yawned. "That won't be necessary! He has some solid references."

"Okay well tell that fool he better stay in line."

"I'll be sure to pass that along."

"I'm serious Shanie! He don't want to see these hands."

"Boy lay back down," Tonya laughed. "Or better yet, go make us something to eat."

"I ain't going to fix anything, I've got breakfast right here… all this chocolate!"

Shane could hear loud kissing noises. "Okay. I'ma let y'all go!" Shane said loudly.

Tonya giggled. "Okay girl, but keep me posted on this Anthony situation!"

Shane shook her head and smiled. They were still going strong.

<hr>

On their first date, she and Anthony went to a lovely seafood restaurant on the water. For dessert, they got sorbet on the Pier and walked and talked for hours. Although they had overlapping business interests, they never talked shop which she appreciated. They talked about books, art and music, but only the sheer love and appreciation of it. She learned that he was a reggae lover and had an extensive collection of Dancehall, Dub, Roots, Ragga and Lovers' Rock.

As they looked out onto the dark waves, Anthony talked Shane through surfing. What he looked for in a wave, what to be careful for and what he does when he first paddles out.

"I'll have to take you out one morning."

"Oh nooo. I'll just watch from the shore."

"Aw c'mon Shane. You've got to try it at least once. It is so freeing! I'll teach you. If you're not feeling it, I'll leave it alone. But try it once."

"Maybe… I know it's freezing out there!"

"Not if you have the right gear."

The next day, a package was delivered to her house. She opened the box to find a lavender and black wet suit. There was a note that read: "It's time to get you wet. Anthony" Shane smirked.

They were meeting for lunch the next day. She had butterflies as she stood in the closet searching for something to wear. This is crazy, she thought. I haven't been this nervous and giddy since… Then she smiled. She didn't feel sadness, only fondness.

The restaurant was walking distance from the university. She'd settled on a casual, olive green smocked A-line dress that fell to her calves with flutter sleeves and a pair of natural, strappy platform wedges. Her favorite denim half jacket would keep her warm should the ocean breeze pick up.

Anthony was there when she arrived, seated at an outdoor table. He wore a cream button down shirt that complimented his dark skin and worn blue jeans. He stood and when she approached the table, he pulled her into a strong embrace.

"Are you okay with sitting outside? We can go in, if you'd prefer."

She was still relishing his embrace and registered surprise that she enjoyed it. "What was that?"

"I said if you would rather eat inside, we can." He smiled and the dimple popped.

So considerate. "No, thank you, this is cool."

He stepped around to pull out her chair. Once she sat down, he scooted her in a bit. He sat down and took her hand.

"So how was class?"

"It was good! We're reaching the halfway point and I think it's going well. This is my first time teaching so at least I hope it is…."

"Are your students engaging with you? With each other? That's usually a good indicator."

"Listen to you! Don't tell me, you've taught before."

"It's been a while, but yes. I taught a few law classes."

"Of course you have Mr. Lawyer, professor, surfer, athlete! What haven't you done?"

He looked at her with a look that scorched her panties and smiled. "Let's look at some menus."

Yes, let's, she thought. And can you throw a bucket of ice water on my ass while you're at it?

They were chatting and laughing and didn't notice when the waitress came to take their order. She stood for a moment or two, then cleared her throat. "Should I come back?" she said, looking from her to him.

"Oh, um I'll have an iced tea and a chicken caesar salad."

"I'll have a fruit salad and a steak hoagie. Do you have lemonade?" he asked not taking his eyes off of Shane.

"Yes, fresh squeezed."

"I'll have one please."

As she crunched her salad, she thought about the wet suit. When she finished chewing, she swallowed and said, "I got your package. You don't waste time do you?"

"Time is not to be wasted," he answered smoothly. "Are you game?"

"I'll try, but you have to be patient with me."

"I promise." And that dimple popped out at her.

They agreed to go surfing that weekend. Anthony would pick her up at 4 a.m. and take her to his favorite spot.

"Four a.m.?"

"Yes. It's a bit of a drive so we've got to get an early start."

Friday night, Shane was in bed by nine so that she would get up for her early alarm. Anthony was there at ten minutes to four waiting patiently out front.

"I am not a morning person and it's too early for my stomach to have coffee."

"Well good morning to you too! You look beautiful."

Shane gave him a half smile. He opened the passenger-side door and she flopped into his truck. There were two boards strapped to the roof.

She took a deep breath. *I guess I'm really doing this!* She'd let Robert and Stephanie know where she was going and sent his contact, just in case. You can never be too safe.

They eased onto some highway and were heading north up the coast. It was dark and the sun was starting to peek out above the horizon. As the road winded closer to the water, she could see the beautiful colors of the sun's grand entrance: gold, pink, orange and lavender. This view shook away the grogginess from her body and she took it all in.

By the time they reached their destination, she could see cliffs in the distance. Anthony drove down into a small cove at the edge of the beach. He jumped out, climbed onto the foot rack and unstrapped the boards. She noticed that one was much smaller than the other.

"I already waxed them. Are you ready?"

She nodded and they traipsed through the cool sand. He gave her a short lesson on the shore. The moves were a lot like yoga. When she first lifted up, she was in the cobra position. If she actually made it to a standing position, she was almost in the warrior pose. She watched as he tethered the board to her ankle, then the larger board to his own.

"Are you comfortable carrying the board?"

"Yes," she was almost yelling over the crashing surf.

"Okay, we'll paddle out together side by side. I'll be watching you the whole time. If you feel unsure, yell out."

And they paddled out past a few rows of cresting waves. They didn't go out far. Shane was a little nervous but was determined to give it an honest try.

"So I'll tell you when there's a wave that I think you should take. When I say go, I want you to paddle with it, then push up on the board like I showed you. Then, remember to plant your back leg first, it'll anchor you. And keep your hands on the board. Are you ready?"

She shook her head yes, but she wasn't sure. Right now they were just paddling lightly over the waves as they came.

"Ok Shane. Here's a good one. Now start to paddle with it!"

Shane tread water and let the wave pass under her.

"What happened?"

"I wasn't ready."

After two more waves came and went, Anthony looked at Shane. "Okay Shane, here comes a good one. Start paddling… NOW, go!"

She started paddling as hard as she could. Once the wave caught her, she put her hands flat on the board and lifted her torso. Then, she brought her planting foot forward so that the ball of her foot was balanced on the board. She brought her other leg forward between her hands and pushed up from her core and using the front foot. Just as she began to raise up from a kneel, she toppled over into the waves.

When she came up, she looked to see where the board was so that it wouldn't bang her in the head. She ducked underwater quickly and came back up just as Anthony made it over to her. Shane wiped her wet hair from her face.

"I almost had it!"

"Yeah, that was a good first try! Do you wanna try again?"

"Yes, but first tell me where I went wrong." Shane hoisted herself back up on the board.

"Next time, keep your hands on the board until you get your feet into position. Once you're up, keep your knees bent. I'm guessing your right foot is your dominant foot?"

Shane shook her head.

"I should've asked. Whichever position your dominant foot is going to be in, plant that one first. That way you will be better centered and it will help your core lift you into position."

The fifth time was the charm. Shane was able to stand and ride the wave for about ten feet.

"Woohoo! That was such a rush!"

"You like that hunh?"

"YES!"

"Okay, let's take a break."

"You're not going to surf?"

"Nah, not today. Today is about you."

They paddled to the shore. When they reached the sand, Shane laid there for a few minutes.

"Kinda tired?" Anthony untethered the board from her ankle, then undid his own.

"Am I? That's a workout for your ass!"

Anthony laughed. "I know. I'll run and grab some towels."

When Anthony returned, Shane was starting to shiver. He scooped her up from the sand. Once she was standing, he unzipped the wet suit to her waist and peeled it from her arms. He wrapped the towel around her torso, rubbing forcefully. Shane unzipped the rest of the suit and stepped out of it. Anthony re-positioned the towel so that it covered her entire body and continued to rub.

"I'm okay. You take off your suit."

He nodded and unzipped his suit. He was wearing some long, bike-looking shorts. His body was ridiculous. Anthony wiped his head, then wrapped the towel around himself.

"I guess we should head back to the truck. You need to put on your clothes and warm up." Anthony stacked the boards and wet suits, then grabbed the bundle.

"My clothes?"

Anthony turned to look at her. "You did bring a change of clothes?"

Shane just looked at him.

Anthony let out a belly laugh. "Shane? How could you not bring dry clothes?"

"I don't know," Shane whined. "I guess I was so focused on the surf gear and it was four in the morning." She was shivering and her teeth were chattering.

"Let's get you warm."

They did a slow jog back to the truck. She climbed in carefully, trying not to get sand everywhere as he started the truck. Anthony turned on the heat and her heated seat.

"Don't worry about the sand. I'll take care of it later." He looked at her and shook his head before closing the door. Shane felt dumb. She was wearing a yoga top and yoga shorts under the towel.

After strapping the boards to the roof rack, he opened the back and found his gym bag. Anthony fished out a shirt and threw it over the seats, to her.

"Put this on. At least it's dry."

Anthony changed clothes behind the truck while Shane maneuvered in the passenger's seat. She chucked the wet towel into the back seat. Anthony had a few dry, clean towels in the back; he climbed into the driver's seat and handed her one.

"You didn't have to laugh at me," she pouted.

"Yes, I did." And he laughed again.

"Okay. Get it all out!"

He pulled out of the cove and they were back on the road.

"I was planning on fixing us breakfast, but you don't have no clothes!"

"You can still do that."

He looked over at her. "Are you sure? I want you to be comfortable."

She shook her head. They were much closer to Anthony's place than hers anyway. It was still early, only 7:15 so the traffic wasn't crazy. They could stop at a Target or somewhere for her to grab something to throw on.

⸻ ∽ ⸻

Anthony's place was unbelievable. A Spanish Revival style home with warm wooden beams that juxtaposed the wrought iron and glass. The front door was a huge, arched wooden door which gave way to a generous foyer complete with a grand staircase that featured intricate, wrought iron balustrades and balconies. There were large arched doorways and wall alcoves throughout his home. The house was light and airy which was helped by the white stucco walls and glass sliders leading to an interior courtyard. The courtyard featured a pool with colorful Spanish tiles, flanked by lush greenery. It sat on at least two acres so it felt secluded.

"Ooh, very nice."

"I will tell my designer that you said so," he chuckled.

He'd dropped the boards in the garage, hung the wet suits on a wall to dry and threw their towels into the washer and started a cycle.

"Make yourself at home. I usually eat something light when I first get back from surfing, then eat something heavier a bit later."

"That's fine, it's early."

He took a variety of fruit from the fridge and pantry and laid it out on the large island. There were three huge, wrought iron pendant lights overhanging it. Shane wrapped her hair in the second towel that he gave her and now unraveled it. Her hair was relatively dry and undoubtedly all over her head.

"Where's the bathroom?"

"My bad Shane. There's a master on this floor. To the left, go down the hall and to the right. There are fresh towels in the bathroom linen closet."

She walked into a large bedroom. When she opened the bathroom doors, it was as if she had stepped into a spa. It was mostly white and glass with earthen mosaic floor tiles that tied in the original architecture of the home. There was a huge egg-shaped tub in front of a picture window overlooking the landscape and an over sized shower with a bunch of nozzles.

There was a small alcove with shelves that had towels and washcloths stacked symmetrically. She spied miniature toiletries on the sink counter. She grabbed a shampoo and conditioner and a shower gel.

That shower touched places she didn't know she had. She let the salt water run off her body and enjoyed the strong spray from the jets. She washed and conditioned her hair, then stepped out of the shower.

She re-wrapped her hair in a towel and wrapped another around her body after drying off. When she left the bathroom, there was a t-shirt and a pair of shorts lying on the bed. Her skin was dry. She went back into the bathroom looking for lotion. She found a bottle and returned to the bedroom. After she lotioned up, she put on the shirt and shorts.

Anthony was sitting at the huge wooden dining room table waiting for her.

"You should've eaten."

"No, I should've waited for you."

There were two fruit bowls made up of sliced bananas, sliced strawberries, raspberries, blackberries, blueberries and granola. There was a smaller bowl that contained Greek yogurt.

"I wasn't sure about the dairy," he said as he pulled out her chair. "So I put it in a separate bowl."

"This looks delicious, thank you. And thanks for the clothes." Shane blushed.

"So you had fun this morning?"

She smiled. "So much fun! I'm mad that I waited so long to try it! I never thought it was something that I'd do… So how long have you been surfing?"

"About ten years," he said between bites. "It is a great way to zone out and de-stress."

After they finished their bowls, Shane started collecting everything from the table.

Anthony stood. "No, thank you. I got it! You relax."

Shane put down the bowls and walked over to a comfortable looking pale blue couch. She laid across it. Oh my God! It was as soft as she'd hoped. She curled up on the sofa and watched as Anthony put their bowls in the sink.

"I am sooo tired!"

Anthony laughed. "Surfing will wipe you!"

He came to sit beside her and she laid her legs across his lap. Shane took the towel from her hair and wrapped her hair into a bun on the top of her head. Anthony began to rub her feet. Her eyes were heavy.

"Do you need a nap?"

She smiled and nodded her head.

"Okay. You chill. I'm going to jump in the shower."

"Okay."

Shane awoke to the smell of something wonderful. How long had she slept? She opened one eye and peeked toward the kitchen. Anthony was fixing breakfast. She looked down and there was a blanket over her. She peeled the blanket back and padded over to the kitchen island.

"Well hello sleepyhead!"

"How long was I asleep?" She glanced at the clock. 11:30.

"Why didn't you wake me up?"

"Why would I do that? You were so peaceful." His dimple popped.

She came around into the kitchen. When she got closer to Anthony, she could smell body wash or cologne. He smelled good. "What are you making?"

"I made some tomato, cheese and spinach omelets and fried potatoes. If you'd like some bacon or sausage, it won't take long to fix."

"No, no. This is great. Where are the plates?"

He pointed to lower cabinets that ran along the wall into the dining room. She walked over then stooped down to grab two.

"Silverware?"

"I've got it." He walked over with forks, knives and two glasses of orange juice. After setting them on the table, he went back to the kitchen bringing two platters: one with the omelets and one with the potatoes.

"I hope you're hungry," he said, putting down the platters. "Cuz I'm starving."

As they ate breakfast, they talked about their lives, their details.

"This house is beautiful! And I love this style of home, but I've never seen one up close."

"Thank you! I'll give you a tour later. Not many people know about Revival homes. They're unique, which is why I bought it."

"Yes, I'd love a tour. Did you do much work to it or was it done when you bought it?"

"Both. It was already renovated to expand the home. I had work done to bring the Revival details back in and some changes for my style preferences."

"Don't get me started on reno talk. I could go on and on…. I restored a Greystone in Chicago. It was a multi-unit and I restored it back to a single family home. It was a lot of work!"

"Wow! I'd love to see it." He paused. "The work I mean…"

Shane finished the last of her omelet. "I appreciate a man that can cook! You threw down on these omelets."

"I love a woman who will eat!" he laughed. "My mother made sure her sons could take care of themselves. By the time we were teenagers, we could cook, clean, do laundry and even sew buttons on our shirts."

"That's what I'm talking about Mom! Are you close with your mother?"

"Yes. We were very close, but she passed away three years ago."

"Oh, I'm so sorry Anthony!"

"Yeah, it was rough… still is, but she had a great life and a lot of people who cherished her."

Shane nodded her head. "Was she sick?" she asked gently.

"No. But she died suddenly, in her sleep. They thought maybe she had an unknown condition and suffered a heart attack, but they couldn't know definitively without an autopsy. We decided against that… it wouldn't change anything…. My Dad is still with us. A little sad, but he has grandchildren and children to keep him busy."

It was quiet for a moment. Shane stabbed at a potato. "So how many siblings do you have?"

"Two brothers: one older, one younger. What about you?" Anthony resumed eating his omelet.

"My father had other children, but I only know one sister. We grew up together but I was alone in my household… that was lonely sometimes. I said that I wouldn't do that to my children and guess what? I totally did." She shrugged her shoulders. "My son Sean was alone with only me to keep him company. I thought I'd have other children someday, but I guess it wasn't in the cards."

Shane took her last sip of orange juice. "Tell me about your children."

Anthony smiled. "I have two boys, Amir and Samuelle; they are 26 and 14. My daughter Naaja is 17. Amir is about to graduate from law school. He's in Pennsylvania. Samuelle is a high school freshman and a jokester who loves movies. And Babygirl… she's finishing her junior year and wants to do everything: swim, dance, debate and draw!" He became serious.

"My children and I are very close and I'm so glad that my ex-wife and I were able to remain on good terms. It really helped them get through the divorce. Don't get me wrong, it was still difficult. But now, we have family celebrations and co-parenting is easy."

"Wow! I admire you two for that." Shane was genuinely impressed. "It's so important! But it takes two mature people who are willing to put their children first."

"Yes, it does. And a lot of hard work."

After they cleaned the kitchen, Anthony fixed coffee. She recognized the sticker on the bag. When it began brewing, she knew the aroma.

"This is the brew that my assistant found!" She laughed at herself. "I shouldn't be this excited about coffee."

"We need to find something else that excites you." He looked at her with the panty-scorching look again. And she remembered that she wasn't wearing any.

He put his arms around her waist and pulled her close. She inhaled his delicious scent and looked up at him. His dimple popped and he leaned down and softly brushed his lips with hers. She kissed him softly, then put her arms around his neck. Shane licked his bottom lip and slid her tongue into his mouth. He kissed her slowly and deliberately, taking his time.

Shane hadn't been kissed that way in a long time. She felt a throbbing between her thighs and began to feel warm.

"Mmmmm," she purred as she broke the kiss. "You're about to get me in trouble."

"This is good trouble!" he laughed. And he kissed her again, long and slow.

This time, when she broke the kiss she backed away from him slightly.

"What's wrong?" he asked.

"Nothing. It's just that if you keep kissing me like that, I'm going to end up face down, ass up," she giggled.

"Now that's a nice visual!"

Shane swatted at him "I just wanna downshift a bit... is that okay with you?"

Anthony hung his head and sighed. "I guess...." He felt her watching him and he looked up, smiling. "I'm kidding, it's cool! I'm not 17; I can control myself. We're still getting to know each other." He held her hands in his. "I like you Shane and I like... this. It's been a while since a woman excited me the way that you do. And I don't just mean sexually."

Shane smiled a big smile. "So what now? I'm not ready to leave."

They relocated to the media room and curled up together in front of the large screen. They watched *Friday* and laughed like they had never seen it.

Before they left, he gave her some sweatpants to change into since they never made it to Target. It had gotten a bit chilly and was overcast.

When he walked her to the door, he leaned down and kissed her cheek.

"When I said downshift, I didn't mean to first gear!" she teased.

Anthony obliged, giving her another long and slow kiss. He savored her.

"Today was a great day," she said emphatically.

"Yes. He said looking at her intensely. "It was. I look forward to the next one." His dimple popped. She could live inside that dimple. She went to bed that night and dreamed of riding the waves and riding Anthony.

The next morning, Anthony sent her a sweet text: **Good morning. You're on my mind. Have a great day!** She texted back as she walked into the classroom.

"Good morning! Let's dive right in. Who's song is up next?"

That afternoon, she called Anthony asking for a rain check. They were supposed to have dinner that evening.

"I'm kinda tired. Can we get together another evening?"

"Yeah, sure. Are you okay?"

"Yeah, I think the last few days are catching up with me. I just need to rest."

Anthony called the next morning to check on her. Shane didn't pick up. That afternoon, he texted asking if she was okay. She responded that yes she was fine, just busy and she would call him later. She didn't. And then a few days passed.

He texted her the next afternoon asking if they could talk. That evening when he called, she hesitantly answered.

"Look Shane. When we met, you told me to cut the shit. So here it is:

I'm digging you and I think you feel the same. If you want to take it slow, that's cool but I don't want to play games."

"Anthony, I promise you that I'm not trying to play games. I just have a lot going on and I- "

"We both have a lot going on. So what! Shane, talk to me. We're grown! If you're afraid, then say that but don't have me feeling like I did something wrong."

Shane was silent.

"Shane."

"Anthony, I need a little time."

"Ok Shane. I can respect that."

Shane hung up frustrated with herself. I need to go to sleep and start again tomorrow, she thought. The next morning, her phone rang early before she began getting ready for class.

"Robert!"

"What's up baby? You must be having fun out there because the only time I've heard from you was when you texted dude's contact!" He laughed.

Shane was quiet.

"Shane. Wassup?"

"Robert, I'm fucking up."

"What?!?"

"I mean, I'm fine, class is fine. But, the guy I met, the one I went surfing with… I'm fucking it up.…"

"Tell me."

Shane laid it out for him as she started getting dressed. Everything. Her reconnecting with Mike. His question, her answer. And now, Anthony.

"Whoa." Robert was quiet for a moment. "I know that was a hard decision for you to make. And I know it was hard for Mike too. But, you took time to think and you made it. Any regrets?"

"Honestly, no. I mean, I know that he's hurt and I regret that. But, it is the right choice for me. We can't go back and I feel like that's what it would've been… I'll probably write a song about it!" She laughed a sad laugh. "But, I'm good with my decision."

"So, how do you feel… about ol' boy I mean? I don't know him, but he and Grover are tight so that's good enough for me."

"I like him. I *really* like him. He's the first person to make me feel this way in a long time."

"Then talk to him Shane! That man has laid it out for you. Don't brush him off because he will move on. And don't think he's not afraid; remember he's putting himself out there just like you."

"Oh shit! I've gotta go! You're going to make me late! Thanks honey." She ended the call and bounded out of the door.

When she arrived home from class, there was a mixed bouquet of white and yellow roses, lilies and lilacs in a vase on the front step. The note read: "Time is not to be wasted." She opened the door and put the flowers on the counter. Shane sat at the counter and scrolled through her call log. Anthony answered on the second ring.

"Hey. I didn't expect you to answer," she said nervously. "I was going to leave a message."

"What's the message?" His voice had an edge to it.

"Anthony, I'm just…afraid. But, let's talk." She paused. "I don't want to waste anymore time."

Anthony canceled his afternoon and drove to Santa Monica. When she opened the door, he pulled her into his arms and shut the door. They stayed that way for a while, neither of them speaking.

That evening, they ordered Chinese. They fell asleep cuddled on the couch. Shane awoke in the middle of night. She shook Anthony and told him to follow her. They climbed into the king-sized bed and snuggled. Anthony fell back asleep, with her head resting on his chest. Shane was wide awake.

After some time, she shook him again. He eventually opened his eyes and must've recognized the look that she had in hers. He leaned in to kiss her and she put her arms around his neck pulling him to her. She kissed him, savoring his tongue and lips while rubbing his head. He slid his hands around her waist and held her tightly.

Shane broke from the kiss and sat up, peeling off her leggings. She pulled her t-shirt over her head, then yanked off her panties. Anthony raised up as she laid down on the bed. He leaned down and kissed the inside of her left ankle. Then, he slowly kissed up to her calf, the inside of her knee, her juicy thigh, then licked her clit. Back and forth over and over until she screamed. Then he began to kiss the inside of her right ankle, up her leg, to her calf, the inside of her knee, her thigh then flicked her clit again and again until she became undone.

He stood and admired her. "You are beautiful Shane Mathews."

He removed his t-shirt and boxers, revealing his slim, fit body. He knelt between her thighs and lifted her ankles to his shoulders. Anthony slowly sank into her. Shane licked her lips and groaned. He continued at that leisurely pace watching Shane's tortured face. Slowly, he began to pick up the pace, thrusting into her as her body quivered. She grabbed his thighs and brought him to her at every thrust. Shane could feel sensations building in her body. Just as it was rising to a peak, Anthony leaned back and pulled Shane onto his lap. They exploded together.

Shane opened her eyes and was almost nose to nose with Anthony. He was smiling.

"I didn't see that coming." He kissed her lightly on the lips.

Shane clenched her eyes shut. She put her hands on his shoulders and raised up from his lap. Wordlessly, she got up and went to the bathroom. As she peed, she promised herself not to overthink it.

When she came out of the bathroom, Anthony was lying on the bed, his dark body amid the cool blue sheets. He opened his arms to her. She climbed up on the bed and went to him; somehow they missed the wet spot. He wrapped her in his arms and kissed all of the soft places that made her feel self-conscious. They fell asleep like two spoons. In the morning, he drove her to class and they agreed to see each other the next evening.

After class, as she was walking to the house, her phone rang. Stephanie.

"I did it!!!!" screeched Stephanie.

"Of course you did," exclaimed Shane. "Congratulations, Dr. Mohel! How do you feel?"

"Honestly? Like a huge weight has been lifted!"

Shane paused. "So have you thought about the 'what now'?"

"I have. But before we get into that, what's up Surfer Girl? You didn't think I was calling just to talk about my dissertation did you?"

"Actually, I did…"

"Well too bad. Besides work texts, I haven't heard from you since you went surfing! Sooo, how was it?"

"It was very cool and exhilarating! I'll definitely do it again, but surfing is a serious full body workout. I need to step up my cardio game if I'm going to keep it up."

Stephanie waited. When Shane didn't continue, she exhaled into the phone.

"And Mr. Dekra? How's he doing?"

"Well, I told him that I didn't need that consult after all."

"Ha, ha. C'mon, I want some details."

"Oooh. Look at you, so nosy!"

"Shane!"

"Okay, okay. I like him. We've been out a handful of times and I'm going to see him tomorrow evening."

"And- "

"And he's very handsome and accomplished and fun to be around. It turns out that we have a lot in common. We have great conversations and I feel good when I'm with him." Shane smiled as she thought about Anthony.

"So when's the last time you saw him?"

"This morning when he dropped me off to class."

"Wait… he lives all the way in Burbank…. Did he spend the night? You can't be leaving out the good shit!"

"Yes Steph. He spent the night. That's all that I'm going to say about it."

"Ok. If that's how you're going to be, then I guess I won't be telling you about Tom."

"Oh, that's how this is gonna go?"

Stephanie laughed. "You show me yours, I'll show you mine!"

And for the next hour, they giggled and gossiped like two girlfriends. However, Shane kept it PG-rated. She was Stephanie's employer for God's sake! She'd save the seedy details for Tonya.

That evening she fixed pasta with vodka sauce and a spinach salad. She ate quietly at the counter, then shifted her attention to her memoir. Shane hadn't spent any time writing lately between class and Anthony. She sighed. He was such a welcomed distraction, but he was a distraction nonetheless.

She'd been ignoring her publisher's phone calls. Shane knew that she owed her more chapters. She retrieved her journal from the bedroom and opened it onto the counter. Shane was still a fan of writing, pen to paper. Sure it took longer, but her words flowed better onto the page like this, at least that's what she believed.

At 15, I was angry…at everyone: my parents, school, society, God. I was losing friends too often to violence and nobody seemed to care. When I looked at the lives of schoolmates, it was like I was from another planet. They didn't have any idea what my world was like and the life and death issues that touched me, my friends, my community. And so I began writing. A creative writing class at my elite school became my solace. I wrote short stories mostly about my life and my world. I was trying to understand my place in it.

As I teetered on the brink of adulthood, I found my soulmate. I thought, finally! My life is getting on track. I finished senior year and headed to

On their next date, Anthony took Shane to hear live reggae music. People crowded into the small venue and packed the dance floor. She was glad that she wore a loose-fitting dress because it was humid and steamy inside. The group played mostly Roots, but would occasionally shift into Ragga and Dancehall styles.

It had been a long time since she'd been out dancing. She liked the way that Anthony held her and moved with her. They stayed on the dance floor for the majority of the band's sets, winding and grinding. He could really move his body. It turned Shane on; she loved a man that could dance. If they hadn't already slept together, she would've given him some!

"I need some water," she said in Anthony's ear.

They left the floor and wedged themselves in at the bar, having lost their table long ago. Shane dug into her purse in search of a ponytail ring. Thankfully, there was one down at the bottom. She could feel that her hair was a frizzy Afro.

"I'll be right back." she excused herself to the restroom.

Luckily it wasn't too crowded and she was able to look into the mirror. She washed her hands then let water pool into her cupped hand. She had to put some in her hair. She laughed. She hadn't done this since she was in her twenties, back in her clubbing days. After dousing her frizzy curls with water, she was able to tame it into a curly bun atop her head.

She returned to the bar and gulped down a glass of water. She strapped her purse across her body and pulled Anthony out into a small, open area beside the bar. They danced and laughed in that spot until they left. They had a great time.

—§—

Class was going well. Her students were polishing up their songs and writing new lyrics all the time. Shane wanted them to understand perspectives from other professionals in the business and learn about functions that they may coordinate with as songwriters. She decided to have a few guest speakers: Grover, composer extraordinaire; Robert, a music publisher and Anthony, an entertainment attorney.

They each attended two classes to talk about their roles in the music industry and explain how they engage with singers and songwriters. Each had a unique style of engagement with the students. They brought a great male energy which was a shift that Shane believed added dimension to the course. Also bringing two business-minded people offered a different kind of balance.

Now, the other creative force, Grover, stole the show of course! His eccentricity and deep knowledge and experience enthralled the students. The way he explained the marriage between composition and lyrics, well no one does it better. She adored her quirky friend.

"Have you and Shane collaborated on any work?"

"How are you in this class and you don't know the answer to that question?" Grover rolled his eyes. "What's your name?" He waited. "Andrew? That's your assignment! Research it."

Andrew's face was beet red.

"Honestly."

The four of them made plans to meet up that evening at an Argentinian grill that Grover knew. Robert was flying out tomorrow and Shane wanted to thank them all for speaking to her class; she also wanted Robert to get to know Anthony a little bit. Their collective energy was exciting and she wanted to keep it going.

The restaurant was dimly lit and moody with huge wrought-iron chandeliers and never-ending brick walls. There was an inviting, smoky aroma that filled the large space as well as laughter and Argentinian, caballero music. Shane didn't complain about the bounty of grilled meat on the menu; the men seemed to enjoy it. The meat prepared on the open flame was fantastic. Although Shane ordered the vegetable platter, she sampled from everyone's plate: filet, spicy sausage and lamb chops.

"Shane, you have a great class. Thanks for inviting me, it was fun!" said Robert, taking a sip of bourbon.

"Yeah! It's been a fun experience." she reflected. "I wasn't sure what to expect but I think it's gone well being my first time out the gate! It's almost time to get back to real life."

Anthony stole a glance at her.

"With that in mind… Anthony, I guess we'll be seeing you in Chicago?" Robert asked, looking up from his plate.

Shane shot him a look, only to be met with Robert's unwavering gaze.

"That's up to Shane. I don't want to put her on the spot."

"Well, if it was up to you?" Robert pressed. "Look, this woman is my sister. When she asked me to come out, I decided that I would have this conversation. I just want to know your intentions."

"Robert!"

"What? We're all grown. If it makes you feel better, I can talk to Anthony later, but the conversation will be the same."

Grover interrupted. "Look, not that it's our business —"

"No it's not!" Shane cried.

Grover put his hand up. "I wasn't finished. I want to hear from Ant too. Y'all are both good friends of mine, more like family. Ant asked about you and I had that dinner party to connect the two of you, so

I've got skin in the game… just like Robert. We're all here, so what's up?"

Shane didn't appreciate this patriarchal bullshit! They were both out of line. "Anthony, don't feel the need to explain." Shane exhaled.

"Shane, I don't want to embarrass you, but I'd like to answer." He paused and looked at Shane. She threw up her hands and took a sip of wine.

"I appreciate that they are concerned and I want them to know that there is no cause for it… Grover, you know me brother. Spending time with Shane is a big step." He turned to Robert. "Shane and I haven't discussed what happens when she leaves. But yes, I would love to be invited to Chicago and spend time with Shane. She is welcome to visit me here anytime. But I don't want her to feel rushed."

"Okayyyyy! That's enough of y'all all up in my business!" Shane did not hide her annoyance.

Grover lifted his glass. The two men followed suit. Shane was last to lift her glass.

"To Shane for bringing us together tonight! And although we 'all in yo business' know that it comes from a place of love." After they clinked glasses, Anthony leaned over and kissed her softly on the lips. Okay, he's sweet. I won't be mad with him, she thought.

———— ❧ ————

Shane wrapped up the class and gave each student her personal contact information.

"Keep in touch with me and each other," she advised. "You never know when you will need or can give help. Everyone needs a hand up sometimes and I have no problem giving one to those who are willing to put in the work. I wouldn't be where I am today if people hadn't helped me."

When she returned to Chicago, it took her a while to adjust to being home. However, Stephanie had everything running smoothly: her calendar and her household.

"Remember, you have the ASCAP Experience in a week. Did you draft your presentation?"

Yikes. Shane had forgotten that assignment.

Stephanie read the look on her face. "Shane! You have to submit your presentation later this week."

"Okay, okay. I've got it… I can use some of the material that I used in the class. It'll be fine."

Stephanie exhaled and shook her head.

"Also, there was a message on your business line from Amara Johnson. Actually she left two messages."

"Oh. That's the family that lives in the DC property. I hope everything is alright."

It turned out that the Johnsons wanted to buy her DC home. Shane was happy to sell it to them, but first she would talk to Sean to make sure he didn't want to keep it.

"We just love it here. This is home… I know that we never discussed it, but we're hoping that you'd be open to selling."

It had been nine years since she rented the house to the Johnson family. It was time to let it go. The house served her well and provided a home for her and Sean. All she ever wanted was for someone to love it as much as they had.

"Yes, I will sell you the house. I apologize that I didn't offer before now."

Shane had her accountant calculate how much the sale price would be to have their mortgage remain the same or close to what they were paying her in rent, factoring in the down payment that they were offering. Her accountant balked at the price, telling her how much she could get for the house.

"Thank you for your counsel. I know what the market price could be, but I don't need the money. And it's important to me to help this family."

The Johnsons were extremely thankful. Shane took the proceeds from the sale and put it in a trust for Sean.

Shane also touched base with Robert. He wanted her to work with an upcoming artist, Valencia. She and Robert had not spoken since the dinner with Anthony and Grover and she was still a little salty with him. But Shane, always the consummate professional, kept her feelings at bay.

"Shane, I want you to meet this young artist. She is something special, I can feel it but she needs some polish. Will you meet with her?"

Valencia needed a breakout song for her first album. After meeting and hearing her voice and sound, Robert knew Shane would be the perfect writer. The young artist had written a few songs that were very good but needed some fine-tuning.

Shane took a liking to her right away. Valencia Marca was a firecracker with a megawatt smile and beautiful energy. She was not much older than Sean. The young woman had stacks of journals filled with poetry and lyrics, drawings. She was a kindred spirit.

"So tell me about yourself," said Shane. "Who are you as an artist?"

To be so young, Valencia was clear about who she was and had a vision of what type of artist she planned to be. As a new artist, it was possible to be influenced and even dictated to by the record label. But, Valencia had leverage. She had a strong following of her MusiCloud and other streaming accounts that made the labels come knocking at her door, trying to outbid each other. And she was not only a singer, she was a songwriter. Valencia was in a great position. Now, she wanted Shane to push her over the top.

"Ms. Shane- "

"No, just Shane."

"Okay. Shane, I'm an artist and my work speaks for itself. I'm not about to be out here showing my ass and gyrating all over the place," she exclaimed, pushing her dark, thick braid over her shoulder and combing a wayward lock behind her ear.

Shane smiled. "Be clear about who you are and know your worth as a person and as an artist. The rest will work itself out."

Valencia unconsciously crossed her legs as she listened, her wide dark eyes absorbing Shane's words. She was focused so her cupie bow mouth had a slight pucker. She shook her head.

"I think I know which songs I want for my first project. It's just a question of getting the execs to feel my vibe."

Shane nodded. "Okay. Show me."

Together they selected a handful of songs that Valencia had written. Shane was impressed with her lyricism and melodic talent. They would focus on those to craft her first project.

A romantic at heart, Valencia really shined with her ballads; but she also wrote about her feelings and experiences as a young woman which made her unique. Everything wasn't a love song or about some object of her desire. She had a critical mind that examines the world through her lens as a Latinx young woman. One of Shane's favorites was *I'ma Keep Dreamin'* which paid homage to Valencia's ancestors and was also a nod to those in the US fighting for their children's immigration rights as DREAMers.

Working with Valencia excited Shane. The young woman's energy was infectious and inspired new songs for Shane as well as content for her memoir. Shane submitted five chapters to her publisher while still in LA. Then, she met with her that following week. The memoir was shaping up and Shane was happy with its direction. Now she was back on the schedule that her publisher originally created so she only had to stay consistent.

The studio at the house was finally finished so she and Valencia christened the space. There, Shane learned that she had perfect pitch and was a natural entertainer. They were able to work whenever they felt inspired. If it got too late, Valencia stayed in one of the guest rooms. And they didn't have to rely on greasy takeout to get them through their sessions. Shane kept a fully-stocked kitchen because she always had guests and friends coming through.

"You always cook. Lemme cook you something Shane."

"I'm not gonna turn that down! But if you're cooking, I want some of that Puerto Rican food you're always bragging about. Lemme see whatchu got!"

Valencia stood at the sink to wash her hands. "Okay but, it depends on what kind of ingredients you have."

Valencia opened the fridge and looked inside. Then she went to the pantry to see what goodies might be hidden.

"Okay Shane, I see you. Where you from with plantains and coconut milk at the ready?"

Shane laughed. "DC and my people are from Maryland. I just enjoy good food!"

Valencia opened the freezer. "Is this beef?"

Shane came and stood beside her. "Um, yes."

Valencia took out the package of ground chuck. "I'm gonna make you pastelon! It's my Mama's recipe… kinda like Puerto Rican lasagna but it's sweet and savory. Where do you keep the spices?"

Shane pulled out the spice drawers for Valencia's inspection.

"Ma you be cookin' up in here… Your spice collection is deep!" she said appreciatively.

Shane opened a cabinet on the island and pulled out a large, glass casserole dish, a cutting board and a mixing bowl.

"The utensils are in those two drawers near you." She pointed them out for Valencia.

"Okay, it looks like this is gonna take a minute so I'ma get us something to snack on." Shane pulled out another cutting board. Then she went to the pantry and came back with two pears and two Granny

Smith apples. She walked past Valencia to the fridge and pulled out a hunk of manchego cheese and a watermelon.

Valencia was slicing plantains and preparing the frying pan. She eyed Shane's bounty and frowned. "Fruit?"

"And cheese and crackers," retorted Shane. "Give it a chance, V."

To make Valencia feel better, Shane went back to the pantry and grabbed a bag of herb popcorn.

"So where are your people from V?"

Shane had been waiting to ask. Some of V's songs talk about the struggles of Latinx peoples, including immigration and she knew V was Puerto Rican and grew up in the Bronx.

"My Mama is from Puerto Rico. I was actually born there. My dad is Colombian. They met at NYU as students. After they got married, they moved to PR cuz Mama was homesick and wanted to be near family."

Valencia finished frying the plantains; they were cooling on a paper towel covered plate. Next, she diced onions and garlic. She reached over and poked an index finger into the plastic-covered ground chuck in the sink.

"What about your dad's family?"

Valencia frowned. "I don't know much about them… They are somehow involved in the drug shit, so my father hasn't been back in a long time." She looked up at Shane. "Stereotype shit right?" She paused. "His parents haven't seen me since I was a baby. Mama said she was afraid when they visited them in Colombia."

She shrugged her shoulders. "So I only know my Mama's family. Some are in New York and some are in PR. I still visit PR when I can." She stopped.

"Where's the cheese? Not that fancy kind there, I need mozzarella!"

"I think I have the shredded kind. Is that okay?" Valencia nodded. Shane took it out of the freezer.

"I know about not knowing family. I didn't grow up with my father or his family, so I don't know that side. Not as dramatic as your story, he just treated my mother badly… I always hoped when I had children, they would have a strong relationship with their father. My son doesn't." Shane sighed.

"That's not on you Ma! I'm sure he knows that."

"He does, but it doesn't make it better." Shane played with an apple slice.

"My Abuela says, 'men will be men'! For a long time, I thought she was just excusing bad behavior. Now I know she just meant that you can't change them. They're gonna be who they are and do want they want to." Valencia clucked her tongue and turned the burner on under a cast iron skillet that Shane handed her for the beef.

⁓

Shane and Anthony continued to see each other long-distance. Despite their busy schedules, they were at a point in their careers where they had flexibility and could travel when they wanted. A weekend flight here. A week there.

Shane had grown quite comfortable writing in Anthony's sun-filled study. And she loved spending lazy evenings in his peaceful courtyard sipping steamy coffee or chilly cocktails while laughing with Anthony. He had given her several more surfing lessons so now she could stay on the board to catch a few waves. They could actually surf together.

When he came to Chicago, they moved in much the same way: they were very selfish about their time together, mostly staying in. But, sometimes they would slip out late-night to The Wild Hare for some live reggae or late on Sunday mornings for its Rum Punch Brunch.

Occasionally they would meet up with Grover or have a dinner date with Imani and Bryan depending on the city. But most of the time, they reveled in each others' company; they were greedy for one another. She loved that they could sit quietly together, enjoying being in each others' space. She would curl up with a book and he would be reviewing contracts or writing a brief. Sometimes she would watch him, his face so serious, poring over a legal document. He'd catch her occasionally and flash his dimpled smile.

Shane enjoyed going back and forth between Burbank and Chicago. Counting down the days until she would see Anthony, it actually kept things passionate and exciting. It was his turn and he'd touch down in Chicago the next evening. She arranged for a car to pick him up at the airport.

"I have to make an appearance at an event, so I'll get to the house about the same time as you."

Anthony left baggage claim, then headed through the double doors to ground transportation. There was a driver holding a sign with his name. As he approached the car, the back window lowered.

"Need a ride?" Shane's crimson lips curled into a smile.

"I thought you had a thing tonight?"

"I lied."

Anthony opened the door and Shane slid across the seat, making room for him. He got in, closed the door and leaned over to kiss her. Shane was wearing lipstick which she didn't often. It was red and he loved it. He had come straight from his office so he was wearing a suit. As she kissed him, she turned to face him and swung her leg across him. She raised onto her knees, straddling him while she pressed the button to raise the tinted glass dividing them from the driver.

"Well hello!"

"Shhhhhh…."

She pushed his jacket off of his arms and threw it onto the empty seat. Shane loosened his tie and kissed him all over his face and neck leaving a trail of red lips.

"I missed you Anthony," she sighed.

He put his hands around her waist and tugged at the knot in the belt of her trench coat. As he loosened it, he saw skin. Shane was only wearing a pair of lacy silver panties under the coat. His eyes bulged and he bent his head to lick one of her nipples. He began to suck it and bit it softly, then moved his mouth to the other breast. His hands were inside her panties massaging her ass, then he made a move to pull them down. She grabbed one of his hands and put it between her legs. He looked at her for a brief moment and smiled a wicked smile; the panties were crotchless. His fingers began to rub her softly.

As he continued to rub her, Shane kissed his bald head and then licked from his temple to the top of his head. She unbuckled his belt and unzipped his pants. His erection sprang toward her. She licked her lips, then bent over and sucked the swollen tip. She sat back up and raised her hips enough to sit down on him as Anthony hissed through clenched teeth. She put her finger to his lips.

"Shhhhh!"

Shane rolled and worked her hips as she held his shoulders for leverage. Rhythmically she would raise up on her knees then glide back down until she grazed his pelvis.

"Ahhh Shane!"

She raised her finger to his lips again. At this, Anthony grabbed her hips and held her tightly to him, thrusting repeatedly as Shane put her head back and closed her eyes. She was lost in their salacious romp and enjoying Anthony's willingness to indulge it. Her skin was on fire and she could feel an exquisite sensation climbing. Shane bit her top lip then leaned over with her lips at his ear.

"Make me come!" she whispered.

Anthony was excited by naughty Shane and happy to fulfill her.

Later that evening, they enjoyed a long and steamy shower together, then laid across Shane's bed. Shane had a taste for deep dish pizza. She'd make them a salad so she wouldn't feel as bad about the thick, buttery crust.

"What do you want on the pizza?"

"Everything," he said, eyeing her.

After she placed the order, they lay talking and laughing. When his dimple popped, Shane stuck the tip of her pinky in it. "This belongs to me."

"What about me? Do I belong to you too?"

Shane reached over and smacked his behind. "I thought that was clear!"

"Maybe I need some reminding?" Anthony licked his lips.

"You don't ever stop!"

"Nope." He grabbed her and began planting kisses all over her face, neck and body. Shane squealed and struggled to get out of his embrace but he had a vice grip. As he held her, his face turned serious and he looked into her eyes.

"I love you Shane." Anthony paused. "I didn't think that I would ever feel this way again… You don't have to say anything, I just –"

Shane put her finger to his lips. "I love you too." She smiled and raised up to sit in front of him. She softly kissed each of his eyelids, the tip of his nose and then his lips. He smiled and she kissed her dimple.

Anthony was the steady kind of man she needed. He made her laugh in a way that she hadn't in a very long time. And though they were in a long distance relationship, she never worried about where she stood with him and knew that he always had her back. There was no drama, no sleepless nights.

A year flew by and Anthony was headed to town to meet Sean. He'd taken an extended leave so that they could start to get to know each other. Shane had already met his two younger children and they loved her; it didn't hurt that they were big fans of hers. Although they were seldom impressed by their father's star clients, Shane was a different story. They were always giddy when they learned that she'd written a song that they liked.

"I can't believe she wrote that song… I LOVE that song… That song in that movie is one of Shane's?"

Sean was glad that his mother was finally spending time with someone. She was happy and that's all that mattered to him. Of course he was eager to meet Anthony, but dude was doing something right and kept a smile on his mother's face.

Shane was anxious for Sean and Anthony to meet. She hadn't introduced Sean to anyone since Chad; that was years ago and the two of them had been close. When the relationship ended, she felt guilty because it was a loss for Sean too. But Sean was a young adult now, so any relationship between him and Anthony would have a different dynamic. Still, she wanted Sean to like Anthony.

Sean was home for the summer and interning for Bryan's architectural firm. He wasn't sure what he wanted to major in but he was strong in math and science; Shane didn't know where that came from! He was also interested in construction and architecture.

By interning with Bryan, he would be able to meet architects and engineers from the firm as well as go on job sites to meet the different trades and craftsmen. It was a great opportunity and he was excited. He had always looked at Bryan as a father figure and Bryan treated him like another one of his children.

After his first day, Sean found his mother in her office.

"Ma, I went to a job site with Bryan today! He showed me the plans and then we walked the site, meeting members of the crew. I have a hardhat!"

Sean held it up. Bryan's company logo wrapped around the side.

Shane listened as he excitedly rambled about all the people whom he met. Tomorrow, they would go to the office to meet Bryan's partner and some staff.

"He said that I could learn the software that they use to draw up plans. And on job sites, I can probably shadow the crew to assist them and learn how to use some tools of their trades!"

Shane was excited that he was so excited. Maybe now he'll pick a major, she thought. But right now she was just enjoying his giddiness. Shane was glad that they never lost their closeness as he got older. Sure, their relationship was different but he never got to an age when he shut her out. They still had their special bond.

Shane smiled at him and wondered how his hair fit under the hardhat. It was a wild, curly halo.

"So a good first day!"

"Yeah! Hey, I'm meeting up with some friends tonight, so I won't be here for dinner. But I won't be out late. I'm meeting Bryan at the office in the morning at 8:30."

"Oh, so I'm on my own is what you're saying."

"C'mon Ma. Don't say it like that!"

"Well how should I say it? When am I gonna get some time?"

"We'll hang out this weekend, I promise. When's Anthony coming anyway?"

"Sunday afternoon."

"See? We have plenty of time!"

He smiled and jogged out of the room.

Shane sighed. I'll see if Imani has plans. Maybe she'll come over for dinner.

Imani and Bryan had dinner plans. "Okay. Another night."

Shane went downstairs to the kitchen to see what she would have for dinner. She opened the fridge. Yes! There was some leftover pesto pasta. She thought Sean had eaten the rest. Good. She'd make some garlic bread to go with it.

Sean came into the kitchen before he left for the evening. He found his mother sitting at the island, enjoying her pasta. He'd showered and was wearing ripped jeans and a camouflage shirt with neon stripes on the sleeves. He wore a pair of Black Doc Martens. His hair was still damp, so it hung limp on his head revealing his fade. No doubt it would spring back into the curly halo quickly in the summery air.

He reached over to grab a piece of bread. Shane smacked his hand.

"Oh, I can't have none?"

"No, you can't." He sulked and walked out of the kitchen. "Have a good night. And be careful!" she called after him.

She picked her phone up from the granite counter and connected the Bluetooth to the sound system. I'll listen to the vocals that Valencia laid down in the studio. They were layered over basic tracks but the heart of the songs was there. Shane closed her eyes and was swaying to a mid-tempo tune when the music abruptly stopped. She opened her eyes to see Anthony standing beside a surfboard on her phone screen.

She answered and his smiling face appeared. "Hey! You're wrecking my flow!"

"Hello beautiful. What flow?"

She laughed. "I was listening to some of V's tracks. What's up?"

"Can't I just wanna talk to my woman?"

"Of course you can… I miss you," she said, smiling into the screen. She made a kissy face.

"I'll be there before you know it."

<hr>

It was Sunday and Shane was planning to cook dinner. She stood looking into the refrigerator. What to cook? Maybe she should run to the grocery store to pick up a few items. Calm down, she told herself. It's not like you haven't cooked for either of them before.

"Ma!"

"Huh? What is it?" Shane turned around to see Sean standing on the other side of the kitchen.

"What's up witchu?"

Shane exhaled and closed the fridge. Then, she sat down at the island and waved for Sean to come sit with her.

"I'm a little nervous about you meeting Anthony. I really want you to like him... And I know it's not up to me, but it's important."

"Ma, you need to chill. It's gonna be fine. You like him so that's what's important."

Shane looked at her son. "I love him, Sean and that scares me. I guess that's why I'm so nervous about you two meeting."

Sean was surprised to hear his mother say this. "Does he feel the same about you?"

"Yes."

"Then there's nothing to worry about. The man loves and respects you. That means he and I already have a lot in common."

Together, they decide on lasagna for dinner. Sean helped his mother make the lasagna which was wrapped with foil and cooling on the counter. Individual spinach salads were in the fridge and the kitchen was clean. Sean would make the garlic bread; he'd had a taste for it since earlier in the week.

*Serpentine Fire* echoed through the house as Shane and Sean played Uno. "You better draw four, SonSon. And change the color to green!"

When the doorbell rang, Shane looked at Sean. She put her cards down and stood up from the island. She headed down the hall to the foyer and opened the vestibule doors. Anthony grabbed her, making Shane squeal.

"I've missed you." He lifted her up and inhaled her scent. She smelled like vanilla and ylang ylang.

She struggled out of his arms. Anthony picked up his luggage and closed the entry doors. Just then, Sean walked into the foyer.

"Hey, how are you, young man?" Anthony extended his arm to shake Sean's hand. "I've heard so much about you, it's good to finally meet."

Sean smiled and shook his hand. The two stood eye to eye. Anthony could see Shane in Sean: they had the same eyes, coloring and face shape. And of course, that hair.

"It's good to meet you man!" Sean bent down and picked up Anthony's bags.

"I've got it man."

"Nah man. Take off your coat and get comfortable. Dinner's almost ready."

"Okay." Anthony looked at Shane, then reached down and removed his shoes. He hung up his coat in the closet and grabbed Shane's hand. They followed Sean down the hall.

"Ma, I'll take these upstairs."

"No baby, take them to the guest room."

Sean stopped. "Seriously, Ma?"

"Yes," she replied.

"Seriously?" echoed Anthony. Shane hit Anthony in the arm.

"Is this cuz I'm here? Cuz, y'all ain't gotta front for me." Sean snickered.

Shane felt scandalized. She put a hand to her chest.

"My bad Ma," he stuttered. "I'm not trying to embarrass you... I'll take 'em to the guest room if you want."

Anthony cleared his throat. "The guest room is fine Sean."

Sean continued down the hall to the guest room. Anthony put his arm around her shoulder.

"It's alright baby. He's a grown man."

"He is not a grown man and he is my baby! That was beyond awkward." Shane's eyes were big.

"Well, he didn't seem uncomfortable. But I understand. We'll get through it." He bent down and kissed her on the tip of her nose. Sean exited the guest room.

"I'm right on time cuz something smells good! What y'all got going on?" He looked at Sean.

"Yeah, we hooked up some lasagna for you."

He walked forward to meet Sean in the hall while Shane collected herself. Anthony followed Sean to the kitchen and sat at the island.

"Do you need me to do anything?"

"Nah. I got it," Sean said as he washed his hands.

Anthony excused himself to the guestroom to wash his hands and freshen up. Shane walked past the guest room and into the kitchen. She looked at Sean.

"Ma, I wasn't trying to be disrespectful. Y'all are long distance and I just thought... I want you to be comfortable."

Shane was quiet. "You caught me off guard. I guess I wasn't ready for this kind of situation."

"My bad. I didn't mean to upset you."

"I'm okay. This is just a new nuance in our relationship, I guess." She gave a nervous laugh.

Anthony came to the threshold of the kitchen. "Is it all clear?"

Shane turned and looked at him. "Yes." She rolled her eyes.

"Okay good, cuz a brother is hungry!"

Sean laughed and took the salads and dressing out of the fridge. Then he opened the drawer getting three sets of silverware, motioning for Anthony and his mother to sit down. They sat beside each other and said grace. Anthony began to crunch loudly. Shane started giggling and Sean looked up from the garlic bread that he was making.

"Damn, you are hungry!" Sean laughed.

"Excuse me y'all. I haven't eaten since lunch today."

Sean smeared the french bread with roasted garlic and butter and put it on a baking sheet. He opened the broiler and slid it in. Then, he turned on the oven light to keep an eye on the bread.

There was a stack of plates on the counter. Sean opened the drawer and grabbed a spatula. He pulled the foil off the lasagna and cut a piece using the spatula, then lifted it onto a waiting plate. The cheese stretched from the plate to the casserole dish. He handed the plate to Anthony.

"Sean, the bread!" Shane reminded him.

He caught it just in time. It was beginning to blacken at the edges. Sean put the bread on a waiting platter. Then, he picked up another plate and loaded it with a piece of lasagna and a chunk of bread.

"Here you go Ma."

Shane hadn't finished her salad but took the plate and sat it beside her salad bowl.

"Anthony, you want garlic bread?"

"Yes, please."

Sean handed him a chunk, then began cutting a hunk of lasagna for himself. He turned and opened the refrigerator to get his salad. He slid the salad across the counter. Then he tore a chunk of bread from the hot loaf and sat it on his plate. He picked up the plate and walked around the island to join Anthony and his mother.

"Y'all did the damn thing with this lasagna!"

"Glad you like it," said Sean. "It's my mom's recipe. She uses spinach and no meat. I've had it this way since I was little… Do you want another piece?"

"Yes, but you sit down and eat. I'll get it myself. Shane, you need anything?"

Anthony picked up his plate and walked to the other side of the island.

"I'd love a glass of wine."

"Yes, ma'am."

Anthony walked to the wine fridge and took out a bottle, sitting it on the counter. Then, he went to the butler's pantry to get a wine glass. And he opened a drawer to find the corkscrew. Sean ate his salad and watched Anthony as he moved comfortably in the space, then snickered.

"What?" asked Shane.

"I didn't say anything."

Shane looked at him.

"Nah, I was just noticing how Anthony knows where everything is… But he didn't know his way to the guest room." Sean started laughing and his mother smacked the back of his head.

"Ma, it's all love. It's jokes!"

"Well I don't like you making those kinds of jokes at my expense! I am your mother."

"Okay, Sean. Let's give your mother a break," said Anthony. He sat the wine glass in front of Shane.

Sean stopped chewing and looked up at Anthony. They looked each other in the eye. Sean nodded.

Anthony opened the bottle and placed the corkscrew in the sink. He walked over to stand beside Shane and fill her glass.

"So do we have any dessert?"

"Dessert?" exclaimed Shane.

"Relax, I'm messing with you. After we finish eating, Sean, maybe we can run out and get something."

"Yeah, that's cool."

Anthony and Sean headed to the store. Sean was still glad to drive his truck since his mother hadn't let him take it to school. He'd wanted folks to see him pushing his black on black Audi Q5, especially the ladies. But, he was in NYC and he'd have to park it on the street; there was no student parking for the dorm. So he was glad to be home, enjoying his ride.

"This is nice," said Anthony, admiring the stitching on the leather seats. "How's the system?"

"Oh, you already know!" said Sean, eagerly turning on the stereo which was synched to his phone. Electric Relaxation flooded the space.

"Whatchu know about Tribe?" laughed Anthony, bopping his head.

"Dude, my mother sleeps and breathes music. If it's good, I know it… I grew up listening to all of her music."

"Right. Your collection is probably more impressive than mine!"

"So where are we headed?" Sean asked.

"I don't know. What do you have a taste for?"

"I thought you wanted dessert."

"Man, I just wanted to give your Mom a minute and for us to get a little time. She's a little wound up about us meeting."

"I know, right? I'm not used to seeing her like this." Sean paused. "My Mom loves you."

Anthony was surprised that Sean shared his mother's feelings, but didn't hesitate. "And I love her. So this visit is really important to me. I want us to get to know each other and hopefully begin to carve out a relationship. I know you're grown, so I'll follow your lead."

Sean nodded. It had been only the two of them for a long time, but he didn't want his Mother to be alone. She deserves someone to love and someone to take care of her; not that she couldn't take care of herself, but she'd done it for so long. He imagined she must be tired. Sean pulled up to a bakery that she liked. He put the car in park and turned off the ignition.

He looked at Anthony. "My Mom deserves everything and I want her to have it. I want to know that you're willing to give her that, nothing less."

Anthony appreciated Sean's honesty and willingness to speak up. He was definitely Shane's son. He smiled.

"That is exactly what I want to give her, everything."

"Aight then. What's for dessert?"

When they got back to the house, Shane was asleep in the parlor. A journal was lying on her stomach and her empty wine glass was on the coffee table. Sean took the apple pie into the kitchen. Anthony shook her gently. Her eyes fluttered open as Anthony stroked her hair.

"Shane."

"Heyyy. What time is it?"

"It's 8 o'clock. We got an apple pie from a bakery that you like."

"Ooooh. That's my splurge place. You must be trying to get on my good side!"

"Always." Anthony kissed her cheek.

"Oh, you can do better than that!"

Anthony leaned down and kissed her, lightly biting her lower lip. "How was that?"

"Better."

Sean talked loudly announcing himself. "Should I put the pie in the fridge or are you going to have some?" He appeared in the doorway between the parlor and the living room.

"I think I'll have just a little piece."

Sean laughed. He knew what that meant. "Okay. I'll put it in the oven for a few."

The three of them ate apple pie a la mode in the parlor. Shane had a refill of her wine. Anthony and Sean drank coffee, black. Yuck as far as Shane was concerned. Sean had pulled out the chess board and he and Anthony were locked in battle. There were periods of silence and deep concentration. Sean's brow was furrowed.

Shane knew better than to interrupt their strategic thoughts with conversation. "Pardon the interruption, but gentlemen I am going to bed."

Sean grunted and Anthony nodded his head slightly. Who knows how long they'd be at it, Shane thought. They didn't need an audience. She rose off the couch and waved.

The next morning Sean was off to his internship. Shane and Anthony had the day to themselves. She decided to take him to her favorite museum. She'd been in the house a lot lately, working in the studio. It was good to get out.

The sun was high and bright and she was with her love. After the museum, they decided to go to The Magnificent Mile and gawk at the tall, intricate buildings. They stood in front of store windows like curious children and walked down the busy sidewalks holding hands.

Then, they had a decadent lunch at her favorite soul food joint. Shane went for the meatloaf and mashed potatoes with a side of fried cabbage. It came with buttery, sweet cornbread. Anthony had fried, bone-in trout, potato salad and collard greens. He put hot sauce on everything! For dessert, they shared a serving of banana pudding.

"You know how to enjoy good food," remarked Anthony.

"That's cuz I'm a real woman."

After they paid the check, they sat and enjoyed the view for a while, taking in the skyline.

"Okay, now let's walk this off!" And they headed toward the Navy Pier and everything in between.

It was late when they got in. They found Sean dancing in the kitchen, lost in the music. He had earbuds in and didn't notice them. Shane tapped his shoulder. He turned and tapped one of his earbuds.

"Hey, what's up Ma? Ant, what's going on?"

"Whatchu listening to?"

"One of my playlists."

"I see you enjoyed the pie." The almost empty pie tin sat on the counter with one, maybe two slices left.

"Yeah, but I saved you some!... What did y'all do today?"

"Acted like tourists. We hit the Mag Mile, then the Pier. It was a beautiful day so I wanted to get out." Shane washed and dried her hands. She opened the cabinet and pulled out a plate.

"Sounds like y'all had fun! Oh yeah, Valencia stopped by not long after I got home. She left something for you. I put it on your desk."

"Oh. She's been working on a few more songs for her album. Maybe that's what she dropped off." Shane was enjoying a slice of the remaining pie.

"I'm not sure, but I know she is fine! Is she single?"

Shane shook her head. "Down boy. That's one of my work associates."

"So, I don't work wit her!" Shane gave him a look. "Ant, the girl is fine! You shoulda seen her."

"Nope. Don't try to pull me in your mess!" Anthony put up his hands and backed away.

"You're too young for her anyway," said Shane looking him up and down.

"Age ain't nuthin' but a number," Sean sang.

Shane started laughing. "Boy, go sit down somewhere!" She swatted his behind.

Her phone started to vibrate. It had actually been ringing most of the day, but she'd ignored it. Shane dug in her purse and answered it. "Imani, I've been trying to catch you girl!" She looked at Anthony. "Yeah, he's here…" She put up her index finger, then headed down the hall and walked upstairs.

"You should get comfortable. She's gonna be a minute!"

Anthony sat down at the island. "So how was your day? Your Mom tells me that you're interning for the summer."

"Yeah, at Uncle Bryan's firm! Today I met a few other architects and engineers on his staff… They were cool. They each explained their role at the firm and showed me a few projects that they're working on."

"Sounds like a cool gig," Anthony said, shaking his head. "You think it's something you might be interested in as a career?"

"Did my Mother ask you to talk to me?"

"Nah man! I'm just curious. She mentioned that you are excited… Just trying to get to know what interests you. Besides, you know if your Mom wants to know something, she'll come out and ask," he laughed loudly.

"Yeah, you right about that! My bad. I guess I'm trippin' a lil' bit… Lemme ask you something, did you always want to be a lawyer?"

"No. For a while, I wasn't sure what I wanted to do. I played basketball in college and majored in business administration. I kinda thought maybe I would do something in the sports industry." He paused. "But then, I took a few political science and business law courses and I began asking questions. I started wanting to know more about the constitution and the law and how it gets applied. I really thought I was going to go into civil rights law… But while I was in law school, I would go to networking events for Black law students and I met a few attorneys that represented athletes, musicians, actors, singers. I'd never considered the entertainment industry; I was intrigued and kind of fell into it. I interned with a firm and was mentored by one of its principals and the rest fell into place, I guess. I liked the work; it was challenging and exciting and I was good at it!"

Anthony stood up from his seat and walked around the island to wash his hands. He headed to the butler's pantry for a bottle of Brough Brothers whiskey and a glass.

He came back to the counter and poured his drink. He looked at Sean. "Sometimes, I wonder if I made the right choice. Should I have gone the civil rights route or some more noble pursuit?" He shrugged his shoulders. "I don't know."

"What I do know is that I was able to make a nice life for my wife and children. We were able to put our oldest through college and law school. We have two more that we have college funds set up for. My children will have no education debt hanging over them. I've lived a comfortable life. And when I no longer felt appreciated or seen, I opened my own practice." He took a sip of his drink and sat down. "And, it's how I met your Mother."

Anthony laughed. "I guess I gave you the long answer. It's okay to not know what you want to do with your life. You're young and it will probably change at least once. My advice is to be open to learning new things and to pick something that excites you."

Anthony stood back up. "I'm heading to the parlor. You coming or are you headed out?"

"I'll be there in a minute."

Sean hung back and wrapped the last piece of pie in foil and put it in the fridge. He switched his Bluetooth to pair with the house system and picked an old school R&B and Hip Hop channel. Then, he headed to the parlor.

"So what do you do when you're not at the internship? Is there a special young lady?"

"Nah," Sean shook his head. "It's a couple of shorties at school that caught my eye, but I'm chilling with that. I kick it with the fellas usually.

We have a few female friends that hang sometimes, but most of us grew up together. My Mom put me in a lot of extracurricular stuff when I was coming up, to keep me busy and I think so I wouldn't be lonely. I met a lot of folks like that and some of her friends had kids too, like Uncle Bryan."

"So what was it like growing up, just you and your Mom?"

"It was cool. We always spent a lot of time together. Even when she started getting busy in her career, she made time for me. I always had "aunties" and "uncles" around and my Grandma. We've traveled to a lot of countries and visited a lot of great places. I know she worried about me, especially since my Dad wasn't around, but I think she did a good job."

Anthony smiled at him. "Seems like she did. I have three children, one's grown but two are still in high school, Samuelle and Naaja. I hope they become as level headed as you are."

"Okay, what'd I miss?" Shane came charging into the room.

"Nothing. We just kickin' it. What's up with Auntie Imani?"

"Oh, nothing. Just catching up… I think we're going to throw a dinner party while you two are in town."

"Here we go!" Sean shook his head. "Ant, get ready. It's about to be a house full of weirdos and bougie people!"

Anthony laughed loudly.

Shane gasped. "Stop!"

"What? You know it's true Ma!"

Shane rolled her eyes. "Don't talk about my friends like that!" She sat down beside him. "I'm only inviting a few close friends to meet Anthony… and Sean, I thought you could invite some of your friends."

"Wait. Are you inviting that fine ass Valencia?"

"Watch your mouth!" Shane hit him with a pillow. "I'm not one of your boys."

"My bad! but is she coming?"

It was Anthony's last week in Chicago and the dinner party was set for the next night. Imani made all of the arrangements: she set the menu, reached out to a caterer, set up the decor and extended invitations. Shane was glad that she only had to show up to her party.

As promised, the guest list was smaller than usual and only included close friends of Shane and Sean. Robert flew in and Valencia was there as well. It was a low key affair with Spades tournaments, good food and good music. One of Shane and Imani's favorite joints catered with crispy, juicy fried chicken, mac and cheese, collard greens, grilled fish, fried cabbage, roasted sweet potatoes and blackberry cobbler.

Shane and Sean were partners as usual, setting a few folks with their prowess. Sean popped his high spade on the table.

"Bam! What y'all got?" There was a collective groan.

"I knew you had me partna," Shane cooed. "They never ready for us!" She cackled and winked at Sean.

"Who got next?" Sean asked, his eyebrow raised.

She heard Anthony's voice over the music and laughter. "Can I get everyone's attention?"

Shane looked up from the dining room table and noticed everyone coming into the room. The music paused and all eyes were on Anthony.

Sean stood up. "Thank you everyone for coming to meet Ant and to welcome me home for the summer. This year was kinda rugged so I thank all y'all that helped me along the way...." He looked from Robert to Bryan and Imani to Stephanie and some of his boys.

"But most of all, I want to thank my Mother." He smiled at her. "Ma, come here."

Shane smiled. She stood up and walked over to her son. He opened his long arms and wrapped her in an embrace. She hugged him and he lifted her off of her feet.

"Boy put me down!" she protested.

Sean let her down and Shane kissed him on the cheek. She looked around.

"Thank you for being our village. I'm so proud of this young man." Her voice trembled a little. "His accomplishments are because of your love and support for both of us. I also want to thank Imani for putting this together for me. I wanted to do something special, not just for Sean, but for Anthony too."

She reached her hand out for him to come to stand beside her and Sean. "I wanted Anthony to meet our family before he leaves."

Anthony sat his drink down on the table. "It's been great meeting all of you. Since I've been here, I see the great support system Shane and Sean have and that makes me happy. And before I leave, I'd like to share something with you."

He turned to look at Shane. "I love you… more than I can express. And I want everyone to know just how much." He briefly looked at Sean and winked. Then, he dug into his pocket and pulled out a box. Shane's eyes widened. Anthony opened the box and took out the most beautiful ring. He gave Sean the box and laid the ring in the palm of his hand.

"Marry me Shane."

Shane looked into his eyes as a tear crept down her cheek. She was overwhelmed, surprised and excited. Technically this was the first time anyone had proposed. Her thoughts about marriage had been complicated for a long time. But with Anthony, it was simple. "Yes."

# FOURTH VERSE

# The Recording Academy

The Recording Academy contacted Shane for a meeting. The big wigs want her to teach the MASTERclass annually. The Academy received an overwhelming response from her students via many unsolicited letters and the evaluations were better than they'd ever seen. Shane was tickled.

She hadn't planned on traveling to LA right now, but since it was on their dime Shane thought, what the hell. She would extend the trip to spend time with Anthony.

When she'd called Tonya to tell her about the proposal, she called on video. They were catching up when Tonya screamed so loud that Shane was sure that her eardrum ruptured.

"Bitch, what is that on your finger?"

"Oh… this?" And she raised her left hand so that it was centered on the screen.

"Aaaaah! He proposed! When did this happen? Why you just telling me? How'd he do it?"

"Okay which do you want me to answer first," Shane said laughing at Tonya's dramatics.

"All of it!"

Shane retold the story of the unexpected proposal at the get-together the previous night.

"So Sean knew and didn't say anything?"

"Not a word. He and Anthony had talked it over and planned it! I didn't see it coming."

"Wow! So Sean is good with Anthony?"

"Gurrrl! They're like Thing 1 and Thing 2. It's cute though… I'm happy." She smiled a radiant smile. "Wait, are you crying?"

"Yes! Cuz you deserve all of this! Ant betta do the damn thang! We need to come out there and meet this man!"

"Well c'mon cuz it's been a while! Let me know when…you know there's space at the Inn for y'all."

"Congratulations Sis! You wait 'til I tell Joe. I told him, Ant is the ONE!!!"

Gail and Chanté were less dramatic but just as tickled as Tonya. She'd told them together on their regular-ish video call. They'd asked a thousand questions and requested that Sean come to the screen so that they could get his take on the proposal and details on Anthony.

"So you approve nephew?" Gail asked looking over her designer frames.

"Yes Auntie. He's cool and he makes Ma happy."

"You're such a great boy, I mean young man!" Chanté exclaimed.

"So when are y'all setting a date?" asked Gail.

"Give me a second to catch my breath! One thing at a time."

⸻ ⚬ ⸻

Shane stared at the clouds through the tiny window. It was such a peaceful view. She sighed. When she returned to Chicago, top on her list was finding a new assistant. That's right. Her irreplaceable Stephanie was moving on…and to NYC. She and Tom were also engaged. Shane smiled when she thought of how they met their future husbands on the very same night. They had no expectations that evening except to have fun.

Stephanie had also made decisions about her career. She would remain an academic, which was her first love. She'd accepted a position as a part-time professor at Columbia University in its Behavioral Science department. It was a great fit for Stephanie; she'd still have time to dedicate to research, and to her new husband.

Shane's eyes brimmed with happiness for her. Stephanie's life was unfolding beautifully. But there was no substitute for Ms. Smarty Pants and she dreaded the search.

Anthony picked her up from the airport. He was her favorite, steamy cup of coffee. His embrace was warm and reassuring. He felt like home.

"How was the flight?"

"You know… it was a flight." Shane never particularly liked flying but had grown used to it. But she had to admit that first-class made it better.

"Are you hungry?"

"I could eat," she said grinning.

"Good cuz Dad put some stuff on the grill."

"I get to meet your Dad today?" Shane asked excitedly. She pulled down the visor to look at her reflection.

"You look beautiful as always." He lifted her hand and kissed it.

"And today, you get a double feature! Amir is at the house too, waiting to meet the great Shane Mathews."

"No pressure at all. You couldn't tell me this morning?"

"I didn't know this morning. This is spontaneous! And the kids will be over later."

"Okayyy. I really wanted to take a shower."

"You still can, but only if I can join you." He raised his eyebrows a few times.

"Anthony! Your family is there and I'm meeting them for the first time."

"And we're grown. You just can't be so loud!"

Shane dug her nails into his thigh and he hollered, knowing that he was the loud one.

As she walked into his enormous shower, she heard the bathroom doors open. A naked Anthony walked up behind her and licked from the base of her spine to the back of her neck. The barbecue would have to wait.

—§—

"Y'all should be good and clean," Amir remarked as they walked into the courtyard.

Shane's face flushed.

Anthony's Dad, Philip, swatted the air with a spatula in Amir's direction. His apron featured grill tongs and a barbecue fork in an X formation and read: Grillmaster, in large letters.

"Don't pay him no never mind. He's just jealous."

He turned to look at his grandson. "If you didn't work so much you'd find you some business. Then maybe you wouldn't be worried about your father's."

Anthony pointed at his Dad.

"Shane, what would you like? Steak, ribs or chicken?"

"I'll take a steak, please sir."

"Don't start that 'sir' foolishness with me. We family!" He walked over to the table. "And I hope you don't like all this newfangled cooking! I believe in cooking a steak proper, not with blood running all over your plate."

"Then you cook it just how I like," said Shane grinning widely.

"I marinated these steaks so it'll be juicy," he reassured her.

Anthony and Amir had disappeared into the house. They were gone for a little while. Shane wondered how the medicine tasted to Anthony now that Amir was serving it rather than Sean. Eventually, they came back with Anthony carrying bowls of potato salad, baked beans and tossed salad. Amir followed behind with baked sweet potatoes, cole slaw and condiments. The outdoor table was already set.

Anthony went back in for a platter and held it as Philip loaded it with grilled meats. Philip closed the top to the grill and hung the utensils on a hook at the far side of it. Then, he untied his smock apron and pulled it over his head. He threw it over an empty chair and took a seat between Shane and Anthony.

"Why don't you bless the table Amir?" His grandfather eyed him.

As everyone began to pass around the bowls and platters of food, Anthony stood up.

"Drinks. We need drinks. Shane, can you help me?"

"Okay, but y'all watch my plate!"

"I gotchu darlin!" Philip unfolded a napkin and gently placed it over Shane's waiting plate.

Once inside the kitchen, Shane turned to Anthony. "Okay, don't keep me in here long so I can get embarrassed in front of your father again!"

Anthony put his arms around her. "Not gonna happen. I spoke to Amir; I don't know what got into him."

"It was a bad first impression and we both know better!" Shane closed her eyes. Anthony kissed her cheeks.

"Let it go baby. You see my Dad isn't trippin'."

Shane exhaled and wriggled out of his embrace. She walked to the fridge and opened the door. "Oooh. Is this your famous lemonade?" She picked up the glass pitcher.

"Yes, honey and mint make all the difference! I'll get glasses and a bottle of wine. Are you okay with drinking wine from these or do you need a wine glass? I don't want to offend your delicate sensibilities."

"Don't mock me… That's fine. By the way, when are the kids getting here?"

"I don't know, a bit later."

They rejoined the men in the courtyard with the beverages. They ate, drank, laughed and the earlier tension was forgotten.

"Are we ready for some wine yet? I'd like to make a toast." Anthony went back inside for a corkscrew.

Philip turned to Shane. "I'll drink one glass for the toast but then I'm switching to bourbon. That's my drink."

Shane smiled as Anthony opened the wine bottle with a flourish. "I don't have any champagne so this wine will have to do." He poured wine in each of the drinking glasses and passed them around.

"I'd like to toast to my beautiful fiancée. Thank you for saying yes and I'm so glad that you are finally meeting the rest of the Dekra clan." Shane beamed and the four clinked glasses. She noticed that Amir's smile didn't quite reach his eyes.

Shane took a large sip of wine. "Thank you Anthony. I'm so glad to be here. I wish Sean could've made it, but he didn't want to miss time from his internship."

"So Shane, you're here for business?" asked Amir.

"Oh yes. I just have one meeting and a contract to sign. I'll be teaching an annual class in Santa Monica."

"What type of class?"

"A songwriting class."

"A MASTERClass," said Anthony. Shane nodded her head.

"So who gets to take this MASTERClass?" asked Amir looking at her.

"People apply and get selected by a committee."

"Is it a free class?"

"No, it's not. However, the contract that I'm here to sign has a stipulation that for every class that I teach in LA, there will be another class offered annually in Chicago which is at no cost to the public."

"Well, how does that work?"

"I will subsidize 50 percent of the cost and the organization will match those funds. But students will still need to apply."

"So what are the selection criteria for students?"

"Okay, okay! Enough work talk," announced Anthony.

"Thank you!" agreed Philip.

"What? Dad, I'm just trying to get to know Shane."

"It sounded more like an interrogation."

"Indeed. Shane, excuse me while I get my bourbon."

Shane smiled, then took Anthony's hand. "It's fine Anthony."

Samuelle and Naaja brought levity to the gathering with their stories and teenage drama. There was a variety show fundraiser coming up and both were participating: Samuelle with a stand-up comedy routine and Naaja with a modern dance number.

"So are you ready for the show?" his father asked, looking from one to the other.

"I stay ready!" replied Naaja.

Shane snapped her fingers. "Well alright then!" She and Naaja giggled.

"Samuelle? Are you gonna bless us with a preview?"

"Naw Dad! I want it to be fresh material for the entire audience." He looked at Shane. "Will you be here for my show?"

"When is it?"

"In three weeks."

Shane shook her head. "No, I'm sorry Samuelle. I have to get back; I'm only here for a week this time."

"So have you two set a date?" Philip asked from the kitchen counter overlooking them sitting in the living room.

Anthony and Shane looked at each other. "No we haven't," answered Anthony. "I guess we need to sit down and discuss it."

Well, where's it going to be, here or Chicago?" asked Naaja.

Shane shrugged. "I guess we have a lot of decisions to make."

"Can I see the ring?" Shane raised her hand to Naaja who oohed and aahed. "My Daddy has good taste." she said approvingly.

"I agree," said Shane.

Amir cleared his throat. Anthony glared at him.

The kids seemed oblivious to the slight. "Shane. How old is your son?" asked Naaja.

"Sean is 19," Shane tried to sound unaffected as she tried to recover.

"Ooooh! I get another big brother!" Naaja looked over and rolled her eyes at Amir.

"Ok. It's getting late." The protests began. "You two can come stay over this weekend, but you need to get home before your mother starts calling. Amir can drop you."

Samuelle made a beeline for the kitchen to make a plate. Naaja and Shane were talking low and laughing from the couch.

"Can I talk to you for a moment outside?" Anthony's voice was low and tight as he spoke to his son.

Philip waved his hand. "Before you go, I have something to say."

Anthony turned to see his Dad stand up from the counter chair.

"When we lost you all's Grandmother, I didn't think I could go on... it's still hard not having Mae here," he said slowly. "Losing her is the hardest thing that I've had to endure but my family helps me heal." He paused for a long moment.

"When your parents split up, I saw that kind of pain in your father. He wondered what went wrong and thought he'd failed all of you somehow. Mae and I consoled him many times until he was strong." He looked around at his grandchildren. "Experiencing the loss of a loved one is devastating, doesn't matter what kind of loss..." He walked to where Anthony and Amir stood.

"Son, I am so happy that you have found someone to spend your life with! Your smile and the way you look at Shane makes me glad." He patted Anthony's back, then he looked at Amir.

"Whatever you're feeling Amir, you need to name it and wrestle it. You have not lived enough to understand true partnership and loss. But that is no excuse for your behavior and I would not be doing my job if I don't call you on it. Understand that it stops here!"

The room was silent and all eyes were on Philip. "Kids, I'll see you soon. Shane, it was lovely to meet you darlin'. Anthony and Amir, good night. I'm going to my room." He grabbed his drink from the counter and walked down the hall.

Shane was up early for her meeting. It was in LA, so she was driving one of Anthony's cars. When she got downstairs, there was a note on the fridge for her. "Eat! Look inside." scrawled in Anthony's writing. He'd made her a fruit bowl with Greek yogurt and granola on the side. She smiled. He knew that she would fly out of there without breakfast, vowing to grab something on the way which meant coffee.

She sat down at the dining room table and ate her breakfast. Shane was visualizing the meeting when Philip interrupted her.

"Good morning!"

She smiled and kissed his cheek as he sat down. "Good morning Philip!"

"It is!" he acknowledged. "Are you ready for your meeting?"

"Yes I am. It should be an easy one and hopefully short."

"Well don't let me keep you. I'll be here when you get back!"

Shane had her contract lawyer colleague give the contract a once over before she arrived in LA. The contract was for three years with an option to renew. Sitting in an opulent conference room, Shane reviewed her stipulations that she'd sent over the week prior, with the group.

1. The Academy would secure the same house for her, if possible.
2. She would teach two per year; the second would be held in Chicago.
3. The Chicago class would be free. Shane would subsidize 50 percent of the cost and the Academy would match the funds. Students would still need to apply.
4. Shane would recruit Black and Brown writers to fill half of the slots. The class would be a recipient of scholarship dollars from the Academy's philanthropic activities.

They agreed to her terms.

Once she left the meeting, she checked her phone before she left the parking garage. There was a text from Grover: When are y'all free for dinner? Anthony undoubtedly told him that she was coming to town.

Shane texted him back: Let me talk to Anthony and get back to you. Then she thought to call Sean but decided to text since he was at his internship.

Hey, just wanted to say hi. Call me later. 🖤🖤

When she returned to Anthony's, Philip was in the courtyard enjoying the sun. He was lying on a chair next to the pool.

He looked up when she opened the sliding glass doors. "How'd it go? Did you get everything?"

She smiled. "I did! I'm so excited! I'm already thinking of ways to recruit people to the Chicago class. We need better representation in songwriting from Black and Brown writers. We have plenty of singers, but not enough writers."

He appreciated her passion. "Writing is where the money's at, isn't it? Unless you're an artist who does those huge tours, right?"

Shane raised her eyebrow. "Right."

"I know a lil' sump'in, sump'in." He smiled and closed his eyes.

She sat down on a nearby chair. "Philip. Thank you for what you said last night… It meant a lot to me, to us."

"Don't mention it. Life is short. I'm not biting my tongue. Amir is young and dumb, but he'll get it together!"

"Have you eaten?" At that, he opened his eyes. "I had breakfast. Why?"

"Cuz I'm fixing us lunch. First, I gotta see what your son has in here."

Shane found some leftover grilled chicken and a few baked sweet potatoes. In the fridge's vegetable bin, she found a head of cabbage. She also took out an egg and a stick of butter. After gathering the necessary tools: souffle cups, mixing bowl, whisk, cutting board and a knife, she turned on the oven.

She went to a cabinet and brought out two glasses. There was just enough lemonade left for the two of them. Shane poured and sat the drinks on the counter.

After scooping the flesh of the sweet potatoes into the bowl, she mashed them. She added brown sugar, cream, an egg, vanilla and softened butter to the bowl and whisked it into a thick, smooth batter. She poured it into three souffle cups.

Philip sat at the island watching her work. "You look like you know what you're doin'! Mae was a baker, so I know."

Shane looked up and rewarded him with a smile.

She checked the pantry and found a canister of flour. She just needed a little. Since Anthony had no pecans, she'd make a streusel for the top of the souffles. She reserved a little of the softened butter so she tossed it with brown sugar and a tablespoon of flour. She sprinkled the crumbly mix onto the souffles.

After Shane chopped the head of cabbage, the oven beeped letting her know that it was up to temperature. She carefully placed the cups on a baking sheet and slid it into the oven. Back in the pantry, she found some veggie broth and a few onions.

"Philip, could you grab a frying pan for me?"

"Sure darlin'." He walked into the dining room and brought a heavy bottomed frying pan from a base cabinet.

Shane put the pan on the range. Back at the counter, she sliced an onion. Then, she returned to the range and turned on the burner. After a minute or two, she swirled olive oil into the pan. She let the oil heat, then tossed in the sliced onions. They softened a bit and she sprinkled them with kosher salt and ground black pepper. When they began to brown on the edges, she added the chopped cabbage and sprinkled in Adobo seasoning, onion powder and a dash of cayenne.

When the cabbage began to crackle, she turned it in the pan. After all sides began to caramelize, she added the broth keeping the burner high. Once some of the liquid cooked off, she turned it down and put a top over it.

"So are y'all gonna have one of those long engagements? Cuz I'm not getting any younger!"

Shane snickered. "Neither am I," she answered as she put two chicken breasts wrapped in foil into the second oven.

"Well you two have to slow down long enough to plan a wedding. I know Anthony stays busy with work and you too, I hear."

"Well since we work for ourselves, we can choose to slow down."

The two of them sat at the enormous wooden dining table for lunch. "I see you know your way around a kitchen, Shane!" exclaimed Philip as he ate another forkful of souffle. "Ooowee! Where you been hiding that some fool didn't scoop you up?"

"Nowhere… I was just waiting for the right one to find me!" She laughed.

When Anthony got home, he found the two of them going through old photo albums, listening to his vintage record collection. Philip was narrating the milestones of his family's photographs. There were sepia pictures of he and Mae as youngsters; black and whites of their pre-teen antics; high school graduation pictures in color and wedding pictures, family pictures, pictures of the boys as children and on and on.

Shane was studying Anthony's high school cap and gown picture. He had a light mustache, a full head of hair and a serious look on his face.

"I see y'all have been strolling down memory lane." Anthony leaned over the back of the couch and kissed Shane's forehead.

"You were so handsome!" Shane ran her fingers over the plastic covered page.

"As in past tense? As in not anymore?" He asked walking around to sit beside her.

She looked up at him. "You aight," she said, tilting her hand from side to side. Then she bust out laughing.

Philip sat in a club chair watching them, his head nodding to the O'Jays. "She used ta be my girrrrl! She used ta be my girrrl," sang Philip. "Not only good looking, the girl was so smart, can't beat her cookin', naw!"

"Aw shucks!" Shane turned her head toward Philip. She snapped her fingers and moved her shoulders and head to the music.

"Oh I could go back in the day… but don't chu go and try to get me in one of those booths!" He winked at Shane.

"You sure? Cuz you can come back to Chicago with me and we can record some tracks. You let me know!"

Philip cackled. "My singing days are behind me. And shoot, they ain't ready for me no way! Ha, haaa!" declared Philip, his voice rising. "I'm going to make myself a drink." He stood. "You want something honey?"

"No, I'm good Dad."

Philip sucked his teeth. "Ain't nobody talking to you boy." He waved Anthony off with his hand.

Shane closed the album and sat it on the low coffee table. She stood up. "You still drinking that nasty bourbon? You should let me fix you a real drink." Shane followed Philip out of the living room and headed toward the wet bar off the kitchen.

"I'll be here," Anthony called after them.

When they returned to the living room, Philip had a glass of his bourbon and Shane had a glass of wine.

"What's for dinner?" Philip asked, looking at Anthony. "Shane cooked lunch." Shane nodded and took a sip of her wine.

Anthony looked at the two of them, looking like partners in crime. "Well I don't know. I guess I better see about it." He headed to the kitchen, rolling up his sleeves. Anthony washed his hands at the sink while shaking his head.

"Oh, I saved you a sweet potato souffle. It's in the fridge. And honey, Grover asked when we could do dinner."

"Grover! Now that's a character!" Philip laughed and sat back down in his chair.

"That he is!" Shane cackled and sipped her wine.

⸺ ৪ ⸺

"So I guess we're officially over?" Grover looked at Shane from across the white linen-covered table.

"I think so," answered Shane.

"C'est dommage," he said woefully. He lifted a spoonful of creamy, lobster bisque to his lips and blew.

"And when are we thinking for the big day? I can put a band together so your music is tight." He looked at Anthony and sipped his bisque.

"We haven't come up with a date yet."

"Okay well, give me some notice so I can move things around if necessary." He put his spoon on the saucer.

"Lemme see that ring Shane!" she wriggled her finger at him. "Somebody's doing something right!"

Shane kicked him under the table.

"Oww shit, I meant Ant was doing right! Damn, that was my shin!"

"That's what you get for being nasty!"

Anthony laughed at the two of them and took a bite of his grilled halibut. After he finished chewing, he grew serious.

"Shane and I talked and we're thinking of a fall wedding."

"That soon? Okay, okay. Just get me a date as soon as you have one."

"The kids are going to be our wedding party, but we'd like you to have a special role in the ceremony." He paused. "Would you be my best man?"

Grover's wide smile answered his question. "I'd be honored brother!" He stood up and walked to the side of the table, pulling Anthony to his feet. He grabbed him in a bear hug. "I'm so happy for you! You got a good one man." he murmured.

He released him and grabbed Shane's hand. "Get ova here woman!"

He lifted her off the ground and kissed both cheeks. Shane squealed.

"We need champagne!" He left the table in search of the waiter.

⁓ ⸙ ⁓

Shane had hoped to do some surfing, but the stormy weather had other ideas.

"How am I gonna become any good if I don't get any practice?" pouted Shane.

"We have plenty of time to get you out on the water." Anthony put his arms around her. She was so cute when she pouted. "After we're married and you're here full time – "

"Whoa, who said I would be here full time? We haven't talked about that." Shane pushed his arms open so that she could look him in the eye.

"Oh… I thought, well I assumed that we'd be in LA."

"Why did you make that assumption?" Shane waited. "Because I'm the woman? I pick up my life and move?"

"I didn't say that Shane! Like you said, we haven't talked about it."

"Well I guess we should because I hadn't planned on leaving Chicago."

That weekend, Samuelle and Naaja stayed over as promised. It was nonstop music, video games and content creation for social. Shane joined the kids in the pool and listened to their dramatic stories about their friends. She loved that the house was so busy and alive. Sean would love this, she thought. Philip seemed tickled with the energy as well.

When they moved the party to the media room, Philip wished them a good night and went to bed. The four of them watched a double feature late into the night, *Black Panther* and *Wakanda* Forever, complete with buttery, salty popcorn, candy and drinks.

The surround sound was awesome making it a true theater

experience. Shane couldn't believe she stayed up for both movies. She needed to get some rest; she had to fly out the next evening.

"When will you be back?" Samuelle and Naaja asked almost in unison.

Shane smiled. "I'm not sure. I have a project to complete with an artist and some chapters to write. Your Dad and I will figure it out." We have a lot to figure out, she thought.

⸎

Sean was in a good routine. He had another six weeks at his internship. He'd decided to major in architecture and he was focused. He'd reviewed NYU's courses to map his next two years; Bryan and some of his staff suggested a few elective courses as well. He also shared his decision with Ant and appreciated the encouragement that he received.

His Mother had been back for about a week but had been keeping long hours in the studio with Valencia. When she wasn't logging studio time, she was writing. He'd find her in her window seat, staring into space with her journal in her lap and pen in hand or in her office, tapping away on her laptop.

He imagined that she wanted to get things off her plate so that she could focus on wedding planning. He knew that Auntie Tonya had been sending her venue options and trying to get her to commit to a date. Imani wanted her to schedule a session with a bridal salon to begin the search for a gown.

"Ma. When are you and Ant going to pick a date? You said you wanted a fall wedding. There's not going to be enough time."

Shane stopped typing and leaned back in her chair. She looked up at him.

"Yeah, about that. I talked to Anthony and told him that we should put the wedding off until next year."

"Why?"

"I have deadlines coming down on me and too much to do. Not to mention this extra course that I decided to teach. The first one is supposed to be this winter. I haven't even started planning for it."

"Then put that off... not your wedding."

Sean sat down in a chair next to her desk. "You always say that we make time for what's important. What could be more important than your wedding?" He waited for her to answer. When she didn't, he pressed.

"And what did Ant say about postponing?"

"He wants what I want."

"But what did he say?"

Shane sighed. "He would rather not postpone it."

"Ok then, don't. I'm here for a little longer, I can help... Let me know what you need."

Shane smiled. "I told Anthony that we can't possibly have a fall wedding and find a venue to accommodate us. He said we should have it at his house."

"Well let's do that! You said that you wanted a small ceremony."

Shane thought for a moment. She looked at her son who was willing to help plan their special day. He is really invested in this, she thought. She picked up her cell from her desk and dialed Anthony.

"Hey baby, you're on speaker. Sean is with me and we're talking about the wedding. Forget what I said... let's pick a fall date and have it at your place. It will make it that much more special."

Sean smiled and nodded.

"Are you sure that's what you want?" She could hear the excitement in Anthony's voice.

"Yes!" she laughed.

"Sean, my man! I don't know what you said but thank you!"

"Just doin' my part. Now y'all need to pick a date!"

"Do you have a minute? We can look at the calendar now," said Shane.

Anthony shared the new wedding details with his father and children. Sean did the same with Tonya and Imani; then, the three of them completed the invitation.

Sean worked with a local printer to get it out, given the short time frame.



Sean became the go-between for Shane with Tonya and Imani, who'd agreed to assist her with the wedding planning. Stephanie would've been her first choice but was busy putting the final touches on her own wedding. Shane and Ant would attend next month in Manhattan. The good news? Stephanie made her a duplicate of her wedding planning binder, so Shane had a template to follow. Best. (Former) Assistant. Ever.

Shane and Valencia had been working feverishly perfecting her songs and the sound of her first project. The label execs were extremely happy with the demo that she presented and gave the green light to begin production. However, they felt that it was missing a breakout song to use as the first single. As Valencia went to work recording the final product, she worried about writing an additional song.

"Shane, we dedicated so much time to this! Now that we have the go ahead, I don't wanna lose momentum."

Shane agreed that they needed to turn something around quickly. They went back to Valencia's trove of lyrics, but nothing was falling into place. They needed new material.

Shane was in her office working on new chapters when her business line rang. It was Robert. He'd been trying to reach her on her cell. It was on do not disturb. He was on his way over with an idea for Valencia's single.

She saw Robert from the window, pulling up to the house. Shane met him at the vestibule and they walked to the parlor.

"I didn't even know that you were in town."

"Yeah. I had a few meetings and a new artist to touch base with. How are you?"

"You know… busy as shit! Trying to finish the first draft of this memoir, plan a wedding and keep V pushing as we work on writing a single."

Robert sat down and motioned for her to join him.

"Shane, you already have a song… You should let Valencia record *Love at Second Sight*." Shane's heart constricted. "I think it should be her first single."

Years ago, Shane told Robert about the song and played a bare bones melody for him on the piano. She never considered selling that song. She looked at Robert.

"Okay, before you say anything, hear me out."

"Robert no!"

"Shane. You told me that you and Mike were the greatest love story never told… this is your chance to tell it!"

He took her hand. "Honey, it's time. This will help you to truly let go… Ant is waiting for you."

Shane sat with tears in her eyes. She sighed.

"Just let her play around with it. See how it feels."

"Let me think about it."

As usual, Robert was right. He usually didn't miss when it came to songs. It was made for Valencia: it was perfect for her tone and range. She took it and made it her own, writing the arrangement. It complemented her mezzo soprano voice and her phrasing was spot on.

The bridge that Valencia penned was spectacular: she switched to a relative key within the key signature and added a guitar solo. Shane reached out to Tom for musician recommendations. Valencia and Tom met and it turns out he was the man for the job; weeks after he and Steph's wedding, he recorded his solo in New York. His bass solo was plaintive and passionate at once.

The producer put his masterful touches on it and the label released the single. It quickly went gold, then platinum, climbing the R&B and Pop charts. Barely making the deadline, the song was nominated for two GRAMMYs and Valencia herself was nominated for Best New Artist.

Shane was glad about the attention Valencia was receiving because of her one-of-a-kind talent. However, Shane was ambivalent and almost indifferent about the nominations. The GRAMMYs were notorious for pigeonholing Black and Brown artists and eliminating or "streamlining" categories so that such artists canceled each other out. That was one of the reasons she became a voting member and was so involved with The Recording Academy. She wanted to educate, affect change and promote representation.

Shane's work was behind the scenes. As a songwriter, her work spoke for itself. Great lyrics didn't have a color. I mean, people could pass on a song once they learned who wrote it, but it seldom happened. Many people knew her name, but most didn't know her. Some didn't even know she was a woman, and Shane was fine with that. She actually preferred it that way. However, she knew this memoir would take away much of her anonymity.

I'm luckier than most,
I have had three soulmates.
One was killed by his best friend's nephew,
The next was running from unseen demons
The last one, I didn't see coming.

I'm luckier than most,

I have had three soulmates.
Although the first one was snatched before he got to live, he changed
my life.
We were young and loved hard, thinking we'd have forever and a
day to get it right.

I'm luckier than most,
I have had three soulmates.
But time was never on our side.
The clock kept spinning and we thought
We would get in sync.
Life had other plans...

I'm luckier than most,
I've had three soulmates.
We stuttered at the start but your patience and clarity made me
forget my fear.
Our lives converged seamlessly and love blossomed naturally,
As though we were meant to be.

⁓

Imani made appointments with a few bridal salons. Tonya flew in to accompany them for Shane's "Say Yes to the Dress" journey. Surprisingly, Sean asked to be included. Shane had been researching the types of gown silhouettes, necklines and fabrics. She knew which types the experts said were best for her body type. She was hopeful that the salon professional and the actual fit would lead her to the right gown.

At the first salon, Shane was nervous as she walked through the racks of gowns with her loved ones and the consultant, trying to select a few to try. It was a small boutique and didn't have many that caught Shane's eye. After trying on two gowns, neither of which were her preferred silhouette, she thanked the consultant for her time and they moved on to the next salon on the list, Jump the Broom.

This salon was larger and Black-owned. The ambience was tranquil and beautiful. Still nervous, Shane answered the consultant's questions and told her which silhouettes she wanted to try.

"But I'm open to suggestions and will lean on your expertise," she added.

Tracey, her gown consultant, was a busty, smiling woman. Her hair was in an intricate, french braid crown and her flowy, lavender dress fluttered around her, as she greeted the group. She wore Crocs and had what looked like over-sized clothes pins, hanging from the hem of her dress and pinned down one sleeve. She also had a straight pin cushion around her left wrist.

"Okay Shane. I want you to take your time and enjoy the process. Today is about you, so let's have some fun!"

Her demeanor was joyous. Not only did she have a different energy than the previous location, she had a different strategy.

"I'd like to divide you into two groups. Ladies and Sean, you look through the showroom to see what you might want Shane to try. I'll take the bride-to-be with me to do a separate perusal of the gowns."

Tonya, Imani and Sean decided to each pick one gown. Then, they would deliberate to see if it made the cut for Shane. Sean saw a few that he liked and imagined his Mom wearing them; he decided to only show two to his Aunties. Once they collectively decided on three, they put them into the fitting room to which Shane was assigned. A placard bearing her name was on the door.

Meanwhile, Tracey and Shane found four to try. An A-line, two Trumpets and finally a ball gown which Tracey had talked her into. Shane confided that she was nervous.

"I'm used to being in the background, not having all eyes on me. To do this, I need to absolutely love the way I look in this dress. And I need to be comfortable!"

The selected seven gowns were different shades: white, cream, antique white and even a pale blush. Shane hated trying on clothes but packed her patience. She wanted to do as Tracey suggested: enjoy this experience. Maybe I should've smoked a jay, she thought.

As the trio waited to see the first selection, they were offered cookies, delicate pastries and finger sandwiches. There was also tea which was delicious and champagne, of course. Because it was a special occasion, they allowed Sean to have one glass.

"Just ONE. We don't need you cuttin' up in here, embarrassing us boy!" said Tonya.

Shane walked out into the gallery wearing the first dress. She climbed three short steps and onto a platform, facing a mirror with several angles. It was cream-colored with a beautiful lace overlay.

"This gown has a Trumpet silhouette with a sweetheart neckline," explained Tracey. "The trumpet is great for an hourglass body type like Shane's because it flaunts the curves. See how the bodice is relatively straight to the hips, then begins to flare at the middle of her thigh?" She shadowed her hand along Shane's hip area. "Also, this type of neckline flatters her collarbone and elongates the neck."

"It's a beautiful dress," exclaimed Imani.

"It is," said Tonya tentatively.

"But not for me," finished Shane.

"Nah," said Sean.

Shane walked down the platform steps and back to the fitting room. It was a lovely gown, but didn't feel like hers. It took about seven minutes to take off and another five to put the next one on. This was a white slip gown with a lacy bodice and Queen Anne neckline. This had to be Tonya's pick.

When she walked into the gallery, Tonya piped up. I knew it, thought Shane. "Ooooh. Look at this!"

Shane climbed up to the platform. She turned slowly so they could see the different angles. As she looked in the mirror, her reflection confirmed that this was not her gown.

"Tonya, I can't wear something like this. My mid-section can't pull this off."

"But you look beautiful. And I like the white on you better than the cream color."

"I agree about the color," said Imani. "But Shane is right. This silhouette isn't right for her."

Tracey interjected. "The slip is usually for a taller bride that has a slimmer frame."

"I like the top part," offered Sean.

"You have great taste," Tracey said looking at Sean. "This is a Queen Anne neckline. It is delicate and romantic and it highlights your Mom's beautiful face."

"This is a no," confirmed Shane.

Two down, five to go.

The next gown was another Trumpet silhouette with a deep V neckline. This one was a pale blush color. Shane was surprised that she actually liked the color; she also liked the deep V.

This time when she entered the gallery, she heard a gasp.

"I like this one!" exclaimed Imani, then she giggled realizing how loud she was. Someone had had a few glasses of champagne. Imani self-consciously combed her auburn hair behind her ear and crossed her legs. She watched Shane on the platform turning slowly. Her hazel eyes narrowed, studying the details of the gown.

"Me too," remarked Sean. "It's different… unique like you Ma."

"This one is also a Trumpet but the flare is more subtle than the first one," explained Tracey. "Also, the bodice is more structured." She looked at the three of them. "What do you think about this one? Shane, what do you think?"

"Turn around!" ordered Tonya. She walked up beside the platform. Shane was looking in the mirror, smoothing the dress across her abdomen. Tonya looked at Shane's reflection and caught her eye in the mirror.

"So what do you think?" Tonya asked her softly. "Is this your dress?"

Shane shrugged, then sighed. "I like it a lot, but I don't know…"

"Next!" yelled Tonya, returning to her seat and grabbing a mini sandwich.

"Well now, wait a minute-" Imani started.

"Nope. She said 'she likes it' and 'she don't know'," said Tonya with air quotes. "This ain't the dress! She's gotta feel it."

"She's right," agreed Tracey. "You gotta be all in," she said looking at Shane.

She held the short train as Shane descended the steps.

As Tracey helped her out of the gown, she asked,"So when's the big day?"

"November 10th. I've never been married so this is all very new. But I haven't felt so sure about anything in a very long time," she said smiling.

Tracey smiled. "The wedding is exciting, but it's the marriage that counts. My husband and I just celebrated our 20th anniversary… he's the best decision I ever made." Her eyes shined.

"Do you have any advice for a wife-to-be?" Shane asked eagerly.

Tracey thought for a moment. "Always be yourself. I probably don't need to tell you that because you're not one of these twenty-somethings so eager to please a man. But… if he fell in love with the real you…" She looked at Shane's reflection as she helped her into the next gown. "It's he, right?"

"Yes, Anthony." Shane laughed.

"Okay, well I wanted to check. I don't wanna make assumptions! Anyway, if he fell in love with the real you, then stay you. He can handle it."

Shane looked in the mirror. She was wearing an antique white, ball gown with a portrait neckline, which fell off the shoulders but covered the top of her arms. "Yikes! I look like the toilet tissue doll that my Grandma used to have in the bathroom."

"PA HAAA HAAAAA!" Her distinct laugh startled Shane, then made her howl. Tracey was trying to gather herself, then she snorted and that sent them both over the edge. "PAH HAAAAAA!!!"

"Oooh girl, I'ma bust this dress!" shrieked Shane.

There was a rap on the door. "Are y'all okay?" Imani asked.

It took a minute for either of them to catch their breath. Wiping her eyes, Tracey finally replied, "yes, we're fine. Shane's gonna pass on showing this one!"

Once the laughter subsided, she peeled Shane out of the gown. Next up was a cream A-line that Shane picked out. It had a Scoop neckline. She wasn't in love with the color, but she really liked the silhouette. Tracey used a few of the over sized pins to nip and tuck the bodice of the dress.

When Shane walked out this time, she was beaming. She carefully lifted the front of the dress as she climbed the steps.

Sean whistled.

"Oh Shane!" Tonya had tears in her eyes.

"Now this is the right cut for you!" said Imani emphatically.

Shane looked in the mirror. The neckline was demure but sexy at the same time. The high waist was working for her, minimizing her midsection.

Tracey agreed. "This looks good on you Shane. It hugs in all the right places and the flare makes it comfortable. How do you feel?"

Shane turned to look at the girls and Sean, her eyebrow raised. "I actually kinda love it but not the color."

"I can check to see if the designer makes it in white… It'll take a few minutes. Do you want me to check?"

Shane nodded.

"I'll be right back," said Sean. And he quickly left the gallery.

"Where's he going?" asked Shane.

"Maybe to the restroom," Tonya shrugged.

"I hope he's not feeling sick from the champagne," said Imani.

Shane sucked her teeth. "Gurrl please! He can handle one drink. You think that boy doesn't drink at school?!"

A few minutes later, Sean intercepted Tracey before she returned to the group.

"Ma'am. This is one of the dresses that I put back before I showed anyone. Have my Mom try it on."

"Okay but I have information on that other gown."

"Just put this one in the fitting room and have her try it. Tell her you're waiting for someone to get back to you." Sean pushed the hanger to the plastic garment bag into her hands. "Please."

Back in the dressing room, Tracey helped Shane to take off her favorite gown and hung it on a waiting hook. "While we wait for an answer, let's try this one. It's another A-line."

This one was white and very different from the previous gown. Once Tracey closed the zipper and fluffed the skirt, she noticed Shane's reflection: tears welled in her eyes.

"Where'd this one come from?"

Tracey didn't answer but opened the fitting room door. "Let's show your family your wedding dress." She smiled and nodded at Shane.

Shane walked into the gallery with tears rolling down her cheeks. She didn't know why she was so emotional. Sean watched as his Mom approached them. Imani had her back turned, picking out another cookie from the tray. Tonya gasped.

"Oh God, this is the dress!" Tonya put her hand to her mouth.

Imani turned around and smiled a big smile.

"Who picked this out?" Shane looked at the two of them.

"Actually, your son brought it to me as I was coming from the office. Let's get you on the platform so we can get the best view."

Sean smiled as his Mother walked up the steps. She looked beautiful.

Shane looked in the mirror, then turned to look at everyone. "This is my dress!"

# Mrs. Dekra

I have a wedding to finish planning! This is too personal and important for someone else to manage all of the details, Shane thought as she opened her eyes and looked at her bedroom ceiling. Now that she was finished with her projects, she wanted her hands in every aspect. She, Tonya and Imani would divide and conquer. Sean was back in New York and he needed to focus on his classes; she and her girls had this under control.

Shane wanted a small and intimate wedding. Only their close friends and some family would attend. The guest list was at 22, not including the bride, groom and wedding party.

She pulled back the down comforter and put her feet on the wool rug. Then, she walked to her closet and opened a bureau drawer, pulling out a yoga tank and pants. Shane always had a lot of moving parts to manage, but she was proud that she'd kept up her yoga practice. It was her time to reset and get centered.

After her session, she jumped in the shower and went downstairs to fix a smoothie. She sipped the banana strawberry smoothie as she walked back up to her office. She opened the planning binder on her desk. Shane recently created a Gantt chart that included tasks divided by categories within a timeline. It correlated to a project that she'd created using software. Also, the tabs in the binder coincided with the categories: music, flowers, photography, decor, catering. Time to delegate. She slurped the last remnants of her smoothie and put the empty tumbler on the desk.

It was still early, but she wanted to get started. I'll see if I can get them on a call, she thought. Maybe a video conference but decided against it. Besides, both of them were at work. She dialed Imani first.

"Hey babe, what's happening?" Imani answered on the first ring.

"I wanted to touch base with you all about these wedding tasks. Do you have about 15 minutes or should I try this again later?"

"No, it's cool."

"Okay, let me get Tonya on the line."

"Wassup ladies!" chirped Tonya. "Is this a wedding coordination call?"

"Ya know it!" answered Shane.

"Okay, let me close my office door."

"You all have the timeline document that I created, right?"

"Yes girl. You know to be a creative you are such an egghead!"

"Don't mock my organizational skills!"

"Okay, okay let's focus," Imani interjected.

"Yes. I'll talk to Grover about the music. I'm sure he has a whole vision, but may need some reining in. I'm also going to see if he can help me with the catering. Lord knows he's been to every restaurant and event in LA so he'll be a good resource. I just have to touch base with Anthony to see if he has a preference in cuisine." Shane paused.

"Imani, I think you should take decor which includes everything that the guests will see when they arrive at Anthony's property."

"Tonya, you have photography, rehearsals and flowers. With regard to flowers, I'd like you to tag team with Imani on that for obvious reasons. I'm going to put Anthony in charge of accommodations for our out-of-town guests."

"What about the wedding party? Who is managing those details," asked Tonya. "Their attire and fittings?"

"I think I'll take that on. Since the party consists of our children, plus Grover, I think that makes the most sense."

"Do you know if Amir is going to participate?" Tonya asked gently. "Has Anthony asked him about it?"

"I still don't know… but I know his Mother wanted to speak with him about it."

"Really?" said Imani, her voice rising. "Good for her! I like her and I don't even know her. What's her name?"

"Simone. She and her husband, Greg, will be at the wedding."

"We need to have a drink with her," Tonya chimed in.

"Indeed," remarked Imani.

"Yes. I haven't met her yet but I'm looking forward to it." Shane circled back to the wedding party. "Since it's an all male wedding party except Naaja, I'm going to focus on her. Anthony can help the men select something that will complement what he's wearing."

"Okay, before we get off I'd like to schedule a weekly call moving forward. Is there a day and time that works for y'all? We can email or text in between or as needed but I'd like to have a regular meeting to review action items and the timeline."

"What about Mondays?" Tonya offered. "That way we can report our progress from the previous week."

"Works for me," agreed Imani.

<hr>

Shane had an upcoming appointment for her first fitting at Jump the Broom. Imani offered to go with her but she chose to go solo. She wanted to have an element of surprise at the wedding. Tracey received her in the lobby.

"How is the bride-to-be?" she said, embracing Shane.

"Good. Busy, trying to keep my shit together. It's a small wedding but it still requires all the things!"

"Your ladies aren't helping you?"

"Yes, of course they are. I just want to be involved in the details…
It's a lot."

"Well, today will be easy. Have a seat and I'll go get your gown."

A few minutes later, a young woman appeared with a cup of tea and
a vanilla scone. She sat it on a coffee table in front of Shane. "Tracey
will be with you shortly."

Shane nibbled on the scone and took a few sips of tea. The tea was
very good and warmed up her insides. It was already quite cold in
Chicago, not Shane's favorite weather. There was soft jazz piped
through the sound system otherwise it was pleasantly quiet. She started
to review tomorrow's to-do list in her head.

"Ready?"

Shane put the cup on top of the saucer sitting on the coffee table.
"I'm following you."

They entered a fitting room where the young woman who brought
her the tea was waiting. "Robin is going to assist us with the fitting
today. An additional set of eyes and hands is helpful so that we can
record any remaining alterations and carefully handle the gown. Our
seamstress will meet us in the gallery in a few minutes to look over the
fit and ask you a few questions."

When Shane looked in the mirror, her eyes began to sting. The dress
looked as if it was made just for her. It hugged her torso and amplified
her bosom. The A-line was delicate in its subtlety and flowed into a
slight train. All the details were there and the few slight changes that
she'd requested. Tracey helped her into the heels that she asked Shane
to bring to the fitting.

"The seamstress left some additional fabric on the inside of the
bodice and skirt in case she needs to let any out at your final fitting.
Our experience has shown us that brides sometimes gain a few pounds
and we like to be prepared."

Shane nodded her head.

"I want you to stand on this step so we can see how it falls."

Robin knelt beside her on the floor and measured the bottom hem in relation to the sole of Shane's shoes. Then, she measured the short train.

"Shane, do you like where the skirt of the gown falls?"

"Yes," was all she could manage. She was overwhelmed by her reflection.

Tracey smiled. "Okay, let's go into the gallery to meet the seamstress."

Shane expected someone older. The woman looked about 30 with short, bronze twists in her hair. Tape measure in hand, she wore a pin cushion on her wrist similar to the one that Tracey wore at their first meeting. The seamstress stood as Shane approached and walked a wide circle around her.

"How does it feel?" she asked, looking at the dress, not at Shane.

"It feels good."

"Are you happy with the length?"

"Yes, I am."

"So let's talk bustle. What type would you like?"

Shane was quiet and stared at her blankly. The young woman looked up at her.

"A bustle is what you see at the back of the gown once the bride is at the reception. It becomes part of the design of the dress and keeps the train out of the way so that she can move freely."

"Oh… I guess I never noticed one before. Is there a type that works best with this style of dress?"

"I would recommend a French bustle but that's up to you." The young woman looked at her and waited.

Shane looked at Tracey for help.

"Maya, can you explain the French bustle and why you would recommend that bustle type for this dress?"

"Okay. The French bustle or under bustle tucks part of the train under, creating what looks like a voluminous tier on the back of the dress. It adds a new detail to the back of the skirt of an A-line gown. It's different from a ballroom bustle that tucks the train under the existing hem, thus shortening the dress. An over bustle takes the train and tucks it over top of the dress so that it is pinned in the center back of the gown."

"Tracey, would you recommend the under-bustle?" Shane asked.

"Yes, I would. I think it is the best choice for this gown."

"Let's do it!"

Maya nodded and Robin took a note. She then approached Shane with the measuring tape, measuring her height, then stopping to measure some points at the back of the dress.

"I like to use ribbons rather than buttons or snaps for a french bustle. They are more secure. When you return for your final fitting, you'll need someone with you to learn how to tie your bustle."

Maya left once she finished her measurements. Shane looked at Tracey with a raised eyebrow as she exited the gallery. They walked back to the fitting room.

"She's an acquired taste," admitted Tracey. Robin laughed.

Shane raised an eyebrow. "I see."

As Shane looked at herself in the mirror, she smiled and thought about her husband-to-be. She would take his last name; it was an easy decision. She'd use Shane Mathews as her professional name.

"Are you sure?" he'd asked on what had become one of their marathon video calls. "I understand why you'd want to keep your last name, especially for business. You don't have to change it… I know you're mine." He'd winked at her.

"I want to… it's important to me."

"Well, okay then future Mrs. Dekra."

At the final gown fitting, Shane asked Robin to record Tracey tying the bustle.

"I just don't want anyone to see the final dress until the wedding," explained Shane.

Tracey made certain to go through the steps slowly and talk through the steps so that whomever tied the bustle after the ceremony would have a clear guide.

—⁂—

Anthony was in Chicago for a quick weekend trip to celebrate her birthday early. It was the last time they'd see each other before the wedding which was in three and half weeks.

"So what do you wanna do?" Anthony raised his eyebrows up and down.

Shane giggled. "Nothing. I want to stay in and relax."

"Got it. Relaxation it is. Are you hungry?"

"I could eat."

"I'm gonna head to the kitchen and whip something up!"

They sat at the kitchen island, eating dinner and making googly eyes at each other.

"I love you Anthony."

"And I love you Shane. I am so honored that soon you will be my wife." He smiled at her.

"Hey, have you guys finished your fittings?"

"Almost. I had Sean's suit sent to a shop in New York and he finished his fitting."

"So why almost?"

"Well." Anthony put down his fork and looked at her. "Amir decided not to be in the wedding. He'll be there…" Anthony added quickly. "But, he won't be a part of the ceremony." He sighed.

"Simone talked to him, but that's the decision he made. I don't know… I'm surprised…. But, as the oldest, he had his Mom and I together for the longest. He was a teenager when we split and it was harder on him. I guess his wounds haven't quite healed."

Shane stared at the counter. Anthony took her chin and lifted it.

"Shane. It's his issue to work through," he said softly. "I know it's not perfect, but our day will be! Besides, my Dad asked to take his place."

Shane smiled a weak smile. "Philip," she said.

"Yes, Philip. You have a new fan!" Anthony leaned in and kissed her lips and the tip of her nose.

The next night, Imani and Bryan brought over dinner from Shane's favorite Chinese spot. They had the best spring rolls! The four of them sat at the dining room table and ate family-style sharing Beef with Broccoli, Hunan Shrimp, Szechuan string beans, Singapore Noodles, Vegetable Fried Rice and spring rolls. She felt like she was going to burst.

"So are you ready Shane?" asked Bryan.

"Why are you only asking me?"

"Cuz you're the one that's never been married!" Imani punched him in the thigh.

"Well, since I've never been married, how can I really know the answer?... If you're asking if I'm having jitters or second thoughts, the answer is no. I love this man and plan to spend the rest of my life with him. So quit being a jerk!"

"My bad."

"That's your friend," remarked Imani, shaking her head while looking at Shane.

"So how's Yanni doing? This is her freshman year, right?" asked Anthony, changing the subject.

Bryan smiled. "She's doing well. You should ask how I'm doing! It's not easy having my baby girl away at school."

"Yeah, it'll be Naaja's turn next year… I'm not ready…."

"Men and their daughters," sighed Imani.

"Oh, I think it's sweet," said Shane. She looked at Bryan. "Yanni will be fine. She has a good head on her shoulders. She knows how to handle those bamas when they start sniffing around!" Shane laughed.

Bryan put his hand on his head. "What? Why would you say that Shane?"

"I'm messing with you Bry, calm down! Just giving you a hard time."

Anthony stood and began clearing the table. "Anyone want a drink or dessert?"

"Yeah. I'll take a drink or two!" Bryan shook his head at Shane and followed Anthony. She shrugged her shoulders.

"Y'all two…" sighed Imani.

Shane waved it off.

"Sooo, how are you feeling?" asked Imani, putting her hand over Shane's. Her creamy skin made Shane's look deep brown in comparison.

"I'm good, really good. Y'all stop worrying after me. This is an exciting time!"

"Okay, okay. So are we gonna get together before you fly out?"

"Ya know iiiit! Just the girls… I'll send something out. Can you help me?"

"You know I got you."

As promised, Shane sent an invite to Imani, V, Gail, Steph and Chanté for a Pajama Jammie Jam. She knew Tonya couldn't make it, but her friend promised to do something together when she reached LA. Chanté couldn't make it either; she was closing on a multi-million dollar deal that she'd been working on for a few months.

Steph and Gail were on the same flight and Imani volunteered to pick them up from the airport. When they arrived at the house, there was raucous laughter; Valencia and Shane had already finished a bottle of wine. The pair were in their PJs. Shane wore a turquoise satin set: a short sleeve, collared button down with white piping and matching wide-legged pants. V wore a similar pink satin set, with matching shorts.

Shane handed out fuzzy, slipper socks to everyone to keep their feet warm. The ladies dropped their luggage in the first floor guest room. They'd figure out sleeping arrangements later.

"Looks like y'all started without us!" Gail sucked her teeth.

"You'll just have to catch up!" retorted Shane. "Go put on your PJs ladies. We'll be here!" And she and V went back to their gossip session.

On the dining room table were treats from Shane's favorite bakery: oatmeal raisin and double chocolate chip cookies and a peach cobbler; bags of her favorite herb popcorn; dishes of roasted cashews; and multiple flavors of sundae syrup and toppings.

There were two gallons of ice cream in the freezer and Chicago deep dish pizza was on the way: one cheese, pepper and onion and one pepperoni, sausage and mushroom. And, of course, the bar was fully stocked as was the wine fridge.

I need to slow down on the wine, she thought. Shane hadn't eaten since earlier in the day. She'd grab a handful of cashews until the pizza was delivered.

Shane bear hugged Gail then Stephanie, then she introduced Valencia to Gail and Imani.

"So how are you Mrs. Juarez? Marriage looks good on you!" Stephanie beamed.

"Why yes, I'm great. You'll know soon enough!"

After the ladies freshened up, they grabbed snacks and joined them in front of the fireplace in the parlor. The doorbell interrupted their laughter.

"Oh good. Pizza's here!" Shane jogged down the hall to the foyer and opened the console table drawer for her wallet. After grabbing some bills, she opened one of the vestibule doors.

She took the steaming pizza boxes to the dining room and then stacked plates beside them. After choosing their slices, the group retired to the parlor again with their plates of gooey deep dish.

"So Shane, what are you looking forward to most?" asked Imani.

"I don't know… nothing big…. Just knowing he's there and he has my back. I mean, that's true now, but I imagine it will feel even more true." She took a sip of wine.

"So have y'all worked out the living situation?" Gail, of course.

"Kinda. We're going to keep splitting our time, at least until Sean finishes school. Then, we'll reevaluate. His kids are still in high school so I wouldn't want him to leave them. I never thought that I'd have a long-distance marriage but, then again, I never thought that I'd get married.... It's what's best for us right now."

Gail nodded her head.

"So where's the honeymoon?" asked Valencia.

"I don't know. It's a surprise!"

"Well how will you know what to pack?"

"Chile please. They ain't going nowhere that's cold! He knows better!" Imani yelled, pushing back her hair. They all laughed as Shane nodded.

"I'm glad to take this break," said Shane. "I haven't had a real break in a while, so I'm going to enjoy it!"

"Okay, but don't come back pregnant!" Valencia wagged her finger at Shane.

Shane laughed. "Oh, they'll be plenty of practice, but there are no more babies coming outta here!" She spread her legs in the air and pointed to her crotch.

Valencia laughed, spitting out some of her drink. "Oh shit, sorry Ma! Lemme get some napkins."

Shane cackled. "Y'all V is getting used to my mouth. We've only spent time in a professional capacity."

"Well shit. You better get ready if you're gonna be around!" said Gail, taking a sip of wine.

"Stop Gail! I'm not that bad."

"You're not that good either," snickered Gail.

"So is the memoir done?" asked Stephanie.

"Spoken like a true former assistant. The first draft…" Shane paused for effect. "is with the publisher!" She took a mini bow.

"Woohoo!" Imani yelled.

"Now, the editor will tear it up. But it's off my plate for now. Hey… where's the music?" Shane asked nobody in particular.

Stephanie picked up a remote from the mantle and turned the system on. It automatically synced to Shane's phone. It was queued to a mix of Reggae, GoGo, Jazz and everything in between.

"Have y'all heard V's album?" Shane looked around. "I'ma play you my favorite cut!" She went to grab her cell.

"Well why can't we hear it live?"

"Oh, well that's up to V.…"

They turned to her.

"Aight, I'll give y'all a lil' somethin'; but then I'm off the clock!"

Valencia stood in the center of the room, closed her eyes and sang the first verse of *Love At Second Sight*. There was a hush in the room.

"Dayum! Baby girl got some pipes!" Gail said appreciatively. "None of that studio voice shit you hear if you turn on the radio."

"WOW!!! We will say we knew you when!" Imani said, clapping.

"Thank you!" Valencia said, dipping into a dramatic bow.

"So are you excited?" asked Stephanie.

"Sooooo excited!" Valencia said, jumping up and down.

Shane smiled. "She has worked very hard. She has a lot to be proud of." She left the parlor briefly to retrieve something from the living room.

She returned brandishing a karaoke microphone. "Who's down?"

"Aw, c'mon after Valencia's performance?"

"That was work, this is play! Besides, this is my party…Get your asses up!"

They relocated to the living room where there was a huge TV screen. Shane and Imani go to the dining room bringing the snacks back with them.

"I'm gonna need more wine for dis," muttered Gail. She headed for the kitchen and grabbed two bottles from the wine fridge.

"Damn! Both of those for you or you sharing?" asked Imani giggling.

"I'm not sure yet," laughed Gail.

Shane pressed the remote and found a karaoke website.

"I'm first," she announced. "Someone please turn down the house lights!"

"Aw shit, Ma is about to perform!" yelled Valencia.

"And you know this… V you better be taking notes!" With that, Shane turned her back to the ladies.

When the music started, Shane dramatically spun to face them. She began slowly stalking toward them, making breathy sounds into the mic. "*If there's a cure for this, I don't want it, don't want it! If there's a remedy, I'll run from it, run from it!*" Shane flung her hair back and forth.

There was a lot of writhing on the floor (more Bey, Me Myself & I) but she was committed. Then she hopped up and started doing a Hustle-esque dance during the disco breakdown. "*I don't want no cure! I don't want no cure!*"

Shane began humping the air and followed up with sequential body rolls. She bowed and melted into hysterical laughter.

"BRAVO!" yelled Imani.

Gail whistled several times.

"Encore, encore," yelled Valencia.

"Okay professor." She stood up shakily and handed the mic to Stephanie. "You're up!"

<hr>

Shane flew to Burbank. The wedding was in four days. Tonya and Joe flew out the same day and they all shared a car to Anthony's.

"There's my Shanie!" boomed Joe.

He walked over and picked her up in a bear hug. "I'm so happy for you honey," he whispered in her ear. He put her down just as quickly as he'd swooped her up.

Imani, who'd been in town for the past week, came over later to go over final details.

"The guests will begin arriving tomorrow. The hotel block is full and I touched base with the site manager to ensure they are on top of it. Since both me and Anthony are staying there, that makes it easier to troubleshoot. Also, Anthony secured transportation for the guests. Five black cars are reserved, which includes one picking up from Simone's house."

"I've been to the cake shop and the design is beautiful. I can't wait to see everything come together!" Imani really was made for logistics and event planning. "The linens, tents, tableware, rental furniture and decor are all sublime. I've reviewed everything in-person."

She looked at Tonya. "Do you have an update to share or do you want me to?"

"You go on ahead. I'm just going to relax here on this sofa."

"Okay so the photographer will be here on the wedding day at noon. Shane, do you want to take photos before or after the wedding?

Shane shrugged her shoulders. Imani exhaled.

"How about he takes a few of you as we tend to you and you get dressed. The pictures of you and Anthony and the children will be taken after the ceremony while guests have cocktails and make their way to the tent."

"I also gave him a recommended shot sheet," interjected Tonya.

"Okay, good."

"Tonya said the florist will be here at eleven am to set up the arrangements. He has a copy of the layout for the ceremony space but we will be here just in case. And the rehearsal dinner? I don't have info on that." She looked at Tonya.

"The party will meet here at three to do a run through of the ceremony, including the minister. It should take about an hour. The dinner is at 7 pm at Barcelona in the Almeca Room. They will serve the dinner family style. It is reserved until ten. I told them that there would be a party of 26 because I wasn't sure if the dinner was limited to the wedding party or to all guests." She turned to Shane. "Let me know because I can adjust it until close of business tomorrow."

"I don't know if we need everyone there, but I would like Anthony's father and brothers as well as my Mother and sister, in addition to the wedding party."

"So, family only?" Tonya was already scrolling through her cell looking for the restaurant's contact. Shane was hesitant.

"It's not a judgment Shane, I'm just trying to clarify. It's your wedding, honey. It's whatever you want."

"I'm thinking… that means Grover will be the only non-family member there… That's a lot of pressure since everyone is just meeting. And that means that I should invite Amir too."

She looked around, thinking. "Let's invite all of the guests today. Ask them to RSVP by mid-day tomorrow so that we have a good number."

"Speaking of Grover, I touched base with him. The band will be here at noon. The caterers will be onsite at seven am. They will coordinate with the company that is bringing the tent and associated decor."

Imani sighed and closed the binder. "So, Shane, do you need anything?"

"No honey. Sit down and have a drink!"

"Can I get in on that?" Joe had been uncharacteristically quiet.

"Yeah. Let's go out to the courtyard and relax, unless y'all wanna head to the hotel?'

"Naw, we can chill for a while."

"Okay. The bar is over there. I'll see what I can rustle up from the kitchen."

The four of them enjoyed sun and laughter into the afternoon. Shane lounged in a chair and savored the moment. She had been going top speed trying to make it here. She wanted to enjoy her friends being altogether in one place and the love that represented.

Imani had a rental so Joe and Tonya left with her for the hotel. Sean wasn't going to be there until tomorrow afternoon Chanté was scheduled to arrive the next morning. She had the house to herself. I'm going to soak in the tub, watch some mindless TV then order something yummy to be delivered, she thought. The house was uncharacteristically quiet. She was used to Naaja and Samuelle entertaining them with their teenage antics and tales and Anthony's booming voice. Soon enough, she thought.

Shane picked Chanté up from the airport. As Shane pulled up to the curb in the arrivals area, she spotted her: tight, blue jeans, a lightweight, olive leather jacket and over sized shades. Her light brown hair was cut in a blunt bob and her long dimples welcomed Shane.

She jumped out of the car and ran to the curb, hugging and rocking with her friend. Chanté laughed and hugged her tightly.

"Look at you all Cali-style with the top down!"

"Yeah, but keep your jacket on because it's chilly once we pick up speed… Girl, let's go before the po-po roll through and give me a ticket!" Shane ran to the driver's side after dumping Chanté's bag into the backseat.

The music played and they were cackling over the wind, just like old times.

"It's so good to see you! You look good… happy…." Chanté said, giving her the once over.

"I feel good! And I'm excited. I haven't been this excited since I moved to Chicago and went into songwriting." She sighed. "I'm marrying a man who is truly my partner and the people I love most will be there to share it with us!" Tears welled in Shane's eyes and the wind blew them across her face. She wiped them away with the back of her hand.

Chanté smiled. "I am truly happy for you sister. So when do I get to meet him?"

"Not 'til the rehearsal dinner, that is if you're coming," said Shane hopeful.

"Girl I'ma be there with bells on! I'm all about you and this wedding."

Shane was glad to have Chanté to herself, if only for one day. She thought about going out to eat, but decided to stay in and cook. They could be comfortable and as loud and obnoxious as they wanted. And the drinks were free!

"So what's up with you?" Shane asked as they lounged in the media room. A random show was on in the background. She absently sipped from her glass of wine.

"Nothing much, just work. You know I closed that deal." Chanté clapped and started doing the snake. "Heyyyy, heyyy," she sang and moved her shoulders.

"That's right! Congratulations! I'm so sorry that I didn't reach out. I've been so wrapped up in my own shit."

"It's fine."

"No it's not. We've always been there for each other, especially to celebrate wins and I missed a big one!" She put her hand on Chanté's shoulder. "Please forgive me."

"Well okay, but don't let that shit happen again! You slippin'!" Chante grabbed a handful of herb popcorn and threw some kernels at Shane. "I can't wait to see Bryan! It's been a long time!"

"Yeah and you're going to love Imani."

"So y'all are tight, hunh?" Shane nodded her head. "You know in school everybody thought you and Bryan were gonna end up together… Did you ever get some a dat?"

"Chanté!" Shane's eyes bulged. "Girl no!"

"C'mon, you can tell me… With his fine, bow-legged ass!"

"No I did not!" She paused for a second. "You know I woulda told you if I did… Sometimes we used to flirt, but that's it!"

"Damn!" Chanté yelled.

"What?"

"I owe Gail $100!"

"Y'all made a bet?"

"Actually, I hounded her so bad, swearing that something happened and she couldn't talk me down. So I made a bet."

"That's what yo ass get!" Shane sucked her teeth, then giggled. Chanté rolled her eyes, then had to laugh at herself. And then, they laughed hard, for a long time. Shane was doubled over, then looked up at Chanté and erupted again. This was what it was always like with them. Hundreds of miles apart and years in between visits didn't diminish their bond.

Chanté took a sip of the margarita that she'd been nursing.

"You need to stop playin' with that drink too! Wastin' my good liquor!"

"You mean your man's liquor!"

She shrugged. "What's his is mine!" And the laughter erupted again. Once they caught their breath, Shane got serious. "How's Amber doing?"

"Girl, she's good. She's staying with her dad while I'm here. She wanted to come, but I needed a break. You know that single parent life!"

"Are things better at school?" A group of girls had been harassing Chanté's daughter for a few months before Amber finally told her Mom. When Amber got into a fight, the school called her parents in for a meeting. When she was threatened with expulsion, Amber spilled. Then it got real. Anyone who has met Chanté knows two things: 1) she has the gift of gab and 2) she's a little crazy.

"Yeah, those little bitches have laid off her. I thought I was gonna catch a case! Tryna talk to their simple Mamas didn't do any good. It just showed me where they get it from. I filed a formal bullying complaint with the school, the school district and charges with the police. Talking about expelling my daughter before you have all the facts. When people fuck around, they find out!"

Chanté took a swig of her lukewarm margarita. "So what we gettin' into while I'm here?"

"Girl, I don't have nuthin' for you besides a spa day and a rehearsal dinner."

Tonya had a spa day planned for the three of them the next day, followed by dinner with Joe that evening. Tonya and Chanté met many times over the years in DC, but hadn't seen each other since Shane relocated to Chicago.

"Lemme find out you've gotten boring!" Chanté curled her lip in disgust.

Shane rolled her eyes. "How long are you here for? I'll have my boy Grover take you out. He's the king of LA!"

"That's what I'm talking about!" Chanté rubbed her hands together.

"Just make sure it's AFTER the wedding! I'd like everyone to be present and functional."

———— ❧ ————

"Girl! I needed this!" exclaimed Chanté as she sipped herbal tea. The trio lounged by the pool in matching plush, white robes. "I've been working nonstop… but then you know all about that Shane… You had to get married to take a break!" Chanté moved her leg as Shane swiped at it.

"I'll admit that my work has taken over my life somewhat." At this Tonya and Chanté looked at each other. "BUT, Anthony has helped me slow down or at least he's made me want to slow down." Shane blushed. "I mean, I didn't have much to do besides work. At least I love what I do!"

"Excuse me," Tonya got the attention of a spa staff member. "Can I get three glasses of champagne over here? My girl is getting married in 48 hours!"

"Tonya, it's early," said Shane.

"Girl, it's never too early for champagne," she muttered. "And we need at least a tiny turn up!" Tonya laughed.

A young man in a seafoam and white uniform carrying a small tray with three glasses of champagne, stopped in front of their lounge chairs. His muscular legs were a burnished brown against his white shorts. And his almond eyes danced as he handed them their glasses.

"Thank you," said Tonya smiling and batting her eyelids as she took a glass.

"Thank you," said Chanté, taking a glass. She looked at Tonya. "Do you ever turn off?"

"What? I was looking for you. Seems like someone ought to…"
Shane laughed and almost spilled her drink.

"Oh, so you got a man for a minute and now you clownin' me?" Chanté looked at Shane.

"Pretty much," she said laughing. "It's your turn Mama! You're just like me working and mothering all the time, not having a personal life. …"

"Okay, okay. We gonna work on Chanté but first we gotta get YOU hitched. Lift your glasses! This toast is to Anthony, my man with the plan! He had you in his sights and did not lose focus," laughed Tonya.

They clinked glasses and took a sip.

"You gotta respect a man who knows what he wants and puts all his energy into it!" said Tonya.

"You are so dramatic!" said Shane, putting her glass on a side table. She laid back and closed her eyes.

"I am so serious!"

Taking a cue from their friend, Chanté and Tonya laid back enjoying the serenity of their surroundings. They'd had body treatments, massages, time in the sauna, facials, manicures and pedicures; they were sated.

"So where's dinner?"

"I don't know. Some place that Joe picked from Grover's recommendations. I like Grover. He seems like a party. I can't wait to meet him!"

"Me, too," Chanté said.

"I'm glad there's Joe because the two of you would be a mess!" Shane said, looking over at Tonya.

"Chanté, are you coming to dinner?" Tonya nudged her.

She opened an eye. "I'm not trying to be a fifth wheel!"

"What are you talking about? It's just me, my husband, Sean and Shane for dinner."

Shane's phone started vibrating. She'd gone to the changing room and snuck it out after their treatments. Chanté gave her a look.

"I'll just check the number to make sure it's not about the wedding." She looked at the screen. Robert. She accepted the call.

"Hey handsome! Are you here?" she whispered. "Okay. I'm at the spa so I can't talk. I just wanted to make sure everything was alright. I'll call you later." She put the phone in the pocket of her robe and laid back. "That was Robert. He just checked into the hotel."

"Ahhh, the work husband. In all these years, we've never met him." Tonya remarked. "Is he single?"

"Yes. He was supposed to be bringing someone but he didn't… I wonder what that's about? I guess I'll find out."

"Shane, why don't you invite him to dinner tonight?" Tonya smiled slyly.

"I'm on it." She texted him the details.

"When is baby boy getting in?" Chanté asked.

Shane checked her phone. No messages. "He should be at the hotel by now. I got a message that the car picked him up from the airport. Lemme text him real quick!"

Her phone vibrated soon after. "Oh. He's with Imani and her family. He says he's going to dinner with them tonight." Shane frowned. "I guess we'll see him back at the house."

They met for dinner at an upscale Mexican restaurant, MX LA. It was near the hotel so the rest of their party was there waiting. Shane and Chanté arrived in Anthony's convertible. Apparently Joe and Robert hit it off: they were in an animated discussion when Chanté and Shane walked in. Joe broke off and walked toward them.

"Joe, this is Chanté, my girl from college."

"Chanté! What it iiiiiiis?" Joe reached in and gave her a hug. "C'mon girl, why you acting all stiff?"

Chanté looked at Shane and Tonya. "Ok, Wow! Both of y'all are on 100!"

"All the time," lamented Shane.

"Aw girl you love it!" Tonya said, looking at Shane. "It's. just. how. we. do!" she said, punctuating each word as she began a low-key twerk.

"We were waiting on y'all. The table's ready," called Robert.

Chanté grabbed Shane's shoulder. "That's Robert?" she whispered.

Shane raised her eyebrow. "The one and only!"

The food and service were fabulous. The combination of tequila, Mezcal and Mexican music enhanced their jubilant mood. They laughed, roasted the bride-to-be and shared memories. Shane was joyous. These people are home to her.

"Shane, whatchu over there grinning about?" Robert asked, chuckling.

"You mean, besides the obvious?" she batted her lashes. "I just feel… full. There is a feeling of abundance surrounding me and I'm taking it in, basking in it! I am grateful for everything and for all of you."

"Awww. We love you Shane!" said Tonya. She raised her glass. "Let's toast our girl. She may not remember, but I made a toast long ago in our favorite little nail shop. I told her that her future was bright. She couldn't see it, but I knew it because of her goodness, her generosity and her talent."

Shane blew a kiss at her. "I remember that day," she said as her voice trembled. "Thank you for always having my back."

"To Shane!" The glasses clinked and Chanté winked at her before knocking back a shot of tequila.

Shane caught Robert glancing across the oval table at Chanté. He'd been sneaking looks all night. Hmmmm, she thought.

"So did you all RSVP for the rehearsal dinner?" Shane asked.

"They did," Tonya answered for the group. "We're all set for tomorrow evening."

"Where's Ant tonight?" asked Joe.

"Oh, his brothers and Grover took him out."

"Uh oh! Maybe I shoulda went out with them!" He laughed and took a sip of mezcal. Then, he jumped up from the table and walked over to Shane.

Shane laughed. "I'm sure Philip is keeping it a little tame."

"Who's Philip?" he extended his hand and pulled her up from her seat.

"My future father-in-law."

Joe put his hand on her waist and began to guide her in an energetic dance to the Mexican music that played throughout the restaurant. Shane followed, throwing her head back in laughter as Joe gyrated and shook his shoulders intermittently. Tonya recorded their antics. Robert walked over to Chanté and extended his hand. They joined Joe and Shane on the small makeshift dance floor.

Shane glanced over at them a few times. They were murmuring to one another. Chanté was smiling, her dimples inviting Robert. Suddenly, Robert spun then dipped her; Chanté did not miss a step and cackled. Shane looked over her shoulder at Tonya who had shifted the focus of her video to the other couple.

Shane whispered to Joe. "I'ma tap out."

She kissed his cheek, then walked over to the table taking the phone from Tonya who joined her husband on the floor. Soon, they were doing some sort of rhumba or what had to be the forbidden dance. Shane shook her head and began recording them. She sighed and sipped her drink watching the four of them on the floor.

Her mind drifted to Anthony and wondered what he was doing. She stopped the video and texted him.

Can't wait to see you tomorrow at rehearsal. 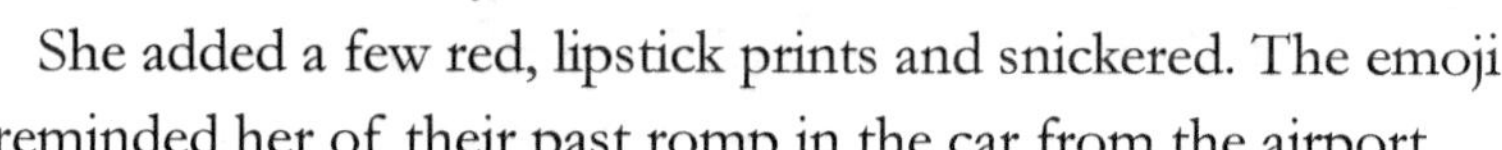

She added a few red, lipstick prints and snickered. The emoji reminded her of their past romp in the car from the airport.

The foursome came back to the table, breathless and chattering nonstop. "Is anyone up for dessert?" Robert asked.

There were a few groans. Shane shook her head.

"Well I guess it's just me then."

The group waited outside the restaurant for an Uber to take them back to the hotel. Shane and Chanté were heading back to Anthony's. Chanté gave Robert a cutesy wave as he climbed into the car.

"Mmm hmm… I see you!"

"Whut?" Chanté smiled as she slid into the car next to Shane.

"Y'all looked cute out there tonight."

"Oh don't get all hype. You know I like to dance…."

"And flirt!"

"Yes, but it's all harmless. Robert likes to flirt too."

"Oh, I wouldn't know. I haven't really seen him engage with many women, outside of work."

"Really?" Chanté was unconvinced. "I would think he has a gaggle of 'em."

Shane laughed. "He's handsome and accomplished, but he doesn't roll like that."

"Interesting…."

Sean got in late that night. Shane was already upstairs in bed when he tiptoed into her room. He leaned over and kissed her forehead.

"Heyyyy," she whispered, groggy. "I missed you tonight. I thought you were gonna hang with us…"

"My bad. Uncle Bryan invited me to dinner; I didn't know Yanni and Bryce would be here. I hadn't seen Yanni in a minute, so I kicked it with them." He paused. "Ant has a dope house Ma!"

She lifted up. "Yeah. I'll show you the guest rooms. Your Auntie is downstairs in the master."

"Nah Ma, I'll figure it out. Get some rest. We'll talk tomorrow."

With that, Shane laid back and drifted off. What she didn't know was that Sean was so late because he and Yanni hung out after the group returned to the hotel. Imani filled her in the next day.

"He left that part out," Shane said, rolling her eyes.

"They young, what'd you expect? They don't need as much rest as we do!"

The pair enjoyed an early breakfast as Chanté and Sean slept in. "They're on east-coast time for real!"

Later the wedding party showed up for a quick rehearsal.

"What's up Shane?" Samuelle ran and gave her a big hug. She squeezed him back. They looked eye to eye. "Hey handsome! How are you?"

"I'm good! Are you excited?"

"Very." She smiled.

Naaja waited patiently for her turn.

"How's my girl?!"

"Good Shane! I'm so excited for you and Daddy!"

"C'mon over here and meet your new older brother."

Shane smiled broadly as she watched Anthony and Sean in the foyer giving each other dap and chatting. Then, Anthony strode towards her dramatically and engulfed her with a bear hug. She inhaled his smell.

"Shane, my Shane."

"Hey baby!"

He released her and stepped back to look at her. "It's been a few weeks, I need to soak you in!"

She blushed and giggled. "It won't be long now, Mr. Dekra!"

"I'm counting the minutes, almost Mrs. Dekra!" He closed the space between them again and embraced her, giving her a long, slow kiss.

"Hellooooo. You were going to introduce us!"

Shane broke from the kiss. "Oh yeah! Sean, this is Naaja and Samuelle. They've been waiting to meet you!"

"What's up, lil' bruh and lil' sis!" He gave Sam a pound and hugged Naaja lightly, giving her a kiss on the cheek. "Are y'all ready for this?" He looked from brother to sister.

"Yes!" Naaja answered for both of them. "We're so ready."

"Um, we're wanted out back," interrupted Grover.

Anthony gave him a look. "My bad Ant! The minister is on a schedule."

The run through was seamless. Everyone stood in their respective places. Sean and Shane walked to the clearing on cue and he escorted her down the yard to Anthony. Anthony took her hand and they walked a few steps to the center and turned to face each other. They stood gazing at one another as the minister gave instructions. Chanté and Imani observed from afar.

"I'm so happy for them!" exclaimed Imani.

"Yeah," agreed Chanté. "It's about time that Shane got her happy ending… Well, new beginning!"

Imani checked her watch and was pleased that they were on schedule. She would touch base with Grover on a few things once they wrapped up the rehearsal.

"So what can we expect at tonight's dinner?" Chanté looked over at Imani.

"Oh, I don't really know. Tonya handled that."

"Sooo we should expect anything! That's what you're saying!" Chanté shook her head and snickered. Imani laughed. "So you know Tonya?"

"Yup! I do…."

The rehearsal dinner was quite traditional and tame. Barcelona was a beautiful restaurant with stone, concave walls and mosaic tile floors. It looked like a huge, dimly lit, but fancy wine cellar. Flamenco music was piped in giving the gathering a festive air while they shared Spanish wine, paella and tapas. They had a private room to talk, laugh and get to know each other. Valencia was snagged by the label at the last minute to do some promotional stuff, so she wouldn't fly in until late that night with her plus one. Tom and Stephanie touched down that afternoon, in time to join the dinner.

Shane tapped her glass with her fork and stood. Everyone quieted.

"Thank you to everyone for being here. Usually the rehearsal dinner is for the wedding party, but I wanted all of you here. Anthony and I wanted an intimate wedding with only our family so you're all here tonight. I'm about to get weepy so I just want to say I love you all."

She took her seat and dabbed at her eyes with her napkin. Then, Sean stood. Shane looked up at him and smiled.

"I want to thank Ant and his family…" He corrected himself. "our new family for welcoming my mother and now me. For a long time, it was just the two of us. That's not to say that we don't have family, but it was only us in our household. I'm looking forward to our family blending and growing. I've always wanted a big family. So I'd like to toast my Mom and Ant! I wish you all the happiness."

Anthony nodded and smiled at Sean. Glasses raised and clinked around the table. Sean smiled and took a sip of Sangria which his Mother allowed. He sat down and looked around at the smiling faces. When he looked over at Yanni, he noticed that Amir was looking at his plate, moving food around.

Before the night was over, Grover, Naaja and Anthony spoke. The two families tentatively chatted and performed the get-to-know-each-other-dance with one another. Shane and Anthony sat together; however, Tonya had placards on the place settings to intermix the family members and spur conversation, including herself and Joe who sat across the table from one another. Chanté and Robert were next to each other. Dorothy was next to Simone and Shane's sister was wedged between Joe and Naaja. Anthony's younger brother sat next to Shane while the older one was next to Joe. Samuelle sat beside Sean and Gail with Greg and Sam opposite them on the other side. Amir sat on the other side of Robert, next to Yanni; and the remaining guests were also intermixed.

Tom surprised the couple with a serenade via acoustic guitar which prompted a turn on the tiny dance floor. Shane melted into Anthony's chest and closed her eyes. A few couples came onto the dance floor as Tom played an encore.

"Tom, that was beautiful, thank you!" exclaimed Shane. "Such an honor to have a GRAMMY-nominated bassist to play for us!" She winked at him and Stephanie as she and Anthony returned to their seats.

As the wait staff began to clear the table, Philip asked that the wine be refilled. He cleared his throat.

"I'd like to make a toast to my son and my almost daughter-in-law." All eyes turned to him.

"Love is precious. It's a gift to cherish and nurture. My heart is full that my son found love again." He looked at the couple. "Take care of each other. That's what it's all about." Everyone raised their topped-off glasses. "To Anthony and Shane!"

Amir slipped out of the private room. He was crossing the main dining room and entering the lobby when Sean caught up to him.

"Yo, Amir. Hold up a minute!"

Amir turned to see his future stepbrother.

"I got something to say to you… Nah, I got two things to say: one, if you're not happy about this union, don't come tomorrow and two, do NOT hurt my Mother's feelings again! Have a nice night."

Sean turned and walked back to the party.

After dinner, Anthony, his Dad and brothers and other guests headed back to the hotel. Sean, his Grandmother, his Aunt and Chanté headed to the house with Shane.

_______ ✺ _______

The day was clear with a light breeze. The sun was high and bright against a brilliant blue sky. Five, sleek black cars inched up to the impressive, circular drive. Guests exited the vehicles and were guided by uniformed, wait staff along the side of the house to the lush acreage in back. The scent of hyacinth and honeysuckle perfumed the air as they made their way to the ceremony space.

There was a smattering of linen covered pub tables each with two companion chairs. Two waiters circulated with wine, lemonade and other cool beverages as well as light finger foods. A band of string and woodwind instruments played light, whimsical music as guests streamed in. Beyond the tables, there were four, neat rows of eight, white wooden chairs, hung with floral sashes. They were separated by a center aisle and flowers cascaded at the ends of the rows inside the aisle.

Huge, fragrant floral arrangements of yellow roses, blush and white lilies and white hyacinths dotted the landscape, framing the ceremony space. At the head of the space was a floral arch, draped with climbing honeysuckle. In the distance were two, white tents.

"This is beautiful," remarked Shane's future sister-in-law to her husband.

My Mother outdid herself, thought Yanni as she stopped a waiter for a glass of lemonade. The colors and textures were sumptuous and elegant. Crisp white, blush and buttercup yellow enveloped the landscape. Maybe she could get her Dad to talk her Mom into finally starting her own event planning or interior design business.

She made her way to a nearby pub table where Dorothy was perched. "Hey Ms. Mathews. Do you want me to get you a drink?"

"Yes honey. Could you get me a glass of ice water please?"

Yanni found another waiter and requested a glass of water. She headed back to the pub table where Ms. Mathews sat fanning herself.

"Where's your brother?" Dorothy asked as she reached the table.

"He's around here somewhere, probably with my Dad. How are you doing?"

There were smiles on guests' faces as they chattered softly and enjoyed the light fare. It wouldn't be long before the ceremony began.

"Heyyy baby boy! Lookin' sharp!" Sean turned to see his posse of Aunties and Stephanie coming through the foyer.

Sean posed in his tailored, charcoal gray, three piece suit; the cut of the jacket highlighted his broad shoulders and narrow waist. He wore a white shirt and blush tie. On his feet were a pair of black Johnston & Murphy Bradford Oxfords, a gift from his almost Stepdad.

He laughed and hugged each of the women. Gail's hug lingered; she hadn't seen him in person since his high school graduation.

"Big day hunh?" Stephanie said stating the obvious. "How's your Mom?"

"Nervous, I think. But she's been smiling all morning. I made her a lil' breakfast before she took a bath to get ready for the glam squad."

"Whatchu know about a glam squad?" Tonya chided and hit his shoulder. "How are you feeling?"

"Good. Excited! But I'm not the one lockin' it down!" He laughed. "Y'all look beautiful. Can I get you anything?"

"No thank you," they said, echoing one another.

"Your Mom did such a great job with you," Gail said softly while playing with one of his wild curls. She kissed his cheek.

"Aight Auntie. That's enough," he said, swatting her hand away. "She's upstairs waiting for y'all."

Gail, Imani, Steph and Tonya quietly ascend the stairs to Anthony's room. They find Shane and Chanté talking quietly. Shane was sitting at a vanity looking at her reflection. She has a serene smile.

Her hair was in wavy tendrils, piled on top of her head in a loose bun. A few curls loosely hang in the back and on the sides of her face.

Shane was utterly breathtaking with a natural face of makeup: a nude pink lip and barely there pink blush on the apple of her cheeks. A sheer layer of mineral powder was pressed on her nose, chin and forehead to tamp down any shine. Her lashes were wispy and pronounced.

"Hey beautiful," called Gail gently.

Shane moved to stand up but Tonya stopped her.

"No. Stay put. Relax. We're here to prepare you." She kissed the top of Shane's head.

"We come bearing gifts," sang Imani holding several packages. The makeup artist and hair stylist, quietly excused themselves taking their tool bags with them.

"Thank you so much!" Shane called after them.

The photographer slipped in as Imani handed a package to Gail and another to Stephanie.

"Where's Dorothy and your sis?" asked Tonya.

"They decided that they would let the girlfriends have the room. We spent some time together last night."

Tonya didn't press and Shane was thankful.

"So you know how this goes. You need something old, new, borrowed and blue."

Stephanie knelt beside the vanity. She handed Shane a small box. Shane took it and removed the top. It was a delicate, cream handkerchief. It had a lace eyelet pattern with SM embroidered on it. They heard the soft click of the camera's shutter.

"It was given to me on my wedding day. I didn't use it, but just in case you need it today. It's your something borrowed."

Shane placed it on the vanity and wrapped her arms around Stephanie. "Don't you make me have to use it now, Mrs. Juarez!" Stephanie closed her eyes and she savored the embrace.

"Okay, me next!" Tonya sidled up beside her.

She handed Shane a small flat box. Shane looked at Tonya, then lightly shook the box. She lifted the top. A midst tissue paper was a slim, sterling silver flask engraved with her initials and an intricate, floral border. Across its flat top, below the neck was an inscription: *A toast to you, my forever Boo*. Shane laughed loudly.

"I know you're on this white wine tip, but every once in a while you'll need a real drink. Trust me! And it's petite so you can take it when y'all travel. Look under the tissue."

There was a garter with an extra wide band in the wedding color palette.

"Put that on. You can slip the flask under your garter if you want a little taste later. Or if Anthony wants a taste before he has a taste!" Tonya did a shimmy. The camera clicked. "Your something new."

Shane shook her head. Tonya blew her a kiss. She looked up to see Chanté and Imani laughing.

"Don't encourage her!" Shane admonished.

Gail stepped forward with a small, but long, narrow box. "This is actually from Anthony and his father."

Shane looked up at her surprised.

"Open it! I wanna know what it is," she whined. "I promised that I wouldn't peek."

Shane opened the box slowly and gasped. There was a diamond necklace with a teardrop sapphire pendant. She stared at it. The photographer inched closer. Click.

"There should be a note."

Under the beautiful necklace, was a small scrolled note.

*To my Shane,*

*My Father gave my Mother this pendant for their 40th anniversary. She cherished it, but only wore it on special occasions. I imagine if she were here, she would be wearing it. The diamond necklace is an update, a gift from me to you. This is your something blue.*

Shane held the note to her chest and looked around the room at her friends. Uncontrollable tears began to spill, streaking her face.

"Aw shit!" Chanté ran into the bathroom for a face towel. "Blot, don't rub," she advised as she rushed back. "Get him outta here!" she yelled pointing at the photographer.

Shane let the tears flow freely. Chanté shooed Stephanie and Gail out of the way. She knelt down and dabbed at her eyes. Shane's face was streaked and mascara encircled her eyes.

"Oh fuck this. We gonna have to start over! Black mascara for a bride?! Amateurs," she muttered.

"Hand me the makeup bag in my purse! Shane honey just let it out. You can wipe your face clean with that damp face towel. I gotchu."

Shane cried into the towel. "Easy Shane. We don't have time for swollen eyes. They gonna think we were in here beating your ass!"

Shane buried her face in the towel and took a deep breath. She exhaled slowly, then handed Chanté the towel. A box of Kleenex was on the vanity. She grabbed one and blew her nose hard.

"Eewww… yeah, handle that Shane. I don't need you snotting after I do your face!"

Shane kicked Chanté in the shin.

"Keep it up and I'll let you go out there looking like who shot John."

Shane bust out laughing. "What kinda country shit is that?"

"Good. Laughter… we can work with laughter!" sighed Imani.

Shane took another deep breath and let it out. "My bad y'all. I was all wound up and that gift from Anthony took me over the edge! But I'm good now." She paused. "What time is it?"

"Oh shit," murmured Stephanie as she looked at her watch. "Chanté, you need to get to work. We're officially behind schedule."

When she finished, Shane looked natural and beautiful. There was no evidence of her meltdown. Shane checked the mirror.

"Well shit! We didn't need a makeup artist!" She turned to face her girls.

"Chanté, her face is beat! You did that!" Tonya slapped Chanté's waiting hand.

"Ok. We better get her in this dress! The rest of the gifts have to wait."

"But what about something old?" protested Imani.

"Her old ass is getting married, that'll have to do," said Gail.

"No, no. The necklace is old AND blue," said Stephanie. "We're good!"

Shane stood and walked into the closet. She came back carrying her gown. Tonya quickly took it from her and laid it on the bed.

Gail and Chanté helped her out of her white, silk robe. Tonya and Stephanie held up the dress as Imani unzipped it. They carried the open gown across the room for Shane to step into.

There was a quick rapping on the bedroom doors.

"What y'all doing up in there? We about to be late!"

"Sean, I'll be out in 10 minutes," she called. "Just a little CP time."

"Okay. I'll be in the courtyard. Let's go Ma!"

Shane carefully stepped into the gown. Imani slowly zipped it while Gail unhooked the diamond choker Shane was wearing and replaced it with the sapphire pendant. Tonya and Stephanie were busy fluffing the skirt while Chanté hunted for her heels in the closet.

Chanté returned with the gold, beaded stilettos in hand.

"Um, keep those for me for pictures later. I'm wearing flats for the wedding."

"WHAT?" shrieked Chanté.

"I'll be sinking into the ground if I wear those. Save 'em for the pictures and reception."

They all stood back admiring her gown. The bodice was simple and smooth Mikado fabric, unembellished. The semi-sweetheart neckline teased at the rise of Shane's breasts, accentuating her bosom. Layers of diaphanous georgette gently flared into an A-line skirt, floating to the floor. Delicate, white rose petals were scattered densely below the waistline then thinned out and ended at calf level. The underlayers of organza flowed behind her forming a small train.

They silently smiled at the lovely bride. Imani quietly opened the door for the waiting photographer. He snapped a few shots of the ladies admiring their friend, then a few shots of the bride before slipping back out. Tonya dug her phone from her clutch and snapped a picture.

"I promise I won't post it until tomorrow!" she cried tearily.

"Okay, okay! We have to go," said Imani, interrupting the quiet. "Ladies, please head to the ceremony space. Use the front door."

"I'm going to help Shane down the stairs, then I'll meet y'all out there." Tonya waved to Gail, Stephanie and Chanté. They quickly left the room.

Tonya shoved her phone back in her purse and tucked the clutch under her arm. She bent down and gently gathered the gown's train in her arms. "Okay Shane, let's get it."

Imani made a quick stop in the kitchen. She opened the fridge and removed a clear, plastic container. It held Shane's floral headpiece: a small crown made of rose and hyacinth petals. Opening the container, she removed the delicate accessory.

Shane descended the stairs with Tonya trailing behind. As Shane headed to meet Sean in the courtyard, Imani stopped her.

"It's perfect," breathed Shane and bowed her head so that Imani could place it at the front of her hair.

"Now, you're ready." Imani smiled and blew her a kiss. "See you out there sis!"

Imani hurried through the foyer and out of the front door toward the ceremony space. Tonya fluffed the train and smoothed it behind Shane. She stood and gave her friend a light hug.

"I don't wanna wrinkle you!" she whispered. "I'll see you soon." Tonya held back tears and smiled. She headed to the foyer and walked out the front door.

Shane closed her eyes and took a deep breath. She felt absolutely beautiful in the dress that her son chose for her. She stepped through the glass sliders and walked into the courtyard. She and Sean would exit through the side entrance and walk to the top of the aisle as they'd practiced.

When Sean turned and saw his Mother, he had the feeling that he'd always had: that she was the most beautiful woman in the world. He walked to meet her, a tear finding its way down his cheek. Shane smiled and wiped it away. They walked to the entrance and waited until they heard the first few chords of the "wedding march." Sean looked down at her and smiled.

"You ready Ma?"

"Yes, I am." The butterflies were colliding in her stomach but her cheeks hurt from smiling.

They took measured steps around the side of the courtyard to the back of the lush property. Once they reached the top of the aisle, the organ music stopped and there was a hush. A beautiful tenor voice sang, *God has a funny way of showing you lessons!*

Her head snapped up and she saw fellow songwriter, Eric Roberson, standing at the end of the aisle, eyes closed. He continued to serenade her in a beautiful a capella. Her gaze left him finding Anthony. He was smiling at her. He knew this was one of her favorite songs. She began to silently weep. Sean gently pulled her elbow to signal her to walk.

*Now I realiiiize, every one that let me down led me to you! Oh bay-beh! All them sleepless niiiights, all the heartbreak I had led me to you!*

Shane focused on Anthony as she walked down the aisle. Cool as ever, he looked so handsome. The sun's rays glinted off his gorgeous, dark brown head. His white, tailored suit jacket and white shirt contrasted his slim, charcoal pants. A charcoal, patterned tie popped against the crisp white. His smile radiated sweetness.

When they reached the clearing at the end of the aisle, Sean turned to her and kissed her cheek. He moved his grasp from her elbow to her right hand. Anthony stepped forward and Sean placed his Mother's hand into Anthony's. Then, Sean stepped to the right to stand beside Naaja in her buttercup yellow gown. Eric took a seat.

The bride and groom stepped forward to the center with Sean and Naaja to their right and Grover, Samuelle and Philip on their left. The minister standing in front of them spoke.

"Who gives this woman to be married?"

"I do," Sean said proudly.

Shane looked into Anthony's face. She studied the crinkle around his eyes and the flare of his nose. His full lips and pearly teeth worked in concert to create the smile that she never tired of, not to mention her dimple. Love shined in his deep brown eyes; its intensity and vulnerability took her breath.

For the first time, she realized this was one of the most important moments that she would ever have. She felt exuberant and shy at once. Eric's lyrics reverberated in her head and her soul. She knew that God hadn't forgotten her.

Shane was staring at her life partner surrounded by their children and the people they loved most. His eyes flitted to the pendant and he swallowed. She took his hand and squeezed it.

"Dearly beloved. We are gathered here today in the presence of God to witness and celebrate the union of Anthony and Shane. God, we ask that you bless this union and shine your love upon them as they begin their life journey together. We ask that you keep them united and strong for the perils that will test their bond and remind them of the vows that they have made. We also ask that you remind their loved ones to stand with them in jubilant and trying times and support them as a family should. We know that you brought these two together for a purpose and that is not for anyone to question or challenge." The minister paused, then looked to his right.

"May we have the rings?" Grover stepped forward and stood at

Anthony's shoulder, between him and the minister. He extended his palm which held the rings.

"At this time, the bride and groom have chosen to share personal vows to one another. Anthony?"

Anthony glanced at Grover as he took the ring from his palm. He drew in a shaky breath, then exhaled.

"Shane. I think I loved you from the moment I laid eyes on you. But I couldn't have known how completely my life would change because of your laugh, your grace and your audacity. You are the first thing that I think about when I open my eyes and the last thing I think about as I drift into sleep. You deserve everything and if it is within my power, it is yours. To say that I love you does not begin to express all that I feel." Anthony took her hand and slid a diamond encrusted band onto her finger. Then he raised her hand to his lips and kissed it. "Take this ring as my vow to you. I promise to cherish you as my wife, all the days of my life."

Shane's mind went blank. She had never felt this way: as if her heart was going to burst in her chest. She closed her eyes and breathed a few slow breaths. When she opened her eyes, she wasn't sure how much time had passed. Anthony's eyes were trained on her.

"Anthony." Her voice was tinny and small. She swallowed hard. "I used to be afraid. I was afraid to trust anyone with my heart and I was afraid to love. And although I asked God to send me someone, I hid behind my writing, my work… my son." Shane stopped and took a breath. "But then you showed up. And even when I pushed, you didn't let me go and you let me know that I was safe with you. Because of you, I know that God did not forget me."

She let out a small sob. Anthony raised his hands and cupped her face, wiping her tears before they fell. They stared at each other for a few moments. Then Shane looked at Grover and nodded. He extended the ring to her. She took the ring and he stepped back. Shane took

Anthony's left hand from her face and held it. She placed a simple platinum ring on his finger.

"This ring is my vow to you. I promise to cherish you as my husband, all the days of my life." She smiled at him and he took her left hand in his and turned slightly to the minister. The minister took their joined hands.

"God bless these rings and the hands that wear them. These rings are a never-ending circle and therefore, a symbol of their bond. Amen."

Sean, Naaja and Samuelle stepped forward and surrounded the bride and groom. "The couple will share words that they've written to their children."

Shane turned her head toward their seated guests and her eyes found Amir. She looked at him briefly, then at Anthony. When she turned her gaze back to Amir, he slowly stood and walked up to join his siblings, standing next to his sister. Shane and Anthony spoke in unison. "Our family is a blended one. It is unique but it is grounded in love." Naaja grabbed Amir's hand. "Today, before our family and friends, we promise to love and support you. There may be challenges that we encounter, but we will do it together as a family. We promise to listen more than we speak and to be slow to anger yet quick to honor you. This is our shared vow to all of you." The four children closed around the couple and they shared an embrace. Philip smiled. After a few quiet moments, they released one another. Shane and Anthony remained in the center, holding hands and turned to face the minister.

"I now pronounce you husband and wife. Anthony, kiss your bride!"

Anthony turned Shane to him. He pulled his new wife into an embrace, then softly and sweetly kissed her on the lips. It was not one of their long, slow lascivious kisses. It was almost chaste but held a promise.

The guests clapped and cheered and they turned to greet them. Imani quickly laid a straw broom at their feet. It was tied with white, blush and buttercup ribbons with honeysuckle vines winding up the handle and hyacinths tucked into it. Shane grabbed Anthony's hand, they looked at one another and jumped.

<hr>

The photographer was sure to snap the traditional photos that Tonya detailed on the shot sheet: bride and groom; bride, groom and parents; bride, groom and children; bride, groom and bridal party; bride, groom and family. But the one that Shane waited for was the one with her girls. They were all together which rarely happened and she was eager to capture it.

"Just be yourselves," she pleaded as they gathered for the photo.

Shane, Chanté, Gail, Imani, Stephanie and Tonya. They posed, showed out and laughed into the camera. A beautiful mosaic of Black women, all skin tones and shapes, in vibrant colors and styles. The pictures were loving and joyful which was exactly what Shane wanted.

Shane pulled Imani to the side. "Thank you for making this day beautiful!" She pinned her friend in an embrace.

"Oh Shane, it was my pleasure. But it wasn't just me!"

"Who are you fooling? I know you spearheaded this so please accept my never-ending gratitude. But, you are my guest so you need to delegate and enjoy yourself!"

"I will. I am! I just need to check on a few more details."

"Okay, but wrap it up. Also, could you do me one last favor?"

"Yes. This is your day."

"When you feel it's appropriate, please make sure the caterers and the wait staff take a break and eat… the photographer too. And also please invite them to celebrate with us if they would like to do so."

After the last set of photos, Shane, Gail, Tonya and Chanté slipped into the house to fasten her bustle. Gail held the phone playing the videoed instructions. The ladies reflected on the ceremony as Tonya and Chanté carefully pulled and looped the fabric into place.

"Eric Roberson though!" exclaimed Gail.

"Anthony is not to be played with," remarked Chanté. "That man could give lessons." They nodded, each confident that their girl was in good hands.

They made their way to the enormous silk tent set up at the other end of the property. As the last of the guests were seated, Shane and Anthony hung back in order to be announced .

"Join me in welcoming for the first time, Anthony and Shane Dekra!" exclaimed Grover.

The band began to play an ebullient piece as they entered to clapping and cheering. The billowy white "walls" were tied back with sashes. Inside were three crystal chandeliers hung above a wooden, dining table set for 30 guests. There were numerous floral centerpieces, candles and ferns atop a blush linen tablecloth.

The spread had a Mediterranean twist with something for everyone: grilled halibut, fire roasted vegetables, peppercorn crusted filet medallions, tabouleh, chilled shrimp and pesto pasta, garlic couscous, roasted corn salad and a mixed vegetable curry. There were also platters of pita bread with hummus, muhammara, baba ghanoush and sun-dried tomatoes.

She nibbled on a few vegetables and hummus, but Shane was too excited to eat. She spent the dinner looking around the table at everyone enjoying themselves. This enormous table was a poem writing itself. She hoped the photographer had candids of this family-style dinner.

"Mrs. Dekra?" Shane realized that her husband was whispering to her. Husband. She smiled.

"Yes?"

"You need to eat. We will be partying this evening and then catching a flight tonight. You need sustenance...." He paused and kissed her lips. "Not to mention for when I get you alone." Her dimple showed itself.

"Okay, okay." Anthony held out his fork holding a piece of a medallion. Shane opened her mouth and took the offering. She closed her eyes and slowly licked her lips for her husband. When she opened them, she knew he would be watching.

"Oh, you don't wanna play with me. I'll take you in the house now and leave folks out here!"

Shane snorted. "Behave Anthony!"

"Stop playin' with me!" he warned.

Just then, Grover tapped his glass with his fork. The table grew quiet. He walked over to the microphone stand.

"My turn!" exclaimed Grover, chuckling. "I know that I'm supposed to say something deep and eloquent but that's not going to happen!" He paused for dramatic effect. "These two gave me a run for my money, especially Shane! Trying to put them together took a bit of finesse. But, obviously, it worked out… I love them both and they make a beautiful couple. So raise your glass to congratulate and give blessings to Anthony and Shane. Que Dieu vous bénisse!"

Shane blew a kiss to Grover who puckered his lips. She giggled as he strutted back to the mic.

"One more thing. I have a housekeeping announcement. We know how we like to eat and get the itis but Imani said to get y'all asses up so they can clear the area for the dance floor and band."

Imani walked over and swatted Grover.

"Owwww! Okay, okay. She didn't say that exactly but you get the point! Everybody get on up and head to the courtyard for the cake cutting. Then we can par-tay!"

"Why couldn't you just invite the guests to join us in the courtyard for the cutting of the wedding cake and drink service?" asked Imani huffily.

"I just did!"

Imani stalked off headed for the courtyard to ensure that everything was perfect for the new couple and their guests. Tonya met her on the way and the photographer hurried behind them not wanting to be the subject of Imani's ire.

When they arrived, it was set up per Imani's instructions. The floral arrangements from the ceremony space had been transplanted giving the courtyard an elegant, romantic vibe. The hyacinths and honeysuckle provided a heavy sweet scent. The pool and lawn chairs had been replaced by the pub tables and chairs with clean linens dotting the deck and patio areas. A bar was set up near the sliding doors to the house. Two bartenders stood at the ready to mix drinks, serve coffee or provide beer and wine service.

The wedding cake was set up on a table in the far left corner, away from the pool. It was simple yet stunning: three, oval tiers with buttercup yellow, buttercream frosting. Fresh blush and white roses are atop the cake and cascade down the side. The base was encircled by buttercream blush and white roses, dotted with honeysuckle buds. The center layer was chocolate, the top and base layers were vanilla with a honey buttercream center. Another small table was set up beside it where the cut slices would be placed with other sweets: chocolates dusted with espresso, chocolate covered strawberries as well as baklava bites.

Tonya and Imani admired the space as the guests began to trickle in. "This is beautiful Imani!" exclaimed Tonya. "You outdid yourself today girl. I know Shane is happy."

Imani smiled. She was happy that Tonya approved. After the cake-cutting, she would find Bryan so they could have a drink. And they would definitely be on that dance floor later. She turned and saw Shane and Anthony enter the courtyard. Shane looked like she was floating. Imani began to tear up. She was so happy for them.

The photographer was busy snapping photos of the crowd, then made his way to the couple and the cake. Shane and Anthony were murmuring and exchanging soft kisses and laughter. Noticing the photographer, Shane picked up the silver cake cutter. Anthony positioned himself beside her and placed his hand on hers. They cut a small slice from the middle tier. Chocolate. Shane's favorite.

Anthony removed his hand from the cutter while Shane cut the piece in half. They each took a piece. She gave her husband a sideways glance, hopeful that he got the message: there will be no shoving of the cake into her face. He winked. With that, they cautiously fed each other cake, then leaned in for a kiss. There was a mixture of applause and the camera shutter opening and closing.

Eager to finally greet their guests, they broke off into opposite directions. Shane knew where she was headed.

"Thank you so much!" Shane hugged Eric Roberson from his seated position. "I can't tell you how much that meant to me!"

Eric turned and stood. "Thank your husband. He came to me and said, 'Eric, you gotta do this for me man. She loves that song!'... I was happy to do it."

"Shane, please meet my wife Shawn." She stood and Shane hugged her. "Thank you all so much for being here, to share this day!"

"Thank you to you and Ant for having us! We love sharing in a couple's happiness and joy. You are such a beautiful and radiant bride." She kissed Shane's cheek. "I look forward to us getting to know one another better."

Shane looked around the courtyard for her husband, spotting him at the bar, getting two flutes of champagne. He nodded and headed over to her. Tonya, Imani and Simone were also at the bar sharing a drink. Shane winked at Tonya. As Anthony passed her the glass, Valencia approached.

"Shane! Congratulations Ma!" She smiled widely and hugged Shane tightly while stomping her feet. When they parted, Shane noticed a young man standing slightly behind Valencia. He and Anthony nodded at one another.

"Oh my God, forgive me! This is Juan Roses Arullo."

Shane extended her hand to him. He stepped forward, grabbing her hand and bringing it to his lips. "Congratulations!"

"Thank you, thank you!" Shane looked at Valencia, her eyebrows danced up and down.

"Stay right here," implored Juan. He rushed to the bar, getting two glasses of champagne. He returned, carefully handing one to Valencia while raising his glass. The three of them followed his lead.

"Felicidades to the bride and groom!" They clinked their glasses and took a sip of the bubbly.

Shortly after, the guests started filing out of the courtyard to head back to the silk tent. When the couple reached the tent, Anthony turned to Shane and extended his hand. "May I have this dance?"

"Why certainly!" Shane took his hand and he whirled her slowly before pulling her close to him. She giggled and looked up at him. His face was serious as he lowered his head and kissed her slowly. The lilting melody of *Love Fell on Me* began to play. She was lost in his embrace. The song ended before she realized their guests were watching. Their first dance.

Their family and friends applauded and looked on, smiling and snapping pictures. The band began playing again and Philip strode over to the couple.

"Son, can I have a dance with your lovely bride?"

"Of course." Anthony kissed her hand then placed it into his father's.

"Darlin' you are glowin' today!"

"I am so happy. I didn't think it could get better," Shane said, smiling up at him.

"This is just the beginning of y'all's story! Now you begin to create memories, the details." He looked down at her necklace. "Thank you for wearing my Mae's pendant," his voice cracked. "It means a lot to me… She would've loved you Shane. Just as I do. You are a blessing to us."

She rested her head on Philip's shoulder. Words escaped her. She looked over to see Anthony twirling her Mother across the floor. Dorothy giggled under the sway of his charm.

"Move over old man. I'm cutting in!" warned Grover.

Philip muttered and walked off but not before hugging Shane and kissing her cheek.

"You have put a spell on these Dekra men!" he said.

"It goes both ways I assure you." They swayed silently for a moment.

"Grover, thank you. Thank you for introducing me to a wonderful man. You saw what I couldn't."

"I can't take all the credit. I was only the co-conspirator. But I love seeing two good people find each other."

"So now we need to find your someone."

"And on that note, I'll hand you over to the young Samuelle."

"Wassup Shane! Y'all did it!" He awkwardly swayed back and forth. Shane looked down at his feet.

"Shane, I don't really know how to dance," he whispered.

"We'll have to work on that. One thing I know is that ladies love a man who knows how to dance." She winked at him. "I can teach you."

"Actually, I was thinking that I might ask Sean."

"Oh right, okay," Shane said quickly.

"I'm sorry. It's just that-"

"No need to explain. I'm sure he'll be happy to help you. It'll be good for you to start getting to know each other. He's here for a few days...."

"Okay, bet!"

"Look, you talked him up! Shane said as Sean sauntered over.

"Lil' bruh, can I cut in?"

"Sure. Shane, see you later." Samuelle waved and was off looking for Bryce, Imani's son.

Sean smiled at his Mother, as he took her hand and slid the other around her waist. He'd loosened his tie and it hung limply around his neck. His top three buttons were undone and he'd retired his vest and jacket.

"You look comfortable!" she laughed.

"Yeah, I had to let go of some layers so I could get loose!" He let her go and spun around.

She giggled. "Okayyyy. You ready!"

"Yeah, I need to holla at Grover so the band can kick it up a notch!" He took her hand and resumed their earlier position. "How do you feel?"

"I feel wonderful." Shane's smile was wide and her eyes shined.

Sean nodded. "Here comes Uncle Bryan. I guess I'll see you later."

Bryan smoothly took Sean's place. "You are a beautiful bride Shane. We are so happy for you!" They swayed silently for a few moments. "I'm glad that our families have one another… when we were partying in college, who knew that our lives would stay connected!"

"I'd hoped and here we are. So many more memories to make. I am eternally grateful to Imani for this one."

Suddenly, Robert approached. "May I have this dance?"

"Of course."

Bryan left in search of his busy wife, ready to get her on the dance floor.

She looked at Robert. "So what's up with Chanté?" she demanded.

"Damn, you don't waste no time."

"My husband told me that time is not to be wasted," she countered.

"Well I agree with him on that. And he wasted none. I'm happy for you Shane, my man came correct. I'm glad you didn't fuck it up!"

"I know right… glad you set me straight! By the way, smooth deflection… I'ma leave it for now, but you betta come correct – that's my girl."

"And I'm your boy!" he said, looking her in the eye.

"It's different." She returned his gaze. "I said what I said." She looked over his shoulder. "Where is my husband?"

Robert jerked his head to the right. Anthony and Naaja danced nearby. Robert steered them in that direction. He nodded at Anthony.

"Can I have a dance young lady?"

"Of course." Robert shook Anthony's hand and hugged him. Then, he extended his hand to Naaja and twirled her away from the couple.

"Mrs. Dekra, how are you?" Anthony pulled her close to him.

"I am wonderful. And you, my husband, how are you?"

"I'm ready to get outta here and have some quiet time with my wife." He gazed at her and smiled, her dimple greeting her.

"Me too." She kissed him lightly on the lips.

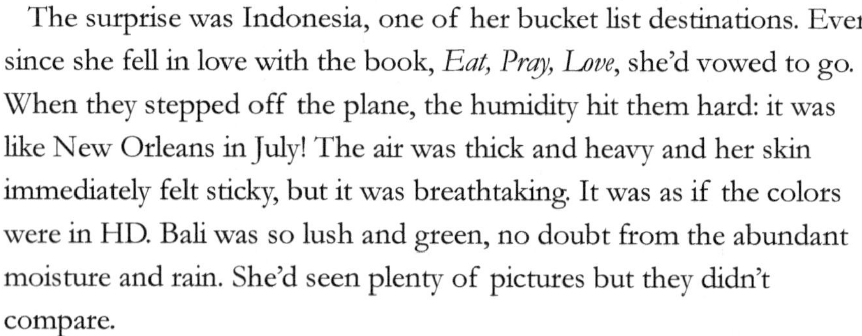

The surprise was Indonesia, one of her bucket list destinations. Ever since she fell in love with the book, *Eat, Pray, Love*, she'd vowed to go. When they stepped off the plane, the humidity hit them hard: it was like New Orleans in July! The air was thick and heavy and her skin immediately felt sticky, but it was breathtaking. It was as if the colors were in HD. Bali was so lush and green, no doubt from the abundant moisture and rain. She'd seen plenty of pictures but they didn't compare.

A driver picked them up in a canary yellow VW 181 and they were off! Shane's greedy eyes devoured the landscape. Traffic was horrendous but it gave her time to see and feel the bustling city of Kuta. The aromas of the food stalls wafted toward them, making her mouth water. There were markets with colorful wares, artisans with hand-crafted wooden carvings, woven rugs and beautiful furniture pieces.

"Are we staying nearby?" she asked her husband who sat watching her as she took in everything.

"You'll see," he winked.

"We are on Jalan Pantai Kuta," offered their driver, Kadek. "This is a popular area of Kuta with shops and the market."

"Well, I wanna come back here and look around."

"And by look around, you mean shop!" Anthony shook his head.

She shrugged her shoulders. "There is so much to see!"

He laughed at his wife's excitement.

"Depending on what you want to see," explained the driver. "Kuta has a lot. Ubud is another nearby city with boutiques and lots of arts and crafts."

Shane's eyes shined. "Kadek, would you be able to show us around a bit?"

"Sure. I will give your husband my information."

Kadek wove through the traffic and it began to open up. The busy, yet picturesque town shrank behind them. They were headed to the town of Seminyak, a quieter, less populated destination with immaculate beaches and some nightlife, if you were in search of it.

By the time they reached their villa, Shane's stomach was growling. Kadek turned onto a gravel driveway that was bordered by glorious palm trees. Then, they pulled into a semi-circular driveway and stopped the vehicle. Shane got out of the VW and looked around. Kadek and Anthony removed the luggage from the trunk.

The sky was a beautiful soft blue and the wispy clouds moved slowly. Soft sun rays shone on coconut trees and curving stalks of bamboo. Radiant clusters of bougainvillea, jasmine and roses scented the air while she marveled at the banana and jackfruit trees. There was such abundance and beauty.

"Are you ready?" asked Anthony, eager to go inside the villa.

"Yeah," said Shane, still studying the natural beauty surrounding them. They turned to wave goodbye to Kadek.

"See you soon," he responded. "Enjoy!"

She shifted her gaze to her husband and followed him to the front door. It was a huge wooden structure that had to have been 20 feet tall, almost as tall as the house. Anthony pushed on the door and it opened slowly turning the huge door to a diagonal position.

"Woooow!" remarked Shane. Anthony turned to look at her.

They entered into a small courtyard with a pond featuring pink sacred lotus floating delicately on its surface. A young woman approached them.

"Rahajeng rauh." She smiled at them and briefly bowed her head. "Welcome, lovebirds." Her words were layered with a strong accent.

Anthony and Shane looked at one another and both dipped their heads in response. A gentleman appeared and took their luggage. The woman removed her sandals and they did the same. She motioned for them to follow her and guided them to a beautiful washroom to wash their hands. Then, she handed each of them a folded, heated towel to wash their faces.

"Come."

She led them deeper into the villa to a dining room. The area was open and Shane could see a man and a woman preparing food. And she could smell the enticing aromas. They sat at a large wooden table set for two.

The two chefs came out carrying several dishes which they arranged before the couple. Shane recognized the grilled prawns, but nothing else. She was excited to try the food. Altogether there were six platters. The woman introduced the chefs and walked them through the dishes.

"This is Koming and Putu. They will be your chefs during your stay. They will be available for breakfast, dinner and evening tea. Please tell me or leave them a note if you plan to be out for a meal."

Anthony and Shane nodded and smiled at the chefs. "Thank you," they said in unison. Realizing that neither of them spoke English, they asked their hostess to translate.

The duo smiled and excused themselves.

"What is your name?" Shane asked their hostess.

"Wayan," she answered.

"Will you all join us? There is a lot of food here!"

"No, it's for you," she explained.

"I know but we won't be able to eat all of this. Please join us," Shane implored.

Wayan shook her head. "This first dish is nasi campur bali. It is a traditional dish of steamed rice served with grilled beef, shredded chicken, tofu, tempe, bean sprouts and sambal. "This one," she pointed at a platter of what looked like fried rice, "is nasi goreng. It is a dish influenced by the Chinese. Next is lawar putih. We stir fry vegetables and mix them with coconut milk and coconut flesh and local spices. These are grilled prawn and a side of sambal which can be very spicy."

There was also a platter of grilled vegetables: string beans, rocket, pumpkin and what looked like sweet potatoes.

"Oh and this is papaya salad. It is sour or tangy because it is made with young papayas. It is like your coleslaw but tastier."

Wayan then said something in Balinese and disappeared. The couple looked at each other and bowed their heads for grace. They were quite hungry.

After they finished eating, they began collecting their plates and headed to the kitchen. As if they rang a silent alarm, Koming and Putu appeared. They waved their hands at the newlyweds, as if to shoo them away. When they went back to the dining table to retrieve the food platters to bring them to the kitchen, Koming came into the room. She shook her head no and took a platter from Anthony and waved them away. Anthony relinquished the platter and nodded at Shane to put the platter down.

With Wayan gone, they looked at the two chefs and said "thank you." The gentleman who took their luggage reappeared to show them to their room.

"This way." He motioned for them to follow. They walked back through the small courtyard and crossed to the other side of the premises. There were white stucco walls with wooden and local accents. The modern villa was a combination of traditional Balinese and modern aesthetics complete with cement and wrought iron elements. There was an indoor/outdoor functionality that employed floor to ceiling glass, allowing the soft sunshine to pour into the spaces.

Hallways displayed intricate wooden carvings that were several feet tall and just as wide. The deep color of the suar wood was magnificent against the white walls. They passed Balinese hand-carved masks and stone sculptures as they followed the gentleman. He stopped, opened wooden double doors with a flourish, then left them.

The king-sized bed was centered on a wood-clad wall with a chevron pattern. The minimalist cement headboard made certain the wall was the star of the show. The bed linen was white with a hand-woven wheat colored throw with matching decorative pillows. There was a wheat colored area rug at the foot of the bed. The room was beautifully understated and framed by glass accordion doors which were open to a small deck awash in sunlight. It looked out onto the turquoise surf and white sand. Two rattan chairs faced the water and were flanked by luscious plants. Palm trees swayed in the distance as the waves rolled soothingly. It was a breathtaking view.

They stepped into the room and walked out onto the deck. To the right was a small pool tiled in cool blues and surrounded by hand painted floor tiles of turquoise and white mimicking the sand and surf. Several colorful poufs of emerald greens and slate gray were scattered next to a lounge sofa. The sofa backed up on a large picture window and a door which led to a hallway to the living room. Hanging ferns spilled from the roof line adding to the ambiance.

Shane looked back at the water and realized that neither of them had spoken since the bedroom doors were opened. She turned to Anthony and stood on her tiptoes giving him a soft kiss. "This is the most beautiful place I've ever seen."

"I knew you would love it… the pictures didn't do it justice… This is amazing!" He took her hand and led her down a short set of stone steps. They passed a row of surfboards and snorkel gear on the way.

Once on the white sand, Shane dug her toes in. It was superfine and velvety.

"Oh, I'm going to be spoiled!" she giggled.

Anthony reached down and scooped her up. "Yes you are, Mrs. Dekra. He looked into her eyes and held her gaze. "I love you."

She smiled at her husband. "Always," she promised and stuck her pinky inside her dimple.

He suddenly let her go, letting her drop a few inches then caught her in the same position.

"Aaaah, Anthony! You play too much!" She hit him on the shoulder.

He laughed, then laid her down on the sand and laid on top of her. He kissed her deeply, then left kisses down her jaw and neck planting kisses across the skin that her scooped neck left exposed.

Shane giggled. "There's gonna be sand all over my clothes!"

"I can help with that." Anthony's eyebrows danced and he began to peel off her t-shirt.

"Ant! We're outside!" She looked around but there was nobody. They had a private beach with their villa. "Oh!" And she began to unbutton the linen shirt he was wearing.

After skinny dipping in the Indian Ocean, they grabbed their clothes and headed back up to their bedroom. As they walked, Shane looked up to see a few palm trees on the roof. Upon closer inspection, she exclaimed, "there's a rooftop area!" She could see the lip of a rattan sunbathing bed. Then, she spied a set of steps that ran along the side of their bedroom.

When they reached the deck, Shane dropped her clothes and shoes. She dug into the pile, then shrugged on her t-shirt and pulled on her panties. She looked at Anthony and waited for him to put on boxer briefs. "C'mon!"

They padded up the steps. Anthony smacked her butt as he followed her up. She swatted his hand away. Once on the roof, they looked out onto Seminyak Beach. The sky, the ocean, the sand. She looked at her husband. "I think we may have to stay."

Anthony took her hand and they walked across the sun bleached floorboards to the waiting sunbed. They stretched across the huge round cushion atop the rattan platform. There were stacked pillows to cushion them. The salty breeze gently dried their damp skin and soothed their travel-weary bodies. As they looked out at the natural landscape their eyes grew heavy.

They awakened to an inky sky filled with stars. "How long were we asleep?" Anthony shrugged and pulled her closer.

"Are you enjoying your honeymoon, Mrs. Dekra?"

"I'm enjoying my husband," she answered, sliding her tongue across his lower lip. He responded by dragging his index finger across her nipple.

"Are you hungry?" he asked.

"Yes, very." And began to plant kisses across his chest and down his stomach. Shane tugged off his boxers and his erection greeted her. "Well hello," she murmured and licked the tip. She wrapped her lips around him and a low moan caught in his throat. I'll get him ready, she thought as she savored her husband's rigidness. She pulled back to the tip and released him then she kicked off her panties and straddled him.

Anthony watched his wife in the starlight. He marveled at her hips and thick thighs. His hands caressed her breasts and watched as her eyes fluttered. Her excruciatingly slow rhythm was pulling him apart but he willed himself to hold on so that he could pleasure her until she was ready. She was so beautiful. She'd stunned him the first time that he ever saw her in that green gown. And now they would spend their lives together.

⸙

"Ooow!" Shane swatted at a mosquito, then scratched her bare butt cheek.

She shook her husband. It was time to go inside. He made a noise but didn't budge.

"Anthony, c'mon! We're gonna get lit up by these mosquitoes." She nudged him again.

She realized they had to be fully awake to walk down those steps. Where were their clothes? She spied them on the deck below. What time was it? It was still dark. I need some water, she thought.

"Ant! Get up baby. I don't wanna leave you out here, but I'm going in!"

He reached out and put his big hands around her waist to pull her to him. She pulled away from his hold, but grabbed his arm. "Let's go sleepy."

They finally trudged downstairs and through the glass sliders. They were sandy and sticky. She had to get in the shower. Anthony stopped at the bed.

"No you don't!" She pulled him toward the bathroom. "We're not gonna ruin that beautiful bed."

She felt for the light in the bathroom and they were bathed in the bright light and white of the bathroom. She admired the egg-shaped tub and promised herself a soak another time. She crossed the bathroom, walking into an enormous shower. She turned it on and the rain shower flowed atop her springy hair. She adjusted the temperature and pressed a few buttons activating the numerous jets.

She heard her husband behind her. He put his arms around her and pressed her against him under the water. The water was hot and felt wonderful. Her body was tired from traveling and from making love to her husband. She smiled. I'm gonna sleep gooood, she thought.

"What are you smiling about?" He smiled back at her.

"I'm happy. I didn't know it could be like this." she sighed.

"What? Didn't know what could be like this?" He was soaping her back in slow circles.

"Life."

He nodded. "So we're gonna enjoy it!"

They lazily lathered each other in the soap, coconut fragrance wafting through the steamy room.  After they rinsed off, she wrapped her hair in a towel. He dried her with the fluffy towel and wrapped it around his wife's short frame. She did the same, wrapping a towel around his slim waist.

They walked into the bedroom and collapsed on the bed. It soundlessly cushioned them.

"This bed!" Shane stretched her entire body appreciating the mattress.

Anthony looked at her. "I'm hungry," he groaned. Then his eyes lit up. "I'm gonna go warm up some food!"

"You go 'head… I'ma be right here.…"

Shane drifted off the sounds of clanking pans in the distance.

"Baby, wake up."

"Whaaat," whined Shane.

Anthony placed a tray on the bed that had a sampling of the dishes they'd savored at their welcome lunch. He sat beside her and loaded a forkful into his mouth. He groaned. "It's better than it was before."

Shane opened an eye and peered at him.

"Sit up baby." He loaded another forkful and held it toward her.

"Anthony, you're going to spill it!"

"Then get up!" he urged.

She slowly pulled herself into a sitting position, her legs like a pretzel. He leaned over, putting the fork to her lips, his other hand cupped under the fork to catch any wayward sauce. And they sat in the middle of the king-sized bed eating leftovers and giggling as the sky began to lighten. They stayed up just long enough to see the sun rise over the water.

The staff came in that morning, but did not wake them. They missed breakfast as they'd missed dinner the night before. The fifteen hour time difference was setting in. Wayan left a note for them on the dining table: the chefs prepped lunch which was in the fridge and if they needed any assistance to please call; they would check back in at dinner time. There was plenty of fresh fruit and beverages in the villa along with a stocked pantry and bar.

Shane and Ant spent the first few days at the villa, enjoying the pool, private beach and each other. The chefs treated them to more local delicacies and even joined them as well as Wayan for an evening meal at Shane's request. Putu prepared a traditional cocktail to toast the newlyweds.

He raised his glass and the rest of them followed. "Selamat Hari Pernikahan!"

"He say, 'Happy Wedding Day!'" explained Wayan. Shane and Ant nodded and clinked their glasses with the trio.

"Semoga Bahagia Sampai Tua!" exclaimed Koming and clinked their glasses again, smiling.

"She say, 'May you stay happy til you grow old together,'" translated Wayan. They all took a moment to sip.

"How do you say thank you?" Anthony asked Wayan.

"Matur Suksma." He repeated it after Wayan. She giggled. "Mah-tour Sooks-mah," she enunciated.

"Matur Suksma," he nodded to Kooming.

"Matur Suksma," Shane repeated, tilting her head to Kooming and Putu. She took another sip of the drink.

"This is good but it goes straight to your head!" Shane put the glass down.

The next day the couple would venture out with Kadek, so they recommended sites they should visit. Shane knew she wanted to go back to the city center they'd passed through on that first day. She also wanted to check out Ubud where the artists were.

——— § ———

Kadek was a great guide! He took them out two days in a row. They went to his hometown of Padangtegal when they visited Ubud. His elders lived in a family compound surrounded by a stone wall. They entered and met some of his elders who insisted that they stay for lunch.

"We must stay," said Kadek. "You honor them by enjoying and sharing the meal."

They walked to an open air pavilion. There were stone pillars encircling the structure. Two long tables and several benches were inside under a thatched roof.

"Where is the bathroom?" Shane asked Kadek.

He shook his head and gestured for them to sit at a table. "Please."

Soon, his aunt brought steaming towels for them to wipe their hands and faces.

"Matur Suksma," said Shane as she smiled at his aunt. She smiled and nodded.

Kadek clapped his hands. "Very good!"

"Show off." Anthony elbowed his wife.

"You just mad that I'm a better student."

They feasted on Tum ayam, a local favorite. The minced chicken was mixed with local herbs and spices then wrapped and steamed in banana leaf. There was also fried rice, sliced fruit and hot tea.

After the meal, they walked a short distance to the courtyard. There were several hewn benches and low slung chairs. A slow breeze flowed, as they sat. They were surrounded by lush plants and flowers. Palm trees and stones bordered the courtyard. Kadek served as interpreter for his family.

"My aunt and uncle wish you love and patience for your marriage. They have been married for 38 years. They say that they have had much more sunshine than storms. The key is to hold onto each other during the storms until they pass."

Anthony and Shane looked at each other. His eyes told her that he would hold onto her and she knew that she would do the same. Shane looked at the elders and bowed her head. Kadek's aunt smiled.

"Kadek, did you grow up in this compound?" asked Anthony.

"Yes. With my parents, siblings, my aunt and uncle's family and my maternal grandparents." Kadek translated the question to his aunt and uncle. They stood up.

"They want to show you around. It would give them much pride."

Anthony stood up and held his hand out to Shane, helping her to stand.

"This area, where we are sitting is the natah. It is the symbolic center of the compound," said Kadek. "Its design and the space between the structures allow airflow and provide comfortable indoor temperatures. All the buildings, especially the homes were designed for maximum airflow. As the air warms during the day, it flows from indoors to out and rises. In the afternoon, the walls, floor and rooms around the courtyard are warm when the temperature drops."

His uncle led the impromptu tour explaining the structures and their significance. "The materials are sourced from nature so they are kind to the earth and provide the benefits that you want for a home: shade, warmth, breathability and strength," translated Kadek. "Materials include grass, teak wood, natural stone and bricks."

Most had thatched roofs but a few were topped by ruddy tiles. Plants and palm trees studded the community as well as fragrant flowers and grass.

"Where we ate lunch, is the bale gede, a place for work to be done and sometimes we share meals here," Kadek explained. "It is open to allow air to circulate. The thatched roof protects from rain but still remains cool." They walked to the next building.

They watched Kadek's uncle gesture and speak in his native tongue. Kadek was pensive as he listened, then conveyed what he'd heard.

"This is the kitchen or paon and it is always situated in the south. It is ruled by Brahma, the Hindu god of fire. The separate structure keeps heat from the living quarters and it is enclosed for sanitation."

"What are the roofs made from?" asked Anthony.

"The thatched roofs are made from sedge grass. The others are shingles made from ironwood, a very strong and durable local wood. The shingled roofs last for 30 - 35 years."

As they rounded the path, three young children ran past giggling and screeching.

"Those are my young cousins. They are the grandchildren of my aunt and uncle."

"This entrance to the compound is called Angkul-angkul. Besides providing security, it keeps out negativity and bad spirits. Some can be very ornate and include statues of Hindu gods. The gap between the building walls and the compound wall reduces the noise from the street."

His aunt and uncle smiled as Kadek took the lead. Not far from the front gate was an enclosed building with an open air area in the front.

"This is the bale dauh or the west pavilion. Direction is important in our culture and religion. We orient buildings in relation to the mountains." Kadek continued. "This is a living quarters. Guests stay here or it is for unmarried boys in a compound."

"The next building is the largest. It is the bale meten where the head of household lives; a section would also house unwed young women of the family. It is also enclosed and has a pavilion. Pavilions in front of the enclosed rooms allow light and promote connectivity between inside and outside. Gardens are usually planted between the buildings to provide a visual connection to nature."

There were pillars across the front of the home. It had a thatched roof and several steps that led up to it. The home was a mixture of wood and brick. The pavilion, which we would call a porch, had a floor made of natural, reddish stone tiles.

"To the northeast, is the sanggah or our house temple where we honor our ancestors. It is also surrounded by a wall which is a portal that divides the spirit realm and this one."

They followed the direction of Kadek's extended hand and could see several buildings that resembled mini pagodas within the wall. There were brightly colored fabrics draped on some and others had gold colored detailing.

Then, they were back in the courtyard and facing one last building.

"And this is the bale dangin or the eastern ceremonial pavilion. It is used for ceremonies and rites of passage."

They learned that there were two wells on the property that provided the family's water. And there used to be a small open structure that served as a granary or lumbung. The landscape design of the compound also reduced the noise level from beyond its walls.

Shane was fascinated by the thought and intention that went into the design. She loved how they respected nature and built to harness it rather than try to foolishly bend it to their will. And their deference to their ancestors was refreshing. She looked at Anthony who was seemingly impacted by the tour as well.

Kadek's aunt spoke, then her nephew turned to them.

"She says we are simple people. We honor our family, nature and the gods. We build this way to stay connected to all three."

"Thank you so much for sharing it with us. We are honored." Kadek translated on Shane's behalf.

Back in the car, they were silent for a while.

"Kadek, thank you," said Anthony, breaking the silence. "Thank you for trusting us with your family. That was amazing."

"You're very welcome," said Kadek smiling. "I knew your spirits were worthy."

They finished the day at the famous Ubud rice fields. It was unlike anything Shane had ever seen. As far as they could see, there was green. They winded their way through terraced and verdant grasses. The fields were bathed in waning sunlight and dotted with slim palm trees.

She and Anthony held hands as they followed Kadek. As they left the gorgeous fields, the sky was purple and pink. Butter-colored streaking ran through the clouds, crowning the purple mountains as a backdrop to the rice fields. In the distance, fog hovered over the horizon blanketing the base of the mountains and tree tops. It was a perfect end to the day.

The following day, they went to many of the tourist attractions. First, they checked out the Kuta Art Market and Kuta Center so that Shane could admire the artisanal wares and, yes, find what she would be taking back with them. She knew she couldn't leave without hand-carved wooden art pieces for their homes. There were pottery, textiles and handmade furniture that would also be purchased and shipped.

Kadek taught them how to greet people. "Om Swastyastu," Shane offered as she met people in the market and slowly looked through every stall and storefront. When they became hungry, they ate sate from a street vendor.

Anthony took a bite of the luscious chicken and moaned. "This is world's apart from any skewer I've ever had in the states. They bought a few more and the three of them continued combing the town, munching on their sate.

"The next landmark I want to show you, we don't even have to leave the car!" exclaimed Kadek.

It was the Dewa Ruci Roundabout, also in Kuta. This huge statue symbolizes the journey of Bimasena. The god Dewa Ruci made a request. Bima dove in the ocean and met Naga (dragon) and they fought. The statue illustrates their underwater battle. His journey shows obedience to the teacher and the struggle to achieve something. They must've circled the statue about seven times to marvel at it.

They craned their necks to see the impressive landmark. "Can we stop somewhere nearby to see it better?"

Kadek pulled onto a street that was an artery leading from the sculpture at the center. They left the car, amazed by the towering scene before them. Shane took a video to capture it, slowly walking in a large arc to get different angles. She would love to get closer footage but there was no way to safely do so.

At the top, was a sculpture of Dewa Ruci, encircled by what looked like a gold aura. Below, Bima wears a crown and stands on the crest of a wave with one hand on the upper jaw and the other on the lower jaw of the dragon. Naga was wrapped around his legs and waist, shooting flame from his mouth.

"At night, it is spectacular! There are colorful lights that shine upon it, bathing it in purple and blue."

After they dropped off Shane's purchases at Kadek's house, they headed for the iconic Pura Petitenget. As they exited the car, Kadek gave each of them a sarong. "You must cover your knees and ankles to visit the temple."

Kadek helped Anthony with the heavy cloth, showing him how local men wear it. He also handed Shane a light scarf to tie around her shoulders which were bare. She'd already tied the sarong around her waist.

Shane was awed by the sheer majesty of the temple. There were three red brick towers: a tall one flanked on each side by an identical smaller tower. Each had an ornate carved door with stairs leading up to it. Gray, stone dragon heads adorned by an elaborate floral headdress hovered over each doorway.

"This temple was built in the 15th century," explained Kadek. "It is a sea temple that spiritually guards our island's perimeter. Our elders said that there was a surrounding jungle haunted by a bad spirit, Buto Ijo. If you went into the jungle, you would get sick. A Hindu priest had the temple built to protect the community from the spirit. "

"Is it alright if I take a picture of the entrance?" asked Shane.

"Yes, go on," he said, smiling and appreciative of her respectful manner. He also snapped a few of the couple in front of the trio of brick towers at the entrance.

The interior of the temple was a large, lush courtyard filled with shrines and small temples. The plantings were manicured and beautiful amidst the ancient stone structures. Their eyes were large, taking in the beauty surrounding them. They silently admired the temple, holding hands and stealing a glance at each other along the way.

A huge statue of Buto Ijo with bulging eyes guarded from the center of the courtyard. He is stone but gilded with jewelry and head wear with a dragon coiled around him. The statue is surrounded by cone shaped shrubs with red and green leaves and other plants. There were several covered altars in the courtyard laden with offerings like incense and banana leaf and sweets.

On the way back to the villa, Kadek stopped at a vendor for laklak, a local treat. Sweet mini pancakes, which are green, are topped with melted palm sugar and grated coconut.

Shane gobbled hers up quickly and took one of Anthony's. "Oh Kadek. We'll have to get these again before we leave!"

Kadek laughed. "A sweet tooth!"

"Yeah Kadek. She acts like she's only gonna have a taste, then eats it all!"

"I do not," protested Shane as she laughed.

"Are there other places you wish to visit while you're here? I would be happy to take you out again in a few days."

"Yes Kadek. That would be nice." Shane nodded her head.

"Okay. I will take your purchases to be wrapped for shipping. When I pick you up, I will take you to inspect them and finish the shipping process."

Back at the villa, there were two massage tables erected in the living area, each held a folded white robe. A temporary hand carved wall was standing behind the tables, blocking the view to the dining room and kitchen. The sweet smell of jasmine filled the room. Wayan was waiting.

"Put on the robes," she instructed. "No clothes."

She left the room and they followed her instructions putting on the heavy robes.

"How did she know when we'd be back?" Shane looked at her husband. He had a knowing smirk on his face. "You are just full of surprises."

Two women appeared and waited as each of them laid face-down onto the tables, positioning their faces into the cradle. The women began to work their tired muscles with their gifted hands.

"Ohhh!" A moan escaped Shane as the woman's hands massaged her shoulders.

They were each awakened to flip onto their backs. Soft linen towels were placed across them for modesty. The massage ended with them being slathered with a grainy exfoliant that included salt but was also sticky with honey. After they were covered with the scrub, they were helped up and into their robes. One woman gestured toward the master suite. There was a temporary paper carpet laid in their path, to keep the floor clean of any errant scrub.

"They take care of every detail," marveled Shane.

The master bedroom smelled like lavender. The bed was freshly made and the sliders were open welcoming the breeze. The white silk curtains billowed gently.

They walked into the adjoining bathroom and dropped their robes. Anthony walked into the shower turning on all of the many nozzles, getting the temperature right for his wife. She smiled appreciatively as she watched his lean chocolate body under the cascade of water. He could feel her eyes on him and turned to her. She joined him in the huge walk-in shower.

"Glad to see me I see!" Shane's lips curled into a wicked smile.

"Always." He opened his arms to welcome her into the steamy water.

As they slowly cleaned each other, the aroma of spices wafted into the room. Their eyes met. Dinner.

That night they had ayam betutu which is slow-cooked chicken seasoned and stuffed with Balinese spices. There was also a platter of grilled string beans, rocket and pumpkin and a side dish of papaya salad.

Shane and Anthony thanked the chef, then God and dug in, happily. There was only the sound of forks and utensils scraping against the plates and platters. After they finished, they sat on the deck of their bedroom and talked in the dark while listening to the surf. Once their eyelids were heavy, they went inside, closing the doors behind them.

"Baby, wake up!" Anthony shook his wife.

"Whaaat? I'm sleep!" He shook her again.

"Baby, c'mon! The surf is great!" Shane opened one eye. The room was still covered in darkness and her husband was leaning over her.

"C'mon!" he urged. "I brought one of your suits."

It slowly dawned on her that he was talking about surfing. This man! She rolled over, her legs tangled in the sheets. She opened both eyes and sat up. There he stood in his body suit; hers lay on the edge of the bed.

"Meet you out there!"

They paddled out together as the sun began to make its appearance. The surface of the water was glassy and there was a light offshore wind. Some spray was coming off the top of the lip and the waves were breaking in one direction. It was perfect.

Shane caught the first one she saw. She had come a long way since that first lesson when she forgot her clothes. She had a good teacher. The memory made her giggle and lose focus. She fell over into the surf and bobbed under to miss the board. When she surfaced, she saw her husband expertly riding a wave to the shore.

The water was a bit cool, but steadily warming. It was softly lapping, clear turquoise spread around her. She hopped on her board and began to paddle back out. She couldn't let Anthony get all the good ones.

A few hours later they lay on the white sand watching the waves break. It was warm now so she didn't have to rush to peel out of her suit.

"I wonder if they have any fruit in the kitchen?"

"You read my mind."

After a quick, hot shower, they dashed into the kitchen. It was still early so they could have their run of the kitchen before Koming or Putu could shoo them off. Shane sat at the kitchen counter and watched Anthony skillfully slice and cube mangoes, pineapples and bananas. He also grabbed a few rambutans and juwet from the fridge. In a wooden bowl on the counter were mangosteen and snakeskin fruit; they would round out the platter.

They hungrily snacked on the delicious fruits, smacking their lips and licking juice from their fingers. The platter was empty and it was nap time. They cleaned a few dishes and retreated to the bedroom. They were awakened by sounds and aromas from the kitchen.

The rest of their stay consisted of more surfing, eating and lovemaking. They ventured out to one or two clubs out of curiosity. And because the water was so beautiful, they also chartered a boat to fish and snorkel. She and Anthony jumped from the side of the boat into the crystal waters. Face-down and holding hands, they explored. There were manta rays, huge turtles, pink and cream-colored coral and fish everywhere. The fish were every size, shape and color, whizzing through the ocean. When they climbed back on board, Shane removed her mask and snorkel and laid back on the deck. "That was A-MA-ZING!" she shouted.

Their second to last day, Kadek returned to take them to ship their purchases and then to visit Ubud Palace, the official residence of the royal family.

"I had no idea Bali had a royal family," remarked Shane.

"Yes. The palace was built in the 17th century in an area of immense spiritual power that radiates light and energy. It also has a Hindu temple for the family to worship."

A long grand walkway was flanked by pools containing lily pads and orchids which led to the front steps and gilded front entrance. The temple's facade looked like a tiered pyramid. The beautiful orange-red brick had sculpted stone wings and cornices that wound their way up to the temple's peak. The front entrance was framed by majestic trees and greenery. A brick and stone wall encompassed the ancient structure.

Shane craned her neck to make out the faces that were featured in each tier of the facade. They looked like gargoyles but Kadek didn't know the details. From the front walkway, they saw two, thatched-roof dwellings as well as a taller one in the distance that resembled a pagoda.

"The architecture and artistry is remarkable," marveled Anthony. "And to think that they were built so long ago and have withstood time…." He spoke with reverence.

Shane and Anthony enjoyed their honeymoon immensely, especially the people they met and the Balinese culture. However, they were anxious to get home and resume their normal lives, as man and wife.

"I'll want to come back someday," Shane said wistfully.

"Then we will!" Anthony promised.

They looked out of the window, watching as emerald-green Indonesia faded into the sparkling Indian Ocean.

# Life Is What You Make It

Stephanie and Tom were expecting a baby! And guess who the Godmommy was? Shane was so excited to soon have a baby in their midst. Although they were hundreds of miles apart, she and Stephanie would close the distance. They talked often, Stephanie peppering her with pregnancy and parenting questions.

"Steph, that was so long ago! And I was alone, you have Tom to talk to and share your feelings with."

"I know, but I want to talk to you about it."

"I get it, but make sure you don't leave him out," advised Shane. "This is an exciting time for the two of you to share. Cherish it together."

She actually remembered a lot from her pregnancy and being a new Mom. Thanks to the memoir, Shane recalled details that she thought she'd forgotten.

Author copies had arrived a few weeks ago, the box was in her office.

"They're heerrrre!" she sang as Anthony brought the box into the parlor.

When Shane first opened the box, she lifted the book and quietly caressed its cover. Sitting at her desk, she thumbed through the pages.

*I felt every jab*
*The flutter of kicks*
*And squirms to find a comfortable position.*

*He suckled my breast*
*My arm, his cradle.*
*Snuggled to my chest*
*You were soothed.*

*Before breath, you knew me.*
*My voice,*
*My heartbeat.*

*The origin of a father's envy:*
*He will never know the splendor of birth*

*Seen through a mother's eyes.*

Later she sat in her window seat and read it cover to cover.

With Tom's career still peaking, Stephanie and baby Yara were regular visitors of Shane's and sometimes they all met up in LA, spending time at Anthony's. Or in Chicago, Stephanie would take over Shane's office with her laptop to submit grades or review student papers. Ever so often, she'd look up to see Yara and Shane stretched out on a blanket across the floor, giggling and playing.

Shane loved to walk the house, softly rocking Yara and sniffing her tiny head. Ohhhh! There was nothing like the scent of a baby. It had been so long, she'd forgotten just how tiny they were! Their little clothes and shoes... She could not remember Sean ever being that small.

Oh, and the naps! Stephanie could leave for hours to visit friends or just to get some me time. She would return to the Greystone to find Yara curled up on Godmommy's chest and both would be sound asleep. Or sometimes, she would find Anthony walking her around the house, cooing and explaining something to her as if she were an adult.

"I think in order to negotiate a signing bonus for my client, I'll need to guarantee a minimum number of tours and sales. What do you think?"

When Tom was between projects, the three of them would visit or sometimes Shane would fly to New York. And as long as there was a sufficient stock of bottles, Tom and Stephanie were able to have date nights and catch shows in whichever city they found themselves.

"I could get used to this. I'm looking forward to being a Grandma, just not yet!"

—— ∽ ——

Many times when Shane was in LA, Philip was in town to spend time with his grandchildren. Naaja was in her second year of college, with Samuelle bringing up the rear as a high school senior. The stage-ready Samuelle had been accepted early to Juilliard to study theater. Amir warmed up to Shane and would visit sometimes. He was engaged to Monifa, an elementary school teacher. As usual, there was a full house in Burbank, which included Simone and Greg. And of course, Grover.

Philip turned out to be the balm Shane didn't know she needed. The two of them had a special bond that made Anthony love her more, if that were possible. After some sweet talking, Shane convinced Philip to move in so that he could spend more time with family. Anthony worked out the details of the sale of his childhood home.

"I'm grillin' today? What y'all want me to cook?" Philip announced.

"Granddad, can I help?" Samuelle wanted to step up his grill game. He thought it was cool and manly. His Granddad had been giving him tips for a few years, but Samuelle still had limited time actually grilling. His Granddad was eager to impart knowledge, but less eager to yield control of said grill.

"I'll make a list. Samuelle, can you go to the store and pick up a few things?"

"Yeah, I got it."

Later that night after the grill had long grown cold, Shane shared a bourbon with her father in law. Over the years, he convinced her to try his drink and she eventually found Uncle Nearest, a brand that she enjoyed. At the moment, he was trying in vain to teach her poker. There was a pile of nickels, quarters and dollars in the middle of the table.

"Shane baby, are you even paying attention?"

Anthony's booming laughter interrupted her train of thought. She scowled at him.

"Yes I am! I just don't understand how to decide when I should ask for more cards or when I should trade some in… It all seems to be very random and based on luck!" She shook her head and huffed.

"Don't worry about all that right now, darlin'. Just focus on the first bet and if you wanna call or fold."

"What's call mean again?"

Philip slumped in frustration. He looked across the table at Anthony. "Am I not explainin' it right?"

"Don't put me in this! You said you wanted to teach her…"

"Stop talking about me like I'm not sitting here! Samuelle, can you help me?"

"Naw, I'm folding!" He threw in his cards and left the table. "Anybody need anything? I'm grabbing a beer."

"Excuse me?" Shane craned her neck in his direction. Then she flashed Anthony a look.

"Shane baby, he's a man. He drinks beer with his friends. Why can't he drink it here?"

She rolled her eyes at him. "You're driving so you better savor that ONE!" she called.

"I wish you'd pay this game the attention you got floatin' everywhere else!" Philip clucked his tongue.

Shane threw in her hand. "I'm folding too… I'll stick to Spades!" She picked up her glass and held it up to Philip. She swirled the amber liquid and listened to the ice cubes tinkle before she took a sip.

Shane and Anthony spent just about equal time between Chicago and LA. Sean was now working at Bryan's firm as a junior architect and dating Yanni, to both family's delight. He held down the fort when his Mom and Ant were on the west coast. His Grandma wanted to be closer, so they'd all convinced her to relocate to Chicago. Rather than move into the Greystone, Dorothy wanted to maintain a separate residence. Shane purchased a condo for her in a nearby neighborhood. They held onto her DC home in Woodridge and rented it.

Shane's phone was ringing. "Baby could you see who that is?" she asked as she pulled on a pair of jeans.

"It's Chanté! You want me to get it?" Anthony yelled from downstairs.

"Yes please!"

"Heyyyy Chanté! How you doing? She's upstairs, hold on a minute."

Anthony appeared in the entrance of their bedroom. He walked over and gave her a peck on the lips, handing her the phone. Shane smiled up at him.

"Hey girl, what's happening?"

"Shane, girl, I got some tea!"

"Talk to me!"

"Are you ready?" Chanté paused for effect. Shane rolled her eyes and waited.

"Robert asked me to move in with him!"

"WHAT?" Shane took the phone from her ear and pressed the button to change to a video call. "Bitch switch over," she commanded as Chanté cackled.

She looked at her friend. "Say what now?!"

"You heard me!"

"So did you give him an answer?"

"I told him I'd think about it."

"What's to think about?"

"You know I'm set in my ways... I don't know if I want to uproot my life for no man!"

"Seriously? Chanté look. You know you hate Florida. How long do you plan to do this long distance thing?"

"You're one to talk!" She exhaled. "I guess I don't want to lose my independence. I've been solo for a long time girl! Suppose I don't know how to do the full-time thing? And cohabitation is something else altogether!"

Shane was silent. She knew where Chanté was coming from. There had been some adjustments when she and Anthony got married. In some ways, he was old-fashioned and she'd had to learn to compromise. And it was a while before they actually lived together for long stretches. But, in the end it was all worth it... growing pains and all.

"I hear you, Chanté. But ask yourself, if you don't move then what's next for you two? Is it a deal breaker for him? And if it is, are you willing to lose him?"

Chanté sighed. She knew that she was being stubborn. She loved Robert and he was worth the risk. She did hate Florida and she'd be closer to Amber who was in DC finishing up at Howard. Besides, it would be an exciting new beginning for them.

"You're right. I'm tripping! And I could get a real estate license there, if I need something to do. Let me call Robert and talk this through."

Shane stomped her feet excitedly. "Yesssss. Let me know how it goes."

"Baby. Guess what?" Shane yelled as she hung up.

⸻ ❦ ⸻

"Are you nervous?" Ant asked his wife.

"No, not really. I've always worked behind the scenes. But, this is the first time I've attended... Well, I guess I'm a little nervous for Valencia."

"But it's your song."

"Not anymore. She made it hers. And this is her big night!"

"Um, I believe that you have a GRAMMY nomination as well. Baby, you can be humble but I'm shouting you out! Your talent is too enormous not to."

Shane smiled as she looked at her reflection in the floor length mirror. The coral, strapless dress she selected was hugging her curves. Her and the stylist agreed on a Trumpet silhouette. She wore a thin metallic belt. Her hair had grown and she let it be. It was a long, curly halo. She had a pale pink lip and blush and a bit of clear mascara, just in case there were tears. Her metallic stilettos were waiting for her in the corner.

Anthony smiled at her reflection and her dimple popped out. He placed a wrap around her shoulders. He looked so handsome: his charcoal tailored suit, shirt and tie gave him a cool, monochromatic look.

She turned toward him. He looked into her eyes and kissed her long and slow. Shane melted into the kiss, then stopped it abruptly.

"Okay, don't start nothin' that you can't finish!" Shane warned.

"Who said I can't finish!"

She slapped his arm. "The car will be here any second now."

"We can roll up the partition," he whispered.

"There you go…!" she said, walking past him to get her clutch from his walk-in closet.

"Me! I'm just stealing a page from your book." He winked at her.

Valencia performed her nominated single that night. Her short, shapely frame looked fabulous in her sheer, lavender gown. Its bodice was studded with Swarovski diamonds as was her hair which was styled in a braided, chignon bun at the base of her neck.

She belted out the chorus and her legato enthralled the audience.

Tears glistened in Shane's eyes. Anthony raised her hand and kissed it. She felt like a proud Mama on several levels. Sean was seated on her other side, smiling. Robert squeezed her shoulder. He sat in the row directly behind them with Chanté who was grinning like a fool.

Stephanie and Tom were also seated nearby. Tom was nominated for his work on an original movie score and his bass skills were featured in Valencia's nominated song. Her village was there cheering both of them. When the presenters read the nominees for Best R & B Song, Shane's stomach tightened.

"And the GRAMMY goes to… *Love at Second Sight* by Valencia!"

Their section roared. Shane stood up clapping and crying. She didn't think that she was supposed to, but she did anyway. She sat down once she saw Valencia on the stage.

"Wooooooo!" Valencia held up the award. "It's heavier than I imagined!" There was laughter from the audience. "Y'all don't know how long this has been my dream! I always knew that I wanted to sing and write songs, so I put all of my energy into it. While my friends were out doing their thing, I was writing in my journals and banging out notes on my little Casio keyboard. Thank you to my parents for their love and support." She waved. "Thank you to God for my gifts."

A happy tear slid down Shane's face. "She did it!" she exclaimed. She turned and looked at Robert. He gave her an imperceptible nod.

Later that night, Valencia returned to the stage to accept the GRAMMY for Best New Artist. An usher came to Shane's row and asked her to quickly come with him. He whisked her to a hidden path which led to the right wing of the stage.

"This is nuts!" Valencia exclaimed at the dais, then she signaled for Shane to come to the stage.

"I have a special thank you to this lady right here, Shane Mathews. SHE wrote *Love at Second Sight*. Yeah, I put a little of my flava on it, but she wrote a beautiful song." There was thunderous applause. Valencia waited. "But what I am really thanking her for is for seeing me and amplifying my voice!"

Valencia put her arms around Shane and kissed her. They posed for a picture before exiting stage left.

Shane hugged her for a long time. She was so proud. She didn't expect to be invited onstage. Valencia's parents were waiting backstage as well as Anthony. Each of her parents hugged Shane as Anthony looked on smiling.

"This is a big night for the two of you!" they remarked.

"And the night isn't over…" Valencia raised her eyebrows at Shane.

This year, there was a new category, Songwriter of the Year; it was long overdue. Shane was one of the many individuals who had advocated for its addition. There were many great songs written that year. Although she was nominated, she didn't expect to win with her first nomination.

"Let's not get ahead of ourselves," said Shane. She walked over to Anthony. "We need to get back to our seats!"

As they walked, Anthony whispered, "It already won Best R&B Song… don't you think there's a good chance that you'll be taking home a GRAMMY?"

Shane shrugged her shoulders. She didn't want to get hopeful. Besides, she loved songwriting and that was enough.

"And the GRAMMY for Songwriter of the Year goes to… Shane Mathews and Valencia."

She found herself in the spotlight once more that night. And over the next few years, Shane penned four more hits for Valencia and they co-wrote a few additional chart busters.

Shane ripped the cardboard from one of Anthony's yellow legal pads. She fanned herself frantically, the heat rising from her damp skin. She rolled her eyes when she thought of her gynecologist explaining that she was in peri- or pre-menopause, who could remember. And how were they even different?

She'd unexpectedly found a confidante in Simone who was a few years older. She empathized and shared some things that worked for her.

"But every woman's different, Shane. Talk to your Mom. What was her experience? Many times heredity plays a role."

Shane sighed. All she knew was that she would wake up and her side of the bed would be drenched. And sometimes, during meetings, beads of sweat would suddenly appear on her forehead and upper lip; it would feel like someone suddenly turned up her internal thermostat. Then a minute later, it would pass as if nothing had ever happened except that Shane would need to dry her brow. But what was worse, sometimes when she and Anthony were hot and heavy and ready to make love, there was a level of dryness that she hadn't before experienced.

"She's not as juicy as she used to be," lamented Shane.

"We'll just have to get her juicy again." Ant kissed the inside of her thigh, but for Shane, the moment would be lost.

Lucky for her, Anthony was not willing to give up so easily; he wanted his wife to feel as sexy as she still was to him. He began to learn all he could about menopause and reached out to his brother's wife who was a gynecologist. She recommended a few books for him to read and a few for Shane. Anthony learned that while menopause and the preceding stages had symptoms that could impact sexuality, there were also psychological issues that could impact his wife and therefore their relationship.

He began to focus on other acts of intimacy such as massages, taking baths together and his favorite, butt-naked spooning! All of these activities had skin-to-skin contact but he made sure to be patient and not make intercourse the end result. And Shane loved him for it because her libido had not taken a hit, only her confidence.

"Are you busy?" Anthony asked her as he walked into her office.

"Just finishing up a draft curriculum." Shane was now teaching songwriting in both locations. "Why, what's up?"

"I was hoping that we could take a drive."

Shane made sure that her work was saved and closed her laptop. "I'm all yours," she said smiling.

As they rode in the car, they held hands and reflected on their day. "Where are we going?" Shane asked.

"You'll see when we get there."

Anthony pulled into the parking lot of a nondescript building. Hand-in-hand, they walked into the front door. The place was stylishly decorated in lush purples and cool blues with metallic elements. She began to notice shelving on the walls and velvet seating interspersed throughout the space. On the shelves were…OMG…toys, adult toys. She turned to look at her husband.

"I thought we could have some fun picking out things that you might enjoy. But, if you're not feeling it —"

"No, I'm into it… This will be fun!" Her eyebrows danced.

Anthony grinned widely. No Holes Barred is a Black-owned adult space that specializes in pleasure and fantasy. He'd made a reservation online after answering a detailed questionnaire about he and his wife's likes and his desired goal for the visit. Based on their profile, they were assigned a personal shopper, Chandra.

Chandra appeared to be near their age, but who could truly tell with her taut, cocoa skin and enthusiasm for sexual pleasure. She accompanied them through the store, describing the products and making recommendations based on their desires. There were candles that melted into sweet-smelling massage oils; yummy-tasting and all-natural lubricants; double vibrators for vaginal and anal stimulation; wireless vibrators that were blue tooth enabled which paired with an app; crystal anal beads; constricting penile sleeves; vibrating cock rings; textured, tongue-like rimming devices; soft clit-stimulating vibrators; riding crops, blindfolds and feathered ticklers. She also showed them natural supplements that might help with Shane's occasional dryness.

After purchasing toys and a few other items, Chandra put their shopping bag into a locked safe. "Your guide is ready for you." She winked. "Have fun!"

Shane looked at Anthony who was grinning like a Cheshire cat. "What guide?"

Anthony ushered her through a door that she hadn't noticed; it was flush with the wall. He removed his shoes and motioned for Shane to do the same. They passed through another door and Anthony checked their receipt, number 10. He found a door marked 10 and opened it for Shane. She looked anxious so he gave her a quick kiss to reassure her.

It was dimly lit by aromatic candles that were placed around the room releasing the scent of citrus and currant. The walls were the luscious purple color they'd encountered in the store. There was a raised, oval-shaped bed in the center of the room, but it wasn't flat. It had the curved topography of the tantric chair that they'd just ordered with Chandra.

Anthony helped Shane out of her leather jacket, then removed his own and hung them on a nearby hook. There was another door in the far corner of the room which opened suddenly.

"Welcome Shane and Anthony," purred a young Black woman dressed in a leather bodysuit. She had a short natural, full lips and wore an eye mask. "When you are ready, please change in the adjoining room," she instructed.

Anthony took Shane's hand. Her eyes questioned him. "Trust me."

They walked into the next room, removed their clothing and put on matching silk robes. He turned her to him and kissed her long and slow. "I promise, it's nothing crazy," he whispered in her ear.

Then, they returned to the other room where their guide was waiting. "Anthony, could you please help Shane onto the bed?" The woman said, less as a question more like a directive. "Please put this blindfold on her."

"Shane, I want you to relax. You are safe in your husband's hands. I want you to breathe deeply until you feel relaxed. Tune in to your body." After a few minutes, Shane laid back, her body relaxing into the contours. Soft, low music began to play.

"Anthony, when you are ready, begin to massage Shane's muscles helping her to relax into her body. Go slowly and focus on one area at a time."

The woman pointed at a bottle of massage oil that was in a warmer, similar to one they had just purchased. Shane's head and upper body were positioned higher than her legs with her butt seated in the dip of the contour. Anthony began with Shane's feet, rubbing one at a time: the arch of her foot, each toe, the top of her foot, her ankle. Then he slowly moved up to each of her calves, then her thighs, one of his favorite parts. As he rubbed her, he could feel Shane relaxing under his hands.

"Good," the woman purred. "Watch how she responds to your touch. If there is an area that gives her more pleasure, linger there."

He moved on to her left shoulder then her right, then to her temples. Then, he lightly began to massage each breast. Her nipples stiffened as he brushed over them. Just then, Anthony noticed that several of their purchases were laid in a row on a side table, at the same height as the bed. Anthony picked up an item and put it in the pocket of his robe. The woman silently handed him their feather tickler and nodded as she gently pulled the belt that held Shane's robe closed.

Anthony gently dragged the feather's tip down her left leg, across her the sole of her foot and up her right sole, then leg, lingering at the inside of her thigh. He watched as Shane sucked in her breath. He tickled the space where her inner thighs touched, then dragged the feather up to her navel and continued up between her breasts. Shane arched her back slightly. He slowly repeated that motion. Then he began to circle her left nipple with the tickler, then moved to her right nipple. Shane gasped. The woman waved her fingers to get his attention, then opened her other hand. She held a delicate chain link length of material which she extended to him. He swapped the feather tickler for the chain link.

Touching the hollow at the base of her neck, he dragged the chain link down the center of her body. He watched his wife's back raise from the arched bed. Again, he thought. He lifted the chain link and let it land softly between her breasts. This time, he let it tickle each breast then dragged it down her torso and let it dip into her navel. Shane grabbed the side of the bed with her hands and let out a moan.

Anthony walked to the top of the bed and leaned over and kissed his wife slowly. As she kissed him, her thighs began to part slightly. He dragged the chain link from her navel to the apex of her inner thighs, letting the slinky material slide down between her legs. Shane moaned again. The young woman silently slipped out of the room. Anthony dropped the chain and slid his fingers into Shane's panties. She was slick and wet. He slid a finger inside.

"Oooooh."

He inserted another finger.

"Mmmmm."

Anthony broke the kiss and walked toward the end of the bed. He hooked a finger on each side of Shane's panties and slid them down and off. There was a leather step stool at the base of the bed. He stepped up on it, sat on the rounded end of the bed and rested each of Shane's legs across his. He spread her thighs and put her ankles on his shoulders.

"She's pretty juicy Shane." He lowered his face and tasted his wife.

He loved her flavor, her scent. It was his favorite. Anthony slowly moved his tongue up and down, back and forth. Shane began to shiver and he paused. Then, he began again.

"Anthony," she pleaded. She removed the blindfold.

"Yes?" he asked innocently.

Shane pulled her legs from his grasp and sat upright in front of him. She rubbed the bulge in his robe, opened it and tugged at his boxer briefs. He removed them. Then, she turned over so that her elbows rested on the elevated portion of the bed and her knees were now in the dip. She leaned forward so that her ass turned up.

As much as Anthony wanted to be inside her, he told himself to be patient. He grabbed her hips, leaned forward and licked her clit from behind. Then, he reached into his pocket and retrieved a string of crystal anal beads that Shane picked out. He paused for a moment and quickly inserted the beads into his mouth. After wetting them, he began licking Shane's clit lightly tickling it with his tongue; he knew what his wife liked. Her breathing began to speed up and become ragged.

He began to gently finger her anus as he continued to taste her. Then, he slowly began to insert the anal beads until three were inside her. He began to increase the speed of his tongue darting in and out and up and down. Shane began to whimper. As the sound became louder, he inserted two fingers and began curling them toward himself. Finally, her legs began to buckle and he pulled out the anal beads.

"Aaaaaah!" Shane collapsed onto the bed.

Anthony pulled off her robe and covered her shivering body with kisses. As she stilled, he walked to the top of the bed, and combed her hair from her face. He smiled at her.

"How are you?"

Shane smiled; she couldn't answer quite yet. Her mind was spinning. She had never had an orgasm like that before! She was drained and energized at the same time. Whoa! After about five minutes, she raised halfway up and looked at her husband.

"What type of freaky shit you got me into?" She cackled as he laughed loudly.

"And where are we? You know what, never mind."

She crooked her finger, calling him to her. He came and stood at the side of the bed. She wrapped her legs around his waist and put her hands on his chest. He kissed her deeply. She dropped one of her hands and gripped his erection and slowly began to swirl her thumb across the head.

He moaned. She released her legs and laid back into the bed's curvature. She widened her thighs. Anthony sat on the lower end of the bed, lifted Shane by her hips and slid forward into the dip. He lowered Shane onto him. She leaned into him, her nipples against his chest, her arms around his neck. Anthony held her as he thrust. Shane hadn't felt this turned on in a long time. She bit his ear and whispered, "Anthony, make me come."

His hips began to thrust harder and faster and she could feel herself unraveling. It. was. coming. fast. and. hard. Her body shook just as he put her down on the bed. She recognized that look of sweet agony on his face.

"SHANE!!!"

They shuddered together and Shane fell back onto the bed. As their breath slowed, they looked at each other and began laughing. "Lawd, I hope this room is soundproof!"

Anthony's love and dedication paid off. Guess what? He kept her juicy. And they made good use of the tantric chair; there was one in each home. He also inspired *Everyday You*, a mid-tempo song that reached number one on the Billboard charts.

*The curves that time has put on my hips*
*My extra thickness you love to tease with your lips*

Sean took an unexpected trip to Burbank to visit Shane and Anthony.

Sean had used his key and walked into the courtyard where Shane was on a lounger beside the pool.

"Well hello handsome," gushed Shane. "You startled me!"

"Hey Ma. I wanted to surprise y'all!"

"Mission accomplished! Ant and Philip are out playing golf… or at least Ant is trying to teach Philip how to play golf." She chuckled and looked up at her son.

"Sit down. Take a load off and stay awhile!" She could feel the nervous energy wafting from his body.

"What's going on?"

"Ma. I think I'm fucking up," he said quietly.

Shane sat up in the lounge chair, bracing herself.

"What I mean is, I think I fucked up with Yanni."

As Shane listened, Sean hung his head and shared how lately he'd been hanging out late and not spending much time with Yanni. He even revealed that he'd been spending time with another woman.

"So what's up with this woman?"

"Nuthin. She's cool, very different from Yanni."

"Are you sleeping with her?"

"Ma, no!" He averted his mother's eyes. "I coulda smashed, I mean, had sex with her but I haven't."

"Does Yanni know about this other woman?"

"Nah Ma. I mean, she wants to know what's up with me though…."

"Well, what is up with you?"

"I don't know Ma… I feel restless… I know I want to be with Yanni but I don't know…"

"What's there to know?" Shane asked him hotly.

"Ma, why you gettin' all riled up? I knew I shoulda talked to Ant!"

"Why cuz he's a man? You think he's gonna tell you different from me?"

"I don't know… maybe!"

Shane swung her legs around so that her body was facing Sean. She looked him directly in the eye. "Do you love Yanni?"

"Ma, c'mon…"

"Do you?" she yelled.

Sean's eyes widened. "Yes, I do."

"Then show her some respect! Tell her if you need some time and let the chips fall where they may. Don't waste her time. Women want honesty… we want to be given a choice, not have the man we love out here creepin' while we're at home wondering what the hell is wrong!"

"Damn Ma. I'm trying to be honest with you!"

"Are you? Cuz all I hear is dumb shit! It sounds like you're scared of something real with Yanni so you'd rather be in the street and hanging with random women to whom you owe nothing… and if that's what you want, then be honest with her, not me. Besides, Yanni's people are our people!"

Sean exhaled loudly and laid back on the chair next to her. She paused.

"Look Sean. Forget all the cool, dumb shit your friends tell you and all the messages that society bombards you with… When you love a woman, I mean the one who loves you in return, respects you and treats you accordingly, you better share your feelings with her: be vulnerable and honest. There is nothing more appealing and strong than a man who knows himself and is unafraid to express his feelings."

She walked to the table for her glass of lemonade and took a long gulp.

"Trust me. Do not risk losing Yanni because of your ego or whatever power you think you may be giving up. Because you will lose her. Don't be 50, still in love with the woman whom you lost because you couldn't get your shit together, then end up settling for less than you deserve. I've seen it happen and it's sad."

Sean nodded. His shoulders slumped and his eyes were sad. "Has that ever happened to you? You lost someone?"

Shane hesitated. "Yes…but for different reasons."

He sat up. "Like?…"

Shane sighed. "Timing for one. We were at different points in our lives. Also, I think we didn't know ourselves enough yet. And for a long time, I thought I'd lost the love of my life… and it was painful."

"Do you mean Chad?"

His Mom laughed softly. "No, not Chad. Long before him. Chad was a good man but he wasn't for me; I would have been settling. And thank God I didn't. Anthony was out there and I didn't know it… I hoped, but I wasn't sure there was anyone for me."

Sean looked at his Mom. "Thank you," he said softly. "I'm going to think about what you said."

Sean went inside to look for something to eat. He was at the counter eating a Dagwood sandwich and chips when his Dad and Granddad came home.

"What's up playa?!" One of Philip's large hands grabbed his shoulder.

"What up Granddad!" he said between chews. Philip beamed. He never got tired of hearing Sean call him that.

"This is a surprise!" said Anthony, grabbing a bottle of water from the fridge. "How long you here for? Long enough to catch some waves with your old man?"

"Maybe." Sean smiled and crunched on a few chips before he wiped his hands. He stood up and gave Anthony a bear hug.

"What's up son? Everything good?"

"Yeah, everything's good."

"Whatchu about to get into? Cuz me and Dad were about to go into the study and roll something." Anthony winked at him.

"Aw bet! I'll meet you in there. Besides I wanna holla at y'all about something."

Shane shook her head as pieces of their smoke inspired rantings floated out toward the kitchen. She went to the cabinet to find her herbal teas; she'd been cutting back on the coffee. Which one will I have this evening? Ah, Oshun's Kiss. That'll do. As her pot whistled, she shook the fragrant tea leaves into the stainless steel strainer inside her special tea cup. She soon retired upstairs with her cup of tea and dialed Gail's number.

⁓

Anthony and Shane Dekra made a decision: they had worked enough. It was time to fully enjoy the fruits of their labor. Shane loved the Greystone, but had long grown tired of the cold. The couple lived in the Burbank home and visited Chicago in the warmer months, spending time with Sean as well as Bryan and Imani. Sometimes Naaja and Samuelle would go to Chicago and stay with Sean when they could get away. Sean and Dorothy would also sometimes join the family in Burbank.

The Dekras also began to travel more often, including domestic trips to visit or meet up with Shane's tribe: Stephanie, Tonya, Gail and Chanté. Not to mention, traveling to new destinations. Anthony was in charge of researching the country, its culture, customs and economic and political landscapes. Shane would scour for accommodations, excursions and dining. But the main purpose of their international travel was to purchase property that was on or near a body of water, a non-negotiable for Shane.

"I always wanted to visit the Seychelles," Shane said dreamily.

"Well let's go!" And off they went on a new adventure. Sometimes, their children would join them on their trips and other times, it was their friends. They had worked hard for many years, so they enjoyed life. They would eventually purchase land and homes in Morocco, Greece, Tokyo, Senegal and Bali, of course.

———s———

"Surprise!"

Their children threw them a 20th anniversary bash. Anthony and Shane planned a quiet trip to their beach home in Kalamata. To their surprise, their children and ten of their closest friends met them there. Imani planned the party to the last detail, letting the deep blues and historic white of the country do the heavy lifting.

Anthony and Shane were in the middle of their stone patio which overlooked the cerulean Mediterranean Sea. Everyone gathered around as they danced in the salty breeze. Shane had whispered to Imani earlier, changing the song her friend had planned for their dance. She gazed into her husband's eyes and felt a catch in her throat. After all of their years together, he still had this effect on her.

Anthony smiled and her dimple showed itself. "Happy anniversary," he whispered, then kissed her lips softly.

She leaned into him and closed her eyes. EWF serenaded them:

*We write a song of love my baby, write a song of love! We write oooh we ooh ooh we ooh ooh wee ooh ooh, write a song of love! Sound, it never dissipates, it only recreates to another place and time!*

Of all the love songs Shane had written over the years, theirs was by far the sweetest. She wrapped her arms around his waist.

Imani even planned a family photo shoot which of course included everyone, dressed in white. These precious memories would later carry Shane through the hard times.

Sadly, they buried Philip and Dorothy within a three-year span. However, Shane felt like she'd lost her mother AND her father. She and Anthony lifted one another up when the sadness lasted a little too long. They found solace in knowing their parents shared great memories with the blended family that they created.

⸏

A decade later, after thirty years of love, laughter and music, Anthony left Shane. Her husband died quietly while they were asleep in their Spanish Revival home. Shane laid with him for a while, inhaling his scent, before calling anyone. She rubbed his smooth head as the doorbell rang. Simone was the first to reach her and they quietly cried together and waited. They embraced one another as the coroner came and left with his body. Later Grover was there, silently making calls.

Grover and Simone stayed with Shane that night despite her protests. Grover regaled them with animated stories of he and Ant's antics as bachelors. The ladies giggled at his theatrics despite sorrow's vice grip on their hearts. After the laughter subsided, there was a collective silence.

"Shane?"

She turned her head to look into Simone's eyes, thankful for the deep friendship the two women forged over the years. Simone leaned over and took her hand. Her eyes landed on Shane's rings.

"I remember when Anthony came to tell us that he was going to propose to you." She smiled, her eyes distant recalling the memory. "As soon as we sat down, I looked at Greg and I knew what he'd come to tell me… He was so excited and I was so happy that he'd found someone to bring him joy again. He deserved it and our children deserved to see both of their parents happy again."

As Simone recounted Anthony's words, Shane could almost hear his baritone. She could feel his excitement in Simone's words and she reveled in the feeling.

The next morning, Shane was up early, putting a kettle on for her tea. Her eyes were sore from lack of sleep and the insistent tears. As she sat at the counter, she heard the entry door close and looked up to see

Sean rushing toward her. She stood and opened her arms, suddenly overwhelmed by a mixture of relief, love and sorrow.

Sean enveloped his mother with his long arms and silently held her. She could feel his heart hammering against her as his body began to shudder from his silent sobbing. Shane waited and rubbed his back. After a few minutes, they parted and sat together at the counter.

"How are you doing?" His eyes searched hers and a silent tear slipped down his cheek.

Shane exhaled softly, but didn't answer. Her sad smile told the truth. She raised her hand and gently held his face. He leaned into her touch, closing his eyes.

Just then, Grover emerged from the first floor master with a drink in his hand. He stood behind Sean and squeezed his shoulder.

"Hey man… You want a drink?"

Sean nodded, his eyes still closed and Grover retreated towards the bar. Shane didn't bother to chastise them about the early hour.

"I got on the first flight out," he said, answering a question she didn't ask. "Yanni and the kids will be out in a couple of days."

Shane nodded and sipped her tea.

"I can't believe he's gone… we just talked the day before…." Sean sighed loudly and put his head in his hands.

Simone appeared and walked into the kitchen. "Hey Sean," she said softly. He stood up and kissed her cheek. They shared a lengthy embrace. Grover returned and pressed a tumbler into Sean's hand. Simone eyed their glasses before speaking.

"I'm going to fix breakfast and everyone…" She paused and looked pointedly at Shane. "is going to eat. We all need our strength. Then I'm heading home and Greg and I will be back later." Simone headed into the kitchen and opened the refrigerator checking its contents. She made a mental note to order some groceries to be delivered in the afternoon.

A few hours later Grover, Sean and Shane waded through the

contents of boxes that Sean had retrieved from Anthony's study. They were laughing and reminiscing as they passed around pictures and a joint. Shane was thankful that the marijuana smoke loosened her laughter and relaxed her nerves. Barrington Levy's strong voice pierced through the haze pontificating about the black roses in his garden. Footsteps made them pause their reverie and they collectively looked to the foyer to see Amir.

He quickly came to the living room, crossing over to Shane and knelt before the sofa where she was relaxing. They locked eyes and the first thing she noticed were the reddened eyelids and bags beneath his eyes. She leaned forward and embraced the eldest of her bonus sons.

The rest of their children and their families would reach the house within the next few days to help make arrangements, with quiet tears dotted by fond laughter. Shane's girlfriends would arrive soon after, wringing their hands unsure of what to do because Anthony was the first of their spouses to pass away.

As much as she loved their home and the life they made there, she couldn't bear to stay. Anthony's scent was infused in the crevices and hollows of that house. His laughter echoed through the empty, whitewashed hallways and reverberated in her heart. Every room bore his indelible mark and added to her insurmountable loneliness.

But how could she leave? They were married on this beautiful property. Philip had shared this home as had Samuelle and Naaja, until they forged their separate paths to create their families and stories. And although the sofa had long been replaced, she recalled lounging and napping on the pale blue one the first time she'd visited this home: Anthony took her surfing and he'd cooked for her and rubbed her feet. She closed her eyes and smiled, remembering how he pursued her patiently and assuredly.

Shane slowly went upstairs and turned left, down the hall past their master bedroom. She opened the door and was flooded by the scent of currant and citrus. She walked into the dark room and waited until her eyes adjusted to the dimness. This was their shared boudoir, inspired by their passion for one another. She sank down onto the tantric chair and leisurely ran her fingers across the studded seams. Although they hadn't used that chair in years, memories crashed her senses. Salty tears soaked her lashes and streamed down her weathered cheeks.

Shane moved back to Chicago, to the Greystone. Valencia visited regularly as did Imani. Gail and Sam would invite her to the City to take in a show or just to catch up, which she did sometimes. They would also meet up with Steph and Tom to eat, laugh and reminisce. Shane was happy to see her friends, but everyone could see the sadness behind her smile.

Shane had recently updated her will and made sure everything was covered to her satisfaction. She'd always appreciated Anthony's keen, legal mind and he'd made settling his affairs effortless. She wanted the same for their children and grandchildren when that time came.

Sean and his family visited every Sunday for dinner. He and Yanni would cook and later clean as Shane watched her grandchildren laugh and banter. She loved their energy and they loved the undivided attention that she bestowed upon them.

Holidays were now spent here which included she and Anthony's children and their families, Simone and Greg as well as Imani and Bryan. Sometimes, Robert and Chanté would make the trip. Every other year, Steph and Tom would join them as well. Once again, the home that she built so long ago was full to bursting at the seams with love. But her heart was missing a vital piece.

# CODA

# What Do You Know About Love?

Shane's eyes were closed and she began to hum.

"Gran Gran!"

She blinked. "Yes baby. What is it?"

"I was calling you. Didn't you hear me?"

Shane looked down at the parer in her hand. She had only gotten through half of the potatoes. She sighed, realizing she'd been meandering down memory lane.

"I'm sorry sweetheart. I must've drifted off...."

"You were asleep?"

Shane chuckled. "No, but I was dreaming!"

"Whatchu dreaming about? A man?" she asked playfully. Her granddaughter, Savonne, looked just in time to see the blush in her cheeks.

"Oooh Gran Gran! You were thinking about a man... Pop Pop?"

Shane immediately felt guilty for thinking of Mike. It didn't happen often: the thoughts ebbed and flowed. She'd tried to stop years ago, but grew to accept them; they truly did not lessen what she felt for Anthony.

Shane motioned for granddaughter to sit down at the counter beside her. She watched as her grand sat down, her cutoff jeans revealing young, toned legs; then, she ran her fingers through her curly mane. To Shane it looked like some sort of crew cut, but long on top.

Savonne was staying with her for the summer. She had an internship at the Chicago Museum of Contemporary Art and asked if she could stay with her. Although she knew Sean and Yanni had put their eldest up to it, Shane didn't mind. She enjoyed her granddaughter's company and there was more than enough room in the Greystone. Besides, the house would be Savonne's one day; Shane wanted it to feel like home.

She'd shown Savonne old pictures and video of what the house looked like when they'd first moved in. Then, stages of the huge restoration with her teen-aged father helping knock down walls and lay tile.

But Savonne's favorite part of the house was the recording studio; she loved spending time there. Her grandmother taught her how to work the sound board and let her record when she wanted to. She knew her grandmother was a big time songwriter and knew all kinds of stars. Her godmother Valencia was one of them and so was Auntie Stephanie's husband, Tom.

There were all kinds of awards in the studio and in Gran Gran's office: seven GRAMMYs, an Oscar, a few ASCAP Awards, a Tony, a special American Songwriting Award, a Lifetime Recording Academy Award and several more. Savonne loved hearing about her exciting life, but even more, about writing songs and poetry.

Since Savonne had been there, her Gran Gran had taken her to most of her favorite places and old haunts that were still around. Shane adored Chicago and wanted her granddaughter to love it too.

Savonne looked at her Gran Gran in anticipation.

"What do you know about love?" Shane asked her.

Savonne snickered and sucked her teeth. "Not much. It's slim pickings out there! Those clowns at school do not interest me."

Shane chuckled. "Don't rush. You have time." She put her wrinkled hand over the young lady's. "I've told you mine and Pop Pop's story. We found each other later in life, after love had knocked us around a bit." She paused.

"Sometimes you can love someone and they can love you, but it's still not enough. You can feel like a failure and, if you let it, it can close your heart to finding love again." She stared into the distance and Savonne could tell that she was somewhere else. "It took me a long time to learn that lesson. But your Pop Pop wasn't afraid to love again. Me… I took a little convincing.…"

"But I am lucky. I have had more than one true love in my lifetime. Some people only get one and even then, they never experience the kind of love that changes your life." She smiled.

"I'm gonna tell you something that my Grandma told me. She said 'in relationships, one person always loves the other more'." Shane looked at her granddaughter. "Vonnee, you won't understand until you love some and hurt some, but remember to let him love you a little more." She patted her hand.

"And that first time you fall in love, promise to tell me all about it. And don't leave out the good parts!" She winked.

"Gran Gran! You are so bad," she said conspiratorially.

"You have no idea!"

Savonne's right eyebrow raised.

"Let me tell you about a time when I was young and fell in love. I met him in Walmart of all places. Can you believe that? I was with um…" She paused. "Tonya. I was with Tonya…"

# DISCUSSION QUESTIONS

These questions were designed to spark discussion in your book clubs or discussions with friends and family.

Who is your favorite character? Why?

With which character did you most relate? Why?

What type of person is Shane?

Would you and Shane be friends? Why or why not?

Shane has been a Single Mother for a long time. How do you believe this impacted her? How did it impact Sean?

Shane has a close-knit group of girlfriends. Discuss their role in Shane's life.

Do you have such a group of friends? Why or why not?

Do you think Shane should have given Mike another chance? Why or why not?

Have you ever experienced heartbreak? Did it hinder you from entering into a new romantic relationship? Why or why not?

Several types of relationships are addressed in the novel. What are they? How do they intertwine or overlap?

There is a saying that "you can't choose your family." Do you agree or disagree? Do you have individuals who are like family, but are not blood related?

Shane is a passionate woman who is comfortable in her sensuality. Can you relate to this? Do you think women struggle with this?

Shane experiences symptoms related to menopause. Is this an issue that you have discussed or heard discussed? Why or why not?

Shane and Robert have a close relationship. Do you think platonic relationships are possible between single adults?

Simone and Anthony are divorced yet have an amicable relationship. They remained a family for their children. Do you think this is possible?

Would you choose Mike or Anthony?

What emotions did you experience while reading the novel?

Did you learn any lessons? If so, what are they?

Did anything surprise you in the novel? If so, what was it?

# Acknowledgments

I loved writing this book! This was a long-discarded goal that I'd all but forgotten until it began to take shape as a novel. I'd been a poet for over 20 years when we relocated from Washington, DC to Costa Rica. In the first few weeks after moving, I found my people: a Black Writer's Group. I cannot convey the excitement that I felt! I began attending weekly meetings, but I mostly listened; I had not written anything for months. But soon after, I began writing poems, here and there. Then, my mind began to clear and my body began to relax. As peace took over, the creativity began to flow, once again.

I was inspired by a fellow writer who'd written a beautiful short story. As I walked by the beach on the way to my weekly meeting I thought, I can write a short story. It wasn't until that moment that I remembered that's how my writing began! In high school, I wrote short stories. So after a 34-year hiatus, I wrote a short story. Then I wrote another and another. My short stories were creative non-fiction; that was my lane within the group. And then, I challenged myself, again. I decided to write a work of fiction.

What began as a short story, became a novel. Writing fiction was so freeing! I could make up the world that I wanted to see and it was a heady feeling. I got lost in the world of Shane and sometimes found it difficult to separate myself. I would have vivid dreams from Shane's perspective and within her life. It was wild.

First, I want to acknowledge my partner, Tsadeek "David", who has always supported my writing and given me opportunity and space to delve into it. Though not a creative, he respects my passion for and love of writing. He also overlooks my obsession with books when I am up at 3 am devouring my latest title. I love you and thank you.

I'd like to thank Gina Foshee for her love of this novel and agreeing to read it 47 times and edit it with love and scrutiny! Your patience and support cannot be articulated. She has been one of my biggest fans from day one.

I'm thankful to Keiona Clark for the custom artwork which graces the cover of this book. Thank you for agreeing to do it. Your talent and perspective will continue to take you wherever you want to go!

Thank you to Akesha Scott, my creative designer and jewelry-making friend. Thank you for the cover and spine designs of this book. As always, you guided me through font selection and layout options like a pro! Thank you for your patience.

Thank you to my daughter Nadiyah who had early discussions with me about sex scenes. You'd think it would've been awkward but we had a great conversation! I'd never written a sex scene and I wanted to treat it with respect. We had conversations about words to avoid and how to determine what was too much.

A huge thank you to my Wolaba Black Writer's Group!!! It was your support and creative energy that made this happen. This group who debates, laughs, shouts and, at times, shed a few tears together meets on Playa Negra Beach to share, write, reflect and provide feedback to the "writer of the week." The talent of these individuals cannot be overstated.

A heartfelt thank you to all the people whom I have ever loved (romantic and otherwise). Those relationships have shaped and informed not only this book, but my life. Once I realized this was a novel, I set out to write something that would inspire forgiveness of oneself and others. We are human and sometimes don't live up to the expectations that we have for ourselves. Sometimes we hurt those whom we love most. The good news is that we can do better. We can learn from those whom we've hurt and from those who have hurt us.* However, this requires patience, maturity and grace. I say this to all of the Mikes, Amirs, Roberts, Simones, Anthonys, Chads and Shanes.

*To be clear, there are some hurts that result from abuse (physical, mental and/or emotional) that may be unforgivable. I'm not talking about these. I'm talking about relationships that end and someone was hurt. We tend to internalize the pain and hold onto these wounds. This stops us from receiving the love and kinship that we deserve! Please, learn to let go. It was not a failure. And be patient. Letting go is a process.

And finally, I want to thank Black Love! I didn't have many good examples growing up, but I had a few. But we know that Black Love exists! It is beautiful, strong and enduring. And as such, it must be uplifted and celebrated. This is a love story. I hope you enjoyed it!

# Love At Second Sight Playlist

The order of these songs is intentional.

Estelle, "Conqueror." Album: True Romance
Erykah Badu, "Ye Yo" (Live Version). Album: Live
India.Arie, "Beautiful Surprise." Album: Voyage To India
Bobby V., "Slow Down" (12" Version). Album: Disturbing Tha
 Peace Presents Bobby Valentino
Rihanna, "Rude Boy." Album: Rated R
Outkast, "Prototype." Album: Speakerboxxx/The Love Below
Vivian Green, "Be Good To You," Album: A Love Story
Maxwell, "Submerge: Til We Become the Sun," Album: Embrya
Lenny Kravitz, "I Belong To You." Album: 5
Corinne Bailey Rae, "Like A Star." Album: Corinne Bailey Rae
Raheem DeVaughn, "Mo Better" (Main Version). Album: Love
 Behind The Melody
The New Birth, "Wild Flower." Album: It's Been a Long Time
Lenny Kravitz, "Believe In Me." Abum: Lenny
Floetry, "Hey You." Album: Floetic
India.Arie, "Ready For Love." Album: Acoustic Soul
Heather Headley, "Always Been Your Girl." Album: This Is Who I
 Am
Sade, "Is It a Crime." Album: Promise
Alina Baraz & Galimatias, "Maybe." Album: Urban Flora
Rihanna, "Kiss It Better." Album: ANTI
Tweet, "Always Will." Album: Southern Hummingbird
Hall & Oates, "Sara Smile." Album: Daryl Hall & John Oates
Mary J. Blige, "My Life." Album: My Life
Lizzo, "About Damn Time." Album: Special
Adele, "Someone Like You." Album: 21
Stokley, "Art In Motion (feat. Robert Glasper)." Introducing Stokley
Kem, "I Can't Stop Loving You." Album: Album II
India.Arie, "Good Mourning." Album: Testimony: Vol. 1 Life &
 Relationship

India.Arie, "Healing." Album: Voyage To India (Special Edition)
Alicia Keys, "Feeling U, Feeling Me (Interlude)." Album: The Diary Of Alicia Keys
Bruno Mars, "That's What I Like." Album: 24K Magic
Alina Baraz & Galimatias, "Can I." Album: Urban Flora
Bushman, "Hear Wah MI Ah Seh." Bushman (Hear Wah Mi Ah Seh).
Anthony David, "Heartstrings." Album: Three Chords And The Truth
Eric Roberson, "She." Album: Music Fan First
Earth, Wind & Fire, "Serpentine Fire." Album: All 'n All
A Tribe Called Quest, "Electric Relaxation." Album: The Anthology
Raheem DeVaughn, "Four Letter Word (Main Version)." Album: Love Behind The Melody
Aswad, "I A Rebel Soul." Album: Aswad
Rihanna, "Loveeeeeee Song (feat. Future)." Album: Unapologetic
India.Arie, "Complicated Melody." Album: Voyage To India (Special Edition)
Tamia, "Can't Get Enough." Album: Between Friends
Leon Bridges, "Beyond." Album: Good Thing
Diana Ross, "Love Hangover." Album: Diana Ross (1976) (Expanded Edition)
Eric Roberson, "Lessons." Album: Lessons
Sheléa, "Love Fell On Me." Album: Love Fell On Me
Curtis Mayfield, "The Makings of You." Album: Curtis
The Baylor Project, "Love Makes Me Sing." Album: Generations
Mali Music, "Heavy Love." Album: Mali Is...
Barrington Levy, "Black Roses." Album: Acousticalevy
Earth, Wind & Fire, "I'll Write a Song for You." Album: All 'n All

# About the Author

Ayoka B. explores the themes of Womanhood, identity, love, loss and family through poetry, fiction and nonfiction. Her writing is vulnerable and honest which resonates with readers. Through her unique lens as a Black woman and DC native, Ayoka seeks to share the untold stories of mothers, sisters, daughters, friends and wives. Her goal is to help people gain clarity and insight into their lives.

This is her debut novel. She is currently working on a second novel, *Bluff*. Set in Costa Rica, it is a supernatural story that is based on historic events and follows the lives of two teen-aged girls who are separated by centuries, yet connected.

Ayoka has a professional background in public relations and strategic communications. She received a bachelor's degree in Communications from Temple University in Philadelphia, Pa. and a master's degree in Public Communication from American University in Washington, DC. Ayoka is a mother and lives with her family in Costa Rica.

Learn more and download the playlist from Spotify or YouTube Music.

www.ingramcontent.com/pod-product-compliance
Lightning Source LLC
Chambersburg PA
CBHW070624300726
48975CB00006B/1914

*9798989732500*